THE BRAKEMAN

C.J. PETIT

Printed in the United States of America

First Printing, 2023

ISBN: 9798375733883

CONTENTS

PROLOGUE

Aitkin, Minnesota
May 8, 1878

Mister Stewart handed the tall, skinny teenager an envelope and said, "You're a good boy, Drew. And I'm sure you're going to grow up to be a good man."

Drew quietly replied, "I'll do the best I can, Mister Stewart," and then folded the envelope and stuffed it into his coat pocket.

After he grabbed his large sack and hung it over his shoulder, Mister Stewart said, "And don't spend your money foolishly, Drew."

Drew smiled, shook the director's hand and replied, "Scots are never foolish with their money, Mister Stewart."

James Stewart laughed, patted Drew on his left shoulder and then watched as the boy turned and left his office.

Mister Stewart let out a long breath before he returned to his desk and sat down. Among his many duties as director of St. Thomas Home for Boys, sending them away when they turned sixteen was the one that he dreaded the most. And watching Andrew Campbell leave the orphanage was easily the most emotionally distressing.

But it wasn't because Drew was the first boy to arrive in the orphanage after he'd been made its director. Drew was also the smartest and most promising boy who had ever walked the halls of St. Thomas Home for Boys. And his kind, generous nature made Mister Stewart feel that Drew was more like his son than an orphan who had been placed under his supervision.

But it was his duty to let each boy find his own way in the world, and he always did his duty. At least he was confident that Drew would succeed in whatever path he chose to follow.

———

Brainerd, Minnesota
May 13, 1882

Drew nodded as he said, "I know it's dangerous, Mister Jones, but I still want the job. I can use the extra pay."

Art Jones shrugged and then said, "Okay. But don't say I didn't warn ya. I ain't seen a brakeman last for more'n a year before bein' tossed off a boxcar and never bein' heard from ever again. It's why the N.P. pays 'em so much. Why do you need the money anyway? I hope it's not 'cause you wanna get hitched."

Drew blushed before replying, "Well, maybe not to get hitched. At least not yet."

Art snickered and then pulled a form from his desk drawer and said, "Go ahead and fill this out. Then I'll take you to Mister Miller. He'll show you how to do the job and assign you to your first train."

Drew sat down and began filling out the form. He figured he'd only have to last a year or so doing the extremely hazardous job. By then, the extra forty dollars a month he'd be earning should be enough to convince Anne's father that he was a good prospect. That assumed he didn't become one of Mister Jones' vanishing brakemen.

CHAPTER 1

Glendive, Montana Territory
April 10, 1884

Drew was studying the gray blanket that covered the sky as he waited for the engineer to blow the whistle. He knew it wouldn't be long before chilling rain began to fall. He only wished it was ten degrees colder so it would come down as snow.

At least there were no passenger cars on this run, so they'd only be stopping for water and coal. While making fewer stops was an advantage, there were two disadvantages for being a brakeman on a freight train. Without complaining passengers, the company expected engineers to make full use of his locomotive's power. And the added speed made Drew's job even more dangerous.

On this run, there were sixteen cars between the caboose and the coal car. And that meant that he had to make it across eight of them when they made each of those stops. Hank Fletcher would handle the rest. At least he had it better than Hank. Because he was senior, Drew enjoyed the comfort of the caboose while Hank had to sleep in a boxcar.

THE BRAKEMAN

When Drew heard the three sharp blasts from the locomotive's whistle, he knew it was time to suit up for the wet weather. So, he hopped onto the caboose platform, opened the door and stepped inside.

After he closed the door, Bill Jensen grinned and said, "It looks like you're gonna have a bad couple of days, Drew."

Drew stepped to his bunk, sat down and then replied, "I've seen worse weather, Bill. So, I'd better get ready before I get on top."

"I reckon so. You've been walking those cars for more'n two years now. Ain't that right?"

"It'll be two years next month."

"I wonder if that's a record for brakemen on the N.P."

The caboose lurched and the train began to move before Drew said, "I have no idea. But pretty soon all of their rolling stock will use Westinghouse air brakes and I'll be out of a job."

"But a lot of those small lines will still be using brakemen, so you could hire on with one of them."

Drew shook his head as he replied, "I'm finished being a brakeman, Bill. I think I've stretched my luck far enough. Besides, I only expected to be a brakeman for a year, and here it is almost two."

Drew pulled off his boots and then pulled on his waders. After slipping the suspenders over his shoulders, he stuffed his boots under the front of the waders before tightening a strap at the top of the waders.

As he hung his customized slicker over his head, Bill asked, "If you only figured on doing the job for a year, why did you stay on so long?"

As Drew began tying the slicker's wide straps around his torso, he replied, "I was planning to save enough money to prove to my girl's father that I could provide for her. But that didn't work out."

Bill snickered and then asked, "Did her pappy still think you weren't good enough after earning all that extra pay?"

Drew smiled as he answered, "No, it wasn't her father who was the problem. Before I even asked for his permission to visit her, she had found a suitor with better prospects."

"That musta been hard to swallow. But why did you stay on as a brakeman?"

"To be honest, after I learned that she'd already married someone else, I felt sorry for myself. And for a couple of months, I took risks that were almost suicidal. Then I figured it was just plain stupid and settled down."

"You sure are the best-equipped brakeman I ever met."

Drew finished tightening his slicker straps and then said, "After I realized sulking wasn't a good way to spend the rest of my life, I took steps to ensure that I could live the rest of my life."

"I can understand your odd slicker and why you wear those waders over your britches, but what else did you do to stay safe when you're running across those boxcar roofs?"

Even though Drew liked Bill, this was only their third run together, and he wasn't about to reveal all of his precautions, so he replied, "Aside from my fur-lined hat and my long-barreled Colt, I keep a sealed tin in my coat pocket with a box of matches."

Bill grinned as he said, "It sounds like you're planning on taking a swim, Drew."

"That's not why I look like a rubberized monk, Bill. When all I have to contend with is the wind, I don't wear the slicker or the waders. But if there's a chance of rain or snow, on they go. Although there have been a couple of times when I've almost been tossed into a river, it's still better than being blown off a roof onto a pile of jagged rocks."

"That's why they pay you boys as much as they do."

Drew grinned as he said, "They must have done some serious cyphering and figured out that it was still a bargain. They calculated that within a few months, they'd save a month's pay."

7

Bill nodded and said, "And some of 'em don't get to collect any pay at all. But let me ask you about those waders. I've been on a couple of trains where the brakemen slid off the roof 'cause of rain or snow. But don't your waders give you less grip up on those roofs?"

"They would if I didn't have a cobbler tap some steel brads into the soles to give me better traction."

Bill looked at Drew's feet and said, "Let me see 'em."

Drew lifted his right foot from the caboose floor and displayed its spiked bottom to the curious conductor.

After Drew dropped his foot to the floor, Bill chuckled and said, "I reckon they're going to come in pretty handy before our next stop at Miles City, too. We got that long downslope before we cross Cabin Creek and then the short one ahead of O'Fallon's Creek. But at least it's pretty level when we cross the Powder River bridge."

"The good news is that I'll only have to brake the caboose and two cars to slow us down."

Bill paused before he asked, "Drew, have you ever had Fast Jack Hickman drive any of your trains?"

Drew shook his head as he replied, "No, and I thought I knew all of them. Is he a new hire?"

"Yup. He used to work for the Denver & Rio Grande but got fired 'cause he rolled in to Castle Rock too fast and one of the brakemen was thrown off a car right in front of a bunch of folks. The Northern Pacific hired him last month but only lets him drive freights."

"I noticed that we were going a little faster than usual on this route, but not excessively."

Bill hesitated before saying, "I know. But there's a rumor going around about Fast Jack that I didn't pay much attention to. I figured it was just a tall tale growing out of that Castle Rock incident. But with the rain about to start falling and you planning to quit, I figgered you oughta know about it.

"Anyway, some of the other conductors heard that Fast Jack keeps a tally on how many brakemen he tossed off his trains. Kinda like those stories about gunfighters notching their pistols' grips for each man they killed."

Drew smiled as he said, "I find it hard to believe myself, Bill. But if Fast Jack sends me flying to my doom, you can ask him for his new total."

Bill didn't laugh as Drew had expected. He didn't even crack a smile which made Drew suspect that the conductor really did believe the rumor.

Bill then solemnly said, "Just be careful up there, Drew."

"I'm always careful, Bill. If I wasn't, I wouldn't be here."

9

Bill nodded before he stretched out on his bunk and said, "I'm gonna get some shuteye while I can."

"I'll be as quiet as a church mouse until Fast Jack blows his whistle."

Bill didn't open his eyes as he repeated, "Just be careful, Drew."

As Bill rested, Drew leaned back against the wall. As he pictured the engineer's face which he'd only seen for a couple of minutes, he thought about his spooky reputation. While he still found it difficult to believe, he knew it wouldn't matter even if it was true. Brakemen fell to their accidental deaths so frequently, no one would notice if Fast Jack was intentionally trying to kill them. Even if they did, they would never be able to prove it even if they bothered investigating which the never did.

He'd been honest when he gave Bill his reason for wearing his unusual, rubberized garb. But he'd made them more watertight than necessary in case he did fall into a river. Of course, there was a much greater chance that he'd land on hard ground, and then it wouldn't matter what he wore. But the waders and modified slicker would give him a chance to survive an unexpected plunge into a river. And the swimming lessons from his days in the orphanage would help, too. But the best way to survive being a brakeman was to avoid being tossed from the roof of a moving train.

Drew then peeled off his close-fitting fur-lined hat and set it on the bunk. After running his fingers through his thick, dark blonde hair, he decided it was time for a haircut. But he'd wait until he returned to Brainerd and have his regular barber give him the much-needed trim.

When he slid his fingertips across his cheek, Drew smiled. His whiskers grew slowly, and their light blonde shade allowed him to go three or four days without appearing unkempt.

Just as Bill began to snore, Drew looked out the small window and saw drops of water sliding across the glass. After noticing the moving moisture, he studied the passing landscape. He estimated the train's speed to be around forty miles per hour which wasn't an excessive speed on level ground. But he knew that until they reached the long downslope before Cabin Creek, the tracks followed a slight uphill grade. So, it seemed as if Fast Jack was living up to his nickname.

———

About ninety minutes later, Drew heard four whistle blasts which was surprising. Usually, he'd only have to brake two cars on this section of track, not four. But he still had a job to do, so he quickly pulled on his hat, folded down the ear flaps and tied the chin strap. After pulling on his gloves, he glanced at Bill and then opened the door and stepped onto the caboose's platform. He closed the door, took hold of the brake wheel and waited for the long whistle telling him to begin braking the cars.

As he stood on the rocking platform, Drew noticed that the train had picked up even more speed than he'd expected after starting its descent to the bridge across Cabin Creek. On his previous runs along this section of track, the engineers always reduced the throttle, yet Fast Jack appeared to be nudging it forward. Maybe that rumor was true after all.

The train was hurtling towards the bridge when one long blast of the locomotive's whistle reached Drew's ears. He quickly began spinning the brake wheel until it reached its stop.

Then he started climbing the ladder, and as soon as his face rose above the roof's edge, he felt the expected blast of cold air and chilling rain. The powerful wind and slick surface forced Drew to crawl along the caboose's roof. As soon as he reached the front edge, he grabbed the ladder's top rung and swung his wader's thick, studded boots over the edge and quickly descended to the platform. In the relative calm between the cars, Drew had no problem leaping onto the boxcar's platform.

It took Drew just fifteen seconds to apply the car's brakes and then begin his second climb. Because of the boxcar's length, crawling would take too long, so he'd have to trust in his wader's studded soles. When he poked his head above the roof, Drew noticed that the smoke pouring out of the locomotive's stack was being blown to the north. So, as soon as he climbed onto the roof, he leaned to his left and began the dangerous trek to the next car.

He soon made it to the front ladder and hurried down to the platform. After hopping onto the next car's platform, he quickly applied the brakes and then reached for the ladder.

But as he made the climb to the roof, Drew realized that the brakes weren't slowing the train as much as they should. When he reached the roof and saw even more smoke pouring out of the stack, Drew realized that Fast Jack was the reason for the brakes' ineffectiveness.

He considered staying on the platform and then seeing what the engineer would do, but he was concerned that the excess speed might derail the train. So, he hurriedly ascended the ladder and started trudging towards the front of the car. Through his squinting eyes, Drew could see the bridge across Cabin Creek up ahead and figured that applying the brakes on this car should be enough to avoid a derailment.

Drew had reached the front of the car and was reaching for the ladder's top rung when the locomotive suddenly slowed, and the cars began to accordion. When his boxcar banged into the one in front of it, Drew lost his balance and traction. In that brief moment when his left boot was just a small fraction of an inch above the slick surface, the strong southern wind was able to knock him sprawling toward the edge of the roof.

Drew fell onto his side and began clawing at the flat rooftop to keep from becoming Fast Jack's next notch.

He felt his right leg drop over the edge but was beginning to inch his way back when the train reached the Cabin Creek bridge. Drew was returning to his feet when his car began to cross the bridge and he was struck by a sudden gust.

The unexpected push sent Drew flailing backwards off the boxcar roof. As soon as he started falling, Drew clamped his elbows against his head to protect it in case he hit the bridge's structure. He watched the terrifying wooden beams flash by just before he plunged into the icy waters of Cabin Creek. The melting snow and spring rains may have turned the creek into a raging torrent, but they also added another two feet of depth. And those extra twenty-four inches of water were enough to save his life.

Drew had struck the water as if he was sitting in a barber's chair. So, after he penetrated the surface, he followed a rapid, curving path, just missing the creek bottom by four inches. As he slowed and began his feet-first ascent, Drew straightened and finally gained some measure of control when he spread his arms and began to fly to the surface.

By the time he popped his head above the surging water and took a deep gulp of precious air, he was already more than two hundred yards away from the bridge. As the icy water carried him quickly downstream, Drew couldn't even see the train. But at the moment, the train and Fast Jack could be in

China for all he cared. What was critically important was to get ashore. So, he began swimming to the eastern bank which was only fifty or sixty feet away.

Drew expected to crawl out of the icy water in less than a minute, but after his first few strokes, he realized that he wasn't making as much headway as he'd hoped. The water was moving so fast that he was barely making progress at all. The realization was disheartening, but he wasn't about to give up. He simply adjusted his time estimate as he continued to slowly swim toward the bank.

After almost three minutes of struggling, Drew thought he was close enough to stand and then walk to onto solid ground. But just as he dropped his wader's boots to the bottom, he entered a large, swirling eddy that pushed him away from the tantalizingly close bank. It was as if Cabin Creek was toying with him.

The eddy hadn't shoved him to the middle of the creek, but to Drew, those thirty feet may well have been three hundred. But he continued windmilling his tired arms through the water while hoping the creek didn't have another trick up its sleeve. But it wasn't Cabin Creek that created his next problem. It was the Yellowstone River.

The Northern Pacific's tracks paralleled the Yellowstone for most of Montana Territory, and Cabin Creek emptied into the long, deep and turbulent river. So, as Drew was nearing Cabin Creek's eastern bank, the creek suddenly turned and then flowed into the Yellowstone River. But it wasn't a peaceful merger. The Yellowstone greedily accepted Cabin Creek's liquid offering, pulling its water and Drew into its own deep channel.

Drew rested his arms as he watched the shoreline fade away and realized that his chances for survival were now almost negligible. As the Yellowstone floated him further downriver, Drew almost laughed at the irony of his situation. He'd bought his clownish-looking rubberized outfit to keep him from being blown off the roof of a moving train. It had not only failed in its intended purpose but was now keeping him alive long enough to contemplate his death.

While some of the chilly water had leaked under his slicker and into his waders, only his hat and coat sleeves were fully soaked. But he could feel the water wicking its way through his coat's fibers and knew it would eventually drag him to his drowning demise. And the frigid water was already beginning to steal his body's heat.

Drew didn't know how much longer he'd be able to stay afloat, but he wasn't about to surrender to the Yellowstone. As the river carried him on its journey to join with the mighty Missouri River, Drew pushed aside the water with his right arm so he could look upstream. The surge of churning water from the melting snow and spring's rains carried a lot of loose debris. It even pulled trees from the ground, and he was hoping to spot one of the river's pine victims floating behind him.

While he didn't see any branches sticking above the surface, he did glimpse something long and narrow bobbing on the water. Drew didn't know what it was but began angling towards the object.

He was about twenty feet away when he realized it was the bottom of a birch canoe. Drew didn't care if its skin had a hole as big as a fist as long as it gave him more buoyancy.

As soon as he reached the canoe, Drew threw his right arm over its bottom expecting it to drop below the water. But it didn't. While it dipped down a few inches, there was still an inch riding above the surface. He knew there must be air trapped inside, and that meant there wasn't a hole in its birch bark skin. That revelation improved Drew's chances for survival which greatly raised his spirit.

With his arm clutching onto the canoe, Drew began kicking his feet to bring him closer to the riverbank. His heavy waders made for slow going but it was his only option. As he began inching towards solid ground, Drew suspected the southern bank was closer but didn't bother looking behind him to check. He wasn't about to try to turn the canoe around no matter how near it was.

His legs were threatening to revolt as the Yellowstone continued carrying Drew and the canoe downriver. But after more than fifteen minutes of his agonizingly slow progress, Drew was just a few short yards from safety. His spirit soared knowing that he'd soon be able to stand when he heard the distant, but unmistakable roar of rapids.

He knew he should abandon the canoe and swim those last few yards but felt an obligation to the birch bark boat that had saved him. So, he ignored the threatening sound of the rapids calling for him and forced his legs to work faster and then began digging into the cold water with his left arm.

The rapids thunderous roar warned Drew he had less than a minute to reach safety before he was sucked into its grip. So, he dropped his feet down and was almost surprised when they touched the riverbed. He quickly began shoving the canoe toward the riverbank as the powerful current tried to wrestle the upturned watercraft away from him. If it won the battle, it would push him and the canoe into the gaping jaws of the rapids.

Using the last ounce of his strength, Drew willed his legs to keep moving and just as he thought he'd failed, the current suddenly abated. He took a deep breath and after the canoe scraped the bottom, Drew looked upriver and about thirty yards away, he saw a small peninsula jutting out from the bank.

Drew slowly walked to the front of the canoe and took hold of its nose. He then dragged the canoe halfway onto the bank before he collapsed onto his back.

THE BRAKEMAN

As Drew gasped for air, the raindrops fell into his open mouth. It was some of the same traitorous spring rain that had conspired with Fast Jack so he could add another brakeman to his list. But he didn't blame the rain for almost killing him, only Fast Jack. As he burned the engineer's face into his memory, so he'd recognize the man and then get his revenge on the sadistic engineer. But to have his revenge, he had to stay alive, and the first step to his survival was to get warm and dry.

When he'd recovered his strength, Drew slowly rose and walked toward a forest of assorted deciduous trees, mostly river birch. The same species whose bark had been used to create his life-saving canoe.

As he made his way into the trees, Drew's first priority was to build a fire, so he began loosening the straps that kept his slicker tightly wrapped around his torso. When he found a reasonably dry spot, Drew removed his gloves, pulled the sealed tin from his coat's right pocket and then made the mistake of squatting. As soon as his butt touched his heels, both of his calves knotted into vicious cramps. Drew grunted before he dropped onto his back and quickly straightened his lower limbs. His legs were covered with the layers of his britches and the thick rubber of his waders, so Drew wasn't able to massage his rock-like calves. All he could do was to allow the muscles to relax on their own.

While Drew waited for his calves to calm down, he scanned his surroundings for fuel for his fire. Birch trees were well

19

known for dropping branches as well as leaves, so there was almost a carpet of fallen branches of assorted sizes. Now that the fire issue was resolved, Drew tried to get a crude estimate of his location. After a minute or so of calculation, Drew figured he was at least four or five miles downriver from Cabin Creek.

He knew the closest settlement was Glendive, but it was around forty miles east of Cabin Creek and on the other side of the Yellowstone. But now that he had the canoe, the Yellowstone River was no longer an obstacle. If it wasn't for the rapids, he'd just ride the Yellowstone's current all the way to Glendive. So tomorrow, he'd fashion a paddle and use the canoe to cross the river to reach the southern shore and the Northern Pacific tracks.

He knew none of the passing trains would stop for him, but that wouldn't matter. After reaching the opposite bank, he'd be able to walk to Glendive. And then he'd surprise Fast Jack Hickman when his train stopped on its way back to Brainerd.

———

Bill Jensen angrily asked, "Why'd you pull your throttle back when we were crossing the bridge over Cabin Creek, Jack? You musta known Drew was up there."

Fast Jack shrugged and then replied, "We weren't slowin' fast enough. He shoulda figured that out on his own 'cause it's part of his job. And you ain't a special agent, Jensen, so back off."

THE BRAKEMAN

Bill glared at the engineer for a few seconds before he turned and then stomped out of the diner.

Fast Jack watched him leave, and was grinning as he finished his supper.

———

Now that his large fire had warmed the air sufficiently, Drew removed his slicker and dropped it onto the ground. Next, he peeled off his hat and then his wet coat and draped them over a nearby branch to dry. After he removed his wet shirt and hung it beside his coat, Drew slid his slicker's suspenders over his shoulders and then picked up his slicker and put it back on without tightening the straps.

After removing his boots which were remarkably dry, he lowered his waders to his knees and then sat down. He tugged off the waders and then removed his socks and pulled on his boots.

He decided his britches weren't wet enough to require removal, so after hanging his socks, Drew sat on the top of his waders. As he waited for his coat, shirt and socks to dry, Drew removed his heavy gunbelt and laid it across his lap. He then slid his heavy, eight-inch knife from its sheath and set it on the waders' left leg. After he released his Colt's hammer loop, Drew slid the long pistol from his holster.

Drew had bought the Colt last year when he noticed it in the display case at Sorensen & Sons Firearms. What had attracted his attention was its unusually long barrel. Jan Sorensen told him that Colt offered customers longer barrels but charged an extra dollar for each additional inch. So, just because it was interesting, Drew paid the extra two dollars and bought the pistol with its 9 ½ inch barrel.

The Colt was the first gun he'd ever owned and had only bought it because he'd almost been robbed by two thugs in Stillwater on his previous trip. But having the pistol wouldn't matter if he didn't know how to use it. So, since buying the pistol, Drew had been a regular at the Sorensen's target range. It was there that he began to fully appreciate the value of those additional two inches of barrel length. On his last practice session, he took ten shots at the hundred-foot target, and seven were within the six-inch-diameter bullseye.

After setting it beside his knife, Drew began removing the sixteen .45 caliber Long Colt cartridges from the gunbelt's leather loops. It wasn't because he wanted to let them dry, he just didn't want them glued to the leather.

———

By the time sunset arrived, Drew had donned his dry shirt and fairly dry coat and hat before stretching out on his slicker. He'd just added more branches to his fire but knew that when he awakened in the morning, he'd need to build it again to ward off the freezing temperatures. Then he'd start crafting his makeshift paddle and when it was done, he'd row across the Yellowstone and then start following the tracks to Glendive.

His stomach was protesting as he closed his eyes, but he promised his deprived belly that when he reached Glendive, he'd eat until it begged him to stop sending food for it to digest.

———

As Drew drifted to sleep, natural forces were underway which would force him to break that promise.

Before the train had departed Glendive, an enormous avalanche had rolled down the face of an unnamed mountain along the Bighorn River. The massive slide of frozen water plunged into the Bighorn which created a ten-foot-high wave that raced toward the Yellowstone. As the snow melted, the river's level began rising until it was two feet deeper than it had been before the avalanche.

By the time Drew had fallen asleep, the temporary flood passed Cabin Creek and just two minutes later, it snatched Drew's canoe from the bank and then carried it downriver to the rapids.

CHAPTER 2

When Drew awakened the next morning, despite the frigid air, he wasn't able to rebuild his fire as soon as he'd hoped. When he tried to sit up, his body ached so badly from his neck down to his toes that he found it difficult to move. At least the rain had moved on, so after it warmed, it should be a pleasant spring day.

It took him almost ten minutes of stretching his muscles and bending his joints before he was able to get to his feet. After emptying his overfull bladder, Drew began gathering kindling. Fifteen minutes later, he stood in front of the flames and visually searched for a forked branch that could serve as a frame for his paddle. After he cut it down to size, he'd wrap the emergency coil of cord which he kept in his coat pocket around the end with the split to create his paddle.

After he spotted the perfect candidate, Drew put on his slicker and after returning the cartridges to his gunbelt's loops, he buckled it around his waist. He walked to the branch, gripped it with both of his gloved hands and then backstepped until the bowed branch suddenly snapped. Drew then slipped his knife from its sheath and cut the thin strip of birchwood that still bound the branch to the rest of the tree.

As he dragged the branch back to the fire, Drew glanced at the river and immediately froze. *Where was the canoe?* He dropped the branch and hurried to the riverbank hoping it was just his memory that had failed him. When he reached the edge of the Yellowstone, Drew quickly scanned the shoreline and soon realized the canoe was gone.

Drew chastised himself for not dragging the canoe to the trees, but now he had to deal with the consequences of his mistake. He stood on the bank for another five minutes as he considered his options. The loss of the canoe meant he'd be unable to cross the Yellowstone, so he'd have to walk along the bank until he could take the ferry into Glendive.

Before Drew walked back to his fire, he looked downriver and felt his stomach twist in a knot when he realized his path was blocked by a tall, steep bluff that ran to the river's edge. That meant he'd have head west and walk the longer distance to Miles City.

But when he turned his eyes upriver, he was disheartened for a second time. The small peninsula that had blocked the strong current was the tip of a tall ridge. And the ridge was really the edge of the foothill of a small mountain. So, he'd have to find another path to reach Glendive.

Drew walked down river for a hundred yards or so before he turned and looked north. Before him was a wide valley with mountains on either side. He couldn't see how far the valley extended, but it was his only way out.

Drew sighed and then headed back to his fire. And now that he wouldn't be reaching Glendive anytime soon, he'd have to hunt for the food his stomach demanded.

After tossing a few more branches onto his fire, Drew pulled his long-barreled Colt and walked deeper into the trees. He'd never even aimed it at anything other than a paper target, so he hoped he didn't hesitate to pull his trigger when he spotted a live animal.

He had the gentle spring breeze in his face as he slowly stepped through the forest. But it was almost impossible to be stealthy as he walked across the carpet of dead birch branches. Luckily, he soon left the river birches behind and entered a mixture of oaks, cottonwoods and pines. The ground was undulating and was slowly rising as Drew continued deeper into the trees.

Drew had just climbed out of a shallow vale when he saw a pair of whitetail hares having their breakfast about thirty feet away. He slowly cocked his Colt's hammer and then set his sights on the fatter of the two rabbits. Drew kept his sights steady as he slowly squeezed his trigger. When his Colt roared, the rabbit he'd targeted fell, and the second bunny scurried into the brush. Drew was pleased that he hadn't hesitated and had been accurate with his shot. He then holstered his pistol and trotted down into the vale.

———

Drew may never have shot a living creature before, but he had skinned and prepared rabbits and other small mammals many times. He'd also plucked and cleaned chickens, geese and ducks while he lived at St. Thomas Home for Boys. It was one of the chores for boys between the ages of nine and twelve. Younger boys were required to perform basic housecleaning while older boys were taught different trades. Drew had been a blacksmith's apprentice for his last three years in the home, but when he left the orphanage, he was unable to find work in the trade.

St. Thomas wasn't like the other orphanages he'd heard about. While the boys were required to work, schooling was also mandatory. They received encouragement and praise when they did well, and when discipline was necessary, it wasn't harsh. By the time they were ten, most of the boys were eager to impress their teachers and other members of the staff. There were a few exceptions of course, but the compassionate people who ran the orphanage still did all they could to help them become good men.

So, using the skills he'd learned at the orphanage, it didn't take Drew long to skin and clean the rabbit. It was just fifteen minutes after he returned that Drew had the rabbit skewered on the end of a branch and roasting over the fire. It was the same branch he'd planned to use as a paddle.

While he rotated the rabbit, Drew wished he'd stored a small pouch of salt in his tin. But neither the tin's contents nor any of his other gear was meant to help him survive in the wilderness. Yet he was very grateful for what he did have. He was sure that none of Fast Jack's other brakeman victims were as well prepared as he was. His waders and belted slicker had saved him from drowning, and the dry matches allowed him to build a fire.

While they had allowed him to survive, what he hadn't mentioned to anyone was what he had stored inside the rubberized pouch he wore beneath his shirt. It contained his savings since he left the orphanage which was originally meant to impress Anne McDuff's father. Inside the waterproof money belt was four hundred and forty dollars in U.S. notes, and another hundred and thirty in gold and silver coins. But that money and the three dollars and sixty-five cents in his pockets would only be useful if he reached Glendive.

––––––

After consuming every bit of the roasted hare, Drew draped his waders over his left shoulder and then left the trees and turned north into the wide valley. As he walked, Drew continuously scanned the landscape. He paid particular attention to the mountains on his right that blocked his path to Glendive. They weren't as tall as the mountains to the west, but he still wasn't about to risk making the climb if he spotted a potential pass. He guessed the furthest mountaintop was about twenty miles away. It would be a five-hour walk before he could turn east to go around the mountains. And it could be even longer if he began seeing lower peaks rise over the northeastern horizon. Drew's biggest hope was to spot a narrow valley or even a canyon that cut between the mountains. But if he didn't find one, he hoped that in five hours, he'd reach level ground.

———

Near the other end of the valley, Boney Remy stood in front of his cabin with his Winchester in his hands and shouted, "Get off of my land or I'll start shooting!"

Bart Early yelled, "You're squattin' on Northern Pacific property! And this is the only warnin' you're gonna get!"

Bart then wheeled his dark brown gelding about, and after the other three riders turned their horses around, the four men rode away heading northeast.

Boney glared at the four mounted men until they were out of sight, before he looked at his daughter and said, "That railroad isn't going to steal our land. We'll make those four thugs sorry if they come back, Gabby."

Gabrielle lowered her Sharps carbine before she and her father turned and entered their cabin. After she closed the door, she hung thr Sharps on its pegs before her father returned his Winchester to their homemade gunrack.

When they sat at the table, Francine asked, "I heard what they said, Boney. I know you and Gabby can shoot, but we can't stay awake all the time. What will you do if they come at night?"

Boney scratched his bearded chin and replied, "I'll figure something out before they come back, Fran. But we can't give up. Your father gave us this land and the damned railroad can't take it away just because the federal government said they could have it."

Francine nodded as she said, "They already pushed my people off their land, but we will not let them drive us off of ours."

Gabrielle then asked, "How many cartridges do you have left, Papa?"

Boney looked at his daughter and replied, "We have almost a half a box of cartridges for the Winchester and sixteen for the Sharps. So, we have plenty of ammunition. But I agree with your mother. They will not come back during the day. They will sneak in at night and try to shoot us while we are sleeping."

Gabrielle glanced at her mother before saying, "Then we will set up traps and other ways to warn us if they come at night."

Boney kissed his daughter on her forehead before saying, "You are a strong warrior like your grandfather, Gabby."

Francine then said, "They are devious men, Bonaparte. They may not give us very many days before they return. Instead of riding back to Glendive, they might camp near the eastern mountains and come back tonight."

Boney replied, "I didn't believe them, either, so we will start making our preparations right away."

Gabrielle asked, "Do you think they will bring more men with them this time, Papa?"

"I don't think so. But even if they do, they won't be able to get within two hundred yards of our home without exposing themselves."

Francine looked at the gunrack as she said, "I wish we had another rifle."

Gabrielle then said, "I wish old Beau was still alive. He could warn us of their approach before they could get close to our home."

Francine smiled at her daughter as she said, "Beau was a good dog, but I wish we could find you a human beau, sweetheart."

Gabrielle shook her head and said, "I don't need a husband, Maman. I am happy living with you and Papa."

Before Francine could express her very different opinion, Boney said, "Let's start preparing for them while we have the time."

After his wife said, "Yes, we must get ready," the Remy family began gathering anything they could use to protect their home from the Northern Pacific hoodlums.

―――――

After walking for more than three hours, the temperature had risen enough to make his fur-lined hat a nuisance, so Drew stopped, removed his hat and stuffed it into his waders.

Drew was in a good mood because he was certain that he would soon reach the end of the valley. Then he'd turn east, and in another day or so, he'd ride the ferry across the Yellowstone and reach Glendive.

With his optimism buoyed, Drew resumed walking at a faster pace and began whistling *Row, Row, Row Your Boat.*

―――――

Boney leaned on his shovel while Francine and Gabrielle covered the three-foot deep hole with branches. When they finished, he began scooping the loose dirt on top until it was the same level as the surrounding ground.

As he smoothed the edges, Gabrielle asked, "Do you think four will be enough, Papa?"

Boney replied, "I think so. But now we will make more surprises for our unwanted visitors."

Francine's hands were on her hips as she stared eastward and said, "They could be watching us with field glasses, Boney."

Bonaparte looked at the distant forest on the other side of the valley and said, "It doesn't matter, mon petit papillion. If they are watching, then they'll know we are willing to defend our home."

Gabrielle snapped, "I want them to come, Papa! Then Maman and I will show them we are not weak women."

Boney chuckled as he said, "And you are a better shot than your old father, too."

Gabrielle didn't dispute her father's claim as it would smack of false modesty. Instead, she honestly said, "Only with the Winchester, Papa."

"And that's only when you fire the Sharps from a standing position, Gabrielle."

Gabrielle quickly changed the topic by asking, "How are we going to protect Jean and Jacques?"

Boney stood and then replied, "They'll be all right where they are. They want our land, not our mules. So, let's return to the cabin and have lunch. We'll string the tripping line just before sunset."

Francine smiled as she said, "And you need to wash before entering our home, Monsieur Remy."

Boney kissed his wife before saying, "Yes, Madame."

As they walked back to their cabin, Boney was thinking about any other tactics those bastards from the railroad might employ to steal their land.

———

Drew's stomach was angrily reminding him that it had been a long time since it had seen anything drop down from his esophagus, but there was nothing he could do about it. He'd seen two small herds of white-tailed deer, but they were well beyond the range of his long-barreled Colt. He'd also spotted a black bear who must be hungry after his long hibernation and was grateful that it was even further away.

Drew suddenly picked up the very faint scent of smoke. He immediately stopped and slowly searched for its source. The mild breeze was coming from the north, but as he stared in that direction, his eyes failed to see what his nose had detected. So, after taking a deep breath, Drew resumed walking.

As he continued walking, Drew wondered who had built the fire that had created the smoke. Knowing he wouldn't find an answer until he saw the smoke, Drew pushed the mystery to the back of his mind. He had more serious issues to resolve, including finding something to quiet his growling stomach.

———

Boney set his empty cup on the table and said, "I don't know when we'll be able to go to Glendive for supplies, Fran."

Francine replied, "We'll be all right, Boney. We can live without coffee, sugar and white flour."

"I know we can, but we're almost out of salt and lard."

Gabrielle said, "I can ride Jean to town for the supplies, Papa. They won't bother me."

Boney exclaimed, "They'll do worse that just bother you, Gabby! Those men have no souls!"

Gabrielle was stunned by her father's almost violent reaction and quickly said, "I'm sorry, Papa."

Boney sighed and then took his daughter's hand and said "It is I who should apologize, Gabrielle. You are a grown woman, yet still do not understand the nature of men. I have failed you as your father."

Gabrielle smiled as she said, "You are the best father a girl could hope for, Papa. And I am not as naïve as you believe. I know enough about men's nature to understand why you would be afraid to allow me to go to Glendive alone."

"Then why did you even offer to go?"

"Because you and Maman need to stay and defend our home."

Francine then said, "Let's not discuss going to Glendive until those men return."

Gabrielle nodded as she replied, "Alright, Maman. We have enough salt for a week or so anyway."

Francine smiled but knew Gabrielle wouldn't be so easily quieted the next time she offered to ride to town. She'd rather face those four railroad ruffians than argue with her daughter.

———

Drew had been focusing on the last mountain that blocked his path to Glendive when he turned his eyes to the center of the valley and saw the tendril of smoke rising into the sky at his ten o'clock position. It was less than a minute later when he spotted the roof of a large cabin. Who occupied it was unimportant. He hoped they would give him directions to Glendive, and he'd be happy to pay for some food, too.

Drew wished he had wings as he seemed that his long legs weren't drawing him any closer to the cabin. It was as if it was floating away at the same speed that he was moving. The thought was so absurd it made Drew begin to laugh.

He was still smiling when he estimated he had about another mile to walk before he reached the cabin. So, Drew had time to decide how to act when he reached its front door. He knew that even without wearing his waders, he looked like a visitor from a different world. So, he stopped and dropped his waders onto the ground and then unbuckled his gunbelt. After setting it on his waders, Drew pulled off his slicker and laid it down before unbuttoning his coat and strapping his gunbelt back on. Then he rolled his slicker and stuffed it into his waders left leg before hanging them over his left forearm.

Now that he no longer presented such a bizarre appearance, Drew resumed his approach to the cabin. As he could see more details, he spotted two mules in a small corral behind the cabin yet still hadn't seen anyone. And their absence bothered him. It was the middle of the afternoon, yet no one was outside working. The cabin was well maintained, and the grounds seemed orderly, so someone should be outside.

He then spotted a stream that ran behind the cabin and then disappeared into a long, deep forest. When he looked to the southwest to find the stream again, he spotted a tall totem standing around a half a mile away. He hadn't noticed it before because it was the same color as the pines behind it. But at this angle, he could see the red face painted on this side of the totem. Drew had no idea why it was there or what it meant but assumed it had something to do with the cabin.

Drew was less than a quarter of mile from the cabin and had yet to see anyone. So, as he continued his approach, he focused on the door expecting it to open at any moment. He was concentrating so much on the door that he wasn't looking where he was walking.

He was still intently watching the cabin when he was around a hundred feet away. And if he'd even glanced at the ground, he would have seen the fresh dirt surrounding one of the Remys' four hidden traps.

Seconds later, Drew's long strides allowed his right foot to reach the center of the disguised hole. And as soon as he put a small fraction of his hundred and eighty pounds onto the foot, it snapped the branches and then dropped three feet into the ground.

As soon as he felt his foot drop, Drew shouted a well-known obscenity and then fell awkwardly to the ground.

His loud, blue reaction startled Boney, Francine and Gabrielle making them leap from their chairs.

Boney yelled, "They're back!" and then raced to the wall to grab his Winchester.

Gabrielle and Francine ran behind him and as Boney yanked open the door, Gabrielle took down the Sharps and cocked the hammer.

Drew was sitting on the ground beside the hole pulling away the sharp ends of the branches to free his leg when he heard the cabin door open. After he turned to greet the occupants, he realized he might not have the opportunity when he saw an older man with a Winchester pointed at him.

Boney didn't recognize the young, blonde-headed man who'd been caught by their trap, but he still kept his repeater aimed at the stranger when he shouted, "Who are you and why are you sneaking up on our cabin?"

Drew forgot about the branches and quickly thrust his hands into the air as he loudly replied, "My name is Drew Campbell, and I wasn't sneaking, sir. I don't even know where I am."

Boney wasn't convinced and asked, "Do you work for the Northern Pacific? And don't try to lie to me."

Drew was about to answer when a tall, stunningly beautiful young woman stepped out of the cabin carrying a rifle. He was so astonished by her appearance that he forgot to reply to the man's question.

Boney reminded him of his failure when he loudly said, "I asked you a question, mister. Do you work for the Northern Pacific Railroad?"

Drew blinked and then replied, "Um, yes, sir. At least I did until a yesterday."

Boney stared at Drew for a few seconds before he asked, "I haven't seen you before, so why'd you quit? And that still doesn't explain what you're doing here."

Drew tried not to stare at the young woman with the rifle as he answered, "I didn't quit. I was a brakeman on a westbound freight train and was blown off the roof of a boxcar as it crossed Cabin Creek. Then I was swept into the Yellowstone before I made it to shore."

Gabrielle was staring at Drew as her father asked, "What the hell is a brakeman and why were you on the roof of a train car?"

Drew sighed before saying, "It will take a while to explain. So, may I take my leg out of the hole before I answer your questions?"

Boney didn't lower his Winchester's barrel before he said, "Go ahead."

Drew looked away from the cabin before he resumed pulling the broken branches away from his leg. After the last pointy piece of pine was out of the way, he lifted his foot out of the hole and then slowly stood upright.

Then he asked, "Is it okay if I pick up my waders?"

Boney looked at the large, rubberized britches with rubber boots attached at the ends of the legs and said, "Go ahead. I've never seen anything like them before. What did you call them?"

Drew hung his waders over his left forearm before he replied, "They're called waders because fishermen wear them so they can wade into streams and get closer to the fish."

Boney tilted his head slightly before asking, "Were you planning on fishing before you fell off the roof of the train?"

"No, sir. I didn't buy them to go fishing. I bought them to keep dry when it was raining, and I had to walk across moving train cars."

Francine then said, "Boney, I think we should continue this conversation inside in case those men are watching."

Boney glanced at the eastern forest before lowering his Winchester and saying, "My name's Bonaparte Remy. And you can tell us the rest of your story in our cabin, Mister Campbell."

Drew said, "Thank you," and then started walking to the cabin.

As he approached the doorway, he wondered who they believed might be watching the cabin and why. But he strongly suspected that the unseen men were employed by the Northern Pacific. But despite his many questions, Drew found it difficult to ignore the dark-haired, incredibly attractive young woman whom he assumed was their daughter.

Boney waited until Drew was close before he said, "Francine, you and Gabrielle can go inside, and I'll follow Mister Campbell."

Francine nodded and entered their cabin, but Gabrielle looked at Drew for another five seconds before she followed her mother.

————

There were no Northern Pacific men or anyone else watching when Drew entered the cabin. By the time he'd fallen into their trap, the four men had already returned to Glendive.

As his three subordinates rode to Finney's Diner to fill their stomachs, Bart Early pulled up in front of the Northern Pacific offices and dismounted.

After entering the building, he walked past the secretary and entered the private office of the director, closed the door and removed his hat.

Ira Butler waited until Bart sat down before he asked, "Did you get rid of them?"

"We didn't get the chance. The old Frog saw us comin' and him and his half-breed daughter were waitin' with rifles."

Ira snapped, "*So what*? There are four of you, and you all have Winchesters!"

"But you shoulda told us they had rifles before we left. And you ain't payin' us enough to get shot, Butler."

Ira calmed down before asking, "So, did you just turn around and leave?"

Bart shook his head and replied, "Before we left, I told 'em they were squattin' on Northern Pacific land and if they weren't gone when we came back, we'd kill 'em."

Ira leaned back and said, "That should keep them awake for a while. But when you go back in a few days, wait until nighttime and burn them out."

Bart nodded and said, "I ain't got a problem with it, but Arnie and Jimmy might balk when I tell 'em to torch the place with them inside."

"Tell them I'll give each of you a fifty-dollar bonus after it's done."

Bart slowly stood, said, "If they balk, you can give me and Cole a hundred each. I'll pay Arnie and Jimmy off with a few ounces of lead," and then turned and left the office.

After Bart closed the door, Ira opened his humidor, took one of his fat Cuban cigars and hoped that after they burned down the cabin, not even one of them returned.

———

Gabrielle hung the Sharps on their crude gunrack and then after her father entered the cabin, she took his Winchester and set it on its pegs.

Boney closed the door and said, "Have a seat at the far end of the table, Mister Campbell."

Drew nodded, and after setting his waders on the floor, he sat on the designated chair.

Before Drew could begin answering Boney's questions, Gabrielle asked, "Would you like something to eat, Mister Campbell?"

Drew smiled and replied, "I'd appreciate it, ma'am. But I think I should explain why I'm here first."

Gabrielle glanced at her mother before saying, "You can do that while I fix a plate for you."

Drew felt surprisingly awkward before he simply replied, "Thank you, ma'am."

Gabrielle smiled and then turned away before Drew looked at Boney and said, "Once a train is moving, it's hard for a locomotive to stop it on its own. So, a brakeman's job is to apply the brakes on each of the cars to slow it down faster. And the only way to do it is to climb across the cars."

Boney's eyebrows rose as he asked, "You climb over the train cars' roofs? Even in the snow and ice?"

"Yes, sir. They pay us a lot more money than regular workers because it's so dangerous and a lot of them still quit after their first trip. And most of the ones who stay on the job don't survive for a full year."

"How long have you been a brakeman?"

"For almost two years, but I was going to quit soon. The Northern Pacific is converting all of their rolling stock to use the Westinghouse air brake system, so they won't need brakemen anymore."

Gabrielle set a glass of water and plate with some cold venison and a piece of cornbread on the table before sitting down.

Drew smiled, said, "Thank you, ma'am," and then drank half of the water in the tall glass.

When he set the glass down, Gabrielle said, "You're welcome, Mister Campbell. My name is Gabrielle, but my parents call me Gabby when they're not angry at me."

Drew's discomfort returned in spades as he replied, "My name is Andrew, but I go by Drew."

When Gabrielle smiled at him, Drew quickly turned his eyes to her father and said, "When the train left Glendive yesterday morning, there was a cold spring rain, so the boxcar roofs were slick. On days like that, I wear my waders and my slicker which has belts to keep it from flapping around in the wind.

"But when we began the descent to the bridge across Cabin Creek, the train was moving too fast. So, the engineer blew the whistle four times telling me to apply the brakes on four cars. I was on the third one when we reached the bridge. That's when the engineer suddenly pulled the throttle all the way back.

"When he did, the train jolted and made me lose my balance. I almost slid off the side but caught myself before I fell. But just when I started to stand, a gust of wind blew me into Cabin Creek. Then it handed me over to the Yellowstone."

Francine quickly asked, "How did you keep from drowning?"

"My slicker and waders kept most of the cold water out, but I still was in trouble until I spotted an overturned canoe. I hung onto it until I was able to make it to shore. I spent the night in a forest and planned to use the canoe to cross the Yellowstone the next morning. But when I woke up, it was gone, so I followed the valley hoping to find a way to reach Glendive."

Before Drew could continue, Francine said, "You can tell us more after you clean your plate."

Drew smiled as he nodded and then cut the venison into small pieces and popped one into his mouth.

As he chewed, he looked at Boney and asked, "Why did you think someone was watching? I got the impression that they work for the Northern Pacific."

Boney replied, "A little more than a month ago, some men showed up with all sorts of instruments. They said that they were worked for the Northern Pacific and were looking for coal. I told them that we owned all the land from the deep gully to the north to the totem in the south. Their leader seemed surprised but didn't argue with me.

"Then a week or so later, Ira Butler, the Northern Pacific manager in Glendive, showed up and told us that the government gave our land to the Northern Pacific, and we had to leave. I told him that the Crows gave us the land, and we weren't going anywhere. Then this morning, four Northern Pacific thugs showed up. They said we were squatters and if we were still here when they came back in a few days, we'd be sorry."

Drew swallowed and then said, "That's not right, Mister Remy. While the federal government does give the railroads land to offset the cost of building the railroad, they lied when they claimed that your cabin is on Northern Pacific property."

Boney's eyebrows rose as he asked, "It isn't?

Drew shook his head and replied, "No, sir. The railroad is only given ten miles of property on each side of their projected routes. So, the Northern Pacific's land grants ended a good nine or ten miles south of here."

Drew continued eating as he thought about the intriguing situation. He was reasonably sure that he was right about the legal issues involved, but he couldn't understand why Ira Butler would make the fallacious claim. And even more puzzling was use of strongarm tactics to force the Remys off their land.

Boney glanced at his wife before he asked, "So, why did Butler lie to us and then send those four men to threaten us?"

"That's what bothers me, Mister Remy. He wouldn't have made that claim unless the Northern Pacific exploration team found a large deposit of high-grade bituminous coal on your land. And that's the best type of coal for locomotives. Then..."

Drew suddenly found the answer to one of his questions and said, "I was wrong. I don't think he lied about the Northern Pacific owning the land."

Boney said, "But you just told us that their land grants ended ten miles away."

"I know. But then I realized that if the exploration team reported finding a large, valuable coal deposit, the Northern Pacific would want to build a spur line to the coal face. Then they'd request land grants for the spur, which would include the entire valley."

Boney sighed before saying, "And that's why Butler told us we were squatting on their land."

Drew nodded, "I'm afraid so. But while he may not have lied, I can't understand his behavior. When Ira Butler showed up, did he say anything other than to claim it was Northern Pacific land and that you had to leave?"

"No, all he did was tell us we had no right to be here."

Drew said, "That's not right. Even if the land grant request had been approved, he shouldn't have just ordered you off the land. How much land did the Crows give you?"

"The northern border is a deep gully, and it runs south to a totem."

Drew nodded and said, "I saw the totem. So, how far away is the gully that marks your northern border?"

"About two miles or so. The western border is marked by the tallest mountain peak, and there's a large boulder in the middle of the valley that marks the eastern border."

Drew did some quick cyphering and then said, "That's at least eight thousand acres. But I doubt the government would consider you legal owners of the land even if you have written proof that the Crow gave it to you."

"I'm sure that you're right. So, they can just force us out after all."

"Maybe not. How long have you lived here?"

"Almost twenty years. Gabrielle was born here, too."

Drew smiled at Gabrielle before saying, "So, even if the N.P. has the land grants and the government won't recognize the eight thousand acres as your property, you still have what they call squatter's rights. That means you'd be able to buy some of the land from the government."

"How much does it cost?"

"A dollar and a quarter an acre, but you'd only be able to buy a hundred and sixty acres."

A disheartened Bonaparte Napoleon Remy quietly said, "Then I reckon the railroad is going to win because we can't afford to buy even twenty acres, Mister Campbell."

Drew heard the undertone of defeat in his voice and then quickly said, "Don't give up hope yet, Mister Remy. Even if the Northern Pacific had their land grants approved, Mister Butler's behavior was wrong. He should have negotiated with you, not just ordered you to leave, much less threaten you."

"Why would he negotiate with us if we can't prove we own our land?"

"Because the Northern Pacific will want to have that spur completed as soon as possible. And you could delay the Northern Pacific's plans by challenging their land grant in court. Even if you lose, which is likely, it would cost them a lot of time because it would involve government bureaucrats.

"So, to avoid any hiccups, what he should have done was to offer you some of N.P.'s other land grants. But what bothers me more than Butler's failure to negotiate was his decision to send those men to threaten you. Did they tell you their names or did you recognize any of them?"

Boney replied, "I've seen two of the four who showed up this morning before, but I don't know any of their names."

Drew said, "Everything about this situation stinks to high heaven. When I get to Glendive, I need to visit the Northern

Pacific offices to let them know I'm still alive. And while I'm there, I should be able to find out what's going on."

"Are you going to walk all that way?"

Drew nodded as he answered, "If I leave in the morning, I should arrive before sundown. I just need to get there before the ferry stops running. After I talk to the Mister Butler, I'll return to let you know what I did or didn't find."

"You don't have to walk, Drew. You can borrow one of my mules. Then you wouldn't have to walk those thirty-five miles when you come back, either."

"You don't know me well enough to trust me with one of your mules. And if I rode a mule into town, those men who threatened you might wonder where I got it. But when I return, I won't be walking. I'll buy a horse and saddle in Glendive."

Boney grimaced as he said, "I wish I could give you some money, Drew. But we need what little we have for supplies."

Drew said, "I saved more than enough of my pay to buy the horse. And if you'll make me a list of what you need, I'll pick them up for you."

Boney was noticeably uncomfortable as he said, "As you just said, you hardly know us, Drew. So, why are you helping us?"

Drew grinned as he replied, "I guess I just want to irritate the Northern Pacific as much as possible."

Gabrielle then asked, "Do you have any family, Drew?"

Drew shook his head and answered, "No, ma'am. My father ran away before I was a year old, and my mother died the next year. I was raised by the kind folks of St. Thomas Home for Boys in Aitkin, Minnesota until I was sixteen. Since then, I've been on my own."

Francine asked, "Did you ever find out why he deserted you and your mother?"

"No, ma'am. And after I left the orphanage, I didn't search for him. If he's still alive, I hope I never accidentally meet him."

After fifteen seconds of solemn silence, Gabrielle stunned her parents when she asked, "Do you have a girlfriend?"

Drew may not have been stunned, but he was definitely put off stride by her question.

So, it took him five long seconds before he was able to reply, "No, at least not now. But I did have a girlfriend a couple of years ago. It was because I wanted to show her father that I wasn't a neer-do-well that I became a brakeman to earn more money. But a year later, she married someone else whom she believed was a better prospect."

"What was her name?"

"Anne. Anne McDuff."

Gabrielle then gave her mother another surprise when she said, "I think you were lucky when she married someone else, Drew. Now that stupid girl can make the other man's life miserable."

Drew smiled as he replied, "Anne wasn't stupid, but she certainly showed her true colors when she accepted Charlie Whitacre's proposal and never even told me."

Francine then asked, "What are your future plans, Drew?"

Drew replied, "I'm not sure yet. I was apprenticed to a blacksmith while I was in the orphanage but wasn't hired by any of the shops after I left. So, maybe I'll see if I can find a smith in Glendive who needs help."

Boney had a good idea why his wife had asked Drew about his plans, so he changed the direction of the conversation by saying, "If those four men are hiding in the forest on the other side of the valley watching, then they'll know you visited us. So, when you're walking to town tomorrow, you have stay alert in case they try to bushwhack you."

"If they accost me, I'll just tell them how I got here, and that you gave me some food and then let me rest overnight."

"I guess that's the best you could do. But do you have a pistol?"

Drew nodded and then unbuttoned his coat, pulled out his Colt and set it on the table before saying, "I'm pretty accurate with it. But until I shot a rabbit for breakfast this morning, I've only used it on a target range."

Boney stared at the handgun and said, "That is the longest barrel I've ever seen on a Colt."

"If a customer wants a longer barrel, Colt charges a dollar per inch. I didn't order this one, I just found it in a gun shop's display case."

"I reckon that'll be good enough to keep you safe on your way to Glendive tomorrow."

Drew holstered his pistol and then said, "I think I'll be safe enough even if I didn't have it. I'm pretty sure those men are back in Glendive already. And I imagine I'll be meeting at least one of them when I visit the Northern Pacific offices."

"Why do you believe they're gone?"

"Because I think Butler would want to know about their visit right away."

"I hope you're right, Drew. But if they are there, we'll be able to see the light from their campfire after sundown, even if they're deep in that forest."

Drew nodded and then said, "I'll be starting out early in the morning and I don't want to disturb anyone. So, do you have a small barn where I can spend the night?"

"I have a lean-to on the side of the cabin for tools and gear, but I don't think my wife will give me a moment's peace if you don't sleep in the cabin."

Drew picked up his waders and then said, "As we both noted earlier, Mister Remy, we hardly know each other. And the lean-to will be a significant improvement over last night's accommodation."

Before Mister or Mrs. Remy, or especially Gabrielle, could argue, Drew stood, quickly stepped to the door and then left the cabin.

Once outside, he took a deep breath and then decided it might be better if he began his long walk now rather than wait another sixteen hours. Then he'd be able to reach town no later than mid-afternoon when Mister Ira Butler, the Northern Pacific manager should still be in his office. So, he tossed his waders over his shoulder and started walking. He also kept his eyes on the ground to avoid falling into another Remy trap.

After Drew closed the door, Francine said, "You should have insisted that he stayed with us, Boney."

"I don't think I'd be able to change his mind, Fran. That young man has backbone. But I'll try again when I ask him to join us for supper."

Gabrielle stared at the closed door as she asked, "Do you think I was the reason he decided to sleep in the lean-to, Maman?"

Francine looked at her daughter and asked, "Why would you even consider that was his reason, sweetheart?"

Gabrielle quietly replied, "Because he knows I like him, and it scared him."

"Why would it scare him, Gabrielle?"

Gabrielle looked into her mother's dark eyes and whispered, "Because he knows I'm a half-breed."

Francine took her daughter's hands and said, "If Drew sees you as anything other than the beautiful young woman you are, then he's not worthy of being your husband."

Gabrielle slowly nodded, but her mother's words didn't erase her belief. She remembered the first time she'd heard the term. She was eight years old and was looking at a jar of peppermint sticks on the counter of the trading post when two boys pushed her away and one of them muttered, 'Stupid half-breed.'

She didn't know what it meant, but it still hurt. When she was sitting on the seat of their wagon between her parents as they drove back to the cabin, she'd asked her mother. Since then, she'd heard more boys and then men call her half-breed as if she wasn't even human. As she grew into womanhood, she understood that men wouldn't want her as a wife, only as a half-breed plaything.

She had finally accepted that her life's path would end in spinsterhood when Drew Campbell entered her life. In the short time he'd been with them, he'd treated her as a woman and not a half-breed. But even he would rather sleep in the cold lean-to rather than stay in their warm cabin where a half-breed slept.

As Drew quickly walked into the setting sun, he had no idea of the effect his decision had on Gabrielle. And it would soon be much worse when she learned he was already gone. If he had realized the hurt that he would cause her, he would have stayed in the cabin until the sun rose.

———

After he'd passed the last of the traps, Drew began following the trail left by the four threatening thugs. He doubted they were Northern Pacific employees, but still couldn't understand why Ira Butler had hired them. As he strode away from the cabin, Drew was surprised his legs weren't as sore or tired as he'd expected and hoped to walk at least ten miles before he rested for the night.

When the tracks passed the forest where Mister Remy thought the thugs might be hiding, Drew knew for certain that they'd returned to Glendive.

Drew had been walking for ninety minutes before he realized he'd forgotten the list of supplies they needed. He didn't want to turn around, so he decided to buy anything they might require.

———

As his wife and daughter set the table, Boney said, "I'll fetch Drew for supper, Fran," and then walked to the door and left the cabin.

After he'd gone, Francine asked, "Do you want me to ask Drew what he thinks about Indians?"

Gabrielle shook her head as she replied, "No, Maman. I'll find a way to ask him."

Francine smiled as she said, "He seems like a good man, Gabby. I'm sure you were mistaken."

Gabrielle looked at the door and quietly said, "I hope so."

She was still looking at the door when it opened, her father entered and as he closed it, he said, "He's gone already."

Gabrielle felt humiliated as she looked at her mother and said, "I guess that answers my question, Maman."

Boney sat down and said, "I can't figure him out. He seemed like an honest man, and I believed every word he said. Now I'm worried that he was sent by the railroad to find out how much supplies we had left."

Francine said, "It doesn't matter now, Boney. Say grace and then we'll share God's bounty."

Gabrielle's head was bowed as her father thanked God for their food but found it difficult to be grateful for anything.

———

After the sun had set and the temperature began to fall, Drew pulled his hat out of his waders and tugged it on. His stomach was beginning to protest again, but at least there were plenty of streams to keep him hydrated.

But as he made his way eastward across the moonlit ground, Drew searched for a reason for Butler's unusual behavior. *Why did he threaten them to vacate their land instead of offering a trade?*

Drew walked for another four hours before his legs gave out. He didn't bother building a fire, but just extracted his slicker, spread it on the ground and used it as his bed.

As he looked at the Milky Way's band of stars overhead, Drew thought about his future. He knew he'd never climb onto moving boxcar's roof again but nothing more. Even though he'd told the Remys that he'd try to find work as a blacksmith, Drew wasn't convinced it was the path he was meant to follow.

Drew thoroughly enjoyed his brief time with the Remys, and especially with Gabrielle. She was the most beautiful woman he'd ever seen. And she had a sharp mind and strong character, too. She was the complete opposite of Anne McDuff.

He'd been instantly smitten by Anne's cute face, blonde hair and blue eyes. She was demure yet flirty at the same time. It was only after she'd secretly rejected him that he realized how shallow she was. Gabrielle had been right when she said he was lucky she'd married someone else.

Drew snickered before asking, "Just how miserable has she made you, Charlie?"

Drew closed his eyes and started planning for his arrival in Glendive. Now that he'd covered at least a third of the distance, he should reach the ferry by early afternoon.

The Northern Pacific had built the ferry across the Yellowstone so the immigrants they were bringing from Europe could homestead on their land grants north of the river. Drew didn't know how many farmers had settled north of Glendive, but he knew four riders had used the ferry earlier today. And when he stepped off the ferry tomorrow, Drew hoped to learn why Ira Butler sent them to threaten the Remys.

CHAPTER 3

Drew's eyelids parted allowing him to see the predawn sky before he realized how cold it was. He yawned and stretched before he sat up and then slowly stood. Drew was sore and stiff again but needed to get moving.

After creating a steaming yellow stream, Drew rolled his slicker and stuffed it into his waders before hanging them over his shoulder. As he began walking, he told his stomach to stop growling but it didn't listen.

It was more than twenty minutes before his leg muscles recovered and he was able to pick up his pace. As he continued following the riders' trail, Drew began calculating how much money he'd need to spend for the horses, tack and supplies. When he arrived at a generous estimate, he unbuttoned his coat and shirt, unsealed his money belt and took out eight twenty-dollar notes and eight ten-dollar bills. Drew then slid two of each denomination into his two coat and two pants pockets.

After his hidden bank was closed, Drew began debating what he would do about Fast Jack Hickman. The train should be west of Bozeman by now, but it should be heading east in three days and would have to stop at Glendive for water and coal. But Drew's priority now was helping the Remys. So, he needed to leave the town tomorrow and may never see Fast Jack again.

He was pretty certain that if he filed a complaint when he visited the Northern Pacific office, they'd do nothing about the murdering engineer. But maybe he could use his survival to his advantage. Drew decided to play it by ear when he talked to the Ira Butler. At the very least, they'd have to pay him last month's wages.

Drew hadn't managed so much as a temporary truce with his rebellious stomach as he trudged his way to Glendive. He'd been walking south for two hours and expected to spot the highest roofs in Glendive. When he did, he should reach the ferry thirty minutes later.

He'd decided to purchase a Winchester if he didn't exceed his earlier cost estimate. When he bought his Colt, Mister Sorensen had let him take a few shots with a Winchester in the hope of selling him the repeater. While he'd been impressed with the rifle's ease of use, he'd been unwilling to part with the twenty-two dollars for the gun and another dollar and twenty cents for a box of cartridges. But now, he'd consider it a wise investment.

———

It was actually forty minutes after Drew first spotted the town when he reached the ferry. But the barge was on the opposite bank of the Yellowstone, and he couldn't see the ferryman. He hoped the operator was in his shack near the southern dock as he pulled his Colt from his holster. He cocked the hammer, pointed it upriver and pulled the trigger.

Just twelve seconds after the loud report echoed across the Yellowstone, Josh Brockman left his shack, spotted Drew and then untied the rope that secured his large ferry to the dock. Drew then stepped onto the empty, northern dock and watched the wide, flat barge bounce its way across the surging water. While he waited, he pulled the requisite fare from his pocket.

When the ferry was close, Drew leapt onto the flat-bottomed craft. And after two years of walking across rocking and rolling boxcars, he had no problem keeping his balance when he landed.

The ferryman was apparently unimpressed with Drew's graceful landing and said, "That'll be ten cents, mister."

Drew handed him the ten-cent piece and after the ferryman slid the coin into his coat pocket, he turned around and began pulling the barge back across the Yellowstone.

Just to feel useful, and without being asked, Drew grabbed the rope and added his own pulling power to make the ferryman's job easier.

The crossing only took two minutes, and after the barge reached the dock, Drew said, "Thanks," and hopped off the ferry.

As Drew started walking away, he heard the ferryman shout, "I appreciate the help, mister," so he turned and waved before he stepped onto the ground.

Now that he was about to enter Glendive, his stomach loudly reminded him of its neglect, but Drew would have to deny it satisfaction for a little while longer. His first stop would be at the Northern Pacific offices.

He'd visited Glendive many times during the past two years but had never stayed for more than a day. So, much of the town was new to him.

As he walked down Main Street, Drew saw a large livery with nine horses and four mules in its corral, so he'd see if any were for sale after getting something to eat. After he'd gotten a room at one of the town's two hotels, he'd have to do some shopping, too.

He passed The Yellowstone Hotel, the sheriff's office, Finney's Diner and then J.D. Arnold Dry Goods and Greengrocer before he saw the Northern Pacific offices.

As Drew told the Remys, he'd met Mister Ira Butler on two of his earlier visits. And he hadn't liked him after their first meeting. So, he was looking forward to surprising the local manager. But he wasn't about to ask him about the Remys or even the coal. Even if the manager answered his questions, Drew was sure he'd be lying. He also suspected that by simply saying he'd met the Remys, it might cause him considerable grief.

Drew stepped onto the boardwalk, opened the door and entered the outer office. After closing the door, he saw the secretary sitting behind his desk but couldn't recall his name.

So, as the secretary stared at him, Drew said, "I'm sorry, but I can't remember your name. My name is Drew Campbell. I'm a brakeman for the N.P., and I was thrown from the westbound freight train that passed through a couple of days ago."

The secretary blinked before he replied, "I'm John Knudsen, Mister Campbell. I'm surprised to see you because we received a telegram reporting your death yesterday."

Drew grinned, thumped his chest and said, "I hate to disappoint everybody, but I'm still breathing. Is Mister Butler in?"

John stood and then said, "Yes, he is. And I'm sure he'll be as surprised to see you as I was."

He then stepped to the manager's door, rapped on it twice before swinging it open and saying, "Mister Butler, you have a visitor who needs to talk to you."

Drew suspected that John hadn't revealed the visitor's name because he wanted to enjoy watching Mister Butler's reaction. But he was sure that he would find it much more enjoyable. And then he'd see what he could extract from Ira after he accused Fast Jack of attempted murder.

Ira was about to chastise his secretary for bothering him when he saw a familiar face enter his office. He couldn't attach a name to the face until he saw the waders draped over Drew's shoulder.

As soon as he realized he was looking at the dead brakeman, Ira exclaimed, "You're supposed to be dead!"

The director's shocked expression had Drew laughing inside, but he didn't crack a smile. He just glared at Ira and angrily said, "That's what Fast Jack Hickman hoped would happen. He knew I was on the roof of a boxcar in the rain when we were crossing the Cabin Creek bridge. When he yanked back the throttle, he probably had a good laugh seeing me fall off the roof. That bastard was trying to kill me just like he murdered that brakeman in Colorado."

Ira didn't want his bosses to send one of their special agents to investigate the brakeman's claim, especially not now. He had to find some way to sweep the incident under the rug but needed time to figure something out.

So, he pointed to one of the two chairs in front of his desk and said, "Have a seat, Mister Campbell."

Drew nodded, set his waders on the floor and as he sat down, Ira said, "That'll be all, Knudsen."

After his secretary closed the door, Mister Butler asked, "Can you tell me what happened, and how you managed to survive the terrifying accident?"

Drew furrowed his brow and replied, "It wasn't an accident, Mister Butler. Fast Jack Hickman tried to murder me. The only difference between him other killers is that he used a train instead of a gun."

Ira took a deep breath, exhaled and then said, "Even if it was intentional, I'm sure you realize that it would be difficult to prove, Mister Campbell."

"Maybe so. But I intend to have him charged, and then we'll see what a jury believes after I tell my story."

Ira was horrified inside but still needed more time, so he said, "Let's not be hasty. Just tell me what happened and how you managed to survive."

Drew nodded and began narrating the story he'd been rehearsing since he began the day's journey. He didn't twist the facts until he reached the point when he crawled onto the shore. In his modified version, he reached the bank in front of the peninsula and never even saw the valley.

Ira barely listened to what Drew was saying as he desperately searched for a way to keep him from visiting the sheriff's office. And there wasn't time for him to arrange for Bart Early's help, either. The only solution he could think of was the most obvious. He'd offer Campbell a bribe but would have to make it appear as if it wasn't one. He didn't believe it would be difficult to convince Campbell because brakemen, like all other common laborers, weren't very bright or well-educated.

So, when Drew finished his story, Ira nodded as if he was sympathetic before saying, "I can understand why you're so angry, Mister Campbell. I'd feel the same way if it had happened to me. But I'd rather that we keep the episode with the Northern Pacific family. I'll notify the head of security about Jack Hickman's attempt on your life, and I promise you he will suffer severe repercussions."

Despite his compassionate tone, Drew could sense the manager's desperation, which actually surprised him. But it also meant that he could push him even further.

He kept his fierce expression as he said, "Even if they fired him, it won't be enough. I want justice, Mister Butler, and I don't think the Northern Pacific can provide it."

Ira realized that this brakeman may not be as stupid as the others yet was still confident that he'd take a bribe. It was just a matter of how much more money it would cost the railroad. But before he offered the bribe, Ira decided to use a mild threat to convince Campbell to forget about the incident.

Mister Butler leaned back and said, "You seem like a smart and reasonable man, Mister Campbell. So, I'm sure you understand the impact of the bad publicity would have on the Northern Pacific if you charged Mister Hickman with murder."

"I don't care about the publicity, Mister Butler. I want to see that bastard pay for what he did."

"You'd probably lose your job if you embarrassed the railroad, Mister Campbell."

"I knew that I'd used up the last of my good luck when I fell into Cabin Creek. So, I decided to quit when I was floundering in the freezing waters of the Yellowstone River, Mister Butler."

After his threat failed, Ira had to return to his first option, so he said, "Then you'll need to find a new job. But there aren't many available in Glendive, so it could be a couple of months before you find work. And until you do find one, you'll need money to survive."

Drew expected he was about to be offered a bribe, but said, "I'll be all right until I find something. The Northern Pacific owes me a month's pay, so that should last me a couple of months."

Ira saw his opening and said, "That's true, but I'm sure if you agree to forget the matter, I could arrange for the railroad to pay your salary for the next three months as well."

Drew was surprised by the size of the initial bribe offer. Three months' pay was a two hundred and ten dollars, but he decided to haggle.

For more than half a minute, Drew pretended to consider the offer before he shook his head and then said, "I'm sorry, Mister Butler. I appreciate the offer, but when I was almost drowning in that icy cold water, I swore that if I survived, I'd make that bastard pay for what he did."

Ira was taken aback by the brakeman's refusal of his offer, but it wasn't his money, so he asked, "Would another six months' pay be enough to let you forget that promise, Mister Campbell?"

Drew had expected the counteroffer to be four months' pay, so when he heard six instead of four, he decided there was no point in continuing to haggle.

He sighed, and then slowly replied, "I reckon I could get a good start with that much money. Maybe I'll start homesteading north of the Yellowstone. I could so some hunting up there, too. When I was walking to town, I spotted an elk that was as big as a bull moose."

Ira was relieved and said, "That's a good plan, Mister Campbell. Let me write you a check for four hundred and ninety dollars. You can cash it at the First Bank of Montana."

Drew nodded, and as Mister Campbell began writing the check, Drew realized that he'd be able to buy a lot more supplies for the Remys.

THE BRAKEMAN

After he finished writing, Ira set the check on the desk to dry, and then grinned and said, "Now don't go to a saloon and spend it all on whiskey and women, Mister Campbell."

Drew smiled as he replied, "That much whiskey and women would kill me, Mister Butler."

Ira laughed but hoped that the brakeman drank and whored himself to death before the sun rose. He then handed the check to Drew and watched the brakeman fold it and slide it into his coat pocket.

Drew then shook the director's hand and said, "I promise I won't say a word about Jack Hickman, Mister Butler."

Ira just nodded before Drew threw his waders over his shoulder and then turned, opened the door and left the office.

While the director was confident that Campbell would honor his promise, he'd have Bart Early or one of his men follow him until he left town. The last thing he wanted was for the undead brakeman to visit Sheriff Hobson. So, five minutes after Drew stepped onto the boardwalk, Ira left his office to find Bart Early.

———

Drew delayed his visit to Finney's Diner because he wanted to cash the check before the bank closed. After he had the unexpected largesse in his pockets, he finally filled his empty stomach. After leaving the diner on his way to The

Yellowstone Hotel, he noticed a hard-looking man following him. He suspected his follower was one of the four men who had threatened the Remys but pretended he hadn't spotted him. After getting his room and leaving his waders behind, Drew left the hotel and walked to the large livery.

When he entered the enormous barn, he found two men sitting at a large crate playing poker. Drew smiled and was just ten feet away before either of them noticed him.

The one who looked up, grinned and then said, "Howdy, mister. What can we do for ya?"

"I was hoping you could sell me a horse and a mule. And I'll need a saddle and a pack saddle, too."

The other poker player replied, "We can accommodate ya," and then threw down his cards.

After they stood, Drew offered his hand and said, "My name's Drew Campbell."

The taller of the two shook his hand and replied, "I'm Jake Tidwell and this is my kid brother, Amos. Let's go to the corral and find your horse and mule."

After Drew shook Amos' hand, he followed the Tidwell brothers through the back door and soon entered the corral.

Jake asked, "Any of 'em appeal to ya, Drew?"

Drew had never owned a horse and wasn't about to pretend that he was an equine expert, so he replied, "You and Amos know a lot more about horses than I ever will, Jake. So, I'll let you pick them out."

Jake grinned and then asked, "We'll do that, but how much are you willin' to spend?"

"Just choose the best of the lot and I'm sure you'll give me a fair price, Jake."

Then, before either brother could choose his horse, Drew said, "On second thought, I'd like to buy two horses and riding saddles and one mule and a pack saddle."

Amos snickered before he asked, "Who gets the second horse, Drew?"

Drew smiled as he replied, "A very pretty young lady."

Jake then pointed to a smaller horse and said, "If she's special enough for you to give her a horse, she'd probably like that chocolate-brown Morgan mare."

Amos then stepped to a taller, black gelding and said, "Now this feller is the one you oughta buy, Drew. He's only six years old and is the best one we've had for a while."

"Then I'll accept your recommendations for both horses. Now I just need the mule and then we'll return to the barn and start haggling."

The Tidwell brothers laughed in stereo before they headed to the corral gate with Drew trailing. His was still surprised by his sudden decision to buy a horse for Gabrielle but hoped she wouldn't be offended when he offered her the Morgan. And it would probably be much worse if her parents were offended.

After almost fifteen minutes of haggling, Drew paid two hundred and forty-five dollars for the horses, mule and the tack. They even included a canteen, a set of saddlebags, a scabbard and a bedroll with each riding saddle. It was an enjoyable way to spend a quarter of an hour.

He said he'd pick them up in the morning and was about to leave when he turned and asked, "Have you heard anything about the Northern Pacific building a spur on the other side of the western mountains north of the Yellowstone?"

Amos glanced at his older brother before replying, "I ain't heard nothin' about a spur. But last fall, some Northern Pacific fellers showed up, and one of 'em was braggin' about findin' a big deposit of high-grade coal in those parts."

Jake then said, "And those four bastards Butler hired went ridin' that way a little while ago, too."

Drew asked, "Do you know them?"

Jake nodded as he replied, "We do but wish we didn't. They're nothin' but trouble. The one who's kinda in charge is Bart Early. The other three are Arnie Williams, Cole Thompson and the last one's Jimmy Lynch, but he ain't as bad as the others. They didn't even hang around together 'til Butler hired 'em for somethin'."

Drew was stunned by what he'd heard but just smiled and said, "I'll see you in the morning," before leaving the livery.

As he stepped onto Main Street, he immediately spotted the man who had been shadowing him. He was a block south and was trying to appear innocuous as he stood on the boardwalk on the other side of the street. Again, Drew acted as if he hadn't noticed the man before he crossed the street and soon entered J.D. Arnold Dry Goods. It only took him twenty minutes to buy two complete outfits, a new shaving kit, and a replacement duffel. As soon as he left the store, he spotted the same, rough-looking man watching him from two blocks away. He only hoped his follower's assignment was just to keep an eye on him.

He continued to ignore him until he disappeared into The Yellowstone Hotel. Once inside, he lingered in the lobby for a minute or so, but the man didn't peek through the window. So, he stepped down the hallway and entered his room. After setting his duffel on the floor, he removed the cash from his coat pockets and dropped the currency on the bed. He then walked to the far wall and hung it on one of the three brass hooks before returning to the bed. He then sat down, leaned over, opened his duffel and removed his shaving kit and the bar of soap. If his follower was supposed to kill him during the night, he may as well be clean and well-shaven.

He unbuckled his gunbelt, rolled it and then buried it under the new clothes in his duffel. Then he pulled the rest of his cash from his pants pockets and added them to the pile on his quilt. After Drew unbuttoned his shirt and removed his money belt, he left forty dollars on the bed and then put the rest of the money into the waterproof pouch. Not that he was planning on taking another swim down the Yellowstone.

Before he left his room, Drew hid the money belt under the mattress and grabbed his shaving kit and bar of soap. When he opened the door, Drew took the precaution of quickly scanning the empty hallway before he walked to the bathroom.

———

Ira asked, "So, he didn't visit the sheriff?"

Bart replied, "Nope. He went to the bank, then to Finney's where he chowed down. After that he got a room at the Yellowstone, he stopped at the Tidwell livery and then did some shoppin' at Arnold's before he went back to the hotel. I reckon he's already asleep by now."

Ira said, "Okay. I guess he's going to keep his promise."

"Do you want me to have one of the boys waiting for him in the mornin'?"

"Just have one stay near the jail to make sure he doesn't pay Sheriff Hobson a visit."

"Why do you reckon he went to the livery?"

"He said he was going to do some hunting north of the Yellowstone, so he probably bought a horse. And if that's what he's planning to do, he'll need to buy a rifle at Gus's too."

Bart grinned and said, "He could buy himself a whole bunch of rifles with the money you gave him, Ira."

"I didn't give him a dime, Bart. The Northern Pacific generously compensated him for his accident."

Bart snickered and then stood and said, "I'll get some chow myself and then I'll tell Arnie to keep an eye on the jail in the mornin'."

Ira nodded and watched Bart leave his office. He was pleased with the way he'd handled the brakeman situation. And in a few more days, Bart and the other three hired killers would solve his other problem. So, when the Northern Pacific survey team arrived, all they'd find is a pile of burnt rubble.

———

In the cabin that Ira wanted reduced to ash, Gabrielle was poking at her salted venison when her mother said, "Drew was only here for a short time, and he obviously wasn't the man you thought he was. You can't go on sulking for the rest of your life, Gabby."

Gabrielle quietly replied, "I know, Maman. It's just that for the first time since I was a little girl, I thought…well, I guess I'm just disappointed, that's all."

Francine looked at her husband and then raised her eyebrows.

Boney took the hint and smiled before he said, "How about if we take some target practice tomorrow, Gabby? You can even pretend one of targets is Drew Campbell."

Gabrielle jerked her head up, looked at her father, exclaimed, *"How can you say such a thing, Papa?"* and then popped to her feet, ran to the door and disappeared into the darkness.

Boney grimaced when he saw the hostile expression on his wife's face, so he stood and said, "I'll go apologize to her, Fran."

"I hope you do a better job with your apology than you did with your idiotic attempt to make her feel better."

Boney didn't dare say another word before he hurried to the doorway, stepped onto the flat stones that served as their porch and closed the door. He didn't see his daughter, so he walked to the back of the house and opened the door to the lean-to.

Gabrielle was sobbing as she sat in the corner hugging her knees when she saw the door begin to open. She quickly began wiping the tears from her face with the hem of her dress but only dried the left side before her father entered the lean-to.

As she wiped her right cheek, Boney softly said, "I'm sorry for saying such a stupid, thoughtless thing, sweetheart. But you have to understand that by their very nature, men tend to say and do stupid things."

Despite her broken heart, Gabrielle smiled and said, "You aren't stupid, Papa. But I'll agree that what you said was thoughtless. And I don't think only men do stupid things, either. How I could believe for a moment that a handsome, kind man like Drew would even like me is proof of that."

Boney kissed his daughter's forehead before saying, "It wasn't stupid, Gabby. I thought he liked you a lot, too. And we both still could be right, too. Maybe Drew had a different reason for leaving. He could have left early just so he could return sooner."

"But why didn't he even say goodbye? He didn't ask what we needed for supplies, either."

"I'll tell you what I'll do. If he hasn't returned in two days, I'll ride to Glendive for our supplies and try to find him. But until then, can you stay out of the doldrums?"

Gabrielle sniffed, said, "I promise to stop sulking, Papa," and then stood and took her father's hand before they left the lean-to.

CHAPTER 4

Drew felt like a new man when he walked out of The Yellowstone Hotel early the next morning carrying his duffel. He still had his waders draped over his shoulders but wore a clean shirt under his coat and a fresh pair of britches over his legs. He was surprised when he stepped outside and didn't spot his follower watching him. He hoped it would stay that way until he crossed the Yellowstone.

After a quick breakfast, Drew crossed the street and entered the Tidwell brothers' livery. As soon as he was framed by the large barn doors, he heard Amos loudly say, "Mornin', Drew. We figgered you'd be anxious to give your lady the Morgan, so your horses and mule are ready to go."

Drew was grinning as he stepped to the two saddled horses and the pack mule. As he rubbed his gelding's nose, he said, "I appreciate your having them ready so early. And you're right about my being anxious to see her again."

After hanging his duffle from a hook on the mule's pack saddle, he hung his waders over the Morgan's saddle seat before he shook their hands and then mounted his black horse.

Drew waved and said, "Thanks again, Jake and Amos," before he walked his animals out of the barn.

He only rode for two blocks before he pulled up in front of J.D. Arnold Dry Goods and Greengrocer and then dismounted.

He spent more than an hour to buy and store all of his purchases. He'd stuffed the four voluminous panniers, and both sets of saddlebags before hanging a twenty-five-pound bag of potatoes and a balancing twenty-five-pound sack of dried beans over the Morgan's saddle. He'd bought everything he could think of that the Remys might need, as well as some things they might consider luxury items. But he didn't consider his tan, broad-brimmed cowboy to be one of those luxury items. Nor did he count the large bag of molasses cookies he stored in his right saddlebag as being excessive.

After he strapped the twenty-five-pound sacks of flour and corn meal onto the pack saddle, he led his horses and heavily loaded pack mule two blocks down Main Street and tied them to the hitchrail in front of Gus's Guns.

The gun shop wasn't as large as the one where he'd bought his Colt, but it was well-stocked. And because of the large bribe he'd received from Ira Butler, he could afford to go a little overboard.

Despite the impressive amount he wound up spending on his purchases, Drew still completed his browsing and buying in less than twenty minutes. But it took him two trips to load the guns and ammunition. He managed to hang the heavy bags of cartridges and maintenance fluids over the Morgan's saddle before he apologized to the small mare. On his second trip, he slipped the Winchester '73 into the Morgan's scabbard before he slid his new, fully loaded Winchester '76 into his gelding's scabbard.

After he mounted the black horse, he looked down Main Street and the only man who seemed to notice him was standing across the street from the jail. Even though Drew was confident he was one of four men hired by Butler, Drew avoided the temptation to wave to him. He just wheeled his horse to the north and headed to the ferry.

Arnie continued to watch Drew ride away until he reached the ferry. Then he turned around and headed to the Northern Pacific office to make his report.

———

Drew had given a silver dollar to the ferryman which included a fifty-cent tip before loading his three animals onto the barge. So, after carrying Drew across the Yellowstone, Josh loudly and sincerely said, "I hope to see you again, mister."

Drew smiled, replied, "I'm sure you will, and then mounted his black gelding, waved to the ferryman and rode north, hoping to reach the Remy cabin by mid-afternoon.

———

Ira said, "From what you saw, it sounds like he's planning on spending a few days up there hunting for that big elk he told me about."

Arnie nodded as he said, "He even bought a spare horse to carry the carcass."

Ira looked at Bart and said, "I won't rest easy until I'm sure he's not going to come back into town. So, when you boys head that way to take care of those squatters tomorrow, I'd appreciate it if you could make sure that he doesn't. You can keep anything he has with him as a bonus."

Bart grinned as he said, "I reckon that even after he bought those horses and supplies, he's still got more'n a couple of hundred dollars left over."

Arnie quickly added, "And he's got those horses and new Winchesters, too."

Ira smiled knowing that Bart and his friends would do what Fast Jack Hickman had failed to do. As far as he was concerned, all of his worries were over.

———

Drew had forced himself to keep a reasonable pace despite his anxiety to surprise the Remys. While he'd been well-treated and raised properly at St. Thomas, it wasn't until he met the Remys that he felt what it was like to be part of a family. Even though he'd spent just a few short hours with them, they made him feel incredibly comfortable. At least Boney and Francine did. Gabrielle, on the other hand, made him a bit nervous, but it was a very pleasant nervousness.

It wasn't anything like he'd felt when he'd been smitten by Anne McDuff. With Anne, he just gazed at her face and listened as she chattered on about things that didn't interest him in the least. And despite all the hours he'd spent with her, Drew doubted if she even knew his middle name or his birthdate.

Gabrielle didn't babble, she said what was on her mind. And Drew wanted to hear much more of what her sharp mind had to say. She seemed to like him, too.

But just a few seconds later, Drew realized he was missing a critical piece of information. In his haste to start his journey to Glendive, he never had a chance to ask if Gabrielle had a beau. And as much as he hoped she wasn't spoken for; he knew the odds that she wasn't were slim. He imagined a young woman who was as beautiful and as intriguing as Gabrielle would have her choice of any of man in the territory. So, he may have misinterpreted her natural kindness and inquisitiveness as interest in him as a man.

And now that he recognized his omission, Drew thought he might have been premature by buying the Morgan and other gifts for Gabrielle. So, as he continued riding north, Drew decided not to offer her the mare until he had an answer to that vital question. If he learned Gabrielle was being courted, it would be far worse than when he'd learned that Anne had married, because he knew he'd never meet another woman like Gabrielle.

———

Since leaving the lean-to last night, Gabrielle had kept the promise she'd made to her father. While she had behaved as if she'd never met Drew, she remained deeply troubled in her heart and soul.

Gabrielle had maintained her cheerful façade as she did her morning chores, and after a quick lunch, she joined her parents as they prepared their large garden's ground for spring planting.

Her father was chopping the hardened soil with a pick axe while she and her mother followed using hoes to break up the large chunks and create shallow furrows. The garden extended a hundred and twenty feet behind the corral and was sixty feet wide, so getting it ready for seeding was a three-day job. And after planting, the garden's proximity to the corral gave them easy access to an abundance of Jean and Jacques fertilizer.

When Gabrielle reached the end of the second furrow, she stood, stretched her back and asked, "Do you want me to fetch a bucket of water, Maman?"

Francine leaned on her hoe as she replied, "That's a good idea. And I think your father would appreciate some water too, Gabby."

Boney punched the point of the pickaxe into the ground before saying, "Water would be good, but it won't make me any younger, Fran."

Francine smiled as she said, "Nonsense. You're just forty-two years old and look as if you're only thirty."

Boney laughed and then said, "I could be forty-four or forty-five for all I know, Fran. And if you think I look like I'm thirty, then you need some strong spectacles."

Gabrielle smiled and then laid her hoe down and said, "I'll be right back."

She wiped the sweat from her forehead before she began walking to the cabin to retrieve the bucket. As she passed the corral, Gabrielle wondered how they'd be able to buy the seed for the garden if they couldn't leave the cabin.

As she headed back to the cabin, Gabrielle was focused on the rough ground to avoid tripping, so she didn't see the rider approaching from the east leading another horse and a heavily loaded pack mule. She soon entered the cabin, snatched the oak bucket from the floor and walked back outside.

Without looking eastward, she turned and began walking to the healthy stream that flowed about sixty yards behind their garden and eventually emptied into the Yellowstone River.

———

Drew had spotted Gabrielle the moment she appeared from behind the cabin, but he was too far away to notice that she wasn't looking back at him. She hadn't waved, so he picked up his gelding's pace hoping she simply hadn't seen him. When he saw her leave the cabin and then walk away, those hopes dropped a few notches.

As he watched her carrying the bucket to the back of the cabin, he spotted Boney and Francine. They just seemed to be standing there waiting for Gabrielle, but he didn't know what they were doing. He then resumed watching Gabrielle and was puzzled when she continued past her parents but soon understood that she was heading to the stream to fill the bucket.

After Gabrielle passed the garden, Boney turned to make sure that those four thugs hadn't returned. When Boney spotted the large dots coming from the east, he said, "I think those Northern Pacific bastards are coming back already, Fran."

Francine turned, and after she found the small, approaching shapes, she said, "I only see one rider, Boney. But maybe the others are waiting in the forest and sent this one to give us another warning."

As they focused on the distant rider, Boney said, "Your eyes are better than mine, Fran. But if there's only one of them, why is he leading two more horses?"

"I have no idea."

Gabrielle lifted the heavy bucket of water, and when she turned around, she saw her parents staring into the distance. She set the bucket down and stared in the same direction. But when Gabrielle saw the distant rider leading two horses, she knew in her heart that he wasn't one of those four evil men. Gabrielle immediately abandoned the bucket and began running toward the cabin.

When she was close to her parents, she didn't slow down as she exclaimed, "It's Drew!" and then hurried past.

Francine said, "I hope she's right, but we need to get our guns in case she's not," and then raced after her daughter before her husband hurried to catch them both.

Drew was less than a mile away when he saw Boney look his way and after Francine turned her eyes in his direction, he was sure they both had seen him. He was about to wave when he saw Gabrielle start running. So, he withheld his distant greeting and watched as she shot past her parents and then saw Mister and Mrs. Remy chase after her.

Drew was close to laughing at the sight, but instead, when Gabrielle reached the front of the cabin, he pulled off his new hat and waved it overhead three times before tugging it back on.

Gabrielle's heart leapt when she saw his enthusiastic hat wave, so she came to an immediate stop and waved back. She still had her eyes trained on Drew when her parents arrived a few seconds later.

She excitedly said, "*Did you see him wave his hat?* I knew it was Drew the moment I saw him!"

Her mother smiled as she said, "I had my doubts until he waved, but now I'm sure you're right."

Boney then asked, "Why is he trailing two horses?"

Gabrielle replied, "It looks like they're both pack animals, Papa."

"If they are, Drew must have spent a lot of his money on supplies."

Gabrielle didn't care about the supplies or horses as she watched Drew. She was so excited that it wasn't until Drew was around a quarter of a mile away before she realized what she must look like after spending the last two hours working in their garden. It was too late to do wash off the accumulated dirt or change into a clean dress, so all she could do was to run her fingers through her long black hair. She had no way of knowing that even her minor bit of primping wasn't necessary.

Drew's hopes rocketed when he saw Gabrielle wave back, but he restrained from pushing his tired horses and overloaded pack mule into a gallop. And he kept them at the same pace even after he saw the big smile on Gabrielle's face.

By the time he pulled up in front of the cabin, all three Remys were smiling. Drew's own smile was as large as Gabrielle's when he quickly dismounted and then tossed his gelding's reins over their short hitchrail.

He forced himself to look at Boney when he said, "I was so anxious to get to Glendive that I forgot about your list supplies. So, I hope I didn't miss anything."

Boney laughed before saying, "It looks like you bought out the store, Drew. But I feel bad about you spending all of your money."

"There's no reason to feel bad, Mister Remy. I didn't spend a nickel of my savings. The generous manager of the Northern Pacific paid for everything you see behind me."

Boney stared at the massive amount of supplies as he asked, "Why would he do that? Does he think I'll give him our land for a load of supplies?"

"No, sir. In fact, I didn't even tell him that I visited the valley. I'll explain what happened in Glendive after we unload your supplies."

Boney said, "Alright. But I noticed you bought yourself a Winchester, too."

"Yes, sir. Actually, I bought two Winchesters."

"I reckon you have your reasons, Drew."

Drew nodded and then he walked to the Morgan and relieved the small horse of the heavy bags of beans and potatoes. It took them another twenty minutes to move all of the supplies into the cabin. After the heavy sacks were stored in the large pantry, they began emptying the bulging panniers.

When Francine took the large jar of honey from her pannier, she cradled it as if she'd found buried treasure before she gently set it on the floor. And that was the first of a long series of surprises as the Remys emptied the leather packs.

Drew smiled as they discovered the two large slabs of bacon, the ten-pound sack of coffee, the large tin of tea, the six cans of sweetened condensed milk, the eight thick towels, and the ten bars of white soap. The twelve-pound sack of salt seemed to surprise Francine, but then she gasped when she found the smaller pouch of peppercorn.

While they'd been emptying the panniers, Drew had granted himself the pleasure of stealing an occasional glimpse at Gabrielle. And each time he did, he found her smiling, dark brown eyes looking back at him and hoped she wasn't happy just because of the supplies.

After everything had been moved to the pantry, Drew opened the two bags he'd bought at Gus's Guns and set the three heavy boxes of cartridges on the floor before taking the bottles of cleaning fluid and gun oil from the second bag.

Boney saw the labels and asked, "That's a lot of ammunition, Drew. Is it because of what you learned in Glendive?"

"No, sir. But I wasn't sure I'd be able to ride into town if I needed more. So, I bought a hundred rounds for my new Winchester '76, and another hundred for the '73 and a box of Long Colt .45s for my pistol."

"We can store them on the floor beneath the gun rack, but I hope we don't need to use them to stop those agents."

Drew almost told him that they weren't agents before he and Boney moved the ammunition and cleaning supplies to the front of the cabin beneath their guns.

Gabrielle then asked, "Can you tell us what happened now, Drew?"

"As soon as I bring in my saddlebags."

THE BRAKEMAN

As he stepped toward the door, Gabrielle quickly said, "I'll carry one, Drew," and hurried to join him.

Drew was surprised but very pleased when she left the cabin with him. He removed his bedroll, and then quickly unstrapped his saddlebags and hung them over his shoulder. After he unhooked his duffle, he stepped to the Morgan's nose as Gabrielle untied the bedroll and then lifted the saddlebags from the small mare's back.

When she turned, Drew was about to ask her if she'd like to have the mare, but before he could utter a word, Gabrielle asked, "Why did you leave without even saying goodbye?"

Drew set his duffle on the ground and then replied, "When I left the cabin to go to the lean-to, I realized that if I left right away, I could walk at least fifteen miles before getting some sleep. Then I could reach Glendive early in the afternoon while the Northern Pacific manager was still in his office."

"But why did you want to sleep in the lean-to in the first place? Was it because of me?"

Drew was taken aback by her second question, so he hesitated before answering, "Sort of. You and your parents had only known me for a few hours, so I could have been an outlaw on the run for all you knew. So, I thought that if I slept in the cabin, I'd make you uncomfortable."

Gabrielle glanced at the open cabin door before she quietly asked, "Do you know I'm a half-breed?"

Drew wasn't expecting her question, so there was a short delay before he replied, "I know your father is white and your mother is Crow, but why should it matter? What's a half-breed anyway? I don't believe there's a single person on the face of the earth who isn't a mixed breed of some sort.

"When I was in the orphanage, I knew a boy named Ralph Johnson whose parents had been murdered when he was four. Their only crime was that his father was white, and his mother was colored.

"Ralph wasn't treated any differently by the good-hearted souls who ran the orphanage. And they never lectured us about looking down on those who are different because it wasn't necessary. Their kindness and acceptance of Ralph as just another one of God's children was the best possible lesson to all of us."

Gabrielle was amazed as she listened to Drew and knew he wasn't just trying to make her feel better. But when he finished speaking, she asked, "What happened to Ralph after he left the orphanage?"

Drew shrugged and replied, "I don't know. He was two years older than me, and after I left, I never met him again. I didn't hear a word about him, either."

Then he asked, "Why did you believe that I would think less of you just because your parents come from different worlds?"

Gabrielle quietly answered, "Because until I met you, every other boy and man thought that way. I believed you were different until you decided to sleep in the lean-to and then left without saying good-bye."

Drew smiled as he said, "I hope you still don't believe it. If you must know, my biggest concern while I was riding back from Glendive was that you already had a beau. I thought you must have had a long line of men desperately trying to win your hand."

Gabrielle laughed before she said, "I didn't even have one, much less a line of them."

Drew was close to asking if he could be the first in that non-existent line but decided it was too early. Instead, he said, "When I bought the black gelding and pack mule, I saw this pretty Morgan mare and I thought that you might like to have her. Is it alright for me to give her to you?"

Gabrielle's eyes widened as she said, "It's more than alright, Drew. I just can't believe you're giving her to me. I've only ridden our mules, so I can't wait to ride her. And she's so pretty, too. I can't begin to tell you how grateful I am, Drew."

Drew smiled as he said, "I'm glad that you like her, Gabrielle. But I think we'd better go inside before your parents think I kidnapped you."

Gabrielle laughed before she said, "My father might be worried, but my mother would thank God that you took me away."

After picking up his duffel, they started walking to the door. Drew wasn't sure Gabrielle's parents would be nearly as pleased as she had been when she told them about the Morgan, but he'd find out in a few seconds.

He followed Gabrielle through the doorway, set down his duffel and the bedroll, and as he removed his new hat, he heard her excitedly gush, "Drew bought the brown mare for me!"

Drew almost cringed when Francine looked at him but then relaxed when she smiled and replied, "She is a pretty horse, Gabby. I'm sure you thanked Drew for his gift and his thoughtfulness."

"Yes, I did, Maman. But I don't think I'll ever be able to thank him enough."

Boney then said, "I'm sure you already have, sweetheart. But let's all sit down, and Drew can tell us about his visit to Glendive."

As Boney and Francine walked to the table, Gabrielle smiled at Drew and then placed the bedroll next to his before taking her seat. As she set the saddlebags onto the floor, Drew took the last open chair and then lowered his saddlebags down.

After he repeated his explanation and apology for his early departure to Mister and Mrs. Remy, Drew began his story by saying, "My first stop after I walked into Glendive was to the Northern Pacific offices. After I identified myself to Mister Butler, I ..."

As he spoke, Drew was interrupted several times, the first was after he told them how much he'd been bribed to keep him from visiting the sheriff. So, it took him almost forty minutes before he finished.

After telling them about his second ferry ride across the Yellowstone, Gabrielle said, "Before we pummel you with more questions, let me get you something to eat, Drew."

As she began to stand, Drew motioned for her to sit back down and then said, "I can wait for supper, Gabrielle. I had some jerky and crackers a couple of hours ago, but I think I'll have a snack now."

Drew then leaned over and untied the straps of one of his saddlebags. He then pulled out a paper sack, opened the bag and extracted a molasses cookie.

Before he took a bite, he showed the open bag to Gabrielle and asked, "Would you like to have one, Miss Remy?"

Gabrielle smiled, said, "Thank you, Mister Campbell," and after she took one of the cookies, Drew made the same offer to her mother and then to her father.

When everyone had a cookie, Drew set the bag on the table. He then created a large semi-circle in his sweet disc and the Remys took their first bites.

As he chewed, Boney asked, "Did you learn anything about their plans, Drew?"

"Not very much. I may have made a lot of money by telling Mister Butler that I was going to visit the sheriff, but it could have been a mistake. He was so worried that I still might go to the jail after I left his office that he had me watched. So, the best I could do was to ask the two liverymen if they'd heard anything when I bought the horses. But that short conversation was very interesting."

"And what did they say?"

Drew took another bite of his cookie before he replied, "They hadn't heard anything about the railroad building a spur, but they did know about the coal deposit. But what was more important was that they knew the four men who threatened you, and even gave me their names. I was reasonably sure that they weren't employed by the Northern Pacific, but the Tidwell brothers confirmed that they were only local ruffians hired by Butler to threaten you."

Boney quickly asked, "Does it matter that much if he only hired them to force us out?"

"It makes a big difference because it means that Butler is doing this on his own."

Francine then asked, "So, if Butler is acting on his own, do you believe the railroad doesn't want our land at all?"

Drew replied, "No, ma'am. One of the Tidwell brothers said a member of the exploration team bragged that they'd found a large deposit of high-grade coal. And Ira Butler's wouldn't have bothered you at all if the Northern Pacific isn't planning to build a spur up the valley and start mining the coal."

Boney asked, "How will we know for sure that they decided to build it?"

"They'll send a survey team pretty soon. After they find the best location for the bridge across the Yellowstone, they'll take the ferry from Glendive, make the ride to the coal face, and then start surveying the route for the construction teams who will lay the tracks down your valley."

Boney said, "We need to worry about Mister Butler's thugs before we start looking for the surveyors, Drew."

Drew nodded but didn't say anything as his mind was occupied with the likely date for the survey crew's arrival and the effect it would have on Ira Butler's hidden agenda.

After Drew hadn't spoken for almost a half a minute, Gabrielle instantly ended his reverie when she touched his left hand and asked, "Are you all right, Drew?"

Drew glanced at his left hand before he smiled and said, "I'm fine. I was just thinking. If the Northern Pacific was going to dispatch the survey crew, they'd notify Butler to let him know they were coming. I suspect he already received that notice and feels pressured to clear the route before they arrive. But that still doesn't explain his behavior."

Francine smiled and said, "I'm glad you know so much about how the railroad works, Drew."

"Not as much as I should. But I wish I knew why Butler chose to threaten you instead of negotiating a trade. He must know that he wasn't following the company's policies. And I'm sure the railroad's big bosses would be furious with him if they knew what he was doing."

Boney asked, "Why would they be so mad about it?"

"The Northern Pacific, like almost all railroads, has had financial problems. But theirs have been worse than most of the others, and one was a massive scandal. And now that their reputation is finally recovering, they couldn't afford to have another scandal, not even a small one. And driving you off your land without offering any compensation would be a scandal."

Francine asked, "But why would a big company like the Northern Pacific be worried about small scandals? I don't think it would cost them anything."

Drew smiled as he replied, "You're wrong, Mrs. Remy. It could cost them quite a lot. While they probably already have the land grants approved for the spur, it could cause them problems with future land grant requests. Land grants used to be approved as soon as they were requested. But some of the railroads took advantage of the law by following winding routes just to get more land.

"So, now those requests are scrutinized more closely and any wrongdoing on the part of the railroad could make the government to turn them down. So, that's another reason why Mister Butler's behavior is so difficult to fathom."

Boney asked, "Can you think of anything that makes sense to you?"

Drew replied, "I'm still trying to figure that out. But two or three years ago, the Northern Pacific had an eerily similar problem when they were laying track to Miles City. It involved their manager and some land the railroad needed to acquire. But the lady who owned it wouldn't give it up. It turned out that she hadn't been told that the railroad needed the land because the manager had his own, very different motives. The issue was only resolved after the manager was shot and killed by the man who is now their sheriff."

Gabrielle asked, "Do you know what happened to the lady?"

Drew grinned and replied, "She is now the wife of Sheriff Ben Arden."

Gabrielle smiled as she asked, "Really?"

Drew replied, "Yes, ma'am," and then he looked at her father and said, "I need to take care of the horses and the mule. Is it alright if I let them share the corral with your mules?"

Boney laughed and then said, "I don't think Fran would be want them to join us in the cabin."

Francine quickly said, "But I do expect you to be staying in the cabin tonight, Mister Campbell."

Drew smiled as he stood and said, "Yes, ma'am."

Gabrielle then jumped to her feet and said, "I'll take care of my own horse, if you don't mind."

Drew glanced at her mother before saying, "You can show me where to store their tack, too."

After they left the cabin, Drew untied the Morgan from the trail rope and handed the reins to Gabrielle before taking his black gelding's reins.

As they started walking, Gabrielle asked, "Why did you buy two Winchesters, Drew?"

"I took advantage of Mister Butler's generosity with the railroad's money to buy a '76 model. This one has a thirty-two-inch barrel, so it has more range and better accuracy. It fires the more powerful Winchester .45-70 cartridge, too. The

Winchester in your scabbard is the same '73 model as your father's, so it uses the same ammunition."

"But you can't fire them both at the same time, so why did you buy it?"

Drew grinned as he replied, "Both saddles came with rifle scabbards, and I didn't want to leave one empty."

As Gabrielle opened the corral gate, she said, "I'm sure that's the reason," and then led her mare inside.

Drew walked his horse and mule into the corral and said, "It does sound pretty feeble, doesn't it? The real reason is that I wanted you to have one with you whenever you went for a ride."

Gabrielle released her saddle's cinch and then asked, "Do you think I'll be in danger even if I'm riding on our land?"

"I don't know when those four thugs will return or what Butler wants them to do, so it's better to be prepared for anything."

"Are you a good shot with a Winchester?"

"I've only fired a few rounds when I bought my Colt, and that was with a '73. So, I'll need to spend some time with my '76 before I can answer your question."

"Now that I have my own Winchester, I'll practice with you, too."

"Alright. But you know that all men consider themselves to be expert marksmen, so don't embarrass me too badly."

––––––

Ira Butler sat in his office with the door closed and stared at the telegram from the head of the survey team that was sitting on his desk. He hadn't expected the survey team to arrive for at least another week, and now everything depended on Bart Early and his three stooges.

He'd begun having doubts about Bart and the others' ability to do the job after they'd been run off by the Frog and his half-breed daughter. If they failed this time, he might not have enough time for third attempt to get rid of them before the survey team arrived. But he couldn't let the surveyors find the squatters, so he had to create a backup plan before those four idiots left Glendive.

As he started working on his hopefully unnecessary plan, the recently resurrected brakeman never even entered his mind. And even though he had concerns about Bart and his three minions eliminating the Remys, to Ira, Drew Campbell had already returned to his grave.

––––––

Drew laid his riding saddle on top of the pack saddle, but when he turned to leave the lean-to, he found his path blocked by Gabrielle.

He smiled as he asked, "Have you decided that I should spend the night in the lean-to after all?"

Gabrielle didn't smile when she replied, "No. I just wanted to ask you something before we return to the cabin."

Drew knew it would she would ask a serious question before he said, "And I'll give you an honest answer."

But her question wasn't as serious as he'd anticipated when she asked, "Why do you still address me as Gabrielle after I told you my parents call me Gabby?"

"I imagine they began calling you Gabby when you were a cute little baby girl, but I don't think it fits you anymore. Now, if you were a grizzled old prospector, it would be perfect."

Gabrielle laughed before saying, "I guess it does sound as if it belongs to a gray-haired, scruffy man."

Drew then said, "Besides, Gabrielle is a beautiful name, and it suits you. But if I were to drop a couple of syllables, I would call you Brie."

Gabrielle smiled as she quietly said, "I like it. So, will you call me Brie instead of Gabby?"

Drew grinned as he replied, "When I don't have time to say Gabrielle."

Gabrielle's warm, dark eyes smiled at Drew for a few seconds before she turned around and walked out of the lean-to with Drew following.

Boney was adding wood to the cookstove's firebox and Francine was kneading biscuit dough when Gabrielle and Drew returned.

Boney closed the iron door and asked, "Were Jean and Jacques pleased to share their corral with the newcomers?"

Gabrielle smiled and replied, "They may not have been happy to share their hay, but they didn't bite them."

As Gabrielle walked to help her mother, her father chuckled before he stepped away from the small cookstove, looked at Drew and asked, "Do you think they'll be coming tonight?"

"I don't think so. When I reached the end of the mountains, I cut across a low foothill so I could see a lot farther. When I looked back toward Glendive and didn't see anyone following me. So, even if they took the ferry right after I checked, they couldn't arrive until after sunset."

"That's good. That will give us at least a day to plan for their arrival."

Drew then asked, "When those four thugs agents showed up, did they have a pack animal with them?"

"No, they didn't. And it was early mid-morning when they arrived. So, even if they left Glendive before predawn and pushed their horses, they shouldn't have gotten here that early. Maybe they brought one and then left it at their campsite."

"That makes sense. And I imagine they'll use the same campsite when they come back."

"That could be anywhere between here and the town, Drew."

Drew nodded as he said, "When I walked to Glendive, I followed their trail most of the way. Now, I'll admit that I'm not a good tracker, so I didn't notice how many horses I was following. But I only lost their trail for about an hour or so after the sun went down, and before the moon rose. So, tomorrow morning, I'll follow their trail again and see if they turned into the forest along that three-mile stretch."

Gabrielle turned and said, "Another pair of eyes will help, so I'll come with you, Drew."

Drew waited to hear if either of her parents objected before replying, "Alright. You're probably a better tracker than I am, anyway. And we can test our Winchesters along the way, too."

Drew then snatched his waders from the floor and said, "Let me get my things out of the way, so no one trips over them."

Boney sat at the table as Drew picked up his duffel and then set it and his waders in the corner of the cabin. After moving his saddlebags, he picked up the two bedrolls and scanned the cabin to find a place to sleep. There was just one bed in the room, and only one inside door. So, Drew assumed the door opened to Mister and Mrs. Remy's bedroom and the lone bed was where Gabrielle slept. And that posed a problem. The large room was cluttered, and the only clear space that would accommodate his large frame was close to her bed.

He decided it would be better if he suffered some physical discomfort rather than making Gabrielle or her parents worry, so he set one bedroll down and then untied and rolled out the other one near the boxes of ammunition. But the bottom of the brown sleeping bag didn't finish unraveling before it reached the cabin wall.

As he untied the straps which kept the second bedroll cylindrical, Gabrielle asked, "How will you be able to fit in there? There's plenty of room near my bed."

Drew was trying to think of a reasonable excuse when her mother said, "Don't be such a prude, Mister Campbell."

When he saw her husband smirking, Drew smiled and said, "I'm not a prude, Mrs. Remy. I was just being considerate."

"You've already proven to be much more than just considerate, Drew. And you'll need a good night's sleep before those four thugs return."

Drew quickly scanned each Remy's face before he slid the first bedroll across the floor and after leaving it about four feet from Gabrielle's bed, he layered the second one over the first.

Once his sleeping location was settled, Drew picked up one of his saddlebags and then walked to the table, sat down and flipped open one of its flaps.

Boney then asked, "Forget something, Drew?"

Drew extracted a small cloth sack, set it on the table and then said, "Yes, sir. I bought these almost on a whim."

He then opened the bag, pulled out a pair of barber's shears and as he handed them to Boney, he said, "Now you'll be able to keep your beard neatly trimmed to impress Mrs. Remy."

Boney laughed and then showed them to his wife and said, "Don't worry, mon petit papillion, I'll remain faithful no matter how many women swoon over me."

Francine shook her head as she smiled and replied, "Trust me, Monsieur Remy, I will not lose a moment's sleep."

Drew then extracted two hairbrushes with enameled backs, handed one to each lady and said, "I didn't see a hairbrush before I walked to Glendive, so I bought these for Mrs. Remy and Gabrielle."

Francine said, "Thank you, Drew. That was very thoughtful, and very useful as well because we just used a wooden comb that Boney made."

Gabrielle then added, "Thank you for yet another gift, Drew. But you're in danger of spoiling me."

Drew stuffed the empty into his saddlebags, and as he closed the flap, he said, "I don't believe that's possible, Gabrielle."

Drew then returned to the serious subject of the pending arrival of Mister Butler's hired thugs when he said, "I'm convinced that Ira Butler is desperate to drive you off your land before the survey team arrives. So, it doesn't make much sense for him to send those four lowlifes out here just to warn you again. Especially after you told them you weren't leaving."

Boney thought about it for a few seconds before replying, "You're right, Drew. Maybe they figured they'd catch us outside preparing our garden. But we spotted them early, so by the time they were within shouting distance, Gabrielle and I were standing in front of the cabin with our rifles."

Drew slapped the table and snapped, "That's it! Butler probably ordered them to shoot all of you, but they figured he hadn't paid them enough to risk being shot."

Francine exclaimed, "*He sent them to kill us without warning?*"

Drew looked at her as he replied, "I believe so, ma'am. I still don't know his motive. But for whatever reason, he seems intent on doing more than just forcing you off your land."

Boney said, "But this time, we'll have four rifles."

Drew shook his head as he said, "Even though they don't know I'm here, or that I added two more Winchesters to your arsenal, I don't think it matters. Even if Butler gives them more money, I think they still won't risk getting into a gunfight. I believe they'll wait until after midnight and then douse the cabin with kerosene and set it on fire."

The room was silent for eighteen seconds before Boney said, "Only cowardly men without souls would do such a thing. But those four all fit into that category. We can schedule watches during the night, and we still have the other traps. What else do you think we can we do to stop them, Drew?"

"I've been thinking about that. It's almost a full moon, so they can't get close without being seen. But the bedrolls would be difficult to spot because they're almost the same shade as the ground. If I'm inside one of them with my Winchester, they wouldn't see me until it was too late."

Gabrielle quickly said, "And I could be in the other bedroll with my new Winchester."

Drew knew it was her right to defend her home, so he didn't try to make her change her mind. Instead, he said, "My biggest concern is that I might balk at a critical point. As I told you yesterday, until I shot the rabbit, I've never even aimed a gun at a living creature, much less a human being. Granted, those men barely qualify as human, but I'm still unsure if I'll be able to shoot them."

Gabrielle said, "I've never shot a person either, Drew. But if those men invade our land, then I'll do whatever is necessary to stop them from burning our home."

When Drew saw the determination in her dark brown eyes, his self-doubts vanished as if they'd never existed. So, he quietly said, "And I promise I won't hesitate, Brie. Not for a heartbeat."

Drew then took a deep breath before he said, "We'll pick out where we'll set up tomorrow."

Gabrielle smiled as she said, "After we search for their campsite."

"Yes, ma'am. And after we test our Winchesters."

Francine then said, "But first, we need to finish preparing supper, Gabby."

Gabrielle flashed a big smile at Drew before she stood and returned to the counter.

Drew shifted his eyes back to her father and they began adding more features to their defenses.

———

Arnie Williams snapped, "Hell, Bart! *Why can't we just sneak up to their cabin, open the door and start shootin'?*"

Bart harshly replied, "Because we'd give 'em a chance to start shootin' back, that's why! Look, if you don't wanna do it, then go back to that hole where I found ya and we'll split your share."

When Arnie just slumped a bit, Bart turned to Jimmy Lynch and sharply asked, "How about you, Jimmy? Do you wanna stay in town? I don't want you comin' along if you're just gonna get in the way."

Despite his inner turmoil, Jimmy nodded and said, "I'm comin'. I ain't got no problem burnin' 'em alive. They're only gettin' what they deserve."

Bart then focused back on Arnie and asked, "Well, how about it, Arnie? Are you gonna man up or start wearin' dresses?"

Arnie glared at Bart as he snarled, "I ain't no coward, and I'll be the first one to start that cabin burnin'."

Bart still wasn't convinced about Arnie's commitment and even less about Jimmy's, but if either of them backed out at the last minute, he wouldn't live long enough to see Glendive again.

But now that all four would be leaving town tomorrow, he said, "Okay then. We'll have plenty of time to get there, so after we eat a big breakfast, we'll pick up the coal oil and head to the ferry. We'll stay where we camped the last time and get some sleep. When it's really late and we know they're sleepin', we'll ride until we're about two hundred yards away and dismount. Then we'll carry the coal oil and splash it all over the front and sides, but not the back where they keep their mules."

Then he looked at Arnie before saying, "And then Arnie is gonna light it up."

Cole grinned as he said, "At least we won't be cold when we hear 'em screamin'."

Bart laughed, but Jimmy and Arnie only managed a weak smile that was closer to a grimace.

––––––

After a filling supper made possible by their fully stocked pantry, Drew and Boney filled the large steel tub in the bedroom with hot water and then washed. When they finished, Gabrielle took a bath and changed into her night dress. Francine then took her turn and bathed in the lukewarm water. After they emptied the tub, Boney and Francine said goodnight and closed their bedroom door.

THE BRAKEMAN

With only the light provided by the flames in the fireplace, Gabrielle slipped beneath her blankets. When Drew slid into his bedroll, he was surprised that he wasn't as uncomfortable as he'd expected to be. In fact, he wasn't uncomfortable at all.

As soon as he was stuffed inside his cloth cocoon, Gabrielle said, "Drew, I've been thinking. You think they'll show up late at night to burn our cabin down, and I agree with you. So, when do you think they'll leave Glendive?"

Drew had been so focused on what to do after they arrived, that he hadn't considered when they would leave town. He suddenly realized that it might play a vital role in stopping them.

He rolled onto his left side before he replied, "I'm glad you asked, Brie. It can make a huge difference in our plans, and I missed it."

Gabrielle shifted to the edge of her bed and looked down at Drew before she asked, "Why is it so important?"

"If they leave Glendive just before sunset, so they can arrive here after midnight, they'll be riding in the dark. Even with the light from a full moon, they might lose their way. So, they'll want to get here before sunset, which means they'll probably return to the same campsite they used the last time."

Gabrielle excitedly said, "And if we find it tomorrow, we could be waiting for them!"

"Yes, ma'am. And we'd be able to catch them with their pants down."

Gabrielle quietly laughed before saying, "I'd rather surprise them with their pants up."

Drew grinned and said, "And after we had them with their hands in the air and our Winchesters pointed at them, we could find out why Butler sent them."

"Do you think they'll tell us? Won't they continue lying and just say they're railroad agents?"

"They would if I wasn't the one asking the question. They'd know I was a brakeman for the Northern Pacific, so there would be no point in pretending to be special agents."

"But what would we do after we captured them?"

"Disarm them, bind their wrists and after we mount them on their horses, bring them to the cabin. Then tomorrow, I'll escort them to Glendive and visit Mister Ira Butler."

Gabrielle quickly asked, "Don't you want me to come with you when you bring them back?"

"No. I think I should do it alone."

"Why? Is it because you'd be embarrassed to be seen with me?"

"Of course not. I'd be proud to be seen with you. I just don't know if the sheriff is partnered with Butler in his scheme. And if he is, I don't want to put your life in jeopardy."

"But what about your life? You're risking your life, and until a couple of days ago, you didn't even know we existed."

Even in the dancing light from the fire, Drew could see the concern in Gabrielle's eyes as he said, "But before then, I didn't know what it was like to have a family. Now that I do, I'll risk everything to protect you and your parents."

"But I don't want you to risk anything, Drew. If we do capture those men, I'm coming with you when you take them back. And don't try to change my mind, either."

Drew realized he'd already lost the argument, so he said, "I won't, Brie. Besides, tomorrow might have all sorts of surprises."

Gabrielle smiled and said, "Ever since you fell into our trap, we've had nothing but surprises."

Drew rolled onto his back before saying, "And I'm sure we'll have many more. Goodnight, Brie."

Gabrielle looked down at Drew for another few seconds before she replied, "Goodnight, Drew," and then returned to her supine position.

CHAPTER 5

The sun had just peeked over the eastern mountain peaks when Drew and Gabrielle waved to Boney and Francine and then rode away from the cabin. Even with their early departure, Drew and Gabrielle still had taken the time to explain their new plan.

After they picked up the trail left by the four unwanted visitors, Gabrielle looked at Drew and asked, "How far did you go before you lost their tracks?"

"I'm good at keeping time in my head, so I'm pretty sure that I walked for more than two hours before it was too dark to see them. That would be around eight miles, so we should start paying close attention in another hour."

Gabrielle said, "I imagine that you have a clock in your head because time is so important to the railroads."

"It is. It used to be a passenger nightmare when the railroads used different times on their schedules. So, just last year the railroads got together and divided the country into four different time zones."

"I've never ridden on a train."

"You're in the majority, Brie. I imagine less than ten percent of Americans have ridden the rails. And I'm not sure I want to board another one myself."

Gabrielle laughed before saying, "After your last train ride, I can understand why you'd be so reluctant."

Drew nodded, and as he looked down at the trail, Gabrielle asked, "How old are you, Drew?"

Drew turned his eyes back to Gabrielle before replying, "I was born on the second of May in 1862. So, in a few more days, I'll turn twenty-two. Why did you ask?"

"I was just curious. And before you ask, I was born on February the sixteenth in 1865."

"And you've lived in this valley ever since. How often have you visited Glendive?"

"After the railroad came, or since I was a little girl?"

"Just after the Northern Pacific arrived."

"I've only gone there twice since then. Most of the time, my father drives our wagon to Glendive for supplies while I stay with my mother."

"I assume that's why you're a good shot, too."

Gabrielle nodded as she replied, "And I do most of the hunting, too. Speaking of that, I'm pretty anxious to try my new Winchester. So, when can we take a few practice shots?"

"Let's wait until we either find their campsite or start back. Okay?"

"Alright. I hope we find it, though."

"So, do I."

———

Bart had bought the two cans of kerosene late yesterday afternoon because he decided to get an early start. But when he found Cole, his most trusted partner was suffering from a severe hangover. So, it was almost nine o'clock when they finally rode out of Glendive. And during their bouncing ferry ride across the Yellowstone, Cole emptied his stomach into the surging water.

As they rode north, Cole still looked green in the gills. Bart hoped he'd be all right after a long nap because he didn't trust Arnie or Jimmy had the guts to do the gruesome job.

———

Just about the time that Cole was heaving over the side of the ferry, Drew pointed down and said, "They turned right into the trees."

Gabrielle saw the change in direction at the same time, so she was already turning her Morgan when she said, "Let's see where they set up their camp."

It wasn't long before Gabrielle exclaimed, "Look at all those other hoofmarks! So, they did have a pack animal with them!"

Drew nodded and assumed they'd have one with them when they returned. And it would be carrying enough kerosene to coat the outside of the cabin.

When they entered the trees, they only had to penetrate thirty yards into the forest before they spotted the ashes left by their abandoned campfire.

After they dismounted, Gabrielle asked, "Now that we've found it, what are we going to do next?"

Drew replied, "Let's tie off our horses, grab our Winchesters and then leave the forest to try them out."

Gabrielle grinned as she led her Morgan to the nearest pine and tied its reins to a stout branch. After she slid her new carbine from its scabbard, she and Drew started following the heavily disturbed ground out of the trees.

Before they reached open ground, Drew asked, "Do you think they'll notice the fresh hoofprints when they get here?"

Gabrielle looked down before she answered, "I don't think so. It doesn't seem much different than it did before."

Drew wasn't so sure but decided to scuff their horse's prints as they walked back to retrieve their horses.

As soon as they reached open ground, Gabrielle looked to the east and asked, "If they are coming today, I wonder when they'll show up?"

Drew replied, "If they left Glendive at the same time that we started riding, then they could be here in another couple of hours."

"Could they hear our gunfire from ten miles away?"

"It's possible, but not very likely. Even if they aren't chatting, the hoofbeats from their five horses would mask the sound of our gunfire. So, they'll probably see us first."

"That's a comforting thought."

Drew smiled, but the possibility that they could be within ten miles was unnerving.

When they had walked about a hundred yards, Drew said, "This should be far enough," before they stopped and turned to face the defenseless army of pines.

Each of them took just six shots during their practice session to minimize the risk of being heard. Drew surprised himself when he hit his target with five of his six and attributed it to the quality of his new Winchester.

When Gabrielle lowered her Winchester's muzzle after burying all six of her shots into her target pine's trunk, she smiled at him and asked, "Did I offend your manhood, Mister Campbell?"

Drew lowered his eyes to the front of his britches and then replied, "I don't feel any lighter, Miss Remy."

Gabrielle laughed, and as they started walking back to the forest, Drew said, "We can decide on our next step while we clean and reload our Winchesters."

Gabrielle looked eastward again as she said, "Alright," then after a short pause, she added, "I know it sounds silly, but I can almost feel them coming."

Drew glanced in that direction and said, "It's not silly at all because I feel the same way. It's almost as if I can see them."

"Then we should begin to prepare for their arrival."

Drew nodded and then began shuffling his boots as they followed their trail. Gabrielle noticed, and without commenting. she began kicking loose dirt over the recent hoofprints left by their horses.

———

Cole was munching on a cracker when Bart asked, "How's your gut doin'?"

Cole swallowed before he replied, "It's okay. I'll be as good as new by the time we leave camp."

"Good enough."

Bart hadn't groused at Cole since he'd discovered him in his sorry state because he couldn't afford to lose him. He hadn't questioned Arnie and Jimmy about their commitment either, but it was for a totally different reason. He suspected that if he challenged them again before they left town, one of them might go to Sheriff Hobson and run his mouth. But if they got cold feet before they left the camp, they'd never have a chance to talk to the sheriff because they'd never see Glendive again.

Jimmy was well aware of Bart's silent threat but didn't believe Arnie had a clue of what would happen if they tried to back out. Now he wished he'd expressed his concerns, only because he might need Arnie's help to get out of the mess that he'd gotten himself into.

Arnie might have listened if Jimmy had talked to him, but right now, he was focused on something that had nothing to do with those squatters.

He was scanning the forests along the foothills when he loudly asked, "Hey, Jimmy. Where do you think that rich brakeman is? I ain't heard any shootin', so he ain't out huntin' yet."

Jimmy hadn't given a thought to the brakeman before he looked at Arnie and replied, "I reckon he's campin' somewhere in those trees. He sure had enough supplies to last him a long time."

"I know, but I sure would like to find him. I don't even want any of his money. I'll be happy just gettin' his horse and one of those new Winchesters."

Bart glared at Arnie as he snapped, "Forget about him! He ain't goin' anywhere, so we can look for him on the way back."

Arnie blew out a long breath before saying, "Okay."

Jimmy felt trapped and the thought of hearing those squatters scream while they were being roasted alive reminded him too much of the hell that awaited him. If he wasn't such a coward, he'd just turn around and ride back to Glendive. But he suspected that even if he splashed some of that coal oil onto the cabin's walls, he wouldn't be riding back to Glendive.

As he rode beside Jimmy, Arnie wasn't concerned about what they'd be doing later that night. He just was wondering what Butler's reason was for hiring them in the first place. He knew about the coal, and that the railroad wanted those squatters off the land. But Butler wanted them dead, not just driven off. While he didn't know Butler's motive, Arnie was sure that Bart did, but didn't trust him and Jimmy enough to tell them what it was.

———

Drew and Gabrielle had been already begun modifying their plan as they led their horses about two hundred yards east of the campfire ashes where they tied them off.

As they cleaned their Winchesters, Drew said, "I'll climb one of the trees near the edge of the forest, so I'll be able to spot them early enough for us to set up."

"How much time will we have after you see them?"

"I figure it'll be more than an hour. But if they don't show up by early afternoon, we'll head back to the cabin."

Gabrielle said, "I want them to come today, Drew."

"So, do I. But while we both hope they'll just throw up their hands, we have to be ready in case they decide to fight it out."

"I'm more than ready, Drew."

Drew smiled and said, "I know you are, Brie."

As Gabrielle began reloading her carbine, she quietly asked, "Was the girl you wanted to marry pretty?"

Drew stopped pushing .45s into his '76's loading gate and replied, "Yes, she was very pretty, which was why she had no difficulty in finding my replacement as quickly as she did."

"What did she look like?"

"She was a little over five feet tall with a nice figure. She had light blonde hair, blue eyes and a cute, round face."

Drew anticipated her next question, and after he shoved in another cartridge, Gabrielle said, "I look nothing like her. But do you still think I'm pretty?"

Drew set his Winchester on his lap, looked at Gabrielle and said, "No, Brie, I don't think you're pretty."

But before she could react, he quickly added, "Anne was pretty, and your Morgan mare is pretty. But calling you pretty doesn't do you justice. You're the most beautiful woman I've ever seen, Brie."

During Drew's second and a half pause, Gabrielle's heart threatened to shatter, but now it seemed to stop beating altogether. She hadn't seen her reflected image since she was fourteen and was looking at a dress through the window of Mrs. Drummond's shop. And even then, her face had been distorted by the wavy glass. Her parents had told her how pretty she was for her entire life, but she knew they would say it even if she was hideous. She still wasn't convinced that she was pretty, but it didn't matter what she believed. She knew that beauty was in the eye of the beholder, and Drew beheld her as a beautiful woman.

Drew was surprised when he recognized the disbelief in Gabrielle's eyes, so before she could say anything, he asked, "Didn't you realize just how beautiful you are, Brie?"

Gabrielle blinked, and then in almost a whisper, she asked, "Do you really believe that I'm beautiful, Drew?"

Drew barely touched her cheek with his fingertips as he replied, "I can't describe how incredibly beautiful you are, Brie. The next time I go to Glendive, I'll buy you a mirror. Then you'll know that I'm not exaggerating."

Brie didn't care about a mirror or anything else after she felt Drew's light touch. She was so overwhelmed with emotions she'd never felt before that she wished time would stop and let her live in the experience.

Drew felt a similar, intense sensation, but still remembered why they were here. So, he slowly took his hand away and said, "We need to get ready, Brie."

Gabrielle sighed, and then nodded and said, "I know. But now I wouldn't mind if they waited until tomorrow."

Drew smiled as he said, "So, do I," and then continued reloading his Winchester.

———

Arnie was right in his belief that Bart knew why Butler had sent them to kill the squatters.

After the exploration team told Butler about the coal, they mentioned that some squatters had built a cabin on the property and had included it in their report. When Ira left

THE BRAKEMAN

Glendive, he was prepared to offer them an entire section of
land north of the town rather than get into a long ownership
battle. But when Boney, Francine and Gabrielle stepped out of
their cabin, his deep hatred overpowered his loyalty to the
Northern Pacific. He wasn't about to give a square inch of the
railroad's property to a white man who married an Indian, so
he just ordered them to leave before he rode back to town.

He knew that Bart shared similar beliefs and soon hired
him, and then had him hire three hard men to rid the valley of
their existence.

Bart hired Cole the same day because he was the meanest
man he'd ever met. Then he'd hired Arnie because Bart knew
he'd killed a man. He almost reluctantly added Jimmy Lynch
who had claimed to have killed two Indians, but Bart had his
doubts. He suspected that Lynch was just trying to earn some
respect by playing the part of a killer.

So, as they approached the end of the short mountain
range, Bart was only confident in Cole, who probably was
already anxious for nightfall. And Bart was just as eager to see
the cabin engulfed in flames while the night echoed with the
squatters' loud wails as they roasted inside.

———

Drew and Gabrielle enjoyed a quick lunch with beef jerky as
its main course and molasses cookies for dessert. Their meal

129

was well complimented by Drew's selection of a perfectly chilled 1884 vintage Montana Territory white.

After their gourmet repast, Gabrielle watched as Drew climbed a tall pine until he was more than thirty feet above the ground. He found a reasonably thick branch, and after sitting on his observation perch, he looked down and waved to Gabrielle.

She bent her neck as far back as her cervical spine would allow and yelled, "How far can you see from up there, Drew?"

Drew loudly replied, "I've got a clear view for around eight miles. But all I can see moving is a large herd of deer a couple of miles away."

"How long are you going to stay up there?"

"Not long. If they don't show up in another half an hour, I don't think they'll be coming, at least not today."

"Alright. But hold on tight, because if you fall, I won't be able to catch you."

Drew chuckled and then shouted, "I've already had my tumble for the month of April, Brie."

Gabrielle laughed before she laid on her back so she could see Drew more comfortably.

Drew scanned the open ground from west to east before he looked back down, and then smiled when he saw Gabrielle's new position. But as much as he enjoyed the view, it wasn't the reason he'd made the climb, so he turned his eyes back to the east.

As he watched for distant riders, Drew tried to recall the faces of the two men who'd kept an eye on him while he was in Glendive. But when the first man's image arrived in his mind, it brought along a new method to confront them, and Drew quickly began fleshing out his new plan. It only took him a few minutes, and he was so excited with it, that he wanted to hurry back down and tell Gabrielle. But he had another twenty minutes to go, so he stayed on his branch and continued his observation.

————

The eastern horizon was still clear when Drew's internal clock told him he'd been branch-borne for thirty minutes. So, he grabbed a higher branch and pulled himself onto his perch.

Then he looked down and smiled as he shouted, "I'm coming down, Brie."

Gabrielle loudly replied, "It's about time."

Drew watched her stand, but before beginning his descent, he took one last look and saw tiny specks on the horizon. He realized that the extra twenty-two inches of height he'd gained by standing had allowed him to see another four hundred yards. If he'd just stepped down to the lower branch, he wouldn't have spotted them, and none of his plans would have mattered.

He forgot about climbing down and studied the moving dots to make sure they weren't deer or a herd of mustangs.

Drew had been watching for more than a minute before Gabrielle shouted, "Aren't you coming down, Drew?"

Drew kept his eyes focused on the specks as he yelled, "I think I see them, but I need to be sure."

Gabrielle wanted to ask Drew how long it would take until he was convinced it was them but didn't want to interrupt him. Instead, she turned and quickly walked to her mare and slid her Winchester from its scabbard.

Drew couldn't identify the specks, but they had continued moving in a straight line which wild critters rarely did. It was enough evidence for him to conclude they were the four thugs. He was anxious to talk to Gabrielle but was still careful as he started his descent.

As soon as he hopped onto the ground, Gabrielle asked, "Is it them?"

"I'm pretty sure it is. But there's no reason to rush because they won't get here for at least an hour. And if they use the same campsite, they won't be able to see us. But while I was up there, I came up with a perfect way to deal with them."

Gabrielle quickly asked, "How did you come up with this perfect plan?"

"After I visited Mister Butler, he had one of those thugs follow me around for the rest of the day. And then had a different one watch me the next morning until I reached the ferry. I'm pretty sure it was because Butler was worried that I might go to the sheriff's office and file charges against Fast Jack Hickman. So, when I confront them, I can accuse them of being sent to murder me to retrieve Butler's money."

"Why did you say, 'I will confront them' instead of 'we', Mister Campbell?"

Drew saw the anger in her dark eyes but smiled before he replied, "Yes, Miss Remy, that's what I said. But let me explain why I used the singular pronoun."

Gabrielle waited for his explanation but didn't believe Drew would be able to dissuade her from playing a part in the confrontation.

Drew said, "After they set up camp, we'll wait until they're relaxed. They might even take an afternoon siesta, so they'll be alert when they leave the camp to burn down your home. Then you'll take your Winchester and walk about ten to twenty yards deeper into the trees before you turn toward their campsite. I'll be watching you, and after you turn, I'll follow a parallel path.

"When you can see their horses, I want you to hide behind a tree but keep a clear line of fire. After I see that you're in position, I'll pull my pistol and enter their campsite. They'll be surprised when they see me, but at least they knew I was somewhere north of the town. But they would never suspect you were with me.

"Then I'll accuse them of trying to kill me on Butler's orders. That should trick them into telling me the real reason they were there. And if I'm lucky, I can use that to learn why Butler wants to kill you and your parents instead of negotiating.

"Then I'll say that I don't trust them and want to take them to Glendive and have Butler confirm their story. But I'll tell them I'm not going to give them a chance to shoot me in the back, so I'll take their guns. After they're disarmed, I'll wave for you to come and bind their wrists while I keep them covered."

Gabrielle begrudgingly admitted that it was a good plan, but still asked, "So, I'll just watch until you need me to tie their wrists?"

"I hope so. But you won't be just watching. You'll be aiming with your Winchester cocked and ready to fire. I don't think any of them will go for their guns, but we have to be ready for that possibility. And if one does, I imagine at least one or two of the others will. So, as soon as I see one of their hands reaching for his pistol, I'll open fire. I'll be lucky if I can get a second shot off, but when you shoot, they'll realize they're in a crossfire and then hopefully the others will drop their guns."

134

Gabrielle asked, "Are you sure you won't hesitate if they do go for their guns?"

"If they do, then I'm sure I won't even think about it before I pull my trigger. It's not the same as if I was going to shoot a man who wasn't trying to kill me."

Gabrielle then looked toward their unseen campsite and asked, "What if they're planning to go to our cabin and start shooting instead of setting fire to it during the night?"

"Then after we see them ride past, we'll get behind them. But I'm convinced they're going to return to their old campsite. Remember what your father said when they visited you the first time? When they saw you and your father standing there with rifles in your hands, they knew at least one of them would die if they tried. And that's why I'm so sure that they'll wait until nighttime and use fire instead of bullets."

Gabrielle sighed and then said, "I'm sure that you're right. But I'll feel a lot better if we don't see them ride by. I'd rather use your new plan than shooting it out in the open."

"We'll know for certain within an hour. So, I'll spread my slicker, so we can sit down and have a pleasant conversation."

Gabrielle replied, "As long as we don't include any topics dealing with those four bastards."

Drew grinned before he stepped to his gelding, removed his slicker from his left saddlebag, laid it across the ground and then sat near hem, leaving the smooth, unbelted end for Gabrielle.

After Gabrielle sat beside him, she smiled and said, "When we return, I'd really like to see what you looked like when you walked across a moving railroad car in your waders and slicker."

"I'll agree to don my rubberized finery on one condition."

Gabrielle grinned as she asked, "And what is that condition, sir?"

"That after I appear in my life-saving garb, you will grant me the honor of courting you. With your parents' permission, of course."

Gabrielle had been expecting Drew to require her to dress in something equally outlandish, so she was prepared to laugh. But when his proposed condition was actually a proposal, she was so stunned that her mind refused to provide a response.

Drew, on the other hand, wasn't surprised when Gabrielle turned into a statue. But he was concerned that he might have gone too far and asked too soon. He should have waited, at least until after they'd dealt with the four phony special agents. He couldn't take it back, so now he could only wait for Gabrielle's response.

It was more than a minute before Gabrielle's brain unscrambled enough for her to quietly say, "I wasn't expecting your answer, Drew. And even if you don't put on your brakeman suit, I'll happily agree to your condition. But may I ask you something personal that might be embarrassing?"

Drew was immensely relieved as he smiled and replied, "I doubt if I'll be embarrassed, so what would you like to know about me?"

"Did you and Anne McDuff... when you were seeing her, did you, um..."

Drew laughed and said, "No, I didn't, Brie. And you'll be surprised to know that even after six months, I never even kissed her."

Gabrielle was too amazed to laugh, but quickly asked, "Was it because you were too shy? I'd be surprised if it was."

"No, I wasn't shy at all. But Anne viewed herself as a proper young lady and would never do such sinful things, at least not with me."

"She believed not kissing made her a lady?"

Drew nodded and replied, "She also dressed as she believed was expected of ladies of proper breeding, even though her father was a baker."

"How do ladies of proper breeding dress?"

"Remember I told you she had a nice figure? While it may have been true, I really wasn't sure. As part of her proper young lady's apparel, Anne also wore the one feminine undergarment designed to enhance a woman's shape, a whalebone corset."

Gabrielle did laugh this time and then asked, "I've never even heard about undergarments with whalebone."

"Neither did I until one of my coworkers in the Northern Pacific maintenance depot told me about them. He said they shrink a woman's waist and enhance her bosom at the same time. I imagine it's worn to impress other women as much as it is to attract men."

"It must be very uncomfortable to wear."

"Anne did seem restricted in her movements. One time, we were sitting on her couch, with a proper gap between us of course, when a mouse ran across her parlor floor. She screamed and then tried to bring her legs onto the couch but couldn't twist far enough to do it."

Gabrielle laughed again as she imagined the scene and then said, "I've been seeing mice and all sorts of little animals scurrying across our cabin floor but never paid them any mind."

"That's another big difference between you and Anne. You have substance, Brie. You're also smarter and have a much stronger character."

"And I guarantee that I'll never wear one of those stiff whalebone undergarments, either."

"I hope not. Besides, you don't need anything to enhance your figure, Brie."

Gabrielle looked at down at the worn, light pink cotton cloth covering her legs and said, "I have three dresses and none of them are very flattering. So, how would you know I have a good figure?"

"Even in your loosely fitting dresses, or maybe because of them, your figure is very, um, distracting."

Gabrielle was surprised when she wasn't embarrassed by Drew's reply. Instead, she was overcome with powerful desires she'd never experienced before. She was thrilled and wanted the sensations to continue but knew this wasn't the time.

Drew was even worse, so before Gabrielle could say anything, he quickly added, "As much as I'd like to continue this conversation, we'd better change the subject, Brie."

Gabrielle was relieved that Drew understood the danger and said, "Okay. So, I'll tell you what little I know about those men."

"That'll help. I know their names and that Bart Early is in charge, but I need to put faces with those names."

"The only one who spoke must be Bart Early. He's shorter than the other three, but heavier. He has black hair and wears a full beard that needs trimming. The scariest one was also the tallest, but he didn't say anything. He just glared as if he wanted to shoot us."

As Gabrielle described each of them, Drew was astounded that she was able to even see their faces as they sat on their horses a hundred yards away. But he wasn't surprised that she could recall the details. Seeing four men threatening you and your parents wasn't an image that could be easily forgotten.

He was convinced that Bart Early had been the man who'd been following him after he visited Mister Butler and was reasonably sure that the second watcher was Arnie Williams. So, the one Gabrielle described as being the tallest and the meanest was either Jimmy Lynch or Cole Thompson. And because Jake Tidwell said that Jimmy Lynch wasn't as bad as the other three, Drew assumed the tallest one and meanest one was Cole Thompson.

So. if they used their old campsite, Drew believed that when he confronted them, he'd probably be listening to Bart Early. But he'd be keeping an eye on the tallest and meanest of the four, Cole Thompson.

———

The tallest and meanest of the four men looked at Bart, grinned and said, "I think Arnie's disappointed 'cause we didn't find that brakeman."

Bart snickered, looked at Arnie and said, "Don't fret, Arnie. We'll find him after we burn out those squatters."

Arnie replied, "I ain't frettin' and I ain't disappointed, neither. But I'm wonderin' where he set up camp. We didn't hear any shootin' or see any smoke from a fire."

Bart pointed ahead, said, "Maybe he's usin' the one we did the last time we visited the squatters," and then paused before he began laughing.

As Arnie snickered, Jimmy just stared ahead. He'd always wanted to be a tough, hard man like his father, even after he'd watched his father being hanged for killing a man with his bare hands. He'd adopted his father's swagger and had gotten into more than a dozen fistfights since he'd arrived in Glendive, but he'd never even seriously injured another man.

But as he rode alongside the three killers, Jimmy no longer remembered his father as a tough, hardened man. He saw him as the man who wept as the hangman lowered the noose around his neck. And when his own face replaced that of his father, Jimmy felt a chill run down his spine. He was only nineteen years old, and the thought of never reaching his twentieth was devastating.

Jimmy wished he'd never accepted Butler's offer, but it was too late now. Even if he was able to ride away when everyone else was napping, Jimmy was sure that Bart or Cole would hunt him down. So tonight, he'd do what he was told but when they returned, he'd pack his things and then leave Glendive and his desire to be like his father behind.

———

Drew was telling Gabrielle about his life at St. Thomas Home for Boys as they looked through the narrow gap between the pines waiting for the four men to ride past.

"Even though it was an Anglican orphanage, they didn't make church attendance mandatory. They only encouraged us to attend services, so almost all of us did."

Gabrielle asked, "Were you one of the exceptions?"

Drew replied, "No. In all the years I spent there, I only missed two services because I had the mumps. I…" then he suddenly stopped and put his finger to his lips.

Gabrielle nodded and just a few seconds later, they watched the four men ride past trailing a pack horse. Then a few seconds later, they heard a distant laugh followed by a man's muffled voice shouting, "I told ya that brakeman wasn't here, Arnie!"

She looked at Drew with wide eyes before he leaned close and whispered, "It sounds like Butler told them to get rid of me, too."

Gabrielle whispered back, "Now we'll have to come up with a new plan."

Drew shook his head before he replied, "No, we won't. In fact, knowing that they actually intend to kill me will make it much more likely that they'll explain Butler's behavior."

Gabrielle was still concerned but just asked, "What do we do now?"

"We stay quiet and relax for a couple of hours. Then we'll pay them a surprise visit."

"Okay. But don't depend on our horses to stay quiet. And I hope they don't come this far looking for firewood."

Drew looked at the horses, said, "I'll get our Winchesters in case they do," and then stood and walked to his gelding.

After he handed Gabrielle her Winchester, Drew sat down and laid his rifle on the slicker.

Gabrielle set her repeater next to his before she said, "I don't hear them anymore."

"We're more than two hundred yards away, so we won't hear them unless one of them shouts again."

Gabrielle stared at the unseen campsite and knew it would be a long two-hour wait, so she asked, "What was it like when you were on the roof of a boxcar as the train raced along the rails, Drew?"

"The first few times, it was terrifying, but it was also exhilarating. After I became accustomed to it, I concentrated on keeping my balance as I fought the wind and sometimes the slippery rooftops."

"Did you ever have any close calls?"

"It depends on what you consider close. I fell fairly often during the first months but never slid close to the edge. But there were six times when I almost joined the ranks of the other lost brakemen, not including the time I plunged into Cabin Creek."

Gabrielle quietly asked, "Did you think you were going to die when you fell?"

Drew smiled as he replied, "I was too busy trying to avoid hitting the bridge to worry about dying. It was after Cabin Creek gave me to the Yellowstone that I began to believe I wasn't going to survive."

"But then you found the canoe."

Drew nodded as he said, "And then I found the canoe. I was horrified when I found it missing the next morning, but now I'm happy that it left me. If it was still there, I never would have found your cabin."

"And you never would have fallen into one of our traps."

"It was a small price to pay, Miss Remy."

Gabrielle felt her new, exciting emotions beginning to return, so she took a deep breath before asking, "So, assuming that your plan works, and we get them tied up, what will be our next step?"

"It'll be too late to take them back to Glendive, so we'll tie them to some trees. Then you can ride home to tell your parents what happened. In the morning, I'll escort them into town and see what happens."

Gabrielle flared as she sharply asked, "And do you expect me to stay with my parents while you take those four evil men to Glendive?"

"They'll have their wrists tied, Brie. And I'm not sure if the sheriff will do anything about it. If he's in cahoots with Butler, he might even arrest me."

Gabrielle knew it was a sound decision, but she still asked, "Then won't it be better if I'm there to confirm what you tell the sheriff?"

Drew shook his head as he replied, "It wouldn't matter, Brie. Even if the sheriff isn't aware of Butler's plan, he's far more likely to listen to the local manager of the Northern Pacific Railroad than to a nobody like me."

"Then I hope we shoot all four of the bastards."

Drew wasn't surprised by what she said, but still hoped neither of them had to shoot any of the four bastards, even though they probably deserved it.

———

Two hundred and thirty yards away, Arnie asked, "Can I use some of that coal oil to start the fire, Bart?"

"Nope. I don't wanna waste any of it. Just pile on some more kindlin'."

As Jimmy and Arnie gathered more twigs and fallen branches, Cole said, "I don't care as much as Arnie, but I wonder where that brakeman is hidin'."

Bart grinned as he replied, "Maybe he rode all the way to the squatters' cabin and is makin' sweet love to that half-breed."

"I wouldn't blame him if he was. She was a mighty handsome half-breed."

Bart spit before saying, "I don't care what she looks like. She's still a half-breed and I don't want her havin' babies who look like her."

Cole snickered and then said, "But her young'uns would be quarter-breeds, Bart. Unless she married some Injun and then she'd have little three-quarter-breeds."

Bart glared and said, "I can't cypher as good as you, but it ain't gonna matter anyway. 'Cause she ain't gonna breed at all after we're finished."

Jimmy was listening as he struck a match and set the kindling ablaze. He may not like Indians or half-breeds, but he didn't think it justified killing them.

Then, as he added dry, broken branches to the burning kindling, Jimmy felt sick knowing that in a few hours, he'd be seeing a much larger, murderous fire. He glanced at Bart and Cole as they happily chatted and wished he really was a tough man like his father. If he was, he'd pull his Colt and shoot them both.

————

Forty minutes after Jimmy lit the match, Gabrielle asked, "Do you smell smoke, or is it my imagination?"

Drew took a sniff before replying, "I didn't notice it before, but now I can smell it. There isn't any wind at all, so their campfire must have been burning for a while."

"It's not that cold, so why would they build a campfire this early?"

"I guess they want to have a hot meal before they have a snooze."

"That's assuming they want to take a nap."

"Even if they don't, I'll still surprise them when I walk out of the trees with my Colt pointed at them."

"If they're going to make a hot meal, do you want to wait a little longer before we surprise them?"

"No. It'll be getting close to sunset if we waited much longer. So, in a little more than an hour, I'll introduce myself and then begin what should be a very interesting conversation."

"I just hope it doesn't start off with a bang."

Gabrielle hadn't intended to make the pun, but when Drew covered his mouth and began laughing, she had to quickly muffle her own laughter.

————

Drew was mistaken when he believed that they were using the fire to cook a late lunch. They'd started the fire to keep them warm while they snoozed in the cool shadows.

With the fire crackling nearby, they laid down on top of their bedrolls and pulled their hats over their faces to get a few hours of shuteye.

While it wasn't long before Bart, Cole and even Arnie were all taking a tour of dreamland, but Jimmy was still wide awake. He could hear Arnie and Cole's snoring, but he still didn't risk taking his hat off. He knew Bart didn't trust him and might be watching him and waiting for him to run. So, as he stared at the dark interior of his hat's crown, Jimmy did something he'd never done before. He prayed that God would send those squatters away before they arrived.

————

Drew looked at Gabrielle and said, "It's time, Brie. Are you ready?"

Gabrielle nodded, picked up her Winchester and then rose to her feet before Drew took his '76 from the slicker and stood beside her.

They looked into each other's eyes for a few seconds before Drew smiled and asked, "Are you sure that you're ready, Brie?"

Gabrielle just nodded and said, "I'm ready," before she turned and walked away.

Drew watched as Gabrielle stepped deeper into the forest and when she was about a hundred feet away, she turned and waved. He returned her wave before he began walking toward their camp at a slow, careful pace.

As Drew passed the pines, he'd glance to his left to check on Gabrielle's progress while still making sure he didn't step on any branches or twigs. Because of their slow approach, it was almost three minutes before he spotted their horses and came to a sudden stop. He didn't see their riders, but he did notice a large can of kerosene hanging from their pack horse's saddle.

When he looked for Gabrielle, he was relieved to find her already standing behind a thick pine trunk. He gave her another quick wave before her return wave let him know that she was in position.

He then began walking closer to find the four men and just three steps later, he spotted them and froze. Even though he'd expected to find them napping, he was still surprised to see the four men laying on their bedrolls with their hats over their faces.

Drew didn't care if they were asleep when he leaned his Winchester against a nearby pine, pulled his Colt and then cocked its hammer before taking a deep breath and resuming his stealthy approach.

As he slowly stepped closer to the resting ruffians, Drew identified Bart Early and Arnie Williams. But he paid special attention to the tall, mean one he assumed was Cole Thompson.

When he was about twenty feet away from the closest one, he stopped, aimed at the tall, mean bastard, and then shouted, "Don't move or I'll shoot!"

All of them jerked, but none tried to go for his pistol. Then Drew loudly said, "You can take your hats off with your left hands, but I'll put a .45 into anyone who reaches for his pistol."

One by one, their left hands lifted their hats off their faces and set them on the ground before all eight eyes looked at him.

Bart Early quickly asked, "Who are you and why are you holdin' a gun on us, mister?"

Drew angrily replied, "You know who I am. You and that other one kept an eye on me after I visited Ira Butler. He gave me six months' pay if I promised not to see the sheriff. And I reckon he hired you to kill me to make sure I kept my promise and get his money back at the same time."

Bart was shaken but quickly argued, "That ain't so, mister. Sure, Butler paid us, but not to come after you. We're headin' to a squatter's cabin to tell 'em to get off railroad land."

"You're lying. I didn't see any cabin."

"I ain't lyin'. You can't see it 'cause it's about six miles west of here."

"Now I know you're lying, mister. I know railroad land grants only extend ten miles from the tracks, so that's not railroad land. Didn't Butler tell you I worked for the Northern Pacific for five years?"

"It'll be the railroad's land pretty soon 'cause they're gonna build a spur line right up that valley. They found a lotta good coal on the land the squatters say the Injuns gave 'em."

Drew paused before asking, "I didn't hear anything about a new spur. And when I was chatting with Butler, he didn't say anything about coal or a spur line, either. And even if that's true, then why didn't Butler just ride out here himself?"

Bart replied, "He came out here and ordered 'em to clear out a few days ago. But they said they weren't gonna move, so he hired us to force 'em to leave."

"That sounds suspicious to me, too. Why would he order them off their land instead of offering them a section of the railroad's land in trade? That's what they usually do to get land they want."

"Why should he offer them anything? They were just squatters."

"Mister Butler knows that even squatters have rights under the law. So, why did he just order them to leave before sending you to force them out? He could lose his job if the bosses back in Minnesota hear about it."

Bart exclaimed, "*How the hell should I know?* He just told us to get 'em off the land!"

Drew glanced at their horses before saying, "I notice you've got a big can of kerosene on your pack horse, so it looks like he wants you to burn their cabin down, too. Did he tell you to make sure they're all inside when you put it to the torch?"

Bart angrily snapped, "*Who cares?* The squatter married an Injun squaw, and they had a half-breed girl. Ain't nobody gonna miss 'em, anyway."

Drew was startled by Bart's reply but quickly asked, "Are you telling me Ira Butler sent you to burn them alive just because of that?"

"You're damned straight he did. He hates Injuns and half-breeds even more'n I do. So, will you lower your pistol now, mister?"

Drew quickly scanned their faces before saying, "I won't believe you until you show me that cabin. But I still don't believe you won't try to shoot me in the back. So, before we leave, I want you all to unbuckle your gunbelts using your left hand and then stand up."

Drew watched as each of them began pulling the end of the belt out of his buckle but failed to notice the tall, nasty man's right hand slowly inching closer to his Colt's grip. After their buckles dropped to the ground, Jimmy Lynch was the first to stand and even put his hands in the air. Then Arnie Williams got to his feet but left his hands by his side as did Bart Early. As Cole Thompson slowly began to rise, so did the lengthened barrel of Drew's Colt.

Cole suddenly pointed to his left and exclaimed, "*Who's that?*"

Drew began to turn his head before he realized it was just a distraction. But the moment his eyes had shifted away, the tall, mean bastard yanked his Colt from his holster and cocked its hammer.

But even though Drew had changed his focus, he hadn't moved his Colt's muzzle even a small fraction of an inch. So, when out of the corner of his eye, he caught the tall, mean bastard bringing his cocked pistol to bear, he squeezed his trigger.

Cole didn't have enough time to be surprised before he felt Drew's .45 slam into his upper chest, just above his breastbone. The lead slug nicked his subclavian artery before pulverizing his first thoracic vertebral body and then creating a massive exit wound as it left his body.

The bullet's impact knocked him back a step and made him reflexively yank his trigger finger. After exploding out of the muzzle, his Colt's .44 ripped across Jimmy's left calf making him scream in pain. As Cole fell onto his back never to rise again, Jimmy dropped to the ground and grabbed onto his leg in an attempt to hold back the bleeding.

As soon as Drew fired, Bart dropped to the ground and grabbed his gunbelt. And before Jimmy fell, Arnie bent over and snatched his Remington '75 from his holster.

Drew had cocked his hammer and watched Cole until he hit the ground to make sure he wasn't going to take a second shot. So, by the time he turned his attention to other three, he was surprised to see Jimmy on the ground gripping his blood-soaked pants leg before he noticed that Bart had dropped to the ground. But he couldn't see Bart pulling his pistol because he was behind Arnie who already was cocking his six-shooter's hammer.

Drew shouted, "Drop the gun!" as he swung his iron sights onto Arnie's chest.

Arnie ignored Drew's loud warning but pulled his trigger before his Remington's barrel was level. The .44 caliber bullet spiraled out of the muzzle and a small fraction of a second later, it buzzed between Drew's thighs without splitting a single thread of his pants' black denim cloth.

Drew didn't know how close he'd come to being emasculated before he fired. His blunt-nosed lead cylinder almost instantly smashed into the right side of Arnie's chest. But because he wasn't standing upright, after it shattered two of his ribs, it began to tumble. It then passed through his diaphragm and pulverized his liver before blasting apart his hepatic artery.

After Arnie dropped his pistol, Drew committed the cardinal sin of believing that the shooting was over. But as he was lowering his smoking Colt, Arnie fell, revealing the shocking sight of Bart aiming it at him. He knew he was too late, so all he could do was hope that Early missed as he cocked his hammer.

Drew was expecting to feel the hammer blow of Bart Early's bullet, but instead, he was stunned when heard the sharp crack of a Winchester and then watched Bart's arm and face fall to the ground. He had completely forgotten about Gabrielle after he began his tense conversation with Bart Early.

Drew slowly released his Colt's hammer when he heard her working her Winchester's lever to bring a fresh round into its firing chamber. When he looked to his left, he saw Gabrielle enter the campsite with her eyes and her Winchester still aimed at Bart Early.

As she slowly stepped closer to her target, Gabrielle loudly asked, "Did you get hit, Drew?"

Drew replied, "No, but only because you shot him first," and then holstered his Colt and began walking to the only one of the four who was still breathing.

Before Drew reached Jimmy Lynch, Gabrielle lowered her Winchester, looked at him and said, "I didn't hesitate, Drew. I just needed to get closer before I had a clear shot."

Drew replied, "I didn't think you hesitated, Brie," and then pulled his knife from its sheath and took a knee next to Jimmy.

Jimmy saw the big, sharp blade and then looked at Drew with wide eyes as he exclaimed, "Don't do it! I wasn't gonna shoot ya, mister!"

"I'm not going to hurt you. I'm just going to cut your britches, so I can see how badly you've been wounded. Okay?"

Jimmy just nodded and then watched as Drew sliced open his already ripped pants. Drew then returned his knife to its leather home before he ripped the cloth apart exposing his wound.

"The bullet just nicked your calf muscle. It'll need to be sewn up, but the best I can do for now is to apply a tight bandage. I'll go check your pack horse for something to use. If I can't find anything, then I'll cut it out of one of your pals' shirts."

"Okay. But they ain't my pals."

Drew said, "You can tell me why you were riding with them later."

Before he could stand, Gabrielle said, "I'll check the pack horse, Drew."

Drew smiled at her, said, "Thank you, ma'am," and then looked back at his patient and asked, "What's your name?"

"Jimmy Lynch."

"Okay, Jimmy, while my fiancée is searching something to use as a bandage, you can start explaining."

"Bart wasn't lyin' when he told ya Mister Butler hired us to kill the squatters. We were supposed to shoot 'em when we came here a few days ago, but Bart said he wasn't payin' us enough to get shot. After we got back, Bart said that Butler was really mad, but he told Bart he'd give us more money to burn down their cabin with them inside."

"Do you know why Butler wanted to kill them?"

"Bart and Cole knew, but they didn't tell me or Arnie 'cause he didn't trust us to go through with it. But a little while ago, Bart said Butler hated Injuns and half-breeds more'n he did, so that might be why he wanted us to kill 'em."

Drew may have been disgusted after hearing Jimmy's reply, but it still made sense. But he kept a calm demeanor as he asked, "Were you going to go through with it, Jimmy?"

Jimmy whispered, "I didn't wanna do it, but I had to do what Bart said or he woulda killed me. You might not believe me, but I was really glad when you showed up. And I was even happier when I saw you shoot Cole. He scared me even more than Bart did."

Gabrielle returned and as she handed Drew a yellowish towel, Jimmy suddenly recognized her and exclaimed, "You're the half-breed!"

Before Gabrielle could react, Drew glared at Jimmy and snapped, "You'd better apologize to my lady right now, or I'll let her show you just how good she is with her Winchester!"

Jimmy almost shouted, "I'm really sorry, ma'am! I don't hate Injuns or half-breeds like Bart did!"

Drew growled, "I don't care how you feel, Mister Lynch. But if I hear you utter that hyphenated insult again, I'll shoot you before she does."

Jimmy didn't dare utter anything, hyphenated or not, but simply bobbed his head for ten seconds.

Drew looked up at scowling Gabrielle and asked, "Should I bandage his wound, sweetheart?"

When she heard how Drew had addressed her, Gabrielle's glower vanished before she replied, "I suppose so."

Drew nodded, tossed the towel over his shoulder and then reached into his coat's left pocket and pulled out his emergency coil of cord. After he used his knife to cut off two pieces of foot-long cord, he sheathed his knife and then folded the towel and wrapped it tightly around Jimmy's wounded calf. Drew then whipped the first piece of cord around the top edge

159

of the towel and wasn't gentle when he pulled it tight and tied the knot.

After binding the towel with the piece, Drew said, "That should hold you for a while."

Then he looked at Gabrielle and asked, "Do you think your mother could suture his wound, Brie?"

"Yes, she can, and so can I. Are we going to take him to our cabin?"

"If you don't mind."

"Alright. But what will you do with the bodies?"

"They can stay here overnight. Then tomorrow morning, I'll borrow a shovel and bury them on the way to Glendive."

Before Gabrielle could ask if he planned to take the wounded thug into town by himself, Jimmy said, "We got a shovel on the pack horse."

Drew quickly asked, "Why do you need a shovel if you were planning to burn their cabin down?"

Jimmy took a deep breath and blew it out before he replied, "Mister Butler said to kill you if we caught sight of ya."

Gabrielle snapped, "*And you wouldn't have had any qualms about shooting him, would you?*"

Jimmy lowered his eyes as he quietly answered, "I ain't never shot nobody before, but I wasn't gonna stop 'em."

Drew stood and then said, "It doesn't bother me, Brie. Can you retrieve our horses while I get Mister Lynch on his horse and clean up the mess on the ground?"

Gabrielle nodded and then gave one long, final glare at Jimmy before she walked away.

———

Forty minutes later, Drew rode out of the forest with Gabrielle riding on his left and an unfettered Jimmy Lynch on his right. Drew had laid their shovel on the ground near Bart Early's body and then hung Jimmy's Winchester in its place on their pack horse.

After they turned westward, Drew looked at Gabrielle and asked, "Are you all right, Brie?"

Gabrielle replied, "Of course, I am. None of them even took a shot in my direction, Drew."

"I know, but I wasn't asking if you were hit. I wanted to know if your soul was wounded."

"It isn't. I hope you don't think it's because I'm soulless, or it's so hard that it can't be wounded."

"I would never think that about you, Brie."

"How about you, Drew? The only living creature you've ever shot was that rabbit. Is your soul wounded because you killed two of them?"

"I thought I'd feel terrible, but I'm not even upset. I guess it's because of what they were going to do."

Gabrielle leaned forward, glanced at Jimmy and then straightened and asked, "Were you afraid, Drew?"

"Only that I might hesitate. Because I knew if I did, you would probably be killed. But once the shooting started, there wasn't enough time for fear."

"There was no time for much of anything. Everything happened so quickly. I think it was less than thirty seconds from the time you shouted until I fired the last shot."

"And I forgot to thank you for saving my life with that shot, Brie. So, thank you, sweetheart."

Gabrielle smiled as she said, "You're welcome," and then added, "When we're close, I'll ride ahead and tell my parents what happened."

Drew replied, "Alright. And when you tell them what they were going to do, you don't have to sugarcoat the reason for Butler's decision to send them."

"Trust me. I had no intention of making it sound any less disgusting than it was."

Drew nodded and was sure that even after Gabrielle repeated what Jimmy had said when he'd recognized her, her mother would still suture Jimmy's wound. While he couldn't predict her father's reaction, he was convinced that tonight, he'd be camping outside the cabin with Jimmy.

———

Boney stared at the eastern horizon and said, "They should have returned by now, Fran. Do you think those four bastards shot them?"

"I'm sure they didn't, Boney. I think Drew was right about their plans. So, I'm positive that Drew and Gabby found their campsite and are waiting for them to show up."

"You're probably right, Papillion. I only hope that Drew's plan for stopping them will work."

"I have no doubts that it will. We've only known Drew for a few days, but I already feel as if he's part of our family."

Boney looked at his wife and said, "So, do I. He's like the son we never had."

Francine smiled as she said, "I'd be happier having him as our son-in-law."

Boney chuckled before saying, "I know it would make Gabby happy, too. She's awfully fond of him, and I think he already cares for her, too."

Francine turned her eyes eastward and said, "And he sees her as the beautiful woman she is and not as a half-breed."

Her husband looked at his wife as he said, "Just as I always have seen you as only a beautiful woman, my love."

Francine smiled and was about mildly contradict his opinion, when she pointed and excitedly asked, "Is it them?"

Boney stared at the dark specks for a few seconds before replying, "I don't know. They're too far away."

"They'll be close enough to identify them in a few more minutes."

Less than a minute later, Francine said, "There are more than two horses, Boney. But I can't see how many of them have riders."

"Do you think those four thugs slipped past Drew and Gabby?"

"No. But we should get our rifles in case I'm wrong."

Boney nodded and then said, "You have better eyesight than I do, so you can keep watching while I go get them."

After her husband disappeared into the cabin, Francine kept her eyes focused on the tiny approaching shapes. Just a few seconds passed before Boney returned and handed her the Winchester.

THE BRAKEMAN

He had the Sharps carbine over his right shoulder as he said, "We ought to be able to count the riders pretty soon, Fran."

Francine replied, "And I don't want to see more than two."

It was less than two minutes later when Francine asked, "Are my eyes deceiving me, or are there three riders on those horses?"

Boney squinted before replying, "I'm not sure, Fran. But if you're right, then it isn't good news."

After another ninety stressful seconds, Francine said, "Now I'm really puzzled, Boney. I'm convinced that there are three riders, but I'm pretty sure two of them are Drew and Gabby."

"Now you've got me wondering how that could be possible."

Francine suddenly smiled and said, "I think Drew and Gabby are returning with one of the four thugs as a prisoner, Boney."

"And that means they must have shot the other three."

"I think so. But I hope Drew and Gabby weren't injured."

"We'll find out in another fifteen minutes or so."

Francine nodded and prayed that she wouldn't be using her needle and thread to close their gunshots wounds after they arrived.

———

They were about a mile and a half away when Gabrielle said, "I can see my parents in front of the cabin, so I'm going to ride ahead, Drew."

"See how fast your Morgan lady can run, Brie."

Gabrielle smiled at Drew and then popped her heels into her mare's flanks.

As Gabrielle raced away, Drew turned to Jimmy and said, "I'm sure her mother will clean and suture that hole in your leg, but don't expect her parents to welcome you with open arms. And after you've been treated, we'll probably spend the night outside."

Jimmy, who hadn't said a word since Drew had helped him onto his saddle, replied, "I ain't gonna complain. They got every right to shoot me for what we were gonna do. But when we get to town tomorrow, are you gonna have Sheriff Hobson arrest me?"

Drew looked at him and asked, "Why would he? Isn't he friendly with Mister Butler?"

"Hell no! I reckon he'd like to throw Butler into one of his cells and forget where he left the key."

"Why? Even if Butler wasn't paying him under the table, local lawmen and politicians usually bend over backwards to keep the railroad's managers happy."

"I heard that Butler was drinkin' with some pals in Happy Jack's Saloon and called the sheriff's wife a squaw. One of his deputies was playin' poker at the next table and told the sheriff what he heard."

"And what did the sheriff do about it?"

"I don't know if he did anything. But everybody knows he ain't fond of Butler and is waitin' for him to give him a reason to toss him in jail."

"But he doesn't know that Butler hired you to murder the Remys?"

"I didn't know that was their name. But I'm sure if the sheriff heard about it, he woulda marched into Butler's office and slapped cuffs on him."

Drew was more than just relieved to know the sheriff wasn't in league with Ira Butler. So, as he walked his black gelding towards the Remys' cabin, Drew started revising his plans for tomorrow.

———

As soon as Gabrielle galloped away from Drew, she stretched her arm high above her head and began waving to her parents. Her Morgan was creating a long cloud of dust and her long black hair was wildly whipping behind her when she saw them excitedly wave back and couldn't wait to tell them what had happened.

She was still a quarter of a mile away when she heard her mare laboring, so Gabrielle slowed her to a less stressful speed. But less than a minute later, she hurriedly dismounted, dropped her reins and then embraced her mother.

After she hugged her father, she hurriedly said, "I have a lot to tell you, but I have to ask you something before I wave Drew in. We had a gunfight with those four men, and the man riding with him is the only survivor. But he was shot in his calf and needs to be treated. Can he enter our home, and will you sew his wound closed, Maman?"

Francine quickly replied, "I'll treat his wound, but I won't allow him to stay in our home after I'm finished."

Gabrielle then looked at her father who then said, "I agree with your mother, Gabby."

Gabrielle said, "Thank you, Papa and Maman," and then turned and waved to Drew.

After Gabrielle waved to Drew to let him know he could bring Jimmy Lynch to the cabin, Francine asked, "Can you tell us what happened, Gabby?"

Her parents were expecting to hear about the gunfight, so they were surprised when Gabrielle smiled and then exclaimed, "Drew wants to start courting me!"

After they recovered from their daughter's unexpected announcement, Francine wrapped her arms around Gabrielle and said, "I'm so happy for you, sweetheart. I was hoping it would happen, but I didn't expect to hear the good news this soon."

Boney then said, "I'm happy for you too, Gabby. But now can you tell us about the unpleasant part of your day?"

Francine stepped back and looked to the east before saying, "We may as well wait until Drew gets here."

Gabrielle then said, "Before he does, Drew wanted me to tell you why Mister Butler sent them to kill us. It's because Papa is a white man and you are Crow, Maman. And I am a half-breed."

Boney's temper flared as he snapped, "That cowardly, hateful bastard! I wish he had enough courage to say that to my face!"

Francine took her husband's hand and said, "But his henchmen failed. And I'm sure our future son-in-law will punish him for hiring them."

Gabrielle quickly added, "And I'll be with him when he does."

169

Francine heard the confidence in her daughter's voice and realized that any motherly dissent would be pointless.

––––––––

An hour later, Francine was suturing Jimmy's wound, and Gabrielle stood watch with her Winchester while telling her mother what had happened.

Outside, as they were unsaddling the seven horses, Drew finished explaining the day's events to Boney. He was starting to strip the pack horse when he asked, "Mister Remy, I know you've lived here for twenty years after the Crow gave you this land. But how much does it mean to you and Mrs. Remy?"

Boney had a saddle in his hands, so after lowering it to the ground, he asked, "It's the only home we've ever had, Drew. Why do you want to know?"

"Jimmy Lynch confirmed that the Northern Pacific is planning to build a spur up the valley to that coal deposit. So, I'm sure the exploration team included your claim to the property in their report. If you're still here when the survey team arrives, the railroad will send someone to offer you a trade which is what Butler should have done.

"The reason I asked how important the land was to you was because even if they let you keep some of it, it wouldn't be the same. Besides the tracks splitting the valley in half, they'd build a small town for the miners nearby, and miners tend to be a raucous bunch."

170

Boney sighed and then said, "I didn't think about that. And even if we fought it, we'd just be postponing the inevitable, wouldn't we?"

"Yes, sir. But would you and Mrs. Remy be willing to leave the valley altogether if you were offered a large tract of land north of Glendive?"

"How far north?"

"The Northern Pacific's land grants extend ten miles on each side of the tracks. So, it would be between five and ten miles north of the Yellowstone."

"That's some pretty land up there, Drew. But how much do you think they'd be willing to give us if we don't have legal proof that we own our property?"

"I really don't know how much they'd offer. But if you'll let me negotiate on your behalf, I believe that I have a good bargaining position with the Northern Pacific."

"Why?"

Drew grinned as he replied, "Remember when I told you how the Northern Pacific wants to avoid scandals? Imagine how big a scandal they'd have if the newspapers learned that their manager sent four men to burn down your cabin while your family slept inside. Then there's my story about how one of their engineers tried to murder me, and then their manager bribed me to keep quiet about it."

"That sounds good. But Butler might hire more thugs to kill you when he discovers you were still alive."

"He won't be able to hire anyone, Mister Remy. When I ride into Glendive with Jimmy Lynch, our first stop will be at the jail. I'll tell Sheriff Hobson what happened, and Jimmy will corroborate my story. But I won't have Jimmy arrested.

"Instead, I'll ask the sheriff to lock Butler in one of his cells and then I'll send a lengthy telegram to the Northern Pacific headquarters letting them know what he did. I imagine one of their executives will arrive within two days to clean up the mess. And I'm the only broom he can use to sweep it under the rug. That's when I'll negotiate on your behalf if you'll let me."

Boney took some time to process all that Drew had told him before he said, "I'd be willing to do it, but let me talk to Fran first because the land was a gift from her father. But I think she'll agree that yours is the best solution."

"I understand. You'll have time to discuss it with her and Gabrielle after Jimmy and I are out of the cabin."

Boney and Francine had already accepted Drew's recommendation that he and his prisoner sleep outside, so Boney just replied, "I'll let you know as soon as possible."

After he picked up the saddle, Boney smiled at Drew and said, "I don't think Gabrielle will object. After all, she won't be living with us much longer, will she?"

Drew grinned and replied, "I hope not."

———

When they entered the cabin, Drew looked at Jimmy, who was sitting on a chair with his severed pants leg and a fresh bandage around his human leg, and asked, "Can you hobble?"

Jimmy slowly stood before he replied, "Yeah. After Mrs. Remy sewed it up, she put a poultice on it that makes it feel better."

Drew nodded, snatched his bedrolls from the floor, and then said, "Then hobble outside with me."

As Jimmy slowly limped away from the table, Gabrielle started to walk behind him when her father said, "I need to talk to you and your mother, Gabby."

Gabrielle turned and asked, "What is it about?"

Boney waited until Drew and Jimmy left the cabin before he replied, "It's about our home."

After leaving the cabin, Drew laid the two bedrolls on the ground along the southern wall of the cabin. He then waited for Jimmy to lay down before he sat on the other bedroll.

As soon as Drew's behind was planted on the bedroll, Jimmy said, "You didn't tell me if you were gonna have Sheriff Hobson arrest me. So, what are you gonna do with me tomorrow?"

"I'll take you to the jail, but not to have you arrested. I'm going to tell the sheriff what happened, and then you can confirm the story. Then I'll ask the sheriff to put you in one of his cells, but only to keep you safe. After I deal with Ira Butler, the sheriff will let you go. Okay?"

Jimmy gawked at Drew for a few seconds before asking, "Are you tellin' me the truth? You ain't gonna have him arrest me?"

"On what charge? You never took a shot at me, Jimmy. In fact, after you leave the jail, you can have your guns back."

Jimmy blinked and then said, "But we were gonna kill you."

Drew shrugged and said, "I'm not the one who has a hole in his leg."

Jimmy sharply exhaled before saying, "I really appreciate you bein' so forgivin', mister. And I promise not to cause you any more trouble."

Drew was confident that Jimmy wouldn't be a problem. But he wasn't sure if he could say the same about Gabrielle after he told her that she'd be staying with her parents tomorrow.

———

Boney asked, "What do you think, Fran?"

Francine sighed and then answered, "I'm sure Drew's right about what will happen when they start mining the coal. And I know he'll do his best when he negotiates with the railroad."

Boney nodded and then smiled at Gabrielle and said, "I told Drew that you wouldn't object because you wouldn't be living with us much longer. Was I right?"

"I hope so. But what did Drew say after you told him that I wouldn't?"

"The same three words that you just used. He said, 'I hope so.'."

As Gabrielle smiled, her father stood and said, "I'll go let him know that he can negotiate on our behalf."

Before her husband started to leave, Francine said, "And tell him and the other one that supper will be ready in thirty minutes or so."

Boney replied, "Yes, mon amour," and then left the cabin.

———

Because of Jimmy's presence, there was almost no conversation during their late supper. And what little there was consisted of general, non-violent or railroad related topics. Drew was relieved but also surprised that Gabrielle hadn't mentioned tomorrow's ride to Glendive.

175

But as he was chewing his last bite of venison stew, Gabrielle asked, "What time will we be leaving tomorrow, Drew?"

Drew swallowed before he replied, "Jimmy and I will be leaving shortly after sunrise," and then waited for her explosive response.

Gabrielle immediately snapped, "*I'm not coming with you?*"

"I wish you could, Brie. But after we get there, it'll take me at least the rest of the day to deal with Mister Butler. Then I'll have to stay in town for another day or two until the railroad sends someone to clean up Butler's mess.

"You told me how uncomfortable you were when you had to go into town. So, how much worse would it be for you to stay in a hotel for a few days, especially if I couldn't be with you? Hopefully, I'll return in three or four days with the deed for some of the Northern Pacific's land."

Gabrielle wanted to argue, but the thought of staying in Glendive for two or three days was enough to make her reply, "Alright. But after you return, you still have to put on your silly brakeman outfit."

Drew was happily surprised with Gabrielle's answer, so he smiled and said, "I'll be more than happy to oblige, ma'am. And after I don my brakeman duck suit, I'll quack a few times as I waddle around the room."

As Gabrielle and her parents laughed at the anticipated vision, Drew stood and said, "Mister Lynch and I will now retire to our moonlit bedroom. So, I'll wish each of you a good night."

Jimmy stood and as he limped towards the door, Drew gazed into Gabrielle's dark eyes for a few seconds and then followed him out of the cabin.

———

In his apartment behind his private office, Ira Butler was sitting in his easy chair reading Mark Twain's *The Adventures of Tom Sawyer.* He was confident that Bart Early would soon put the torch to the squatters' cabin. But he wasn't sure when they'd return because it might take them an extra day to find the brakeman. Ira was curious about how many would be coming back, but he didn't care if only two rode into town.

All that mattered was that when the survey crew reached the end of the valley, all they would find was a pile of charred rubble.

CHAPTER 6

Drew waved to Gabrielle and her parents before he and Jimmy began their five-hour ride to Glendive. He didn't bring a pack animal, but in addition to his Winchester '76, he had Jimmy's '73 model hanging on the left side of his saddle and his gunbelt in his left saddlebag.

After they'd ridden a mile or so, Jimmy asked, "What if Butler spots us before we reach the jail?"

"Then after we visit Sheriff Hobson, I'll probably have a harder time finding him."

"When you do, he'll most likely shoot ya as soon as you lay eyes on him."

"You're probably right. So, I hope he doesn't see us."

"If Sheriff Hobson does what you ask him to do, how long do you figger I'll have to stay in jail?"

Drew grinned as he replied, "Maybe for just the night. Of course, that's providing Ira doesn't shoot me."

Jimmy stared at him and asked, "Ain't you worried about bein' killed?"

"It doesn't help to worry about things before they happen. And when it does, there usually isn't time to worry."

"I was plenty worried before you showed up yesterday. I know you must hate me, but I'm really grateful for how you're treatin' me."

"You should be more grateful to Mrs. Remy for suturing your wound. She did a better job than most doctors."

"I know. But I was so scared that I forgot to thank her when she finished. So, when you get back, can you thank her for me?"

"I will. Now don't take this as an insult to your manhood, but you don't seem to have the hardened character of an outlaw."

"I ain't insulted 'cause I guess I ain't cut out to be one."

"Then why did you ride with those three?"

"I've been tryin' to be like my old man since I was just a squirt. He was..."

As Jimmy told his life's story, Drew began to understand his motive for joining the three genuinely evil men. He also believed that Jimmy regretted being part of the plot and was even becoming sympathetic for the would-be outlaw. But he was certain he wouldn't feel a bit of sympathy when he buried the other three. He did hope that their carcasses had already been dragged off by some large, hungry carnivores.

179

———

Boney set the can of kerosene on the floor and said, "We've got enough coal oil to fill our lamps for at least six months, Fran."

Fran replied, "As opposed to being splashed on our home and to burn it down. They didn't have much food, but they did bring some useful supplies with them."

Gabrielle then said, "We have four more horses, their tack, three more Winchesters, and three pistols, too. But I'd trade everything just to keep Drew safe."

Boney smiled as he said, "Now, Gabby, Drew knows what he's doing. I'm sure everything will turn out fine."

"I hope so."

———

After taking less than an hour to bury the three bodies in a single, shallow grave, Drew and Jimmy were now close to turning south toward Glendive.

In Glendive, Ira Butler had just entered Finney's Diner. After taking a seat at his usual table and placing his usual order, Ira unfolded his fresh copy of *The Yellowstone Gazette.* He quickly read the front page which held nothing of interest.

When he opened it to the second page, he began reading an interesting, but sordid article. It was about a working girl who'd been hanged for stabbing to death a non-paying customer in the town of Bismarck. The Dakota Territory town was not only a stop on the Northern Pacific route but had also been renamed by the railroad to attract German immigrants.

When he read that the victim's name was Gavin Campbell, he snickered and said, "I reckon it ain't a good time to be named Campbell."

He was still grinning when he moved on to a story about the new lumber mill being constructed west of town.

———

As they turned south, Drew asked, "How's your leg?"

Jimmy glanced down at his bandaged calf and then replied, "It hurtin some, but my back tooth hurt a lot more before Abe Sessions yanked it out a couple of months back."

Drew looked at Jimmy and asked, "Is Abe Sessions a dentist?"

"Nope. Abe's a wrangler on the Harrison ranch. He's pulled a lotta teeth before, but they all came outta horses' mouths."

Drew rubbed his cheek and decided to buy a toothbrush after dealing with Ira Butler.

———

On his way back to his office, Ira stopped at the Western Union office to check his box for new messages and found two waiting for him.

He snatched them from the small cubicle and without returning the telegrapher's wave, he left the office and turned onto the boardwalk. Ira suspected that one of them was from the head of the survey team to let him know when they'd be arriving. He wouldn't know who'd sent the second telegram until he pulled it out of its envelope.

After sitting behind his desk, Ira opened the first envelope, slid out the folded sheet and read the message. As he'd expected, it was from Ed Osmos, the lead surveyor. He was surprised when he read that the team would be arriving much earlier than he'd expected. Their train should pull into the station early tomorrow afternoon. Suddenly, Ira became very concerned about when Bart and the others would return. He'd have to know that they'd done their job before that survey team took the ferry across the Yellowstone.

He was still thinking about the potential problem when he opened the second envelope. It was from the head of security, and as he read the telegram, Ira realized he had a much larger problem. In addition to the survey team, their train would be carrying Warren Adams, a Northern Pacific special agent. But it was the agent's assignment that made his visit so troublesome. It was also very puzzling.

The chief of security had dispatched Adams to investigate the death of brakeman Drew Campbell, which was highly unusual, if not unique. And almost as strange, Ira couldn't understand why the agent was coming to Glendive to investigate Campbell's death, when he'd fallen off the train after it left Glendive. Besides, all he had to do was to interrogate the engineer when he returned to Brainerd.

Just a few minutes ago, Ira was having breakfast and enjoying the story about a whore being hanged for stabbing a different Campbell to death. Now he had to avoid facing the noose himself and cursed himself for not notifying headquarters that the brakeman had survived.

Ira didn't know the agent, but maybe he'd be susceptible to a bribe. It would be the easiest solution, but an enormous risk as well. If Mister Adams was honest, offering him a bribe would ensure his arrest and eventual hanging.

Ira knew there was only one solution to his multi-faceted dilemma. Bart Early and his thuggish companions had to return before the train arrived and confirm that they not only burned out those squatters, but also killed Drew Campbell. *But if they hadn't returned, what would he tell the special agent?*

Ira only pondered that question for thirteen seconds when a revelation provided the answer and his desperation vanished.

He would tell the agent that Campbell had survived the fall and walked into his office. And after receiving his last month's pay, he'd quit, taken the ferry across the Yellowstone and ridden north. His secretary would confirm the story and so would anyone else in town the agent might interview.

But the best part of his life-saving plan was that when the survey team found the burned pile of rubble, he'd suggest that Drew Campbell was the murdering arsonist.

Ira grinned as his quietly said, "Before he left my office, Mister Adams, Campbell said how much he hated half-breeds. So, I imagine he was the one who set that cabin on fire."

———

Drew handed Jimmy a large strip of jerky and then ripped a chunk from his own salty, dried beef.

As he chewed, Jimmy asked, "What are you gonna do now that you ain't gonna be a brakeman anymore?"

"I apprenticed as a blacksmith, but I don't think I'll work iron for a living. Did you do learn a trade while you tried to be a hoodlum like your father?"

Jimmy shook his head as he replied, "Like I told ya, I just wanted to be like my pa. So, after he was hanged in '81, I came to Glendive and then hung around town causin' trouble. And I bragged about doin' really bad things that I didn't do."

"And that's why Bart Early asked you to join him."

"Yeah, it was. I figgered I was finally gonna make my old man proud of me, but I didn't measure up."

"You're lucky you didn't, Jimmy. Now you can start doing things that will make you proud of yourself and not your dead father. And if you have a son of your own someday, he can be proud of you, too."

Jimmy didn't reply but looked at the tall ex-brakeman and saw the kind of man he wanted to become. A man other men admired and were proud to have as a friend.

As Drew ripped off another bite of jerky, he was unaware of the enormous impact he just had on Jimmy Lynch. Instead, he continued studying the landscape along the western mountains' foothills. He'd examine it even more closely when they reached the Northern Pacific's land grants. He wanted to find the best land for Boney and Francine, and hopefully to share with Gabrielle.

———

Ira was startled when John Knudsen opened the door and said he'd was going to lunch. After his secretary closed the door, Ira looked at the large clock on his wall and was surprised when the two hands told him it was 12:26 pm. He wasn't hungry enough to return to Finney's, so after he heard the outer door close, Ira reread the two telegrams.

After putting them in his desk's center drawer, Ira began estimating the earliest time that Bart and his terrible trio could return. They would have returned to their campsite in the wee hours of the morning and most likely wouldn't have started back until mid-morning. It was a least a four-hour ride, so they could reach the ferry within the hour.

The unknown factor in his estimate was the second part of their assignment. Ira wasn't able to factor in how much time they'd spend looking for Campbell. So, they might not return until after the survey team's train arrived, and the special agent paid him a visit.

To reduce that disastrous possibility, Ira decided that if they didn't return before sundown, he'd take the ferry early tomorrow morning and then ride north to look for them. But this afternoon, he'd sit on the library's bench watching the ferry hoping to spot riders coming from the north. And if he did, Ira suspected there would be no more than two men, and they'd be leading a small herd of riderless horses.

He still wasn't very hungry when Ira stood, grabbed his hat from the coat rack and then left his office.

———

Jimmy pointed and excitedly said, "There's Glendive, Drew!"

Drew was surprised when he heard Jimmy address him with his shortened Christian name but even more so by his enthusiasm.

So, he said, "I thought you'd be worried when you spotted the town, Jimmy."

"I woulda been if I didn't trust you to keep your word. But after talkin' to ya, I'm sure you didn't lie to me."

"Telling the truth is a lot easier than lying. When you lie, you have to remember two things: the lie and the truth."

Jimmy grinned and said, "You sound like a preacher or maybe a lawman, Drew."

"I'm not as forgiving as most preachers, and I don't have the skills to be a lawman. But I was good at being a brakeman until I left the job and the roof of that boxcar."

Jimmy was still grinning as he looked for the ferry that would carry him and Drew across the Yellowstone. He was actually looking forward to meeting Sheriff Hobson and listening as Drew talked to him.

Drew was looking south as well but was concerned about what might happen when he and Jimmy entered the jail. He had based his plan on what Jimmy had told him about the sheriff and his strong dislike for Ira Butler. But Jimmy had only heard about it second hand, so it might be nothing more than inaccurate gossip. And if the rumor wasn't true, then Drew might find himself in a locked cell with Jimmy.

So, as much as he hated doing it, Drew asked, "Is Sheriff Hobson's wife an Indian?"

Jimmy looked at him and asked, "I thought you liked Indians?"

"I don't like or dislike all Indians, just as I don't like or dislike all white folk. They may look different than we do, but inside, they're the same. Some are good and others are bad. Some are smart and others are stupid. It's the same for colored people and Orientals, too."

"Are you sure you ain't a preacher?"

Drew grinned as he replied, "I'm sure. But since I was knee-high, I was taught to be fair-minded by the good people at St. Thomas Home for Boys."

"You're an orphan?"

"My father abandoned us when I was about a year old, and my mother died from diphtheria the following year."

"Do you even remember their names?"

"My mother's name was Emily Maureen and my missing father's name was Gavin James."

"Do you reckon he's still alive?"

"I really don't care, Jimmy. Now back to my original question. Is Sheriff Hobson's wife an Indian?"

"I ain't sure, but she sure looks like one. She has black hair that she wears long."

"So, how confident are you that the story you told me about the sheriff not liking Butler is true?"

"I'm pretty sure. Even Bart and Arnie heard about it."

Pretty sure wasn't good enough for Drew, so he said, "Hold up, Jimmy."

After they brought their horses to a stop, Drew reached into his saddlebag, pulled out Jimmy's gunbelt and handed it to him.

As Jimmy wrapped it around his waist, he asked, "Why are you trustin' me with my pistol?"

"I'll tell you after I give you your Winchester."

Drew then detached the scabbard holding Jimmy's Winchester and passed it across to its owner.

As Jimmy tied it in place, Drew said, "I gave you your guns because I changed my plans. Where do you hang your hat when you aren't causing trouble?"

"I have a room at Bascom's Boarding House. Why?"

"When we enter Glendive, I want you to go to your room while I visit Sheriff Hobson. Stay there until I come and get you, which shouldn't be too long."

"I thought you wanted me to tell the sheriff what Butler ordered us to do."

"I still do. But there's a chance that the gossip about the sheriff hating Ira Butler is poppycock. If it is, I want to find out before I tell him what happened. But if you walk in with me, I doubt if I'll get the chance."

"Okay."

Drew nodded and then smiled and said, "Let's go for a ferry ride."

———

Ira Butler was sitting on the library's bench chewing on a toothpick as he stared north, hoping to spot Bart's boys. He'd been optimistic for the first half an hour but was now fading into pessimism.

He pulled out his pocket watch, opened it and mumbled, "I'll give you 'til two o'clock, Bart."

After he snapped the cover closed and slid it back into his coat's small pocket, Ira decided to stretch his legs. So, he stood and began stepping north along the boardwalk. He was passing the barber shop when he spotted two distant riders north of the Yellowstone. He came to a sudden stop and stared at them for almost a minute before he grinned, spun on his heels and hurried back to his office.

Even though Ira had only seen two riders, he assumed they had to be Bart Early and that evil bastard Cole Thompson. No one else could be riding from that direction, and he'd suspected that Bart might be returning with only one of his partners. So, between his preconception and his anxiety to hear Bart's report, Ira overlooked the obvious clue that would make him realize his error. He had overlooked the absence of any trailing horses.

Ira was almost giddy by the time he entered the outer office, so when his secretary looked up at him, he grinned and cheerfully said, "And good afternoon to you, John."

John blinked before saying, "Um, good afternoon, sir," and then watched his boss bounce past him and disappear into his private office.

John was surprised by Butler's first use of his Christian name and by his unusually ebullient mood. He was even more puzzled when Mister Butler left his office door open, especially considering all of his recent, troubling behavior.

But he expected that Mister Ira Butler wouldn't be so cheerful when Mister Warren Adams arrived with another, unannounced traveling companion. John Knudsen then smiled before he continued reviewing the latest dispatch notices.

———

Drew and Jimmy led their horses off the barge, and Drew handed the ferryman a fifty-cent piece. After Josh Brockman expressed his gratitude, Drew tipped his hat before he and Jimmy mounted their horses and rode off the dock.

As they approached the town's outskirts, Drew said, "I'll take Main Street, but I think it'll be better if you used one of the side streets to get to your boarding house. So, let's split up."

"Okay."

As Jimmy angled his horse away, Drew focused on Main Street. He'd decided to split up because he suspected that Ira Butler would be anxious for his hired killers to return and might be watching. Butler would want to hear the good news that they'd roasted the Remys alive and murdered the troublesome brakeman.

Drew was still scanning the busy main thoroughfare when he reached the jail and dismounted. After looping his reins around the hitchrail, he stepped onto the boardwalk and then opened the door to the sheriff's office.

Deputy Sheriff Jack Pope was hanging a new wanted poster when he heard someone open the door. He quickly stabbed the upper corners of the poster onto the nails and then turned just as Drew entered.

"What can I do for you, mister?"

Drew stepped closer before he stopped and replied, "I'm Drew Campbell. I used to be a brakeman for the Northern Pacific..."

Drew was interrupted when Jack exclaimed, *"You're that feller that fell off the train and almost drowned, ain't ya?"*

"I am. Anyway, I headed north to do some hunting and four men tried to kill me, but I got the better of them. So, I need to talk to the sheriff."

Jack was wide-eyed as he excitedly said, "He's in his office, so I'll go fetch him!"

Drew was halfway through a nod when Deputy Pope shot away, ran past the three cells, opened a door and entered the sheriff's small office. Drew listened as the deputy rapidly repeated what he'd just been told, and then heard the sheriff's terse reply. Then a few seconds later, both lawmen left the office and quickly stepped towards him.

Sheriff Bob Hobson was a couple of inches shorter than Drew, yet probably outweighed him by ten or fifteen pounds. But he had the appearance of a man who was born to be a lawman. So, before the sheriff spoke a word, Drew instinctively believed him to be an honest man, and the rumor about his dislike for Ira Butler was probably true.

Deputy Pope took a seat at the desk before Sheriff Hobson stopped before Drew and asked, "You said you were waylaid by four men but killed 'em all? But it looks like you didn't even get a scratch. So, do you expect me to believe that a feller who only helped slow down trains could outshoot four outlaws?"

Drew glanced at Deputy Pope before replying, "It's a long story, Sheriff. But before I tell you what happened, can you give me your opinion of Ira Butler?"

Sheriff Hobson's eyes narrowed as he growled, "If it was up to me, I'd lock that bastard in one of my cells and toss away the key. Why did you wanna know?"

"Because everything I'm about to tell you involves Mister Butler. And when I'm finished, you may get your wish."

The sheriff quickly said, "Pull up a chair and tell me what happened."

Drew nodded and after the sheriff perched on the corner of the desk, he took a seat on one of the two straight-backed chairs.

Drew began his long story by saying, "After I fell from the train…"

———

As Drew narrated the chain of events that would culminate with his return to Glendive with Jimmy Lynch, Ira was becoming even more anxious as he waited for Bart Early to enter the office. It had been more than an hour since he'd spotted the two riders, so they should have arrived in town by now. He then began drumming his fingers on his desk as he stared at the wall clock. *Where the hell was Bart Early?*

After another fifteen seconds of finger tapping, Ira huffed and then stood, grabbed his hat and then left his office and walked out the front door without giving his secretary a glance. Ira then turned left and began walking north along the boardwalk. But after taking just six steps, he came to a sudden stop when he couldn't see any signs of Bart. It was as if he'd vanished before he reached the ferry. Ira was beginning to worry when he realized that Bart must have gone to his room at Bascom's to clean up. So, he rapidly walked to the end of the boardwalk and then turned left onto Fifth Street.

When he spotted Bascom's Boarding House, there was only one horse tied out front. And it wasn't Bart's. Ira wasn't sure, but it looked like Jimmy Lynch's animal. Then he remembered that Bart had told him he wasn't sure if Jimmy or Arnie Williams would have the stomach for the job. Ira then suspected that Jimmy had come running back to town rather than do the job he'd been paid to do.

Ira's anger began to rise as he stepped closer to the horse and noticed that there was a Winchester hung on the other side of the saddle. When he reached the gelding, Ira laid his hand on its warm shoulder to confirm it had recently been ridden. He then slipped the Winchester from its scabbard and stepped down the short walkway. He knew which room was Bart's, and Bart had mentioned that Jimmy's was across the hall. So, it was time to have a chat with Jimmy Lynch.

———

After he'd limped into his room, Jimmy had hung his hat and coat, and then unbuckled and removed his gunbelt. After setting it on his plain pine dresser, he laid down on his bed.

After he laid his head on the pillow, Jimmy closed his eyes and pictured Sheriff Hobson's face when Drew told him what had happened. He smiled and hoped everything worked out as Drew planned. And he wanted it to happen quickly because he was getting pretty hungry.

Jimmy was drifting off when the door opened. He opened his eyes expecting to see Drew, but was terrified when he saw Ira Butler enter the room carrying a Winchester.

Ira closed the door and stepped towards the bed with the carbine's business end pointed at Jimmy.

Jimmy quickly sat up and snapped, "*What are you doin' here?*"

Ira glared at him as he replied, "I was going to ask you that question. Why are you here and Bart isn't? Did you run away because you were too squeamish to set fire to those squatters?"

Jimmy's mind was racing to create a life-saving answer as he stammered, "I...I didn't run off. I...it's just that I got hurt."

"How'd you get hurt, Lynch? Did you break your foot when you were trying to run away?"

"I told ya. I didn't run away. It was after we set fire to the cabin. I was steppin' back 'cause it was so hot and then stepped into a hole and twisted my ankle."

"That still doesn't explain why you're the only one who made it back."

"Bart and the others were lookin' for that railroad feller. And Bart told me I was useless and to ride back on my own."

Jimmy's quickly developed fictional account sounded plausible to Ira, so he asked, "But you saw that cabin go up in flames, didn't you?"

Jimmy grimaced as he replied, "Yes, sir. And I don't wanna hear screamin' like that ever again."

Ira was relieved that the squatter problem was gone and then asked, "Do you know if the other three found the brakeman?"

Jimmy shook his head and replied, "No, sir. But I'm pretty sure they knew where he set up his camp. So, I reckon they'll finish him off before sunset."

Ira believed that he'd learned all he could from Jimmy Lynch. He was about to toss the Winchester onto his bed when he remembered that he'd seen two specks on the northern horizon, not just one.

So, he quickly asked, "Did you ride back alone, Lynch?"

Jimmy blinked and then replied, "Yeah. Like I told ya, everybody else wanted to find the brakeman."

"Then maybe you can explain why I saw two riders coming from the north."

Jimmy was close to panic and hurriedly said, "You musta been seein' things, Mister Butler."

Ira might have accepted that possibility, but seeing the fear in Jimmy's eyes not only dismissed that likelihood, it also put the lie to everything else Lynch had just told him.

He shoved the Winchester's muzzle a few inches closer to Jimmy's face and then exclaimed, "You've been lying about everything, Lynch! Tell me the truth or I'll put a bullet between your eyes!"

Jimmy knew he should be terrified as he looked down the inside of the repeater's barrel, but he wasn't. He was through being a coward. He wanted to be proud of himself.

So, instead of trembling with fear, Jimmy glared at Ira and said, "You ain't gonna shoot me, Butler. If you did, Sheriff Hobson would have you sittin' in one of his cells before sundown."

Ira was stunned by Jimmy's transformation, so several seconds passed before he said, "Maybe not. But if you don't tell me what happened, then I'll have Bart Early pay you a visit."

Jimmy smiled as he said, "That ain't gonna happen either. 'Cause Bart, Cole and Arnie are all dead and buried."

Ira snapped, "You're lying again, Lynch! *Do you expect me to believe that you killed all of them?*"

"Nope. We were ambushed by that brakeman you wanted us to kill, but I got away. And I reckon he might be payin' you a visit pretty soon, too."

It was Ira Butler who now experienced a growing sense of panic. But before his mind descended into chaos. he asked, "Did Campbell ambush you before you reached the cabin?"

Jimmy nodded as he replied, "He was waitin' at our campsite yesterday afternoon, so we never got close to the cabin."

Ira threw the Winchester onto the bed before he whirled around, ripped open the door and fled into the hallway.

Jimmy quickly grabbed his Winchester and cocked the hammer in case Butler returned. But as he stared at the open doorway, Jimmy realized that he'd made a mistake by telling him about Drew. And if Drew hadn't told him to stay put, he would have limped as fast as he could out of the boarding house, mounted his horse and ridden to the jail to warn him. Now, all he could do was hope everything still worked out as Drew had planned.

———

Ira was convinced that Jimmy Lynch had told the truth about the ambush. So, as he hurried back to his office, he frantically tried to think of a way out of his self-created trap. He now realized that Drew Campbell was his biggest problem. And if Campbell was on his way to town, he'd surely visit Sheriff Hobson first. So, when he reached Main Street, Ira stopped and looked north. He was relieved when he didn't see any riders coming from the ferry, so he quickly turned and stepped onto the boardwalk. Once again, Ira had overlooked a vital clue. He'd failed to account for the man who was riding beside Jimmy Lynch.

After entering his office, he looked at his secretary and said, "You can take the rest of the day off," and then walked into his private office and slammed the door shut.

John was curious about what had panicked his boss and stared at the doorway for almost a full minute. He then stood, walked to the wall and took his coat down from the brass hook. As he slid his arm through its sleeve, he hoped Mister Butler wasn't planning to take the evening's eastbound train. He'd been looking forward to seeing his face when Mister Adams and Mister Alistair MacLeish entered the office tomorrow afternoon.

———

Because of the sheriff's constant interruptions to either ask questions or express his disgust with Ira Butler, Drew wasn't even halfway finished with his long narration.

So, rather than wasting another hour, Drew asked, "May I ask you for a favor, Sheriff?"

"It depends on what kind of favor, Mister Campbell."

"I know you want to arrest Mister Butler and charge him with conspiracy to murder, but I'd appreciate it if you just held him in one of your cells for a few days."

Sheriff Hobson's eyebrows rose as he asked, "You don't want me to arrest him for tryin' to kill you and the Remys?"

"At least not yet. I need a few days to try and use his despicable behavior to help the Remys."

"How is that gonna work?"

"After he's in your jail, I'll wire the Northern Pacific main office and let them know they have a problem. I know they're about to build a spur to the coal deposit on the Remys' land. But if the government learns what happened, they might deny their request for the land grants which would include that coal deposit."

The sheriff grinned and said, "I reckon I can just let him enjoy a few days in one of my cells while you do that."

"Thanks, Sheriff. If it's alright with you, I'll leave now and visit Mister Butler while he's still in his office."

"Do you want me to come along?"

"No, sir. He probably thinks I'm dead again, so I'd like to surprise him with my second resurrection."

Sheriff Hobson chuckled before saying, "Now I really want to come along, but I reckon you earned the right to bring him in."

Drew stood, said, "I'll finish telling you the story when I return with Mister Butler," and then pulled on his hat and left the jail.

———

Mister Butler was sitting behind his desk and was no closer to finding a solution to either of his problems. But after he sat down, he took the precaution of opening his bottom desk drawer and taking out his Smith & Wesson Model 3. After he verified that all six chambers were full, he set it on his desktop and resumed his desperate search for an solution.

He was contemplating doing exactly what John Knudsen suspected he might do and boarding the eastbound train when he heard the outer office door open. Ira didn't know who had entered, but still grabbed his pistol, pointed it at the door and cocked the hammer.

Drew was surprised that Mister Knudsen wasn't behind his desk, but it wasn't important. It may even be better if he didn't witness his meeting with Ira Butler.

He then took a deep breath and stepped toward the closed door, but just before his hand touched doorknob, he froze. He didn't know what had stopped him or why, but Drew wasn't about to tempt fate. So, he slowly stepped to the side of the doorway and slid his Colt from its holster.

He then shouted, "Is anybody here?"

Even though Ira knew someone was in the outer office, when he heard Drew's loud, unexpected shout, he jerked in surprise. His reflexive reaction pulled his right index finger back which released his pistol's hammer.

So, just a small fraction of a second after Drew yelled his question, the door exploded. Splinters flew as the .45 caliber bullet crossed the room, shattered the front window, crossed Main Street and burrowed into the outside wall of the Lassiter brothers' butcher shop.

Drew was stunned but wasn't about to open the door. And he didn't dare move in case Butler fired again. So, he just waited and tried to figure out how Ira Butler knew he was coming. And as much as he didn't want to believe it, the only one who could have told him was Jimmy Lynch.

Inside the office, Ira was recovering from his pistol's unexpected blast. He hadn't heard anyone scream or fall to the floor, so he knew he hadn't hit anyone. *But what if it was Drew Campbell out there?* If it was, then he'd go running to find Sheriff Hobson. Ira couldn't let that happen, so he quickly stood, cocked his pistol's hammer and then slowly stepped toward the wounded door.

Drew could hear Butler's muffled footsteps and took one step further back from the doorjamb which put his back against a wall. Even though Butler had fired, this wasn't anything like the deadly situation he and Gabrielle had faced yesterday. So, instead of cocking his Colt's hammer, he lifted his pistol overhead and focused on the doorknob.

Ira grasped the other side of the doorknob and slowly turned it clockwise. When its inside mechanism reached its stop, he hesitated, took in a deep breath and gradually pulled the door open. When he looked through the foot-wide gap, he didn't see Drew Campbell or anyone else outside. As more of the empty front office came into view, Ira believed that the unknown visitor must have run away in abject terror.

And he was sure that the gunshot would attract Sheriff Hobson, so he had to be ready with his tale of an accidental discharge before he arrived. But now he had to be absolutely certain that he was the only one in the office when that bastard lawman showed up to question him. So, with his cocked pistol leading the way, he resumed his measured exit.

Drew's heart started pounding against his ribs when he'd seen the door slowly start to swing into Butler's office. After a tense four or five seconds, it stopped moving, and a gun barrel emerged followed by Butler's hand.

Ira knew there was only about three feet of space on the right side of the doorway, so as he carefully entered the outer office, his attention was to his left. He'd almost finished scanning the room when the lights went out.

Drew watched Ira Butler collapse, and then holstered his pistol, took a knee and rolled Butler onto his back. He then laid his hand on the manager's chest and was relieved when he felt a strong heartbeat.

———

Sheriff Hobson was talking to Deputy Pope when he heard the muffled report from Ira's unintentional shot. He turned his eyes to the front of the jail and asked, "Did you hear a gunshot, Jack?"

Deputy Pope replied, "I heard somethin', but I ain't sure it was a gunshot."

The sheriff leapt to his feet and then hurried to the wall and grabbed his hat from its peg. Before he pulled it on, he said, "I'm gonna head down to the N.P. office to make sure Butler didn't shoot Campbell."

"Do you want me to come with ya, boss?"

Sheriff Hobson yanked his hat on and said, "Stay here. If I ain't back in fifteen minutes, then you can come lookin' for me."

Before his deputy could reply, the sheriff opened the door, turned right and hurried away. Jack Pope then left his seat behind the desk to close the door.

———

After Drew stood, he looked through the broken glass and saw folks already gathering on the other side of the street. He wasn't about to carry Butler to the jail, and he couldn't leave the office in case Butler regained consciousness. So, he just waited until someone had the courage to enter the office to ask what had happened.

Drew didn't have to wait long. Just a few seconds after he'd decided to stay put, Sheriff Hobson rushed through the door.

The sheriff stopped, glanced at the unmoving Northern Pacific manager, and then looked at Drew and sharply asked, "*Did you kill him? What happened?*"

Drew shook his head as he replied, "He's not dead, Sheriff. I just tapped him on his head. When I got here, his secretary was gone, and his office door was closed. After I loudly asked if anyone was here, Mister Butler put a bullet through the door and then it broke the window."

"He shot at the door without even knowin' who you were?"

"He must have been expecting me to show up. I suspect that Jimmy Lynch told him what happened yesterday."

"Did he say anything before you knocked him out?"

"No, sir. But I need to talk to Jimmy Lynch right away, so you can ask him when he comes to."

"I'm lookin' forward to askin' him a few other questions, too. So go ahead and ask Lynch."

Drew stood and then asked, "Where is Bascom's Boarding House?"

"On Fifth Street. Just turn left and it's the first side street."

Drew said, "Thanks," and then walked through the open doorway and turned left.

As he headed toward Fifth Street, Drew ignored all of the stares from the growing audience. But when he heard hurried footsteps coming from behind him, Drew stopped and then turned to loudly dismiss his curious follower when he recognized John Knudsen.

John stopped and asked, "Did you shoot Mister Butler?"

"No, I didn't. He tried to shoot me, but all I did was give him a knock on the noggin with my Colt. Sheriff Hobson's is waiting for him to wake up, so were you planning on having me arrested?"

"That thought never entered my mind. I was surprised when I saw you leave the office, but I was also very pleased. I have much to tell you, so may I walk with you, Mister Campbell?"

Drew's curiosity shot into stratospheric levels as he replied, "You may. And I imagine it has something to do with the four lowlifes Ira Butler sent to murder the Remys."

As they began walking, John quickly asked, "Did they succeed?"'

"No, sir. The Remys are doing well. But three of the four are dead and buried, and I'm on my way to talk to the last one. Did you know what Butler had ordered them to do?"

"I knew he was meeting with Bart Early and others, but I only suspected it had something to do with a family of squatters. However, I did know that he had paid you a bribe to prevent you from seeing Sheriff Hobson."

As they turned onto Fifth Street, Drew said, "I'm not surprised. Are you telling me this because you want me to return the money to the Northern Pacific, Mister Knudsen?"

"Heavens, no! But can we stop, so I can tell you what I did about it?"

As soon as Drew came to a halt, John said, "For quite some time, I suspected that Mister Butler had been treating the Northern Pacific as his personal bank account. But it was difficult for me to prove until he gave you the check for seven months' salary. And when I looked at the check's stub and saw that Butler had written that it was for repairs on the water tower, I had proof of his chicanery. Then I sent a telegram to the chief of operations reporting Mister Butler's duplicity."

Drews eyebrows peaked as John continued his explanation by saying, "In the telegram, I had to include the fact that you were still alive. The reply arrived at my home yesterday and the head of operations informed me that he was dispatching a member of his staff to deal with Mister Butler.

"And because the conductor on your train charged the engineer with intentionally trying to send you to your death, the head of security is sending a special agent, too. They'll both be on board the survey crew's train which will be arriving early tomorrow afternoon."

Drew was pleasantly surprised hearing that a member of the operations staff was already on his way. He wouldn't need to send the telegram and he'd return to the Remys sooner than he'd expected, too.

He then replied, "That's good news. But why did you think it was so urgent to let me know?"

"I didn't want you to leave town until they arrived."

"I wasn't planning to leave for a couple of days, anyway. I told Sheriff Hobson what had happened, but only asked him to hold Butler in one of his cells for a day or so before having him charged with conspiracy to murder."

John was surprised and quickly asked, "You were? How could you prove that he sent Early and the others to kill the squatters? Do you believe you'll be able to convince the last one to testify against him?"

"Jimmy Lynch told me that he would, but now I'm not so sure. I think he might have told Butler what happened and then warned him I was coming."

"I didn't see anyone enter the office before I left twenty minutes ago. But Butler was gone for most of the afternoon."

"Then I'll give Jimmy the benefit of the doubt when I ask him in a couple of minutes. Are you going back to the office?"

"I'd rather come along and hear what he tells you. Oh, and you don't need to send a telegram."

Drew nodded and then resumed walking to Bascom's Boarding House. As he approached Jimmy's horse, Drew hoped that Jimmy hadn't warned Ira Butler of his imminent arrival. But he still wasn't about to stand in front of his door when he knocked. Then he realized he didn't know which door opened into Jimmy's room. And he doubted if John Knudsen knew where he lived either, so he didn't bother asking him.

But when he and John entered the boarding house, Drew was relieved when he saw a heavyset woman sitting on a couch in the small parlor knitting a hideous pair of orange socks.

Drew removed his hat, approached the woman and asked, "Excuse me, ma'am. Could you tell me where I could find Jimmy Lynch?"

The woman's eyes never left her knitting as she replied, "He's in number four."

Drew said, "Thank you, ma'am," and then he and John stepped down the narrow, dark hallway and stopped in the space between room number two and Jimmy's room.

After forcing John back, Drew rapped on the door and loudly said, "Jimmy, this is Drew. Are you awake?"

Jimmy was startled but was immensely relieved when he heard Drew's voice, and quickly replied, "Yeah, I'm awake. But is everything okay?"

The tone in Jimmy's reply was enough to convince Drew that he wasn't going to walk into a bullet, so he said, "Everything's good," and then lifted the latch and opened the door.

As Drew stepped into the small room, Jimmy slowly swung his legs off the bed and then said, "I was really worried, Drew. Butler showed up with my Winchester. Then he pointed it at me and asked me how come I was back, but the others weren't."

As John walked through the doorway, Drew asked, "What did you tell him?"

Jimmy ignored John and replied, "I told him that I hurt my ankle, so Bart sent me back while they went lookin' for you. It looked like he was believin' me when he asked how come he saw two horses instead of just one. And then he said I was lyin' and he'd shoot me if I didn't tell the truth."

"So, you told him what happened and that I was coming to see him."

Jimmy nodded as he replied, "Yeah, I did. But it wasn't 'cause I was afraid. Not even with my Winchester's muzzle just a couple of feet from my nose. It was 'cause I wanted to scare him. So, I told him that the others were dead and buried. And when I told him you were on your way, I made it sound like you weren't in town yet."

Then, after a short pause, Jimmy quietly added, "I just wanted to do somethin' that made me feel proud of myself, Drew."

Drew slowly smiled and said, "You earned the right to be proud of yourself, Jimmy. Not many men would have challenged a man who had a gun's muzzle a couple of feet in front of his eyes."

"Then you ain't mad at me?"

"No, sir. And the good news is that Mister Ira Butler is lying flat on the floor of his office after I tapped him on his head with my Colt. When he wakes up, Sheriff Hobson will escort him to the jail and fulfill his wish to toss him into one of his cells. So, it's safe for you to leave and go grab some lunch."

Jimmy glanced at John before he asked, "Are you comin' with me, Drew?"

"Not this time. Mister Knudsen and I have to return to the Northern Pacific offices."

"Okay."

Drew tipped his hat before he and John turned, left the room and then the boarding house.

As they walked east along Fifth Street, Drew asked, "Are you going to be the next manager, Mister Knudsen?"

"I hope so. But I don't know if Mister MacLeish will promote me or bring in someone else."

"Who is Mister MacLeish?"

"Alistair MacLeish is the man the head of operations sent to handle the mess."

Drew smiled and said, "That's a good Scottish name. My best friend at the orphanage was named Alistair, but he was only there for a couple of years. One day, Alistair Ferguson's aunt and uncle arrived and took him away. They seemed like nice people, so I was happy for him. But I was still sad, and I think he was, too."

Then Drew chuckled before saying, "Enough reminiscing. I hope Mister MacLeish gives you the job because you're an honest man, Mister Knudsen."

As they turned onto Main Street, John said, "Thank you. And feel free to address me as John. May I call you Drew?"

Drew replied, "Of course. Let's find out if Ira Butler is awake and talking, John."

John grinned and replied, "Let's."

The crowd gathering outside the Northern Pacific offices had grown in the last ten minutes, so Drew and John had to push their way through the human blockade before they reached the office door.

As soon as they entered the outer office, Drew found himself almost face-to-face with Deputy Jack Pope, who quickly said, "He woke up a couple of minutes ago, and we moved him to his office. The sheriff's talkin' to him, and I'm keepin' folks out."

Drew said, "I need to talk to him, too," and without asking permission, he stepped past Deputy Pope and walked to the smaller office with John following closely behind.

Ira hadn't said a word until he saw Drew step through the doorway and exclaimed, "I had to shoot! You were going to kill me!"

Drew said, "You missed," before Sheriff Hobson asked, "Did Lynch warn him?"

"Only when Mister Butler had a Winchester aimed at his nose. But even then, it wasn't intentional. So, are you going to put him in one of your cells now, Sheriff?"

"I was just waitin' for you to get back. And after I lock him up, you can finish tellin' me what happened."

"I'll do that."

As Sheriff Hobson took hold of Ira Butler's right elbow and lifted him from his chair, John asked, "May I come with you, Drew?"

"It's alright with me, but it's Sheriff Hobson's jail."

As the sheriff perp-walked Ira to the doorway, he said, "Come along, Mister Knudsen. I need to talk to you, too."

Deputy Pope took hold of Ira's left elbow before they escorted their prisoner onto the boardwalk and turned left. Drew and John followed six feet behind in case Mister Butler decided to resist being incarcerated.

As they stepped along the dry pine boards, John quietly asked, "Why do you think the sheriff wants to talk to me, Drew?"

"I imagine he'll want to ask you the same questions that I did a few minutes ago."

"Oh. Then I guess it'll be okay."

––––––

The sun was setting when Drew and John left the sheriff's office. As Drew was untying his gelding's reins, John asked, "Would you join me and my family for supper, Drew?"

Drew smiled as he replied, "I appreciate the offer, John. But after I leave my horse with the Tidwell brothers, I'll just grab something at the diner. Then I'll get a room at the hotel and get some rest."

"I understand. But you don't need to get a hotel room, Drew. Butler had an apartment built behind the office, and I don't think he'll be using it any longer."

"I'll do that. And maybe I'll search the place before I make use of his bed."

John replied, "I'll see you in the morning, Drew," before he waved and walked away.

––––––

Drew spent a half an hour talking to Jake and Amos Tidwell about all that had happened before he walked to the diner to have his supper.

When he finally entered the dark Northern Pacific offices, Drew needed visual assistance to help find the apartment. So, after setting his stuffed saddlebags down, he struck a match and lit the lamp on John Knudsen's desk. He then carried it into Ira Butler's private office, and after checking the wall clock which informed him it was 9:17, he spotted the door to Butler's apartment.

Drew opened the door and when he stepped inside, he was surprised by the almost luxurious furnishings. He closed the door and walked across the room and opened the door to another room, which he assumed was his bedroom.

His assumption was proven to be correct when he saw the bed, but Drew wondered why Ira Butler needed the enormous four-poster. He set the lamp onto the polished surface of a maple dresser before he lit the lamp on one of the bed's two side tables.

Even though the quilt-covered mattress was calling to him, Drew's intense curiosity overcame his need for sleep, so he began to search the apartment.

He quickly went through the dresser drawers, but unsurprisingly, he didn't find anything interesting. Then he took the lamp from the dresser and returned to the front room. After setting it on the top of the maple rolltop desk, Drew sat in its matching maple chair and opened the wooden curtain.

Drew reached into the top right cubicle and removed the folded papers. He was disappointed when none of them were incriminating in nature.

He remained disappointed as he read the remaining cubbyholes' papers and those that he found in the small drawers beneath the rows of maple boxes. When Drew opened the top right drawer, he found it empty, as were the middle and bottom drawers. He didn't expect to find anything when he slid the top left drawer open, so his level of disappointment didn't get any worse when he saw the bottom of the drawer.

After Drew closed the empty middle drawer, he yanked open the large bottom drawer and was surprised to see the front cover of a single green ledger. He took it from the drawer, set it on the desk's foldout surface and opened it to the first page.

It was a standard accounting ledger. The first column contained dates starting with September 17, 1882. The wider second column contained descriptions. The next column, which was intended to be used for costs was empty. But the one for expenses was full, as was the last and widest column. Butler had listed his explanation for each expense in the right-hand column, and Drew was astounded that he'd even written them. *Why would he document his illegal behavior and then leave the ledger where it could be so easily found?*

After quickly reading the first page, Drew flipped it over to scan pages two and three. The entries ended halfway down the third page, but it was those last few that Drew found most intriguing. They included the payments Butler had given to Bart Early with an explanation of the expense, and the bribe he'd had to give to 'the dead brakeman'. The last entry was the added cost Bart had demanded for torching the Remys' cabin. When he read the comment column in that row, Drew's stomach twisted even though he knew why he'd offered Early more money. Butler had written, 'told him to send those filthy squatters to hell where they belonged'.

Drew closed the ledger before he returned it to the bottom drawer and then slowly pushed it closed. He pulled the rolltop cover down and then stood, blew out the lamp and returned to the bedroom. As he undressed, Drew tried to understand why Butler had kept a record of his misdeeds.

As he slid beneath the heavy blankets and the thick quilt, Drew doubted if he'd ever learn the reason why Butler decided to create the self-incriminating ledger. So, as he laid his head onto the goose feather pillow, Drew forgot about the green book and filled his mind with very pleasant thoughts about Gabrielle.

————

In the darkness of the Remys' cabin, Gabrielle had been under her blankets for almost an hour but was still wide awake. When she had watched Drew ride away early that morning with Jimmy Lynch, she worried that Drew had made a terrible mistake. Even though Drew had both of Lynch's guns, Gabrielle believed that Drew still should have bound his wrists. But now, all she could do was to pray that her fears were groundless.

As she stared at the almost invisible ceiling, Gabrielle was engulfed by loneliness. She had never felt so isolated and lost before, and it was disturbing. Gabrielle began to believe that Drew would never return from Glendive. But when she started to descend into the depths of depression, she suddenly sat up and whispered to herself, "Stop it! You're behaving like…like Anne McDuff. Do you want to make Drew ashamed of you? Now, get to sleep and dream about your wedding night."

Gabrielle smiled before she laid back down and then pulled her blankets to her chin and closed her eyes.

CHAPTER 7

After Drew opened his eyes, it took him almost a full minute to realize where he was and how he'd gotten here. After making the bed as he'd been doing each morning at St. Thomas, Drew poured enough water from the full pitcher of water into the wash basin to clean and shave. Then he quickly dressed, hung his saddlebags over his shoulder and left the bedroom. Before leaving the apartment, Drew removed the ledger from the rolltop's bottom drawer and slipped it into one of his saddlebags.

John Knudsen wasn't at his desk when he entered the outer office, so Drew decided to have breakfast at the diner. As he stepped along the boardwalk, Drew began adding details to his negotiating position with the Northern Pacific.

Because the Remys had no proof of ownership, the twelve sections of land given to them by Francine's Crow chieftain father carried little weight in the negotiations. But as Drew had explained to them earlier, he had a lot of other bargaining chips. And Ira Butler had unwittingly provided the most valuable chip by keeping a record of his misdeeds. He only planned to use the ledger if he wasn't satisfied with their best offer. But a lot would depend on Alistair MacLeish, the man who would be representing the railroad in the negotiations.

221

———

After having a filling breakfast, Drew thought about visiting the sheriff, but decided to talk to John Knudsen first, so he headed back to the N.P. offices.

When Drew entered the outer office, he found John sitting behind his desk writing.

As Drew took off his hat, John looked up, smiled and asked, "Did you get a good night's sleep, Drew?"

Drew grinned as he replied, "I slept like a bear in January. That was the largest and most comfortable bed I've ever seen. Have you seen another one like it, John?"

As Drew sat down and set his saddlebags on the floor, John answered, "I can't make a comparison because I've never seen it. Mister Butler made it clear that no one was to enter his apartment."

"Who kept it clean and changed the linen?"

"Believe it or not, Mister Butler did his own cleaning. But he'd have me take his linen and dirty laundry to Mrs. Procter's to be washed."

"Do you want to explore his apartment when you have some time?"

"I wasn't planning on it, but now I have to see his enormous bed when I have the time."

John set down his pen and then asked, "What are you going to do now that you decided to give up the rewarding life of a brakeman?"

"I'm not quite sure. A lot depends on the deal I can get for the Remys."

John leaned back and said, "You told me that they were given more than eight thousand acres by the Crows. But you must realize that you'll be lucky to get a quarter section of land for them in exchange, Drew. And even if I'm fortunate enough to be promoted to manager, they'd fire me in an instant if I offered them even a full section."

"Normally, I'd agree with you. But I believe I have the upper hand in any negotiations."

"Why?"

"How long have you worked for the Northern Pacific?"

"Just for a couple of years. But I've read all of their policies and procedures, including the standard practice for obtaining occupied land."

"I'm sure you have. I've been working for the railroad for five years, and all I've learned came from talking to laborers, conductors, and engineers. And many of them have been working on railroads for most of their lives. So, I understand the hidden processes that aren't written in any manuals."

"Such as?"

"I'm sure that you know that everything is about money. And for the railroads to make money, they need the land grants to sell to immigrants. And the politicians in Washington are the ones who decide if they get them or not. So…"

Drew then continued explaining the reason why he was confident that he'd be able to almost blackmail the Northern Pacific into giving the Remys much more than a quarter of a section of land.

When he finished his long-winded explanation, John shook his head as he said, "I reckon you do have them over a barrel, Drew. And now I understand why you asked Sheriff Hobson to just lock Butler in a cell without arresting him. But I do have one more question. You only met the Remys a few days ago, so why are you bending over backwards to help them?"

"At first, I was sympathetic to their situation and wanted to help them defend their property rights. And I wasn't happy with the Northern Pacific either. But now I'm trying even harder because I intend to marry Gabrielle Remy and settle down on some of their new land."

John's eyes widened as he grinned and said, "At least that's a more reasonable reason. So, how much land are you hoping to convince the railroad to give them?"

"I'll settle for less than half the acreage they were given by Mrs. Remy's father. I'll show you which sections I believe would satisfy them."

Drew stood and walked to the large, sectioned map on the far wall. When John stepped beside him, Drew pointed at one of the ten sections of land grants above the Yellowstone River.

Then he said, "I'll ask for five sections, starting with the northernmost," and then he tapped four more surveyed squares before saying, "And then these four."

John stared at Drew as he said, "That'll block off two government sections, so effectively you'll be asking for seven square miles of land."

Drew smiled and said, "The Northern Pacific won't care. And I'm going to ask for more than just the land, too. I'll ask them to build two houses and a barn to replace the cabin they've called home for twenty years."

John chuckled before saying, "I thought you were a little crazy for thinking they'd agree to five sections of land. But now I know you're ready for the loony bin, Drew."

"Why? They're going to be sending construction crews and a lot of material to build the mining village. So, it won't cost them much to construct two small houses and a barn."

John was still smiling as he walked back to his desk while Drew continued to study the map. There were several reasons why he'd chosen those sections. It was good land with plenty of water and deep forests along the foothills. But more importantly, it was almost a mirror image of the land given to them by Francine's father. And he didn't believe that the Remys would mind losing a few thousand acres. Especially if he was able to coerce the railroad into building them a new house and barn.

Drew tapped the map, and then turned, walked back to the desk and plopped onto the chair.

John then asked, "What will you do if they refuse to give you anything, Drew? You have to anticipate that possibility."

"It seems they already have the land grants approved, so it's more likely than I had previously believed. But I still have the potential scandal as a bargaining chip. And I think they'd rather give up some land that was given to them rather than reading a newspaper story about one of their employees sending men to burn a family alive."

"I hope you're right, Drew."

Drew stood, pulled on his hat and then picked up his saddlebags before saying, "So, do I. I'm going to head down to the jail and talk to Sheriff Hobson."

"I have to finish my order for a new window. Will you be coming back?"

Drew draped his saddlebags over his shoulder, replied, "Yes, sir," and then gave John a short wave before leaving the office.

———

Gabrielle and her father had just finished moving the last of their stored hay into the corral when she asked, "Papa, do you think Drew is all right?"

Boney wiped the sweat off his brow with his shirtsleeve and then answered, "I'm sure he's fine. What makes you believe otherwise?"

"I think he trusted Jimmy Lynch too much. When they left, Drew didn't even tie his wrists."

"Drew knows what he's doing, sweetheart. Besides, he had Lynch's pistol and his Winchester. And don't forget that Lynch has a bad leg, too."

"I know. But I still have a bad feeling about it."

Boney smiled as he said, "Don't fret, Gabby. I'm sure Drew will return tomorrow with good news."

Gabrielle looked at her Morgan and said, "I could ride to Glendive, Papa. Then I'd know for certain."

"You know that would be a foolish and dangerous thing to do, Gabby. Remember why Drew didn't want you to come with him?"

227

"I remember, Papa. But I'm not worried about strange men anymore. I'm only worried about Drew."

"But Gabby, he said he'd be gone for at least two days. So, just for your parents' peace of mind, will you please forget about riding to Glendive?"

Gabrielle sighed before replying, "Alright, Papa. But if he hasn't returned by sunset tomorrow, I'm leaving the next morning."

"And your mother and I will come with you."

Gabrielle kissed her father on his cheek before taking his arm and escorting him out of the corral.

———

Sheriff Hobson grinned as he said, "Mister Butler doesn't seem to like his new accommodations. He wasn't even happy with his breakfast."

Deputy Pope snickered before saying, "He didn't get much sleep with old Tom Walker snorin' so loud in the next cell, neither."

Drew asked, "Did you have to stay here all night to watch him?"

"Nope. Willy Smith had the night shift. He headed home before you got here."

"Is he another deputy?"

"Yup. But he's a lot younger than me and he's only been on the job since October. So, he's still learnin'."

"How much younger is he?"

Jack looked at the sheriff who replied, "He'll turn twenty in September."

Drew smiled and said, "That's even younger than I am. But I'm sure he's already a better lawman than I could ever be."

Sheriff Hobson said, "He's doin' okay, but you did a damned good job takin' down those four bruisers."

"I only shot two of them, Sheriff. If it hadn't been for Gabrielle, I wouldn't be here talking to you."

"But you still shot two of 'em while they were firin' at ya. Not many lawmen I know woulda been able to do that."

Drew shrugged before saying, "Hopefully, I'll be able to let you know whether or not to charge Butler after I meet with the Northern Pacific representative this afternoon."

"I won't mind leavin' him in the cell for another month or so before you decide what to do about him, Drew."

Drew stood, said, "I understand why you wouldn't mind. But I don't want to wait another day before I ride out of town, and then turned and left the jail.

———

As the train carrying the survey crew and their equipment hurtled westward, Special Agent Warren Adams asked, "So, are you sure that the brakeman who survived that fall is the same Drew Campbell you knew as a kid, Mister MacLeish?"

Alistair nodded as he replied, "I'm sure. After I read John Knudsen's telegram, I went to personnel and checked his employment card. When I confirmed his identity, I was surprised he was just a brakeman because he was the smartest person I've ever met. And he was the kindest, too.

"He was my best friend at St. Thomas until I left the orphanage when I was adopted by my aunt and uncle. Now I'm really anxious to talk to him about his life after he left the orphanage, and why he took the most dangerous job in the country."

"I'm looking forward to talking to him, too. It sounds like we have a real mess on our hands courtesy of Mister Ira Butler."

"I hope we can manage to keep it from spreading. And I imagine that much of it will depend on what's happened since we received Knudsen's telegram."

"Butler doesn't know I'm coming to investigate his embezzling. So, do you think Butler would try to kill your friend because my boss wired that I was being sent to investigate Drew Campbell's death?"

"I never met Butler, so I don't know what he's capable of doing. But we'll find out in a couple of hours. And if he even tried to kill Drew, I'll see him hanged."

Warren was startled by Mister MacLeish's reply, but just nodded and then looked at the Yellowstone River through the car's dirty window. He hadn't met Ira Butler either, but if he was as crooked as he appeared to be, Warren wouldn't be surprised to learn that Mister MacLeish's childhood friend had mysteriously disappeared.

————

Drew had accepted John's invitation to share lunch with his family. Of course, more time was spent answering his wife and two sons' questions than eating. After thanking Susan Knudsen, Drew returned to the Northern Pacific offices with her husband.

After entering the windowless office, Drew asked, "Do you want me to come along when you greet Mister MacLeish and Special Agent Adams?"

John thought about it for a few seconds before replying, "I think it might be better if you waited in Butler's private office."

"Alright. But before their train arrives, I need to go to Arnold's and pick up a few things. If you're not here when I return, I'll just wait in the smaller office behind a closed door."

"Just don't take too long perusing the shelves, Drew."

Drew smiled, said, "I know what I need to buy, John," and then stood, hung his saddlebags over his shoulder and exited the office just two minutes after sitting down.

After walking through the store's front door, Drew headed straight to the personal hygiene aisle to buy a toothbrush and a tin of tooth powder. He wasn't about to visit Abe Sessions, the horse dentist. He took a tin of tooth powder from the shelf but as he reached for a boxed toothbrush, Drew wondered if Gabrielle would be offended if he bought one for her. He decided he could always claim that he'd bought them both for himself when he showed them to her. And he couldn't give one to her unless he had two more for her parents.

After taking the three additional toothbrushes and another tin of tooth powder, Drew stepped further down the aisle and selected a large hand mirror for Gabrielle. When he gave it to her, and she saw her reflection, she finally would realize just how beautiful she truly was.

While he had told John he wasn't going to waste any time perusing, Drew decided to quickly scan the rest of the stock to make sure he hadn't forgotten anything. But after three minutes and forty-one seconds of busy browsing, Drew hadn't increased the quantity of his selections.

After paying Ben Arnold two dollars and eleven cents, Drew left the store and headed back to the N.P. offices. When he turned onto the boardwalk, he saw John Knudsen leave the offices and head to the station.

Drew soon stepped into the outer office, walked past John's desk and after entering Butler's private office and closed the door. He set the sack and his saddlebags on the floor and then sat behind the desk. After pulling off his hat and setting it on the desktop, Drew leaned back and hoped he wasn't going to be riding back to the Remys with bad news.

While he waited for John and the two N.P. visitors, Drew unbuttoned his shirt and then removed and opened his money belt. He pulled out all of the bills and gold pieces and began counting. He was almost surprised when he finished. He still had seven hundred and sixty dollars, not including the bills and silver he had in his pockets.

Drew quickly calculated that if he failed to make a trade with the Northern Pacific, at least he'd be able to buy them the quarter section of land around their cabin. But just securing their home would be terribly disappointing to the Remys. *And how would Gabrielle feel about his failure?* Now he wished he hadn't filled them with so much hope.

Drew deeply inhaled and after sharply exhaling, returning his cache to the money belt. He then opened his ledger-bearing saddlebag and slid the waterproof pouch bank inside before stuffing the bag of purchases into the other saddlebag.

Now, all he could do was to wait for John Knudsen to return and was introduced to the two Northern Pacific men. Drew was sure he'd get an indication of what to expect when he was able to look into the eyes of Mister Alistair MacLeish.

―――――

Their train was already slowing when Warren asked, "Do you think Butler will be waiting for us at the station?"

Alistair replied, "Maybe. But after receiving your boss' telegram, he might have taken the first westbound train and is already on his way to Oregon."

"If he skedaddled, then we'll be met by John Knudsen. And maybe your friend will be on the platform, too."

Alistair nodded and would be happy just knowing Drew was still alive. And even though he hadn't seen Drew for more than ten years, Alistair believed he'd be able to pick him out of a crowd, even if he'd grown a healthy beard. But for no particular reason, Alistair was convinced that Drew was clean shaven.

He was still trying to imagine what Drew looked like when the locomotive's whistle announced the train's imminent arrival to the Glendive station.

―――――

John Knudsen watched the locomotive squeal and hiss past the platform and after the coal car rolled by, he turned his eyes onto the lone passenger car. He assumed the survey team would use the back exit, so he focused on the front door.

Less than a minute after the train stopped moving, A thin young man wearing a well-tailored dark suit left the car, and John assumed he was Mister MacLeish. He was followed by a shorter, older man who also wore a dark suit, but had the look of a lawman. John took a deep breath and stepped toward the special agent and the man who had the power to promote him to Butler's open position.

Alistair saw a man walking towards them but waited until Warren Adams had stepped onto the station's platform before turning to greet either Ira Butler or John Knudsen.

John stopped, smiled and as he offered his hand, he said, "Welcome to Glendive. I'm John Knudsen."

Alistair shook his hand and said, "I'm Alistair MacLeish, and this is Special Agent Warren Adams. Where is Mister Butler?"

"He's in jail, sir. A lot has happened since I sent the telegram, Mister MacLeish. And I'd rather explain everything in the office."

Alistair nodded and said, "Alright. But do you have any news about Mister Campbell?"

As they began walking, John smiled and replied, "Yes, sir. And it will be Mister Campbell who will tell you most of the story. He's waiting for us in what used to be Mister Butler's private office."

Alistair exclaimed, "*He's here?*"

They stepped off the platform before John answered, "Yes, sir. And he's the reason Mister Butler is in jail and not in his office."

Alistair was even more anxious to be reunited with his childhood friend but resisted the urge to jog to the office, and just matched John's steady pace.

———

The arriving train's whistle had penetrated the walls of Butler's private office. So, Drew knew it would be a matter of minutes before the door opened and he'd meet Mister MacLeish and Special Agent Adams. Since he'd accepted the possibility of failure, Drew had focused on the greater likelihood of a successful negotiation. And if he reached an agreement, the level of success could vary wildly.

As Drew listened for footsteps in the outer office, he began to create mental pictures of Alistair MacLeish and Warren Adams. He pictured the special agent as almost a taller but younger version of Sheriff Hobson. When his imagination created Mister MacLeish, Drew smiled when he envisioned a rotund, balding man with a full beard wearing a black suit with a gold watch chain across his maroon vest. And he'd be wearing a bowler hat and have a fat cigar in his mouth.

Drew was close to laughing when he heard the front door open, and then voices as John Knudsen escorted his visitors into the outer office. He calmed his surprising nervousness and waited for John to open the door.

But when the door did open, it wasn't John Knudsen who stepped through the doorway. Drew quickly stood and assumed the well-dressed young man was Mister MacLeish who looked nothing like his preconception. On the other hand, Alistair's expectation of Drew's appearance was almost perfect.

Alistair smiled, and as he offered his hand, he said, "It's good to see you again, Drew."

Drew was well beyond simple confusion as he stared at Alistair and tried to recall when they'd met. It surely wasn't at a social event in Brainerd or anywhere else. But as he shook hands with Mister MacLeish, Drew suddenly made the Alistair connection.

Alistair saw the expected confusion in Drew's eyes and about to tell Drew he was also Alistair Ferguson until he'd been adopted by his aunt and uncle when he saw Drew's puzzlement disappear.

Drew smiled and then asked, "Didn't I use to call you Fergie?"

Alistair laughed before replying, "Yes, you did. But I couldn't come up with a nickname for you, so I just called you what everyone else did. And I'm very happy to see you again."

"I'm glad to meet you again after all these years, too. Have a seat and tell me how you managed to become a well-heeled gentleman."

Alistair said, "I may be well-heeled, but I'm far from being a gentleman. But we need to talk about what happened here before we share personal information."

"Of course."

As Drew and Alistair sat down, John and Warren Adams entered the smaller office carrying chairs.

After the other two men were seated, Alistair said, "When we received John's telegram, it created quite a stir among the higher ups. It wasn't as bad as the fiasco that the land manager created in Miles City a couple of years ago, but the possibility of another scandal caused great concern.

"The head of security was going to dispatch Warren to investigate Butler, and my boss wanted to send a different staff member to handle the mess he'd created. But when I read your name in the message, I volunteered. We believed it was just a matter of embezzlement until we stepped off the train a few minutes ago and John told us that Butler was in jail. He also said that you were the reason for his incarceration. So, will you explain what happened after Ira Butler bribed you?"

Drew nodded and then said, "After Fast Jack Hickman intentionally caused me to fall off the boxcar roof, I plunged into Cabin Creek. Then…"

John knew most of the story, but as Drew spoke, Alistair was fascinated but shocked what he heard. Yet he was also impressed and proud of his friend's actions and decisions.

While Warren was equally stunned by Drew's revelations, he knew his assigned task just became more difficult. He'd expected to quietly bring Butler back to Brainerd. Bur now he needed Drew Campbell to drop any of the serious charges against Butler, so he could carry out the orders his chief had given him in a very private meeting.

As he'd anticipated, Drew was asked many questions during his lengthy monologue. But when he finished talking about his return to Glendive with Jimmy Lynch, Drew was interrupted by a question from an unexpected source.

He smiled and said, "My stomach just asked me when I was going to finish yapping. So, can we continue while we have lunch at Finney's Diner?"

Alistair grinned as he replied, "I'm pretty hungry myself. So, before my gut decides to revolt, let's move to a food-filled location."

They stood and after Drew pulled on his hat, he hung his saddlebags over his shoulder before they left the building.

As they walked to Finney's, Alistair said, "You look like a cowboy, Drew. Do you always wear a six-gun and carry your saddlebags?"

"I've worn my Colt since I was waylaid in Stillwater a year ago, but the saddlebags and my cowboy hat are new."

"And you're obviously handy with your pistol or those four thugs would have succeeded."

"And if Gabrielle hadn't been a good shot with her Winchester, I wouldn't even be here."

"Are you planning to marry her, Drew?"

"As soon as possible. But a lot will depend on how successful I am in my negotiations with the Northern Pacific on behalf of her family."

Alistair looked at Drew, smiled and then said, "As you'll be negotiating with me, I'm sure that they'll be very pleased having you represent them, Drew."

After Drew's surprising reunion with his childhood friend Alistair Ferguson, he'd failed to recognize him as Alistair MacLeish, the man representing the Northern Pacific.

So, he looked back at Alistair, grinned and said, "I forgot that you were a Northern Pacific big shot, Fergie."

"I'm far from being a big shot, Drew. I'm just a senior staff member in operations. And while I do have the authority to negotiate for the acquisition of the property claimed by the Remys, my offer will be reviewed by my boss. So, I'll need to be less generous than I'd like to be."

"I understand. But I believe I have some very powerful bargaining chips that will give you a lot more leeway with your boss."

Alistair was very curious what Drew might have which would allow him the leeway. But even if it wasn't as impressive as Drew seemed to believe, Alistair was willing to risk his position to help his friend.

———

As Drew continued telling his story while eating his lunch, Fast Jack was stepping down from his locomotive in Bismarck. After hopping to the ground, he pulled off his heavy gloves and headed to the station. After checking for track changes, he'd have lunch at Ophelia's.

But as he entered the operations office, Horace Bent looked at him from behind his desk and said, "Dan Jones will be taking over for ya, Jack."

Jack snapped, "*What do you mean, he's 'takin' over'?*"

"Just what it sounds like. He'll be driving your train for the rest of the run."

"And what am I supposed to do, sit there and watch?"

Horace shook his head as he replied, "Nope. You're never gonna set foot in a Northern Pacific locomotive again, Jack. And I reckon no other line is gonna let you drive any of theirs, either. You've been fired for killin' Drew Campbell."

Fast Jack exclaimed, "I didn't kill him! He just fell off 'cause it was rainin'!"

Horace shrugged and then said, "The bosses seem to think you made him fall off on purpose. So, what you tell 'em ain't worth a hill of beans."

Jack snarled, "They still owe me a month's pay."

Horace smiled as he said, "You can't board your train, but you can ride in a boxcar on the next one headin' back to Brainerd to collect what they owe ya."

Jack jammed the envelope into his overall's pocket before he stormed out of the station manager's office. He stomped across the platform and almost knocked over a small boy before entering Bismarck. He hoped to find that traitorous conductor Bill Jensen and teach him a lesson.

He hadn't spotted Jensen before he entered Ophelia's Restaurant and sat down at a table. He knew that his days as an engineer were over, but he had to return to Brainerd to collect his things. Then he'd find some way to get even with Jensen, and if he knew where Campbell's body was, he'd kill him again.

———

After leaving Finney's diner, Warren asked, "When are we going to talk to Butler?"

Drew replied, "Probably not until tomorrow."

Warren asked, "What charges did you file against him, Drew?"

"None. At least not yet. I asked Sheriff Hobson to hold him because I suspected the N.P. would want to avoid the scandal, especially after the one in Miles City a couple of years ago."

Alistair grinned as he said, "And I'm sure you withheld pressing charges because of your deep affection and loyalty for the Northern Pacific."

Drew chuckled before asking, "I may not have had altruistic reasons for not charging him, but was I right in believing that the bosses back in Brainerd want to keep this as quiet as possible?"

"That's why I'm here. So, is that your best bargaining chip?"

"No, sir. It's just one of many."

"You have even sharper swords to dangle over the railroad's iron heads?"

Drew nodded as he replied, "And the one that could be the biggest headache for the N.P. is also very difficult for me to believe that it even exists."

John glanced at Drew and couldn't recall anything that Drew had told him thus far that was hard to believe.

They entered the office and after John closed the door, Alistair said, "John, your first tasks as the new manager will be to have the window boarded up and then order a new sheet of glass."

John quickly asked, "I'm replacing Mister Butler?"

"Don't you believe you're qualified for the position?"

"I'm sure that I am. I was just a bit startled."

"Good. I'll notify the personnel department when I return."

As they returned to the inner office, Drew was smiling because of Alistair's surprising manner of notifying John of his promotion. Drew had been surprised by the adult Fergie's appearance, but his mischievous sense of humor hadn't changed.

After returning to their seats, Drew asked, "Did you and Warren want to pick up your travel bags and get rooms at the hotel before we start negotiating, Fergie?"

"Our bags are already in our rooms at The Yellowstone Hotel courtesy of Ed Osmos, the head of the survey team. So, tell me what you expect from the Northern Pacific."

"I told you the Remys were given their land the Crows, but I didn't mention the dimensions of the property. After Mister Remy pointed out the boundaries, I estimated it to be at least a dozen sections."

Alistair's eyebrows rose as he said, "That's more than eight thousand acres."

Drew nodded and then said, "We both know the size of the property is secondary because their ownership isn't recognized by our laws. But if the Remys decided to fight for their land, they could present a strong legal argument.

"More than twenty years ago, Mister Remy married a beautiful Crow maiden named Bilichilee. Her father, a powerful Crow chief, gave them the land as a wedding present. And this was long before the Crow agreed to move to the reservation. So, to resolve the issue would require the involvement of the Bureau of Indian Affairs and possibly other federal agencies."

Alistair smiled as he shook his head and said, "Which would take a lot of time."

Drew nodded as he said, "And bureaucrats love to waste time even more than politicians. So, I'm sure that the N.P. doesn't want to get dragged into court to argue the validity of their claim."

"But as much as I'd like to offer them an equal amount of land, I'm sure you understand that the deal would be rejected by my superiors."

"I wasn't going to ask for twelve sections, Fergie. I already picked out the five sections of Northern Pacific land grants I'd accept in trade."

"That's still a hard sell, Drew. So, what else can you give me to ensure their approval and keep me from being fired?"

"The obvious is that I won't press charge against Ira Butler. That alone should be enough to satisfy the big boys back in Brainerd. But I'll also forget about Fast Jack Hickman's attempt to kill me."

"Jack Hickman already has been fired. But you could still have him charged, so it's still a valid point."

"How could they fire him? He may push that locomotive, but it still shouldn't return to Brainerd for another couple of days."

"We brought a replacement engineer with us and left him at Bismarck."

Drew grinned as he said, "I'm sure Fast Jack accepted the news gracefully."

"I'm already convinced they'll agree that the five sections you chose is a fair bargain. But a few minutes ago, you said that you had a bargaining chip that was difficult to believe even existed. Yet none of your arguments seemed unusual. I assume you've saved the irrational one as the convincer."

"Not intentionally. But before I show it to you, I have one more request."

Alistair rolled his eyes before saying, "Go ahead."

"I want the N.P. construction crews to build two small houses and a barn on one of the five sections."

Alistair then surprised Drew when he said, "That's reasonable. The Remys will need to replace their home, and I imagine the second house is for you and Gabrielle."

Drew replied, "That's the idea," and then bend over, released the straps on his saddlebag and pulled out the ledger.

He slid it across the desktop and said, "I found this last night in the bottom drawer of Butler's rolltop desk. As soon as you read the first entry, you'll understand why I couldn't understand why it even existed."

Alistair glanced at Warren before he opened the ledger. As soon as he started reading, his eyes began widening. Just as Drew had when he discovered the ledger, Alistair couldn't believe any rational person would keep a written record of his crimes. But unlike Drew, Alistair read each entry before flipping the page. After reading the second page, he was no longer astonished by Ira Butler's misdeeds. But when he read Butler's final confessions, he was stunned.

Alistair closed the ledger, handed it to Warren and said, "After you read this, keep it with you until we return to Brainerd."

Warren nodded, and as he opened the green cover, Alistair looked at Drew and quietly said, "I've been ordered to keep this situation quiet, but the man deserves to be hanged, Drew."

"I know. But it's more important to me that the Remys are happy with the agreement."

Alistair looked at John and asked, "Can you get one of those small land grant maps and some sheets of blank paper, John?"

John nodded, said "Yes, sir," and then hurried to the outer office.

Drew may have placed Ira Butler's fate behind the Remys' happiness, but he was still concerned about what would become of the soulless bastard. If he wasn't going to be prosecuted for any of his crimes, the worst the Northern Pacific could do was to fire him, which already happened. And if he remained in Glendive, Ira Butler would become a constant danger.

He was searching for another way to punish Butler when Warren closed the ledger and said, "I've never seen anyone do anything this stupid. Tomorrow, when we talk to Butler, I want to hear why he incriminated himself like this."

Alistair replied, "I doubt if he'll tell us, Warren."

Drew was about to offer his opinion when John returned with the folded map and four sheets of blank paper.

After he set them on the desk, Alistair unfolded the map and asked, "Which five sections did you choose, Drew?"

Drew touched each of his selections before Alistair grinned and said, "That'll block access to two sections of the government's land, too. So, effectively they'll be getting seven sections. Where do you want the houses and barns located?"

Drew replied, "Section L162-8. About a hundred yards east of that creek."

Alistair nodded and then picked up a pencil and marked the locations before setting the pencil down and asking, "Can we switch places, so I can write the agreement in pen, Drew?"

Drew stood, said, "Yes, sir," and then he and Alistair traded chairs.

Alistair dipped a pen into the bottle of ink, but before he began writing, he said, "John, after I finish, can you make me two copies? I promise to keep it concise."

"Yes, sir."

As Alistair created the document which would give the Remys a new home, Drew wondered just how concise his friend would be. He was reasonably sure that Alistair wouldn't include any of the sordid reasons for the generous agreement. He assumed he'd wait until he returned to headquarters where he could explain to his boss why it was necessary.

Less than five minutes later, Alistair slid the completed agreement to Drew. As he'd suspected, it was a bareboned legal document that only included the trade of the Remys' land for the five sections of land grants. But Drew was pleased when he read that Alistair had included the two houses and a barn in the last paragraph.

He then looked up and asked, "Do Mister and Mrs. Remy have to sign it?"

"They do if they want to have their names put on the deed. But before you have them sign it, it has to be approved by my boss. The reply should also include instructions for Warren from the head of security about what to do with Ira Butler."

"Then after you receive the reply from your boss, we'll visit the jail and then I'll ride to the Remys. Can I have them sign all of the copies there and bring them back? Or do they have to sign them here?"

Alistair grinned as he replied, "You can just return with the signed agreements, and I'll take the risk that you won't forge their signatures, Mister Campbell."

"So, if everything works out, I should be back the day after tomorrow."

"Then I'd better send the telegram requesting their approval and what they want us to do with Ira Butler. And when I return from the Western Union office, you can tell me about your life after I left St. Thomas."

John smiled as he said, "And you can tell me about yours after you became Alistair MacLeish, Fergie."

Alistair laughed, stood and as he headed for the door, he snatched his hat from the coat rack as he passed.

John then picked up the agreement, said, "I'll start making those copies," and followed Alistair out the door.

Warren watched John leave before looking into Drew's eyes and saying, "When that reply arrives, I'm sure they won't want Butler charged. They'll just order me to escort him back to Brainerd on the next eastbound freight train."

Drew was surprised after hearing what Warren said, but he didn't argue the point. It wasn't because he disagreed with his opinion, either. When Warren said that he'd be escorting Butler on the next eastbound train, Drew felt the hairs on the back of his neck come to attention. The coldness in his eyes, combined with the chilling undertone in his voice suggested that Warren would ensure Butler never set foot in Minnesota. And if that was Warren's intention, Drew wasn't about to dissuade him.

So, Drew just asked, "How long have you been a special agent, Warren? I've met a lot of them, but I would remember if I'd even seen you."

Warren's fearsome personality disappeared before he replied, "I was hired in '79. But since '82, I've spent most of the time working undercover."

"Are you married?"

"Not yet. I spent too much time on the road to have a family. But next month, I'm going to be assigned to the director's staff, so I'll probably find a good woman and settle down."

Drew smiled as he said, "It was only after I dragged my carcass out of the Yellowstone River that I found a perfect woman."

Warren grinned and replied, "I hope I don't have to fall off a train to find mine, Drew. But just hearing how you talked about her, I'm sure you still felt lucky for dropping into Cabin Creek."

"It was a small price to pay."

Warren then radically changed the course of the conversation when he asked, "May I see your long-barreled Colt?"

Drew nodded, and then pulled back his coat, slid the pistol from his holster and handed it to Warren.

Warren slid his fingertips along the top of the extended barrel and then said, "I imagine this gives you a little more range but a good deal more accuracy."

Drew nodded as he replied, "I get good results at a hundred feet. But I'm not sure how much more power it has than a standard Colt."

———

Alistair slid the small black book back into his coat pocket and then stepped to the telegrapher and handed him his long, confusing message. While telegrams were supposed to be kept private, many organizations developed private codebooks to ensure the confidentiality of their sensitive communications. And this was the most sensitive telegram Alistair had ever sent.

So, the operator wasn't surprised when he read what Alistair had written. He simply counted the letters before saying, "It comes to a dollar and ten cents, sir."

Alistair placed a one dollar note on the counter before dropping a dime onto the George Washington's head. The telegrapher slid the money into his cash drawer and then turned around to face his key set. As he began tapping out the code, Alistair listened closely to ensure the dots and dashes were correct. When using a codebook, one wrong tap could radically change a sentence's meaning.

After the telegrapher received an acknowledgement code, he returned the message to Alistair, who thanked him before walking out the door and onto Main Street.

As he headed back to the Northern Pacific offices, Alistair was confident the agreement would be approved. But he would be surprised if they decided to have Butler charged. Yet unlike Warren Adams, Alistair believed that Ira Butler would return to Brainerd as a free, but unemployed man.

———

The sky was a deep red when John headed home while Drew, Alistair and Warren walked to Finney's for supper. When they entered the diner, Alistair introduced Drew to the head of the surveying team. Then Ed Osmos introduced the rest of his six-man team before Drew, Alistair and Warren walked to the only open table in the far corner.

After placing their orders with the harried waitress, Alistair asked, "Why on earth did you decide to be a brakeman, Drew?"

"I was working in the maintenance shop when I met a cute, blonde girl who seemed to like me…"

Drew only needed a few minutes to review his life's history after leaving St. Thomas because it was so unremarkable until he took his unexpected bath in Cabin Creek.

He finished just before their meals were set on the table, so as they dug in, Drew asked, "How did you become Alistair MacLeish, Fergie?"

"I was summoned to Mister Stewart's office one morning and there I met my mother's brother, Angus MacLeish and his wife Mary. They were happy that they found me and told me they were going to adopt me. I wanted to tell you about it, but they whisked me away."

"Why didn't you write to me after you arrived at your new home?"

"My new parents told me it would only make you sad because you weren't adopted."

"They were probably right. So, how did you land a spot on the head of operations staff at such a young age? I'm sure you're qualified, but skills and abilities aren't usually sufficient to rise to such a lofty position."

Alistair smiled and replied, "Uncle Angus is the vice president in charge of procurement."

Drew chuckled before asking, "Do you have a family of your own now?"

"I'm married to a wonderful woman. Her name is Alice, and we have a six-month-old baby boy we named Andrew James."

Drew didn't dare ask why they'd christened their son with that name, so he just said, "That's a good Scottish name, Alistair."

"I think so, too. Even my parents approved of our choice."

Drew looked at Warren and asked, "If the powers that be don't want me to have Butler charged, when will you escort him back to Brainerd?"

Warren had just stuffed a large chunk of meatloaf into his mouth, so he held up a finger as he rapidly masticated the mostly meat mouthful.

After swallowing, he answered, "As soon as the next eastbound train pulls into the station."

Drew nodded and asked, "Are you going to put him in restraints?"

"No, I'm not. If he wants to run off into the wilderness, I'm not going to chase after him."

Alistair suddenly realized what Drew had already suspected. And like his friend, he had no objections to whatever Warren planned to do with Ira Butler.

———

THE BRAKEMAN

After supper, Alistair and Warren entered The Yellowstone Hotel while Drew returned to what used to be Ira Butler's apartment.

As he lay in the enormous and exceedingly comfortable four-poster, Drew smiled and said, "If the agreement is approved, I'll ask for one more, small favor just for you, Brie."

Drew laughed but knew a lot depended on what was in the telegram from the head of operations. While Alistair seemed confident that the agreement would be approved, Drew hoped that he hadn't asked for too much. Of course, there was the unexpected advantage of having Alistair's adoptive father being a Northern Pacific vice president. Maybe he should be more optimistic, but the Remys future hinged on the approval. And so did his future with Gabrielle.

CHAPTER 8

The anxiously awaited reply was received by telegrapher Mitch Henderson while Drew was sharing breakfast at Finney's with Alistair and Warren.

After writing down the strange sequence of letters, Mitch folded the message, slid it into an envelope and then had Timmy Patterson take it to the Northern Pacific office.

John was rearranging his new private office when Timmy entered the outer office and loudly said, "I got a telegram for Mister MacLeish."

John rushed through the doorway and said, "I'll take it, Timmy."

Timmy handed him the envelope and hopefully waited for a nickel tip but would be satisfied with a penny.

John knew he was being overly generous when he laid a dime on the boy's palm, but he could afford it now that he was the manager.

Timmy gushed, "Thanks, Mister Knudsen!" then sprinted out the front door.

John was more reserved when he exited the office but was very curious about the envelope's contents.

———

Alistair and Warren were laughing as Drew described his waddling walk away from the canoe in his duck-like outfit when Drew saw John enter the diner.

He quickly said, "I think John has their reply, Fergie."

Alistair spotted John just before he arrived, handed him the Western Union envelope and then sat down and said, "This was just delivered."

Alistair quickly opened the envelope, removed the folded message and then pulled the codebook from his coat pocket.

Even though he knew the reply was in code, Drew was surprised by the brevity of the message when Alistair unfolded the sheet. There were only two lines of gibberish following the cleartext address.

Drew focused on Alistair's face to see his reaction as decoded the message. Alistair's brows didn't furrow as he deciphered the first line, but halfway through the second, Alistair barely nodded in acceptance. He then folded the paper and stuffed it and the envelope into his coat's pocket along with the codebook.

Alistair smiled at Drew as he said, "They approved the agreement. So, after you pick them up, you can take them to the Remys and give them the good news."

Alistair's smile disappeared before he said, "But they still don't want you to charge Ira Butler with any crimes, Drew. So, you'll need to go to the jail and let the sheriff know before you leave."

Drew nodded and replied, "And I'll tell him that Special Agent Adams will be taking him to Brainerd where he'll face charges of embezzlement. Then Warren can take custody of him when the next eastbound train arrives."

Warren said, "That'll work, Drew."

After leaving payment for their morning meals on the table, the four men left the diner and headed to the sheriff's office. As they stepped along the dry, pine boards, Drew was curious about Ira Butler's reaction would be to the news. John was hoping that his ex-boss briefly believed he'd be getting his job back before Drew told Sheriff Hobson that he'd be facing charges in Minnesota. He was the only one of the four who still expected Mister Ira Butler to disembark in Brainerd.

Drew was the first to step into the jail, and before Alistair crossed the threshold, Sheriff Hobson exclaimed, "*What took you so long, Drew?*"

Drew waited until the others were in the room before he replied, "I had to wait for Mister MacLeish's boss to approve the deal for Mister and Mrs. Remy, which he did in a telegram that arrived a few minutes ago."

"So, are you gonna charge him with conspiracy to commit murder and attempted murder when he tried to shoot ya?"

Drew looked past the sheriff and saw Ira Butler in his cell glaring at him as he answered, "No, I'm not going to press charges, Sheriff."

After he noticed Butler's smug look of satisfaction, Drew said, "But the Northern Pacific wants to charge him with embezzlement. So, let me introduce you to Special Agent Warren Adams who will be bringing him back to Minnesota for trial."

Sheriff Hobson was disappointed that Butler wouldn't receive the punishment he deserved. But he was pleased that the Remys would benefit from the agreement Drew had negotiated on their behalf.

He shook Warren's hand and asked, "Do you want me to keep him locked up 'til you take him in custody?"

"I'd appreciate it, Sheriff. I'll check with the dispatcher for the next eastbound train and then I'll return to let you know when I'll be picking him up."

"Do you wanna borrow some leg irons and manacles?"

"They won't be necessary, Sheriff."

Sheriff Hobson then had the same revelation that both Drew and Alistair had experienced earlier, and hoped he wasn't mistaken in his belief.

After Drew introduced him to Alistair, he said, "I've got to make a five-hour ride to the Remys, so I need to get going."

Sheriff Hobson snickered and then said, "I reckon it ain't gonna take you even four hours to get there, Drew."

Drew smiled, said, "Probably not," and then glanced at Butler before turning and heading to the door.

The others had to hurry to catch up but soon they were bunched together as they headed back to the windowless Northern Pacific offices.

After passing The Yellowstone Hotel, Drew said, "I need to tell the Tidwell brothers to get my horse ready. It won't take long."

John then said, "I know you're anxious to leave, Drew. So, I'll put all of the copies in an envelope and bring it and your saddlebags to you."

Drew didn't protest but just smiled, waved and then angled across the street to the Tidwell brothers' livery. Once he entered the large barn, he spotted Amos and Jake in his black gelding's stall. Amos was brushing his horse's coat while listening to his brother advocating his opinion that gelding a stallion was almost blasphemous.

Drew was grinning as he quietly approached the brothers, and then stopped and loudly said, "I know I sure wouldn't want to be stripped of my manhood."

Jake and Amos were startled by Drew's unnoticed arrival, but then laughed before Amos said, "I'm a lot older than you and I ain't about to lose any of my private parts, neither."

Jake then asked, "Are you leavin' town, Drew?"

"Yes, sir. But I'll be back tomorrow."

"Then we'll get your fine feller ready to go."

Amos and Jake then walked to their storage room, and Drew followed. Amos lifted his saddle from a shelf while Jake gathered the rest of his tack and Drew retrieved his Winchester.

As they prepared his gelding, Drew answered their questions about Butler's incarceration after the shooting in the N.P. office. The horse was only missing his saddlebags when John stepped into the livery with Drew's saddlebags draped over his shoulder and an envelope clutched in his left hand.

John handed the saddlebags to Amos and then gave the envelope to Drew who said, "Thanks, John."

"You're welcome. Alistair and Warren went to send telegrams to their bosses, but they should be here shortly to see you off."

Drew grinned, slid the thick envelope into his coat pocket and then said, "It's not as if I'm boarding a ship for Europe, John."

"You probably won't see Mister Adams again, so he just wants to thank you for stopping Butler. I reckon your boyhood friend just wants to make sure you don't fall off your horse as you seem to have a problem with your balance."

Drew chuckled before Amos handed him his reins and said, "See ya tomorrow, Drew."

Drew replied, "Thanks, Amos. And you too, Jake," and then led his black gelding out of the livery.

He and John had just stepped onto Main Street when they were greeted by Alistair and Warren.

Warren shook his hand and said, "I hope things all work out for you and Gabrielle, Drew. If you ever return to Brainerd, pay me a visit in the security offices."

"I'll do that. And while I'm not sure if I'll ever set foot in Minnesota again, you'll know where to find me if you pass this way again."

"Count on it. And thanks for conking Butler on his thick skull. But I'm even more grateful for the ledger that confirms all of Butler's shady actions. And while we're crossing the Dakota plains, I'll see if I can get him to explain why he kept the incredibly stupid record."

Drew nodded and then shook Alistair's hand and said, "I'll see you tomorrow with the signed agreements, Mister MacLeish."

Alistair was smiling as he watched Drew mount his horse and then wave before his friend rode north along Main Street. He hoped Drew would return with Gabrielle, so he could meet the extraordinary woman who'd taken possession of his heart so quickly.

———

As Gabrielle stared to the northeast hoping to see a distant rider, her mother smiled and said, "Even if Drew was successful with his bargaining, he won't return until much later, Gabby."

"I know, Maman. But I'm still worried about what that evil Ira Butler might do after Drew rode into town."

"I understand. But you have to trust that Drew will be ready for anything Butler might try. And as your father promised you, if he hasn't returned before sunset, we'll leave for Glendive early tomorrow morning."

Gabrielle sighed before she looked at her mother and said, "At least we'll be able to get there faster now that we can ride instead of taking the wagon."

"And we'll each have a Winchester, too."

Gabrielle grasped her hoe and as she began breaking up the clumps of dirt, she said, "If Butler had someone ambush Drew, I'll shoot the scheming bastard with my Winchester."

As Francine resumed her work, she hoped Drew was all right. She knew that if Gabrielle shot Butler, they wouldn't hesitate to hang her. Despite Butler's heinous crimes, they would take her to the gallows simply because she was a half-breed.

———

The ferryman was a bit disappointed when Drew had only given him a quarter for the fifteen-cent crossing. But Drew hadn't noticed before he led his gelding off the northern dock, mounted and then set him to a fast trot. While Sheriff Hobson had suggested he'd make the five-hour ride in only four hours, Drew was hoping to better that mark.

Yet even in his anxiety to see Gabrielle and her parents, Drew wasn't about to start woolgathering. He still paid close attention to his surroundings, but it wasn't to avoid being bushwhacked.

He'd been angling to his right until he estimated he was about a mile from the forests on his left before he returned to a northerly heading. He was searching for the creosote stakes left by the Northern Pacific's surveyors. If he spotted one, he'd be able follow the others, and when he reached the sixth marker, he'd be riding across Remy land.

He'd ridden for almost thirty minutes when he caught sight of one of the blackened, short poles sticking out of the ground. When he reached the marker, he turned and estimated the distance to the Yellowstone at three miles. So, this was probably the eastern corner of the third section of land grants, which was owned by the federal government.

Drew smiled before resuming his ride. He soon noticed the marker that had been pounded into the ground in the eastern corner of the fourth section, which was available for purchase from the Northern Pacific.

It was less than an hour later when he reached the edge of what would legally become the Remys' property after the deed was recorded. He slowed his horse as he closely studied their southernmost section. Drew imagined all of the game that must call the distant forests home and then admired the wide creek that crossed the middle of the land. Even though he'd examined it as he and Jimmy rode to Glendive, now that it belonged to Mister and Mrs. Remy, it seemed more beautiful.

Drew's admiration of the landscape continued to grow as he rode north. The two government sections which were only accessible by the Remys were just as impressive as the others. Even the two sections which he'd only requested to restrict access to the two government sections were better than he recalled.

Drew had been so occupied with evaluating the land that he was surprised when he realized he had long passed the last marker and was able to turn westward. He then looked at his shadow and realized it was already past noon, so he nudged his gelding into a faster pace.

———

Gabrielle lifted an overflowing spoonful of stew from her bowl, quickly cleared it of its contents, and as she chewed, stuck the spoon back into the bowl and held the next mouthful over the bowl in preparation for consumption.

Francine said, "You'll get a tummy ache if you don't slow down, Gabby."

Gabrielle wiped an escaping stream of gravy from the corner of her mouth before she swallowed and said, "I'm not a little girl anymore. So, I won't get a tummy ache, Maman."

As her daughter cleaned off the spoon, Francine replied, "I know you're not a girl anymore. But eating too fast won't make Drew return any sooner. Besides, what will Drew think if he sees you with gravy stains on the front of your dress?"

As Gabrielle checked the front of her dress for evidence of dripped gravy, Boney looked at his wife and asked, "Do you think Drew is on his way, Fran?"

Francine wasn't about to add to Gabrielle's worries, so she quickly answered, "I'm sure he is. So, we should see him well before sunset."

Gabrielle hadn't found any evidence of gravy on her dress, so she resumed eating as her father asked, "Do you think the railroad agreed to everything that he hoped to get for us?"

Francine doubted if it was possible, so she honestly replied, "I'll be happy if they offered us one section of land on the other side of the eastern mountains, Boney."

Boney nodded and then said, "We'd have to build another cabin, too, sweetheart."

"I know. But we could take everything from our cabin with us before the tracks reached our land."

Gabrielle then said, "I think Drew will get them to give us more than one section of land. I believe he'll get us at least three sections, and even have a new cabin built on one of them."

Francine smiled as said, "Maybe he'll have them build another one for your new home, too."

Gabrielle knew her mother had only suggested the possibility to make her happy, but the idea still made her smile before she replied, "We'd need our privacy, Maman."

As her parents laughed, Gabrielle resumed eating her stew, but at a slightly slower pace. But she was still anxious to leave the cabin and resume her observation of the eastern horizon.

———

Drew had just returned his canteen to his saddle when he spotted the Remys' cabin about four miles away. And for the first time in his life, Drew felt the warmth of homecoming.

He couldn't see anyone moving at this distance but still focused on the log building as his gelding carried him closer with each stride.

It was another ten minutes before he spotted one of the Remys standing alone near the cabin's northern wall. While it could be Mrs. Remy, Drew believed he was looking at Gabrielle, so he yanked off his hat and enthusiastically waved it high overhead.

Gabrielle had just spotted Drew when he suddenly appeared out of the shadows. So, as soon as she saw his excited, distant greeting, she almost left the ground as she waved just as wildly and shouted, "Drew's back!"

Her parents hurried out of the cabin and immediately saw Drew as he made his rapid approach. When they reached Gabrielle, Francine said, "He appears to be happy with the agreement."

Gabrielle didn't take her eyes from Drew as she said, "I don't care what the railroad gave us, Maman. Drew is all that matters to me."

Just a few minutes earlier, Drew was excited about telling Mister and Mrs. Remy about the agreement. But when he was close enough to see Gabrielle's face, there was no room in his mind for even a whispering thought of anything other than her. And as much as he wanted to scoop her in his arms and kiss her, Drew knew he had to exhibit restraint, especially with her parents standing beside her.

When he was less than a quarter of a mile from the cabin door, Drew reduced his horse's pace. But it was only ninety-three seconds later when he pulled up, quickly dismounted and dropped his reins.

Boney grabbed his hand and said, "We're glad to see you, Drew."

Drew grinned as he replied, "I've got great news, Mister Remy."

As soon as Mister Remy released Drew's hand, Mrs. Remy surprised him when she embraced him, kissed him on his cheek and said, "Welcome home, Drew."

"I'm glad to be home, Mrs. Remy."

Despite Francine's unexpected hug and buss, Drew was still unsure about how he should greet her daughter. But when Drew turned toward Gabrielle, his mild dilemma vanished when Gabrielle threw her arms around him and kissed him as if he was her beloved husband returning from a long war.

Drew wrapped his arms around her and lifted her two inches from the ground. Fourteen seconds later, their lips parted, and Drew let her feet return to the earth.

271

He then smiled and said, "I'm happy to see you too, Brie."

Gabrielle quietly replied, "You still have to wear your brakeman suit, Drew."

Drew laughed before he released Gabrielle, turned to her parents and said, "I have a lot to tell you, including the details of the agreement with the Northern Pacific. But I need to take care of my horse first."

Boney said, "We'll come along, so you can start telling us."

Drew nodded, took his reins in his right hand, and they began walking to the corral. Before Drew spoke a single word, Gabrielle grasped his left hand which delayed his narrative for another five seconds.

After he regained focus, Drew said, "When I rode into Glendive with Jimmy Lynch…"

———

Drew was still talking when they entered the cabin, but he hadn't even reached the second day of his stay in Glendive. Nor had he mentioned any of the details of the agreement.

After they sat at the table, Drew set his saddlebags on the floor and then continued his lengthy monologue. He was telling them about waiting in Butler's office to meet Special Agent Warren Adams and Mister MacLeish when Gabrielle left the table and returned with a glass of water.

As she set it on the table, Drew smiled and said, "Thank you, Miss Remy."

Gabrielle sat down and replied, "I hope you won't be addressing me as Miss Remy much longer, Mister Campbell."

"As you reminded me, ma'am, I still have to don my duck suit and waddle around the cabin."

As Gabrielle and her parents laughed, Drew quickly emptied the glass of the much-needed, cold liquid before saying, "When the office door opened, Mister MacLeish entered and said, 'It's nice to see you again, Drew'. I couldn't recall meeting him before, but after I looked into his eyes, I realized he was my best friend when I was in the orphanage."

Francine asked, "Didn't you remember his name?"

"He was adopted by his aunt and uncle, so he changed it from Ferguson to MacLeish."

Boney said, "That must have helped with the negotiations."

"It did. But the agreement still had to be approved by his boss at headquarters. So, I still had to put all of my chips on the table to ensure it was acceptable. The telegram approving the agreement arrived this morning, and John Knudsen, who will be the railroad's new manager, made three copies."

Drew reached into his coat pocket, pulled out the thick envelope and said, "I brought the original and the copies with me for you and Mrs. Remy to sign. I'll bring them back to Glendive tomorrow and after Alistair MacLeish signs them for the Northern Pacific, I'll have the land registered for you at the county land office."

When Drew slid the folded sheets from the envelope, he understood why it was so thick when he discovered that John had included the small, surveyed map that Alistair had marked.

He unfolded and spread the map across the tabletop before placing his index finger on Section L162-8 and saying, "This is where you'll have your new home."

He then touched the other four sections which would soon become their property and said, "These will be your land as well. Sections L162-9 and L162-7 will still be owned by the federal government, so technically homesteaders still could settle there. But to access the land, they'd have ask for your permission. So, effectively you own seven sections, not five."

Boney stared at the map and quietly said, "I know you told us what you wanted them to give us in exchange for our land, but I still didn't believe it was possible."

Gabrielle then touched the three small marks on L162-8 and asked, "What are these, Drew?"

Drew smiled as he replied, "The ones that are parallel to the creek are where the Northern Pacific's construction crews will build two houses. And the one in the middle is where they'll build the barn."

Francine exclaimed, *"They're going to build us a house?"*

Before Drew could reply, Gabrielle said, "No, Maman. They are building us two houses," and then looked at Drew and asked, "Is the second one for us, Drew?"

"Yes, it is, Brie."

Drew took a deep breath before saying, "On my way from Glendive, I found the pegs that marked the corners of your new property, and it's some of the prettiest land I've ever seen."

Boney was still staring at the map as he said, "You've done so much for us, Drew. We'll never be able to repay you."

"You already have, Mister Remy. You've given me what I never thought was possible. You've given me a family."

Then he looked at Gabrielle before saying, "And much, much more."

After a few silent but meaningful seconds passed, Drew unfolded the four agreements and gave one to each of the Remys before saying, "It's a very short document, but it'll make the land legally yours and for the Northern Pacific to build the houses and the barn."

Boney asked, "When will they start to build them, Drew?"

"The survey crew will probably show up in a couple of days to mark the path for the tracks. That will take them three or four days. Then the engineers and a large construction crew will arrive to design and build the bridge across the Yellowstone. That will probably take them a week or so. Then they'll start building the spur line up the valley. They're pretty good at laying track, so it should take them less than a week to reach the coal face.

"Then they'll have to bring in all the equipment and materials to build the miner village and the coal mine itself. Hopefully, they'll construct the houses and barn at the same time. So, I'd guess you'll be able to move to your new home in six weeks or so. But I'll talk to Alistair tomorrow to get a better estimate."

Gabrielle asked, "Are you sure they won't build the bridge where the ferry is now and run the tracks right past our new property?"

"I suppose it's possible, but there are a few reasons why it's not likely. The first is that by following the valley directly to the coal face, they'll get another forty sections of land from the government. It's also about ten miles shorter, so it'll save them material, time and money. The last reason is that the valley will require fewer trestles to cross the gullies and streams."

Gabrielle smiled as she asked, "You've really thought this out, haven't you?"

"I tried not to overlook anything."

Boney then said, "You told us that Butler is being taken to Minnesota to be charged with embezzlement. But do you think when he's released from prison that he might return to get revenge?"

Drew had a short mental debate about expressing his suspicion that Butler would never reach Brainerd, and decided to say, "I doubt if he'd pay the twenty-six dollars and fifteen cent fare after spending three years in prison. Especially as some of that money would profit the Northern Pacific."

"I guess you're right, but can you have them notify you when he gets out?"

Drew nodded and said, "I'll ask Alistair tomorrow."

Gabrielle quickly asked, "I'm coming with you, aren't I?"

Surprisingly, Drew hadn't anticipated her question, so he didn't have any prepared arguments. But he immediately realized that the situation was much different now than it was the last time he'd denied her request.

So, he smiled and replied, "Of course, you are. But only if your parents don't object. They might want to come along, too."

Francine spoke for her husband when she said, "We'd be delighted to join you and Gabby, Drew."

"Good. And I'll be proud to introduce my family to Alistair MacLeish, who was my boyhood friend Alistair Ferguson."

Drew then folded the four sheets and said, "You can sign these when we meet him," and then returned the unsigned agreements to the envelope leaving the map spread across the tabletop.

————

Ira Butler wasn't in the best of moods as he packed his new travel bag and asked, "How come we're taking a freight train instead of the scheduled passenger run? It's only an hour behind that freight."

Warren replied, "Because I don't want you mingling with paying passengers. Besides, it'll get back four hours earlier."

Ira had much more things he wanted to say to Adams, but he didn't want his traitorous secretary to overhear a single word. But once he and the special agent were alone, he'd speak his mind.

Ira knew why Campbell hadn't had him arrested or charged with murder. And when he stood before those pompous bastards at headquarters, he was confident he'd be able to make them forget about the embezzlement, too. Ira even believed he'd be able to extract a sizeable sum from them in exchange for his silence. It was just a question of the amount.

But even if they didn't pay him off, Adams had surprised him when he allowed him to empty his bank account. So, the Northern Pacific already had bankrolled him to the tune of twelve hundred and sixty-five dollars. Yet the money wasn't nearly enough to pay for the humiliation he'd suffered. As soon as he walked out of the Northern Pacific headquarters building, he start planning for his return to Glendive. And then he'd make Knudsen, Campbell and those savage squatters pay for ruining his life.

———

As Gabrielle and Francine prepared supper, Drew removed his boots and slipped his feet into his waders. After sliding the straps over his shoulders, drew tightened the belt around his waist and then picked up his slicker. Gabrielle was already grinning as she watched him lower it over his head and then begin tightening the three wide straps around his torso.

Drew smiled at Gabrielle as he plucked his fur-lined hat from the top of his saddlebags and slowly pulled it over his dark blonde hair.

Gabrielle started giggling when Drew tightened the chin strap and then bent over and arched his back which made his posterior protrude as if he had been born with a natural bustle.

Boney and Francine began to laugh when Drew started his exaggerated waddle and then added a rhythmic series of duck quacks as a final touch.

279

Drew made two silly circuits before he stopped, stood straight and after removing his hat, spread out his arms and executed a deep bow.

Gabrielle clapped and exclaimed, "Bravo!" before her parents joined her in a round of applause in appreciation of Drew's impressive performance.

Drew smiled, tossed his hat onto his saddlebags and then began the laborious process of removing his duck suit.

As he transformed from water fowl back into human form, Drew was happier than he could ever have imagined. He now had a family, and soon the wonderful young woman helping her mother cook upper would soon be his wife.

While he still wasn't sure how he'd earn enough money to support Gabrielle, he was optimistic that he'd soon find a way. Drew removed his waders and as he pulled his first boot, he saw nothing but happiness in his future. And most of it was because of the dark-haired young woman who'd stolen his heart even before he knew her name.

What Drew couldn't have known was that there were now two men who were determined to destroy his plans and end his life.

_____

One of those men was sitting in the caboose of a fast-moving freight train as it sped along the tracks heading east.

The train had already entered Dakota Territory and would soon cross the Little Missouri River.

Warren was sitting across from Ira when he pulled a cigar from his inner coat pocket and a match from his left coat pocket. He was well aware of his prisoner's long romance with cigars and when he bit off the end of the cigar, he noticed the almost lustful longing in Butler's eyes.

So, before striking the match, Warren asked, "You smoke cigars, don't you, Butler?"

"Yeah, but mine are in my humidor back in my apartment. I know you don't like me much, but I'd appreciate it if you'd let me have one of yours."

"I still don't like you. But I reckon it won't hurt to give you one, Butler."

Warren extracted another cigar and handed it to the long-time cigar smoker.

Before striking the match, Warren said, "After they're lit, we'll smoke them on the platform."

Ira nodded and anxiously waited for the secret agent to light the match, so he could take that first soothing puff.

After their cigars were glowing, Warren opened the caboose door and then followed Ira onto the back platform.

Butler was already satisfying his tobacco craving when Warren closed the door.

Ira then smiled and said, "You know they aren't going to charge me with embezzling or anything else, don't you?"

Warren blew out a cloud of smoke that quickly dissipated in the wind before asking, "Why do you think they won't, Butler?"

"They won't do anything about the embezzling for the same reason they didn't want Campbell to charge me for trying to have him and those squatters murdered."

Warren didn't give Butler the satisfaction of appearing to be angry or disappointed but was focusing on the landscape that was rapidly passing behind Ira.

Ira then snapped, *"Didn't you hear me, Adams? I'm* gonna walk out of there with a smile on my face and a lot more money in my pocket."

Warren calmly said, "You aren't going to get another dime from the Northern Pacific, Butler."

As Ira glared back at him, Warren tossed his cigar away, and then quickly pulled a derringer from his jacket pocket and cocked the hammer.

He then pointed it at Ira's face and exclaimed, "Give me your wallet, Butler! Now!"

Ira was shocked into immobility as he stared at the small pistol. *Adams was robbing him!*

After he recovered from the stunning development, Ira slowly slid his thick wallet from his inner coat pocket, handed it to Warren and then said, "You can't shoot me, Adams. The brakeman and the conductor will know you did it. And even if you kill both of them, you'll still hang."

Warren shoved the wallet into his left coat pocket before saying, "This money doesn't belong to you. But I'm not going to shoot you, Butler."

Ira was furious about the money but wasn't about to challenge Adams when he had that derringer pointed at his face. When he met with those lofty Northern Pacific executives, he'd use Adams' theft to increase his bribe demand.

Ira then asked, "If you aren't gonna shoot me, would you mind just letting me finish my cigar before we go back inside?"

Warren saw the first support beams of the Little Missouri bridge and loudly replied, "You're not going through that door, Butler. You're going for a swim."

Before Ira could understand what Adams meant, Warren rammed his left elbow into Butler's chest knocking him sprawling backwards to the edge of the platform.

Ira felt himself tipping over the edge and desperately tried to grab the railing when he felt Warren's boot strike his abdomen. As he fell, Ira screamed and began flailing his arms as if he'd learn to fly. He'd only fallen six and a half feet when his left foot struck one of the crossties. The hard contact made him tumble head over heels for the next sixty-eight feet before he hit the cold water with an awkward, but almost perfect belly flop.

Warren had followed Butler's fall until he created the enormous splash. He then released the derringer's hammer and returned it to his coat pocket before he opened the caboose door and stepped inside.

As he closed the door, Warren looked at the brakeman and the conductor and then said, "Mister Butler tried to escape by jumping off the platform, but he didn't notice we were crossing the Little Missouri. I don't think he survived the fall."

Both men nodded as Warren sat down, opened his satchel and removed the green book. He opened it to the first blank page and began writing his report which would be the last entry in Ira Butler's ledger. His written report wouldn't include the manner of Butler's 'accidental' death, nor the amount of money in Butler's wallet. But he would provide both details to the chief of security. No one else would ever know the method of Butler's execution. And even they wouldn't recognize the ironic aspect of Ira Butler's death.

———

After her father closed their bedroom's door, Gabrielle sat on her bed and watched as Drew created his double-bedroll mattress.

When he finished, Gabrielle was surprised when he sat next to her and then pulled his saddlebags close to his feet.

She smiled and asked, "Did my welcoming kiss make you believe you could share my bed, Drew?"

Drew grinned as he replied, "No, ma'am," and then opened one of his saddlebags and removed the hand mirror.

Before he gave it to her, he said, "When I told you how beautiful you are, you seemed to believe it was just my opinion. So, now you can see for yourself."

"I don't care what anyone else thinks about my appearance, Drew."

Drew just handed her the mirror and waited for her to see her reflected image.

Gabrielle kept her eyes on Drew's face for almost a half a minute before she slowly turned to look in the mirror. Even in the flickering light from the fire, for the first time in her life, Gabrielle saw an undistorted view of her face.

As Drew watched, she touched her right cheek and then slid her fingertips across her jawline before she set the small looking glass onto the bed.

Gabrielle then looked at him and softly asked, "Was it just my handsome face that attracted you, Drew?"

"I'm not going pretend that I wasn't overwhelmed by your appearance when I first saw you. But if you weren't such a wonderful person, I wouldn't want to marry you, Brie. Anne McDuff taught me a valuable lesson. It's what's inside that truly matters."

Gabrielle smiled and asked, "So, you'd want to marry me if I was a good-hearted woman who looked like a frog?"

Drew grinned as he replied, "Maybe if she was a handsome frog."

As Gabrielle lightly laughed, Drew said, "When I was in the store, I bought myself a toothbrush and a tin of toothpowder, and I though you and your parents might like one, too."

"I'm sure they'll be grateful. A toothbrush and powder are a lot better than a finger and salt."

Drew reached down, extracted three of the toothbrushes and one tin of powder and set them on the small table beside her bed.

Gabrielle smiled, and with her dark eyes just sixteen inches from his, softly said, "Thank you, Drew."

Her quiet expression of gratitude was hardly flirtatious, but Drew knew he was entering dangerous territory. So, he surprised her when he quickly said, "Goodnight, Brie," and then slid from her bed.

As he was slipping into his bedroll, Gabrielle looked down, and almost mournfully said, "Goodnight, Drew," and then laid her head on her pillow.

Drew hoped Gabrielle understood the reason for his hasty exit. He was reasonably sure she expected a goodnight kiss, but he suspected that even a quick smooch would demolish his already weakened emotional and physical dam. Just sitting close to Gabrielle in her nightdress had been bad enough.

So, as he stuffed himself into the bedroll, Drew knew he'd have a difficult time falling asleep. It was going to be a long night, and there would be many more before the houses and barns were finished.

———

It was early in the mid-morning when the Remys and Drew rode away from the cabin. Drew and Gabrielle were riding in the center with Boney on Drew's right and Francine on Gabrielle's left.

As they headed into the morning sun, Drew described how he and Alistair had become friends at St. Thomas which led to a long conversation about his life at the orphanage. Drew shifted the subject when he asked how Boney had met his wife.

The turn south toward Glendive created another change in topic when Boney asked, "When will we reach our new land, Drew?"

"We're following my tracks that I left behind yesterday, so we should spot the first marker in about ninety minutes or so."

Francine loudly said, "I want to see where they'll build the houses and barn."

Drew smiled as he said, "When you see it, I'm sure that you'll be pleased with the location, Mrs. Remy."

Boney then said, "I'm already pleased with what I see, Drew."

Drew nodded and then looked at Gabrielle wondering why she'd barely spoken since they left. He didn't believe she was worried about visiting Glendive but was hesitant to ask what was bothering her with her parents riding alongside.

So, he smiled and asked, "Do you think it's time we gave our horses names, Brie?"

Gabrielle nodded and then replied, "I suppose so. What will you call your gelding?"

"In honor of my impressive performance last night, I'll christen him Mallard."

Gabrielle's sullen mood evaporated before she smiled and said, "That's different. I haven't given much thought to a name for my lady yet. Any suggestions?"

Drew scratched his chin for a few seconds before replying, "I was going to recommend Hen, but how about Henna?"

Gabrielle laughed then said, "She wouldn't be happy with Hen, but I'm sure she'll be satisfied with Henna."

Drew was relieved that she was in a better mood and hoped that whatever was troubling her was only temporary. But if it wasn't, he'd ask her about it when they were alone.

———

John Knudsen was almost finished rearranging his new office when Alistair stepped through the doorway carrying a small, heavily bound package.

After sitting down before the desk, he said, "This was just delivered to me by the conductor of this morning's westbound train along with a note from Warren Adams."

John sat down and asked, "What's in it?"

"I don't know. Alistair wants me to give it to Drew when he arrives. He didn't say I couldn't open it, but judging by amount of cord he used, I suspect he wants Drew to be the one to find out what's inside."

"Did the conductor say how he got it?"

"He said the station manager in Bismarck gave it to him last night when they were taking on coal and water. The station manager also passed along Warren's very specific instructions. And he seemed to believe that there would be severe penalties if he didn't follow them."

"What do you think is inside, Alistair?"

"I have no idea. But we'll find out when Drew shows up in a couple of hours with the signed agreements."

John nodded and then said, "I was impressed by everything Drew's done since he walked through the door. He's an exceptional young man."

"Even when we were young boys, I knew he was special. That's why I was so surprised when I discovered he was working as a brakeman. He could probably do a better job as head of operations than my boss."

John grinned as he said, "He'll probably be a lot happier living in that new house with Gabrielle than he would sitting in a big office."

"I don't doubt it. He didn't have the same opportunity that I had been given when I was adopted, but I still wish he'd found a way to make better use of his incredible abilities."

"He's still young, so I reckon he'll find his calling before long."

Alistair knew if he asked, his adoptive father would be willing to find a well-paying position for Drew. But now he was equally sure that Drew would decline any offer he believed he hadn't earned.

———

Drew pointed to the first marker and said, "That's the northeast corner of your property, Mister Remy."

Francine exclaimed, "It's beautiful, Drew! We've passed by this ground many times before, but I never fully appreciated how lovely it is."

As they continued riding toward the next stake, Drew smiled knowing that their center section's landscape was even nicer. He noticed that Boney was examining their new property in detail, and when Drew looked to his left, he found Gabrielle and her mother studying the land as well. He was still smiling when he shifted his attention to the front to pick up the next marker.

After identifying the stake that marked the start of the government's section, Drew didn't point it out as it really didn't matter. For all practical purposes, it was still their land.

But six minutes after passing the stake, Drew loudly said, "We're just entered the middle section where they'll build the houses and the barn."

Boney excitedly said, "Let's head west to see where they'll be built!" and then angled his horse to the right.

The others immediately turned their animals in the same direction and when they were about two hundred yards from the wide stream, Boney slowed, turned to Drew and asked, "Is this the spot?"

"Those marks on the map were just a quick approximation, Mister Remy. You and Mrs. Remy can choose the exact location any time before the construction crews arrive."

Boney nodded and then turned his horse due south again before slowing his gelding to get a closer look at potential building sites.

As her parents searched for the best location, Gabrielle looked at Drew and asked, "What will the houses be like when they're finished?"

"I asked for small, two-bedroom houses with a separate kitchen, but didn't specify the size. But they'll be constructed of finished lumber instead of logs, so they'll be easier to maintain."

"But they won't keep out the cold as well, will they?"

"It depends on how they're constructed. Would you rather they built log cabins?"

"No, I was just curious."

Drew wished that he'd been more specific in his demands, but if the houses only had a single outer wall, he'd pay to have an inner wall added.

———

It was early afternoon when they reached the ferry, and after handing the grateful ferryman a silver dollar, Drew and the Remys led their horses onto the bouncing barge.

Drew assisted Josh as his boat rocked and rolled its way across the Yellowstone River. Two minutes later, the ferry was reached the southern bank, and the four human and four equine passengers slowly disembarked onto the unmoving dock.

After thanking Josh for a successful crossing, they mounted, and headed to Glendive.

Drew looked at Gabrielle and was relieved that she didn't seem nervous before saying, "Alistair will be waiting for us at the Northern Pacific offices. After the agreements are signed, we'll all go to Finney's for lunch. Okay?"

Boney nodded and replied, "Alright. Then after lunch, we'll go to the courthouse and get the deeds registered. Is that right?"

"Yes, sir."

They soon entered Glendive, and as they passed the jail, Gabrielle asked, "I'm happy about the new land, Drew, but I still wish they'd put Butler on trial. He deserved to be hanged."

Drew simply replied, "I agree with you, Brie."

But he didn't add his suspicion that Ira Butler would face a one-man jury named Warren Adams who would convict him for his crimes. He wasn't aware that Special Agent Warren Adams already had carried out Judge Adams' sentence.

They soon dismounted before the Northern Pacific offices, tied their horses' reins to the hitchrail and stepped onto the boardwalk. Drew opened the door and after Gabrielle and her parents stepped into the outer office, he followed and closed the door.

Alistair turned just as Drew entered John's office and was surprised when he saw Gabrielle cross the threshold behind him followed by Mister and Mrs. Remy.

He and John quickly rose before Drew smiled and said, "Fergie, I'd like to introduce you and John to Mister and Mrs. Remy, and especially to my fiancée, Gabrielle Remy."

Despite Drew describing Gabrielle as the most beautiful woman he'd ever met, Alistair was still stunned. And what was most astonishing was that she'd done nothing to enhance her appearance. She was wearing a threadbare, yellow dress and her long black hair was scattered across her shoulders and back after the long ride.

He was still staring at Gabrielle when Boney offered his hand and said, "It's nice to meet you, Mister MacLeish. Drew told us a lot about you, and he considers you the best friend he's ever had."

Alistair turned his attention to Boney, shook his hand and said, "I've never had a better friend either, Mister Remy. And I'm sure you're happy to have him join your family."

"We're more than happy, Mister MacLeish."

"Well, I'm pleased to meet you, Mister Remy."

Alistair then smiled at Francine and said, "And it's a pleasure to meet you as well, Mrs. Remy."

When he looked back to Gabrielle, he said, "I can see why Drew was so quickly smitten, Miss Remy. He's a very lucky man."

Gabrielle smiled as she replied, "He already was lucky when Anne McDuff decided to marry someone else."

Alistair laughed before saying, "Let's get the agreements signed before we get distracted."

As Drew took the envelope from his coat pocket and laid the agreements on the desktop, John and Drew moved more two straight-backed chairs closer to the desk. After Boney and Francine sat down, John dipped a pen into the bottle of ink and handed it to Alistair. He quickly autographed each of the

295

agreements before giving the pen back to John who dipped it into the ink bottle and handed it to Boney.

After Francine gave the pen back to John, Alistair said, "While the ink is drying, I have something to give you Drew. It's from Warren and was delivered this morning."

Drew's eyebrows rose as he watched Alistair pick up a small package that must have been bound with four feet of cord.

When he picked it up, Drew asked, "Do you know what it is, Fergie?"

"I don't have a clue. I'm pretty sure Warren wanted you to open it."

Drew nodded and as ten eyes stared at him, he slid his knife from its sheath and began slicing the cord. After the knotted cord fell to the desktop, Drew peeled away the thick butcher paper and found a folded sheet of paper and a man's black leather wallet.

Drew unfolded the sheet and read:

Drew:

Ira Butler tried to escape from the moving train. But he mistimed his jump and plummeted into the Little Missouri River where he met his death. Before he fell, I relieved him of his wallet which you are now holding in your hand.

296

I'll include my decision to send it to you when I report to my boss. After he reads all of the contents of his ledger that you gave to me, I'm sure that he'll agree that you earned whatever you find inside.

Thanks for your help,

Warren

Drew didn't open the wallet, but just handed the letter to Alistair and said, "Ira Butler didn't make it to Bismarck."

Alistair looked at Drew for a few seconds before he began reading Warren's letter. Twenty seconds later, he gave it to John Knudsen who immediately focused on the page.

Drew looked at Gabrielle and said, "Ira Butler is dead. He tried to escape, but the train was crossing the bridge across the Little Missouri River when he jumped."

Gabrielle wasn't in the least upset but still asked, "Didn't he see the river before he leapt?"

Drew shrugged and replied, "It was probably nighttime."

"Oh."

Drew already knew it was probably late afternoon when the train reached the bridge but didn't want to make them believe that Warren was a cold-blooded murderer.

Alistair didn't believe Butler had tried to escape or that he'd accidentally fallen either, but he'd earned his fate. But he did believe that Warren was acting on orders from the head of security after the head of operations had updated him on the situation. But even if Warren hadn't received any such order, Alistair didn't blame him for what he'd done. Ira Butler should have been hanged.

After John returned Warren's short letter to Drew, he asked, "Are you going to see how much money is in the wallet?"

The wallet's weight alone suggested that it held a substantial amount, even if they were mostly singles. But to satisfy everyone's curiosity, Drew nodded, flipped open the wallet and pulled out a thick wad of cash from each of its two pockets.

Boney whistled and said, "That's a lot of money, Drew."

Drew quickly thumbed through the U.S. currency and then returned them to the wallet before sliding it and the letter into his coat pocket and then quietly saying, "It's more than twelve hundred dollars."

Alistair noticed Drew's deep embarrassment and could almost feel Drew's sense of guilt, so he quickly said, "You earned every penny of that money, Drew. Warren wouldn't have sent it to you unless he believed it as well. So, just smile and decide what you'll do with it. Okay?"

Drew glanced at Gabrielle before he managed a weak smile and said, "I guess so," and then asked, "Do you want to have lunch before we go to the courthouse, Fergie?"

Alistair replied, "That's a good idea. I'll take one copy of the agreement with me, leave one here with John, and Mister and Mrs. Remy, you'll need the other two. One will stay with the land office and the other is your copy."

Alistair picked two copies from the desktop, handed them to Boney and then opened his valise and placed his copy inside. He then closed the case, stood and waited for Boney and Francine to stand before they walked out of the office leaving John sitting behind his desk.

As they walked to the diner, Drew looked at Gabrielle and when she turned her eyes to him, he silently indicated that he needed to talk to her in privacy.

Gabrielle nodded and assumed Drew was going to give her the money. Then he'd ask her to pass it on to her parents believing that they'd be reluctant to accept it from him.

After finding a table at the diner and placing their orders. Alistair said, "The team from Ainsworth in Washington already built a quarter-mile long siding and a turnaround. And today, the survey team is marking the location for the bridge. They'll return this afternoon and take the ferry tomorrow morning. They should finish in three days, but the engineers and construction crews will arrive tomorrow afternoon to start work on the bridge.

"Then after the bridge is finished, which should take less than a week, they'll begin laying track for the spur to the coal face. So, in less than three weeks, you should see the work crews preparing the ground for the rails."

Boney grinned and said, "That's almost exactly the same estimate Drew gave us."

Alistair smiled at Drew as he said, "I'm not surprised. For a brakeman, he knows more about railroading than most of the men who run the show."

Drew was close to blushing as he asked, "So, when will you be returning to the place with the men who run the show?"

"I'll be leaving on tomorrow's 8:40. I'd like to stay for a few more days, but I'm anxious to return to Alice and Andrew."

Francine asked, "After only knowing Drew as a boy, did you name your son after him?"

Alistair glanced at Drew before replying, "It's a good Scottish name."

Drew marginally changed the subject by saying, "I'm sure Alice is anxiously waiting for your return as well, Fergie."

Before Alistair could make Drew even more uncomfortable, their orders arrived.

As they began eating, Drew looked at Boney and said, "After we're finished, I'll take the horses to the Tidwell brothers and then meet you in the courthouse."

Gabrielle quickly said, "I'll come with you, Drew."

Drew smiled at Gabrielle before saying, "It sounds as if you don't trust me with Henna."

"I want to make sure she isn't put in the same stall as an enormous, lonely stallion."

As her parents and Alistair laughed, Drew winked at Gabrielle and wondered if she understood why he needed to talk to her privately. While he was planning to ask her to give her parents half of the money in Ira Butler's wallet; it was of much lesser importance than his primary reason for wanting to have a private conversation.

———

There were no protests when Drew said he would pay the three dollars and twenty-five cents for their meal. So, he left four dollars on the table before they left the diner.

After Alistair, Boney and Francine crossed the street to the courthouse, Gabrielle asked, "You're going to give me half of the money Mister Adams sent you so I can pass it on to my parents, aren't you?"

Drew grinned as he replied, "You're a very perceptive woman, Brie. Yes, I'd like to give you six hundred dollars, and you can explain to your parents that it's only fair. After all, Butler tried to kill them, too."

"I think you could convince them yourself, Drew. But I'll agree to act as your go-between."

Drew said, "Thank you, Brie," just before they reached the hitchrail and began untying the reins.

As they led the four horses to Tidwell Brothers Livery, Drew said, "But asking you to give the money to your parents wasn't the main reason I wanted to speak to you privately, Brie."

Gabrielle was surprised yet filled with hopeful anticipation as she could think of only one reason that could be more important than making her parents happy. And one that would make her even happier.

Drew took a deep breath before saying, "Last night, before I left your bed, I really wanted to kiss you. But I knew I couldn't."

Brie quietly said, "I was hoping you would and was disappointed when you didn't. You must have known I wouldn't be offended. So, why did you just say goodnight and leave?"

Drew stopped a block away from the livery and then replied, "Because I wasn't sure I'd be able to control myself if I kissed you. I was already, um, excited just by being close to you. And you were so…so, well, I just couldn't trust myself."

Gabrielle smiled as she asked, "Was it only because you were worried that my parents might hear us?"

Drew gaped at Gabrielle before answering, "I guess it was part of the reason. But mainly, I didn't want you to think that I was only satisfying my urges."

Gabrielle asked, "Don't you know that I have urges of my own that need satisfying, Drew?"

"I do. But I haven't even told you how much I love you, Brie. And I didn't want the first time you heard me say those words was when I was overcome with physical passion. It's important to me that you understand that I love you as a whole person and not just because you're so incredibly beautiful and desirable."

Even though she'd been hoping that Drew would admit his feelings for her, Gabrielle was still overwhelmed by how he'd expressed his love.

She touched his cheek and softly said, "And I've loved you from the first day, Drew."

Drew took her hand and said, "After I hid in my bedroll last night, I knew I'd have a hard time falling asleep. Then I realized it would be another month before our home was finished, which meant that I had another thirty difficult, frustrating nights ahead of me. But this morning, I realized that I didn't want to wait another month. I don't even want to wait another day."

After a short pause, Drew looked into Gabrielle's dark eyes and asked, "After we leave the land office, could we stop at the justice of the peace's office and have him marry us, Brie?"

Gabrielle had barely recovered from Drew's last emotional broadside, so it took her a few seconds before she was able to say, "I'll be the happiest woman on the face of the earth to have the justice of the peace marry us, Drew."

Then, in the middle of the afternoon while standing in the center of Main Street with four horses watching, Andrew Campbell wrapped the soon-to-be Gabrielle Campbell in his arms and kissed her.

A few pedestrians and two teamsters smiled at the sight, but Drew and Gabrielle weren't embarrassed. To them, the rest of the world no longer existed.

When their lips parted, Drew smiled and said, "We'd better take the horses to the livery."

Gabrielle nodded before she and Drew took the reins of the four patient horses.

Less than a minute later, they entered the large barn, and Drew spotted Amos entering a stall carrying an armful of hay.

He didn't see Jake, so he loudly said, "Amos, I have some horses that need boarding."

Amos dumped the hay and left the stall before he grinned and said, "We can use the business, Drew."

Then he smiled at Gabrielle and asked, "Do you like the pretty mare that Drew picked out for you, ma'am?"

Gabrielle replied, "I'm very happy with her."

Then Amos looked at the horses and asked, "Are my eyes lyin' to me, or did the other two used to belong to Bart Early and Arnie Williams?"

Drew nodded as he answered, "Your eyes didn't deceive you, Amos. And Cole Thompson's horse is in the Remys' corral with their mules."

"I'm sure they'll all be happier bein' with you instead of those lowlife snakes."

Drew said, "At least they won't have to worry about being hit by a stray bullet anymore," and then handed Amos his two reins and added, "We'll be back to collect all of the saddlebags in about an hour or so."

After Amos took Gabrielle's reins, he said, "I'll have 'em waitin' for ya."

Drew tipped his hat and said, "Thanks, Amos," before he and Gabrielle turned and left the livery.

As they started walking to the courthouse, Gabrielle said, "I can't wait to see my mother's reaction. May I tell my parents the wonderful news, Drew?"

"Of course, you may. And when you give them the money, you could say it's sort of a reverse dowry."

"A reverse dowry?"

"It'll be proof that I am more worthy than all of the other suitors who desperately wish to marry their incredible daughter."

Gabrielle was still laughing when they stepped onto the boardwalk and then a few seconds later, they entered the county courthouse. Neither of them had visited the large building before, but after reading the office directory on the wall, they headed to the stairs. The land office was room 207, and the justice of the peace was closer to the stairs in room 201.

As they passed room 201, Drew glanced through the open doorway and was pleased when he saw the justice of the peace at his desk.

When they entered room 207, Alistair smiled and said, "We're almost done here. Glad you could make it before we left."

Drew replied, "We chatted with Amos Tidwell for a little while."

As the clerk handed Boney his copy of the deed, Drew looked at Gabrielle and thought she was about to burst like an overfilled balloon as she anxiously waited to tell her parents.

So, he was surprised when her mother asked, "Are you as happy as I am, Gabby?" and Gabrielle only replied, "I'm happy too, Maman."

But as soon as they all left the land office, Gabrielle hurried a few steps ahead, and then turned to block their way and said, "Before we leave, Drew and I want you to come with us to room 201."

Francine glanced at her husband before asking, "Why do you need to go to room 201?"

Gabrielle broadly smiled as she replied, "It's the office of the justice of the peace where Drew and I will be married."

Gabrielle's expectation of her mother's astounded, yet joyful reaction was met, if not exceeded when Francine's eyebrows shot up and she exclaimed, *"You're going to be married?"*

Then her father added his own excited response when he quickly and loudly shouted, "I'm going to be a grandfather!"

Alistair just grinned, shook his friend's hand and said, "Congratulations, Drew."

"Thanks, Fergie. I'd be honored to have you as my witness."

"It will be my honor, Drew.

Drew nodded and then took Gabrielle's hand before they walked past rooms 205 and 203 and then entered the office of the justice of the peace.

J.P. Elliot Gladstone looked up from his desk as Drew said, "Miss Gabrielle Remy and I wish to be married."

Drew expected to be told the fee and then to be asked to fill out the necessary forms, but Mister Gladstone just continued to stare at him.

When the J.P. hadn't spoken for ten seconds, Drew said, "Miss Remy and I wish to be married, sir."

Elliot Gladstone leaned back in his chair, looked at Gabrielle and said, "I don't marry half-breeds."

Drew was ready to explode when Gabrielle laid her hand on his shoulder and whispered, "It's okay, Drew."

Drew was still furious but didn't want to make a scene, so he just glared at the man on the other side of the desk and growled, "You're a half-wit and shouldn't be sitting in this office."

Then just to irritate the ignorant official, Drew pulled Gabrielle into his arms and kissed her with as much passion as he had earlier. When their long kiss ended, he smiled at

Gabrielle, and then took her arm and followed her parents and Alistair out of the office.

As they descended the stairs, Gabrielle quietly said, "I don't think either of the ministers will marry us either, Drew."

Drew replied, "I wasn't going to ask them, sweetheart. As far as I'm concerned, we don't need the territory's approval. If we receive your parents blessing, then I'm sure God will give us His as well."

Gabrielle squeezed his arm and said, "I feel the same way, Drew."

After leaving the courthouse, Alistair said, "You should make a formal complaint to the mayor about him, Drew."

"It wouldn't matter how loudly I complained, Fergie. Nothing will make a man like that change."

Boney snapped, "I wanted to punch the smarmy idiot in the nose! It shouldn't matter what he thinks, he still should have done what the county is paying him to do."

Francine smiled and said, "You seem to forget that we were never officially married in accordance with the laws of the Territory of Montana, Bonaparte."

"I haven't forgotten. But I'm still angry about it, Francine."

"I don't mind, but let's get our room at the hotel."

C. J. PETIT

Drew then said, "Our saddlebags are waiting at the livery. We can pick them up on the way."

Boney nodded and as they headed to the livery, Drew decided that he and Gabrielle weren't going to ask for two rooms at The Yellowstone Hotel. And they weren't going to share one, either.

After picking up their saddlebags, they crossed the street and soon entered the hotel. Before they reached the desk clerk, Drew asked, "Mister and Mrs. Remy, may I speak to you?"

Alistair understood he wasn't to be privy to the conversation, so he said, "I need to start packing," and then waved before heading to his room.

Drew and Gabrielle then stepped to the sitting area where they set their saddlebags on the floor, and then sat down and waited for her parents to sit on the couch.

After Boney and Francine lowered their saddlebags to the floor and sat down, Drew said, "I was furious when the justice of the peace refused to marry us. And even if he was ordered to perform the ceremony, I wouldn't give him that honor. Gabrielle said that neither of the ministers would marry us, either. So, I'm asking for your blessing to marry Gabrielle in the eyes of God."

Boney smiled as he said, "As my beloved wife just reminded me, we were never considered to be married by the territory. And we believe God has already consecrated your marriage, so of course you have our blessing."

Drew looked at Gabrielle who, despite her plain dress and unkempt hair, looked more like a bride than any woman wearing a white silk, veiled gown standing at the altar of a cathedral could equal.

Drew then stood, stepped in front of Gabrielle and took her hands before he quietly said, "I, Andrew Douglas Campbell, promise to love, honor and cherish you until death we do part and then reunited in heaven."

Gabrielle hands were trembling as she softly said, "I, Gabrielle Marie Remy, promise to love, honor and cherish you until death we do part and then reunited in heaven."

Drew then leaned over and gently kissed her before whispering, "I love you, Mrs. Campbell."

Gabrielle felt tears slide across her cheeks as she barely whispered, "And I'll always love you, my husband."

Drew then gently lifted Gabrielle from her chair before looking at her parents who were now his father and mother and not in-laws.

Francine was dabbing at her eyes with a handkerchief and Boney was trying to prevent a single tear from leaking as he stood and shook Drew's hand. Then Francine gave him a big hug and kissed him on the cheek as Boney embraced his daughter. As Francine wrapped her arms around Gabrielle and kissed her, Drew picked his and Gabrielle's saddlebags and draped one set over each of his shoulders.

After Boney picked up his and Francine's saddlebags, he grinned and said, "I guess we'll only need two rooms now."

Drew shook his head as he replied, "No, sir. You'll only need one. I have other sleeping arrangements planned for me and Mrs. Campbell."

Gabrielle looked at her new husband and asked, "You do?"

Drew grinned as he answered, "Yes, ma'am," then looked at Boney and said, "After we know your room number, we'll leave to drop off our saddlebags and meet you for supper."

Boney nodded and then he and Francine walked to the desk clerk to get their room.

Drew looked at Gabrielle and said, "I think you'll be pleased with our accommodations."

Gabrielle replied, "I'm so excited that I won't care if it's a dark cave, Drew."

Boney turned and said, "Room 18."

Drew waved and then took Gabrielle's arm and walked out of the hotel.

As they walked south along the boardwalk, Gabrielle was curious where they'd be spending their wedding night. She continued scanning the buildings on both sides of the street until they neared the Northern Pacific offices. Then she remembered that Ira Butler had an apartment built behind his private office. And even though the despicable man had slept in the bed where she and Drew would consummate their marriage, Gabrielle couldn't care less. Drew was going to make love to her and nothing else mattered.

Drew hadn't had a chance to tell John Knudsen of his plans to use the apartment but didn't think he'd object. He had asked John if he was planning to move the furniture from the apartment to his house. After he received a negative reply, Drew asked him if he could buy the four-poster bed for their new house. Not surprisingly, John had refused to let him pay for it and promised to have it sent to the house when it was ready. So, as they entered the outer office, Drew was anxious to see Gabrielle's reaction when she first laid eyes on their enormous marital bed.

John was just leaving his new office, so when he saw the front door open and then Drew and Gabriel step inside, he smiled and said, "I was just about to head home. Did everything go smoothly at the land office?"

Drew set his hat on the desk as he replied, "Mister and Mrs. Remy are now the legal owners of five square miles of land."

"That's great news. While you were gone, Jimmy Lynch stopped by looking for you."

"Did he tell you what he wanted?"

"No, but he said it wasn't important. I told him what had happened to Butler, but I didn't mention the money or the agreement in case he decided to pay you a surprise visit."

Drew set the saddlebags down before saying, "I'm sure he wouldn't have bothered me if you had told him, John. But I have a favor to ask of you. Gabrielle and I wanted to get married, but the justice of the peace apparently only marries white couples. So, he refused to perform the ceremony."

John's brow furrowed as he said, "That's not up to him, Drew."

"I know. But we're not going to press the issue. After receiving Gabrielle's parents' blessing, we married ourselves. And rather than taking a room at the hotel, I'd like to spend the night with my bride in Butler's apartment. Is that alright with you?"

John smiled as he replied, "Of course, it is. And I promise not to disturb you in the morning."

"Thanks, John."

John shook his hand and said, "You're welcome, and congratulations to you and Mrs. Campbell."

Gabrielle was a bit surprised but very pleased when she heard John address her as Mrs. Campbell. So, as John started to walk to the coat rack, Gabrielle gave him a warm smile which made him miss a step.

John quickly donned his coat and hat, and then waved to the newlyweds before opening the door and leaving the office.

Drew picked up their saddlebags, hung them over his shoulders and then took Gabrielle's hand and stepped into the small office.

After Drew kicked the door closed, they walked to the apartment door. Gabrielle was looking at him with a gentle smile as Drew opened the door and escorted her inside. Gabrielle was surprised when she saw the nice furniture but didn't see a bed. But before she could ask Drew, he led her another door which she knew must open to the bedroom.

As soon as they crossed the threshold, Gabrielle gasped at the sight of the oversized four-poster and then quietly exclaimed, "I have never seen a bed even half that size before!"

Drew set their saddlebags down before replying, "I was a bit stunned when I saw it, too. It's also the most comfortable bed I've ever slept in, but that's not saying much."

Drew then pulled her into his arms and said, "And after our house is finished, the bed will be moved into our bedroom."

Gabrielle smiled as she said, "Then it had better be a big bedroom, Drew."

"If it's not, then we'll use the front room as our bedroom."

Gabrielle glanced at the bed before whispering, "Do we have to wait, Drew?"

Drew replied by walking to the small closet, opening the door, and then took off his coat and hung it on a hook before unbuckling his gunbelt and setting it on the closet floor. As Gabrielle unbuttoned her coat and set it on a chair, Drew took a spare blanket from the closet shelf then carried it to the bed. As he spread it across the covers, Gabrielle understood why he'd covered the beautiful, thick quilt with the replaceable blanket.

Drew then stepped in front of Gabrielle, gently took her chin in his hands and quietly said, "I love you, Brie," before gently caressing her lips with his.

———

Eighty-seven minutes later, as she sat beside her husband on the couch in the hotel lobby, Francine asked, "Have you seen the apartment, Alistair?"

"No, ma'am. Even John Knudsen hadn't seen it until Butler was gone. He was worried that Ira Butler might have set a booby trap. But when he finally got a look, he said he was stunned to see an enormous, four-poster bed he estimated must have taken almost a quarter of the floor space."

Boney grinned as he said, "I reckon that's why they're a little late."

Francine said, "If it's that large, I wonder where Butler found a mattress to fit it and linen to cover the mattress."

Alistair smiled and said, "I suspect that the bed, mattress and linen were probably purchased by the Northern Pacific and shipped in on one of their trains."

Francine was thinking about the difficulty in washing such enormous linen when Drew and Gabrielle entered the hotel. As soon as Francine saw her daughter's radiant face, she knew Gabrielle and Drew had consummated their marriage.

The Remys and Alistair were rising from their cushioned furniture when the couple arrived.

Drew assumed they all understood the reason for the delay, so he just smiled and said, "Let's go to Finney's and have our supper."

As they began walking to the door, Alistair asked, "Are you paying again, Drew?"

"It was my intention. Did you ask because you wanted to treat us to supper?"

Alistair grinned as he replied, "Nope. Now that I know you'll be paying, I'll order the most expensive item on the menu."

Everyone was laughing as they left The Yellowstone Hotel and headed to the diner.

———

Jimmy Lynch was already having his evening meal, but not at Finney's Diner. He was sitting on a tall stool in Happy Jack's Saloon munching on bar food while nursing his flat beer. His choice of dining locations wasn't out of necessity. It was for the same reason he'd gone to the Northern Pacific offices looking for Drew. He was lonely.

After Drew left his room, Jimmy spent a long time examining the years he'd wasted trying to emulate his father. During his self-evaluation, Jimmy realized that the few men he considered friends were just drinking partners and nothing more. If he had died with the others, none of them would give a hoot.

But Drew was different. Jimmy already considered him to be a true friend. Drew had not only treated him better than he deserved, but he'd also shown him the error of his ways. He'd even quickly forgiven him after he'd almost gotten Drew killed by telling Butler what had happened.

So, the only reason he'd visited the Northern Pacific offices was to talk to his friend. While he wasn't able to talk to Drew, he did spend a few minutes talking to John Knudsen. Jimmy had been startled when he learned that Butler had died while trying to escape. Then Mister Knudsen surprised him when he said that he had been given Butler's position. But he hadn't said where Drew was staying, so Jimmy has assumed he'd already left Glendive.

Jimmy grabbed one more pretzel before he stood and headed to the door. He snapped it in two and was chewing the salty snack when he stepped into the cool evening air and then limped back to Bascom's Boarding House. Maybe he'd make the long ride to the Remys' cabin tomorrow.

———

Alistair asked, "So, will you all be seeing me off in the morning?"

Drew grinned as he replied, "We only have a five-hour ride tomorrow as opposed to your three-day-long torturous train trip. So, I think we can delay our departure to wish you a pleasant journey."

"At least I'll be staying inside the passenger car as opposed to running across the roof."

"I finally learned my lesson, so I won't be doing that again."

Alistair then asked, "What will you do with your life now that you're no longer a brakeman? You'll need to find a job so you can provide for your bride, you know."

Drew smiled at Gabrielle before replying, "I'll figure something out. But I'll be pretty busy for a while."

"I'm sure you will. But at least you won't need to worry about income for a while, either."

"That's true. Ira Butler's bribe alone will be enough to keep food on the table for a couple of years. But I still need to work. I just hope to find something that I enjoy doing."

Gabrielle said, "You have the knowledge and the ability to do just about anything, Drew."

Drew returned her smile but didn't say what he wanted to do more than anything else, at least not until they returned to the apartment.

Instead, he placed a gold half-eagle on the table, and said, "We'll meet you in the lobby, and if we have time, we'll have breakfast before we escort Mister MacLeish to the station."

As everyone rose from their seats, Alistair said, "If John didn't have to go to work, I doubt if and your bride would leave the apartment before my train left Montana Territory altogether."

Drew didn't argue the point as they donned their coats, and the men pulled on their hats. Drew took Gabrielle's hand before they left the diner.

CHAPTER 9

John was grinning when he quietly entered the outer office in the morning. But before he removed his hat, he spotted a note sitting on his old desk. He didn't pick it up, but after reading it, he turned and hurried out the door to reach the station before the 8:40 train left.

———

Alistair set his travel bag and satchel on the platform, and then shook Drew's hand as he said, "You may not want to board another train for the rest of your life, Drew, but I expect to receive a steady stream of letters."

Drew smiled as he replied, "I promise to send at least two letters…every decade."

Alistair laughed before he looked at Gabrielle and said, "You're his boss now, Brie. So, you make sure he writes more frequently."

Gabrielle smiled as she replied, "I'll crack the whip to make sure that he does, Fergie."

John hopped onto the platform and spotted Alistair as he was shaking Boney's hand. He was gulping for air when he reached the small gathering, so he was grateful when Alistair took pity on him by speaking to Francine.

Drew smiled but granted him a few seconds before he said, "I see you got my note, John."

John nodded and replied, "I was surprised you and Gabrielle had already left the apartment."

Alistair shook John's hand and said, "I'm sure you'll do a good job as manager, John."

John replied, "A squirrel could do a better job than Butler, but at least my account books will be accurate."

The locomotive's bell began clanging, so Alistair picked up his heavy travel bag and satchel, and then said, "Good luck to each of you," before he turned and boarded the first passenger car.

Drew took a deep breath before he took Gabrielle's hand and said, "Let's go home."

As they walked off the platform, John asked, "Do you need to stop at the office, Drew?"

"No, sir. We dropped our saddlebags with the Tidwell brothers on our way to breakfast."

They were strolling down Main Street when Drew asked, "Now that you're the manager, will you do me a favor, John?"

"What can I do for you?"

"Not so much for me, but can you help Jimmy Lynch find a job? He needs work, even if it's only cleaning out the office or the train station. I'll even leave enough cash to pay his salary for six months."

John looked at Drew and he said, "I'll see what I can do. And you can hold onto your money until your next visit."

Drew smiled and said, "Thanks, John. You're a good man."

John felt like a good man as he waved and then turned into the N.P. offices.

A few seconds later, Boney asked, "Why are you helping him, Drew? He and the other three were coming to kill all of us."

"He wasn't like the others, Mister Remy. I believe he wants to change his ways and become a productive citizen instead of a drain on the community."

Boney chuckled and said, "It looks like you've already chosen your path in life, Drew. You sound as if you're well on your way to becoming a preacher."

Drew grinned as he replied, "Jimmy Lynch said I sounded like a preacher or a lawman. I told him I wasn't as forgiving as a preacher and didn't possess the skills or abilities of a lawman. But I'll find something that suits my fancy and pays me enough to support your daughter in elegant style."

———

After picking up their horses at Tidwell's and paying their exorbitant two-dollar fee, Drew exchanged another fifty cents for the ferry ride across the Yellowstone.

Soon after leaving the dock, Drew spotted wagon ruts stretching northward and said, "It looks like the survey team is following our trail."

Francine asked, "So, they'll reach our cabin before we do."

"Maybe. They're moving a lot slower than we are because of their wagon, so we should spot them pretty soon."

Gabrielle asked, "Do you think the ferry will shut down after they build the bridge for the spur line?"

"That's a good question. I guess it will depend on how much the ferry will be used after they build the spur. But it's the only source of income for Josh Brockman, so I imagine it'll keep running until it sinks and is taken away by the Yellowstone."

Gabrielle smiled and said, "And then, just like you, the ferryman will need to find a new line of work."

Drew grinned as he replied, "But he probably won't have a beautiful young wife to support."

Francine then said, "After we were married, Boney was able to support me without having to find a job, Drew. Nature put food on the table and provided the furs which gave us the money to buy whatever else we needed."

Drew then asked, "Did you build the cabin by yourself, Mister Remy?"

Boney answered, "I pretty much just supervised the Crows who did all the hard work. Since then, all I had to do was to chink the walls and fix the roof. Fran and Gabby helped a lot, too."

"Well, they did a great job building it, and you kept it in good shape. I know it must have taken a lot of hard work to make it look as if it was built a couple of years ago, not a couple of decades."

Francine looked at Drew, smiled and said, "We didn't mind the hard work, Drew. It was our home."

"Will you miss your cabin, Mrs. Remy?"

Francine sighed before replying, "I suppose I will. But change is inevitable. And if it wasn't for you, we would have lost the cabin and probably our lives."

Drew nodded as he recalled the many quirks of fate that led to this moment. *What were the chances that he'd fall into a deep creek when Fast Jack attempted to kill him? What if he wasn't wearing his duck suit which kept him alive long enough to latch onto the overturned canoe?* And then, after the Yellowstone stole the canoe, the mountains forced him to follow the valley where he met the Remys. And if just one of those coincidences hadn't happened, Butler's murderous plan would have succeeded.

Drew began to wonder if they were just a series of coincidences, or if it was the hand of God that sent him to protect the Remys. Then he looked at Gabrielle and was convinced that he'd been sent to save one of His angels.

Drew's brief pontification was interrupted when Boney loudly asked, "Before they start building our new house, will they ask us where to start, Drew?"

"Probably. But to be sure, we'll drive a stake at the center of the location for each house and the barn."

"Why only one? Wouldn't it be better if we marked all four corners with stakes?"

"In the agreement, the Northern Pacific is only obligated to build two houses and a barn. I guess I should have specified the size. So, if they only build two tiny shacks and an oversized lean-to for a barn, you can blame me. But I trust that Alistair will ensure nothing like that happens."

Then he grinned and added, "Besides, his adoptive father is the vice president for procurement."

Boney chuckled and then said, "That'll help."

———

About an hour later, when they spotted the survey team on the northern horizon, Francine smiled and said, "Now we can be sure they won't visit our cabin."

Drew smiled as he replied, "And I hope they don't think we're a gang of highwaymen and start shooting at us if we get too close."

Gabrielle patted her Winchester's stock as she said, "That would be a big mistake, Mister Campbell."

"I'd prefer not to get into another gunfight, Mrs. Campbell. Let's stay back about a mile or so."

Gabrielle winked at Drew and then smiled to let him know she wasn't serious.

———

Seven hundred and twelve miles away, Fast Jack Hickman entered the administrative offices in the headquarters building of the Northern Pacific Railroad. His foul mood hadn't diminished since he'd boarded the boxcar in Bismarck. And except for when he'd slept, it had intensified with each passing mile.

He stepped to the nearest clerk and slapped his dismissal papers on his desk.

Arnold Eckersley didn't even look at Fast Jack as he read the sheet and then said, "After I sign it, just take it to the finance department, and they'll give you your pay."

Fast Jack watched the clerk sign the sheet and wanted to give the smarmy fancy boy a hard smack in the face. But he had to behave himself until he had his pay in his pocket.

When Arnold held out the signed paperwork, Fast Jack snatched it from his hand, spun on his heels and then stomped out of the office and headed to the finance department.

What added to his fury was his frustration knowing he wasn't able to make anyone suffer for his humiliation. Bill Jensen, the bastard who had ratted him out, would be almost impossible to track down. And the brakeman who had caused all of his woes was already dead. At least Drew Campbell had allowed him to end his days as an engineer with an even dozen kills.

As he walked down the hallway, Fast Jack grinned and said, "I'd like to see any of you gunslingers beat that."

When he entered the finance department, Jack headed for the smallest clerk and after tossing his dismissal paper onto the desktop, he said, "You gotta pay me."

Jerry Hopper looked up, smiled and said, "So, you're Fast Jack Hickman."

Jack was surprised that the clerk knew him as Fast Jack because it wasn't written anywhere on the paper, so he quickly asked, "How'd you know they call me that, mister?"

"Word gets around. I heard all of those stories about how you tossed brakemen to their deaths, too. So, I find it ironic that you were fired for trying to kill a brakeman who then turned up alive and well."

Jack was stunned and stared at the clerk for a few seconds before he exclaimed, *"Are you tellin' me that Campbell ain't dead?"*

Jerry initialed the sheet and then replied, "That's what I heard."

"That ain't possible! I saw him fall into Cabin Creek."

Jerry shrugged and then handed him the sheet and said, "Take this to the cashier's cage."

Jack took the paper and slowly walked to the cashier wondering if it was possible that the brakeman was still alive. He gave the completed sheet to the cashier, who then counted out six ten-dollar bills and three five-dollar notes before he had Jack sign a receipt.

After he stuffed the currency into his coat pocket, Jack seemed to be in a trance as stepped towards the door. *Could Campbell have survived the long fall into the surging, icy-cold water?* It was after he left the headquarters building that Jack

329

C. J. PETIT

remembered Campbell wore that odd-looking outfit to protect him from wet, cold weather. That would increase his chances of survival, but Jack still found it difficult to believe it was enough to keep Campbell from drowning. But if he was alive, Jack would make sure the brakeman didn't stay that way much longer. But before he could take his revenge, he needed to confirm what the clerk had told him.

————

They'd been following the survey crew for more than three hours and when they spotted the cabin and then saw the wagon come to a stop. The two men in the driver's seat stepped down, and as the four riders were dismounting, one of them waved.

Drew laughed as he pulled off his hat, waved back and after tugging it back on, he said, "I guess they figured out we're not outlaws."

Boney said, "They're in the middle of the valley right across from the coal. So, I reckon they decided to have lunch before they started."

Francine then said, "We should let them know who we are, too."

Drew said, "That's a good idea. I don't think that they will cause any trouble, but I want to get a quick read on them to be sure."

Gabrielle looked at the six men and felt none of the anxiety she'd experienced when the exploration team had suddenly arrived more than a month ago. And it wasn't because of the Winchester strapped to her saddle. It was because she was riding beside her husband.

When they reached the wagon and pulled up, the man who had waved stepped away from the others, smiled and said, "I'm the leader of this gang of cutthroats. I'm Pete Murphy, the lead surveyor for the Northern Pacific."

Boney replied, "It's nice to meet you, Mister Murphy. I'm Bonaparte Remy, and this is my wife Francine, our daughter Gabrielle and her husband, Drew Campbell."

Pete stepped closer, shook Boney's hand and then looked at Drew and said, "The story of your survival is filling the gossip chain all along the N.P. route, Mister Campbell."

Drew leaned down, shook the surveyor's hand and said, "I imagine so. Mister MacLeish told me that you surveyed the ground for the bridge across the Yellowstone yesterday. Did you find an acceptable location?"

"Yup. And if the exploration team's report was accurate about the terrain, we should reach the river in two days."

Drew grinned as he said, "I did my own survey of sorts when I walked the entire valley, and I'm sure you'll be pleased with the level ground."

Pete nodded, said, "Well, I'd better grab some chow before we get to work," and then returned to the wagon.

The other members of the team were rummaging through one of the packs in the wagon as the Remys and Campbells rode by.

When they were out of hearing range, Boney asked, "What did you make of them, Drew?"

"Mister Murphy was friendly, and the rest of the team accepts him as their leader. So, I'm confident they'll behave themselves. Besides, they should be out of sight before sundown."

Gabrielle then said, "None of them were wearing pistols, and I only saw two Winchesters in the wagon bed. I thought they would have had more firearms for protection."

Drew hadn't recognized their shortage of firepower and was impressed that Gabrielle had noticed, so he said, "That is a bit odd. Even if they weren't worried about renegade Indians or a gang of outlaws, they'd need protection against packs of wolves or hungry grizzlies."

Boney then said, "Speaking of grizzlies, before you showed up, Drew, I spotted some tracks left by a real giant near the totem. Their Winchesters would only make him mad if they tried to shoot him, but it's more likely that they'll never even see him."

"If they're '76s like mine, it might take three shots, but they'd be able to put him down. And I imagine that even your Sharps would need two slugs to do the job."

"Judging by the size of those prints, it might need three. But I'm not about to hunt for that monster just to find out how many bullets it'll take."

Gabrielle was looking at their cabin as she said, "He may hide from the survey team, but I hope he doesn't get hungry enough to attack our mules, Papa."

"The gray wolf pack that marked the northern valley as their territory is a bigger threat to Jean and Jacques, Gabby."

"I know, Papa."

Drew had spent almost his entire life in towns or on the rails. So, as he'd listened to Boney and Gabrielle discuss the sharp-toothed predators, he finally had a glimpse into the day-to-day dangers faced by the Remys and other families who made their homes in the wilderness. Even the large Indian villages weren't safe from hungry animals who could sneak into their lodges at night.

———

They found the two mules and spare horse unharmed by bears or wolves when they dismounted outside the corral.

After stepping down, Francine looked at Boney and said, "Gabby and I will carry the saddlebags inside and prepare lunch while you and our son take care of the horses."

Boney kissed Francine before saying, "As you wish, my princess bride."

Francine laughed before she began untying the straps holding her saddlebags in place.

Drew smiled at his own princess bride before kissing her and saying, "I promise to be gentle with Henna, sweetheart."

Gabrielle rolled her eyes before she started to remove her own saddlebags. After Drew and Boney gave their saddlebags to their wives, mother and daughter soon disappeared around the corner of the cabin.

As the menfolk began stripping the four horses, Drew looked at their wagon and asked, "How many trips do you think it will take to move everything from the cabin to your new home, Mister Remy?"

"I reckon it'll take at least three if we bring the cookstove. And we'll have to take it apart first."

"I was just curious, Mister Remy."

Boney set his horse's saddle on the ground before saying, "Now that you're officially part of the family, you shouldn't address me as if I was just an acquaintance."

Drew knew the issue would come up sooner rather than later, so he quickly asked, "Would it be alright if I used the Scottish version of Papa and Maman?"

Boney grinned as he replied, "That will be fine with me, and I'm sure that Francine won't mind, either. So, how do Scottish children address their parents?"

"They call their mothers 'mom' and their fathers 'dad'."

"Then I'll be your dad and Francine will be your mom."

Drew smiled, said, "Thank you, Dad," and then lifted his saddle from Mallard's back.

———

After leaving Northern Pacific property, Fast Jack had gone to Parson's Place, which was the nearest drinking establishment, and a common gathering place for N.P. workers.

By the time he'd emptied his third mug of beer, he'd not only received confirmation that Drew Campbell was still alive, but he had also learned that the undead brakeman no longer worked for the railroad and was now living in Glendive.

After leaving the saloon, Fast Jack paid a visit to Sorensen & Sons Firearms where he spent twenty-four dollars of his pay for a new Winchester and a large, one-hundred-cartridge box of .44-40 ammunition.

Even though Jack's frustration had faded away, his anger hadn't lessened a tiny bit. Yet he wasn't about to sneak into a boxcar on the next westbound train. He'd need to empty his bank account and then pick up a few more necessities. He'd figure out how to rid the world of Drew Campbell while he was on his way to Glendive.

———

Francine smiled as she replied, "Of course, I don't mind. And at the risk of offending my husband's French forebears, I like it better than maman."

Gabrielle looked at Drew and said, "And maybe I'll become a mom in nine months."

Drew's face reddened which elicited mild laughter from Boney and Francine.

Gabrielle was surprised by his reaction, so she laid her hand on his and said, "I didn't mean to embarrass you, Drew."

Drew smiled before saying, "I guess it's because I grew up in a church-run orphanage."

Francine asked, "Didn't they teach you about men and women, Drew?"

"Only the rudimentary facts, and only on the day before we left. But I learned a lot more when I was working in the Northern Pacific maintenance shop."

Just as his face was returning to its normal hue, Gabrielle smiled and said, "And you learned more than enough to please me, Drew."

As Drew's face quickly darkened into a shade nearing maroon, Boney took pity on his fellow male and asked, "Do you want to go hunting in the morning, Drew?"

Drew greatly appreciated his new dad's empathetic rescue as he replied, "I'd like that. Are you going to bring the Sharps in case we run into the grizzly?"

"I'll carry my Winchester, but I'll hang the Sharps over my back."

Francine wanted to have a mother-daughter chat, so she said, "Gabby and I will catch up on the laundry and do some baking while you're gone."

Gabrielle understood her mother's real motive, but still said, "And now that we have a lot of soap, we can finally get all the dirt out of our clothes."

"Let's use some of the soap to wash the dishes while our husbands fetch a few buckets of water."

Boney grinned and said, "We've got our orders, Drew."

Drew stood and replied, "I'll get the buckets, Dad," and then walked to the sink and picked up both of their large oaken pails.

As they left the cabin, Drew said, "When I bought the supplies, I should have picked up a couple of tin pails."

"We've managed with these two for a long time, Drew. When we need a lot of water, we have Jean or Jacques carry our water bags."

"After we move, we can dig a well between the houses and build a windmill to pump water into a large cistern."

"That's a big job, Drew, but I think we can do it."

Drew nodded, and as they walked past the garden, he envisioned the two small houses, and a new, larger garden. A garden which was being irrigated with water drawn from under the ground by the windmill-driven pump.

It was a pleasant, peaceful image, but Drew knew he'd still need to find his calling, and not just to earn a living. He had enough money in his pocket to last for years, but without work, he'd still feel empty.

―――――

The sun had ended its shift and the moon had taken charge of the sky when Boney carried a lamp into their bedroom and closed the door.

After Gabrielle slid beneath the covers, she lifted the blankets in excited anticipation of her husband's arrival.

But Drew remained standing as he looked down and asked, "Are you sure the bed can support both of us, Brie?"

"It may not be nearly as comfortable as that four-poster, but it's probably stronger."

When Drew glanced at the closed bedroom door before joining his wife, Gabrielle suspected that it wasn't the bed's construction that was bothering Drew.

So, after he lay down beside her, Gabrielle quietly said, "You don't seem as enthusiastic as you were last night, Drew. Is it because my parents are on the other side of their bedroom door?"

"I admit that it does make me, um, uncomfortable. I suppose it's a bit prudish."

"It's understandable considering your upbringing, Drew. But I have a very different childhood experience. Ever since I was a little girl, I've been hearing my parents making love. So, to me, it's just part of living. And I'm sure they'll be surprised if they don't hear us behaving as newlyweds."

Drew pulled Gabrielle into his arms, kissed her and then whispered, "We don't have to shake the walls, but we can't disappoint mom and dad."

———

The survey team was nowhere in sight when Drew and Boney headed to the forests.

After they crossed Boney's split log bridge which spanned the two-foot-deep stream, Drew asked, "Do you do any fishing, Dad?"

"I've caught a few nice-sized trout using the net in the lean-to."

"The creek running behind our new houses is deeper and wider, so I imagine it's full of trout. So, maybe I'll finally wear my waders for their intended purpose."

Boney grinned as he said, "But don't wear your slicker because it'll scare off the fish."

Drew chuckled before saying, "I'll only wear it if I'm fishing in the rain."

A few minutes later, they entered the trees. And it wasn't long before they heard loud gobbling coming from the south. They cocked their Winchesters before they began slowly walking toward the flock of turkeys.

It wasn't long before they spotted the large birds in a small clearing and stopped moving. There were four large toms with their tail feathers fanned out as they tried to woo as many of the eight hens as possible. The ladies were playing hard to get as they studied the four boys as each of them tried to prove he was the best choice for a mate.

In addition to their visual performance, the males were also gobbling and spitting to impress the hens. And both sexes were so focused on mating that they were unaware of the two humans lurking just a hundred and twenty feet away.

Boney looked at Drew and signed that he would shoot the tom on the far left. Drew nodded and silently replied that he would aim at the smaller tom on the right.

After selecting their targets, Boney and Drew leveled their Winchesters. Drew waited until his father-in-law fired before squeezing his trigger. Before the two toms dropped to the ground, the other turkeys spread their wide wings, took to the air and soon disappeared into the forest.

Boney and Drew trotted into the clearing and when they reached the turkeys, Boney looked at both of them before he said, "Did you try to shoot him in the head, Drew?"

"If I hit him anywhere else with my '76, it would have ruined a lot of meat, Dad."

"That's some mighty fine shooting, Drew."

Drew nodded before picked up his tom by the neck and asked, "Do hens lay eggs during mating season?"

"I reckon some of them do. Do you want to look for their nests to get some eggs?"

"It's still pretty early, so we have the time. And if we returned with some eggs as well as the turkeys, I'm sure it would please our wives."

Boney grinned as he said, "Okay. Let's see if we can find some eggs. But it sounded like you already pleased Gabby last night, Drew. And more than once, I might add."

Drew didn't even blush as he replied, "And she pleased me even more, Dad," before they began their egg search.

———

Almost as soon as the cabin door had closed, Francine smiled at her daughter and said, "I shouldn't have been surprised by Drew's reaction when you revealed that you were no longer a virgin, Gabby. But apparently, his lack of experience with women didn't affect his lovemaking."

Gabrielle sighed before she replied, "Maman, even though you told me how wonderful it was, I still was overwhelmed when Drew and I first made love. From the very start, I knew he was, um, ready, but he didn't rush. And even when I thought I couldn't wait another second, he continued to excite me. I felt as if I was about to lose my mind by the time that we consummated our marriage."

Francine quietly asked, "And was it the same for you last night, sweetheart?"

Gabrielle closed her eyes as she answered, "It was better the second time, and the next one was even more exciting."

Francine giggled like a schoolgirl before she said, "Maybe you should have Drew give lessons to your father."

Gabrielle laughed but was already dreaming about tonight's couplings.

————

It was Sunday, so after he and his family returned from church, John Knudsen decided to pay Jimmy Lynch a visit. He wasn't about to offer him the open secretary position, even if he could read and write. But they'd start building the bridge on Tuesday, so he'd see if Jimmy would be willing to work as a common laborer. If Drew was right about his decision to turn over a new leaf, he should accept the offer. And after the spur was finished, John would find Lynch a better position.

When he was about to knock on the door of Jimmy's room in Bascom's Boarding House, John wasn't expecting an immediate response. Despite Drew's optimistic opinion, John still believed it was likely that Jimmy Lynch had staggered out of one of the town's three saloons in the wee hours of the morning.

So, after he just tapped a couple of times, John was surprised when he heard hurried footsteps on the other side of the door.

343

But when Jimmy swung it open, he seemed disappointed when he saw John and then said, "Oh. Come on in. What can I do for ya, Mister Knudsen?"

After John entered the room, he was surprised a second time when he noticed how tidy it was. Even Jimmy's boots were placed neatly at the foot of his bed.

He removed his hat and said, "Drew Campbell asked me to talk to you about a job."

"Is Drew already gone?"

"He married Gabrielle Remy on Friday and left yesterday."

"Oh. Why did he ask you to give me a job?"

"He believes you want to change your ways and that doing honest work will help."

Jimmy grinned as he said, "It sounds like somethin' he'd do. I told him he sounded like a preacher, but now he's actin' like one, too."

John smiled as he scanned the room and spotted three books laying on the side table. When he read the titles, he couldn't imagine that they belonged to Jimmy Lynch.

So, he asked, "Did you like Charles Dickens, Jimmy?"

"Not all of 'em. But I kinda feel like Oliver Twist, so I like that one."

John was puzzled and asked, "How is it that you read novels like *Oliver Twist* but talk like an illiterate cowhand?"

"I reckon I talk this way 'cause my father did. But he was drunk a lot, so I spent most of my nights readin'.'"

"You learned to read on your own?"

"I had two years of schoolin', but I liked to read 'cause I could make believe I was someplace else."

John smiled as he said, "Oliver Twist didn't have it any better, Jimmy."

Jimmy glanced at his small library before saying, "When I was a young'un, I read fairy tales and adventure stories. I only started to read Mister Dickens' books a couple of years ago."

John then asked, "Can you do arithmetic as well, Jimmy?"

"Yes, sir. But I ain't very good with fractions."

As John reevaluated his earlier decision, Jimmy asked, "So, what kinda job will I be doin'?"

"Would you like to be my secretary, Jimmy?"

Jimmy took a breath before replying, "Um, Mister Knudsen, I'd like to work with ya, but I don't think it's a good idea. I mean a lotta folks in town know I rode with Bart Early and the others to murder those folks and Drew. But I think it'd be okay if I helped build that new spur. And my leg's already doin' better, so I can do the work."

John knew Jimmy was right and was impressed with his honesty, so he replied, "The construction team will be arriving tomorrow afternoon. So, come to my office after lunch and when they get here, we'll talk to the foreman. Okay?"

Jimmy nodded, and then John surprised Jimmy when he offered his hand, and as they shook, he said, "I'll see you tomorrow afternoon, Jimmy."

Jimmy watched as John pulled on his hat and left the room. After he closed the door, he walked to his bed and sat down. He'd been hoping that Drew would stop by, but after the short conversation with Mister Knudsen, Jimmy was no longer disappointed because he felt as if he'd made another friend.

He briefly looked up at the ceiling before he lowered his eyes to the floor because it seemed more appropriate and then said, "I ain't like you at all anymore, Pa."

———

Drew and Boney returned to the cabin carrying the two turkeys but no turkey eggs. It took them more than an hour to pluck, clean and prepare the birds before presenting them to their wives.

Soon, Drew's tom was roasting in the small cookstove oven, while Drew removed the meat from the second and cut it into smaller pieces. When he finished, he dumped the chunks of turkey along with the chopped gizzards into a large pot of salted, boiling water. When he stepped away from the cookstove, Francine added a few cups of rice.

The cabin was filled with mouth-watering aromas and lively conversation as Francine and Gabrielle continued cooking while Drew and Boney cleaned their Winchesters.

After their repeaters were serviced, Boney and Drew left the cabin to replenish their diminishing wood pile and do all of the chores necessary to keep the horses and mules healthy and content.

As they cleaned the corral, Boney looked at their half-tilled garden and said, "I reckon there's no point in planting our garden now. And it'll be too late to prepare and seed a new one by the time we settle into our new place."

Drew asked, "You're really going to miss your cabin, aren't you, Dad?"

"I know we'll be better off living in a nice house on land we legally own, but this has been our home for more than twenty years."

"Maybe it would have been better if they'd never found that coal."

Boney smiled as he replied, "But if they didn't, you wouldn't have fallen into our trap."

Drew chuckled, said, "And then fallen in love with Gabrielle," before he resumed shoveling the unused fertilizer out of the corral.

————

Fast Jack was having lunch at Mama's Kitchen when he overheard four men talking about building the spur line near Glendive. After one of them mentioned that at least they'd be riding in a passenger car when their work train left tomorrow afternoon, Jack smiled.

He quickly cleared his plate, gulped down the last of his coffee and then dropped a quarter on the table and hurriedly left the diner. When he returned to his room, he'd finish packing, and after he cleaned out his bank account in the morning, he'd pick up some food for the trip and then sneak into one of the full boxcars.

The work train would only be stopping for water and coal, so he should reach Glendive in a couple of days. Then he'd just walk into the first saloon he saw, and as he enjoyed a beer, he'd find out where Campbell lived. And if the timing was right, he'd shoot the ex-brakeman and still be able to hop onto the work train after it unloaded its cargo and the workers.

As Fast Jack headed back to his room, he was confident that, in a few days, he'd finally get to add the surviving brakeman to his total. His only disappointment was knowing he'd never get the chance to make it a baker's dozen.

———

After enjoying a filling turkey and baked potato supper followed by a lengthy cleanup, the two couples adjourned to their respective beds.

It wasn't long before Drew heard familiar sounds coming from the bedroom, so as he embraced his wife, he said, "You'd be surprised to know that I'm not blushing, Mrs. Campbell."

Gabrielle slid her fingers down his torso as she replied, "Then let's join the symphony, Mister Campbell."

Drew didn't say another word as his baton was already poised and ready to conduct the overture.

———

The train carrying the engineers, the work crew and a long line of boxcars and flatbed cars loaded with equipment and material, rolled into Glendive at 2:37 in the afternoon.

The men who would build the bridge soon filed out of the passenger car to have a late lunch. The head engineer and the foreman turned into the Northern Pacific offices while the rest of the hungry men hurried to be the first to reach Finney's Diner.

John was sitting at his old desk in the outer office talking to Jimmy Lynch when Rupert Gorman and Abe Cloverfield stepped through the doorway.

John stood, and as he shook the lead engineer's hand, Rupert said, "I'm Rue Gorman, the head engineer. This is Abe Cloverfield, the foreman who's really running the show."

John said, "It's good to meet you both. I'm John Knudsen, and I just took over as manager."

Rupert replied, "We heard about Butler's shenanigans and his accidental fall into the Little Missouri River."

As John shook the foreman's hand, he said, "This is my friend, Jimmy Lynch. And I'd appreciate it if you'd add him to your work crew, Mister Cloverfield."

Abe nodded and after shaking Jimmy's hand, he said, "We could always use more help. We'll be moving the train in a couple of hours, so just show up at the station and look for me."

Jimmy smiled as he replied, "Okay, Mister Cloverfield."

Rupert said, "Abe and I are going to get some chow if there's any left. We'll be starting work in the morning and after we set up our camp, we shouldn't be a nuisance to the townsfolk. The next work train should be pulling out of Brainerd shortly, but it won't stop in Glendive until it heads back. So, you won't see any of the next batch of workers."

John said, "I'm sure there'll be a string of loaded freight cars passing through until the spur is completed and the mining operation is finished. Then we'll start seeing loaded coal cars rolling by."

Rupert grinned, said, "That's what we hope will happen," and then he and Abe left the office.

John sat down before Jimmy said, "Thank you for telling them I was your friend, Mister Knudsen. I guess I'd better go to my room and pack some spare clothes."

John smiled as he said, "You are my friend, Jimmy. Good luck on the job."

Jimmy grinned and then grabbed his hat, tugged it on and hurried out of the office. As he walked back to his room, Jimmy wondered what Mrs. Remy used on the poultice. In addition to reducing the pain and helping it heal faster, Mrs. Remy said it would almost melt the threads making them easy for him to remove. While he didn't consider Mrs. Remy to be a witch, he believed she'd concocted a medicine that was nothing less than magical.

———

Eighteen minutes later, Fast Jack Hickman felt the boxcar jolt before the work train began to move. He'd found a perfect hiding place in the back of the car under a small crane.

As the train picked up speed, Jack huffed and then grumbled, "I'd get this train to Glendive a lot faster than the gutless feller workin' this locomotive's throttle."

He then stretched out on his bedroll and started to work out the details of his plan. As he filled out his scheme, Jack failed to allow for the possibility that Campbell might live miles outside of Glendive. It was an oversight that would render his plan virtually useless.

———

By the time another turkey supper was being served in the Remys cabin, Jimmy Lynch was helping to build the bridge's work camp, and Fast Jack was fast asleep as the train carried him across the Dakota Plains.

CHAPTER 10

April 24, 1884

Earlier in the day, despite using Gabrielle as an intermediary, the Remys had firmly rejected Drew's offer of half of Ira Butler's money. So, as the family rode away from the cabin early in the afternoon, Drew was thinking about what he could buy for them that would cost six hundred dollars. The problem was that he couldn't think of anything that cost that much.

After tying a yellow rag to the top of the stake, he stood, smiled at Gabrielle and said, "That should be in the middle of our new home's front room, Brie."

Gabrielle took his hand, said, "I can almost see it, Drew," and then pointed and added, "And the barn will be over there, and my parents' house will be close, but not too close."

Boney said, "I won't even mind watching them build that miners' camp before they start working on our houses, Drew. Do you think that they'll they show us the plans before they start?"

"When the construction crew shows up, we have to tell the foreman about the stakes anyway, so I'm sure we'll get to see them."

Francine was looking at their stake as she said, "Maybe they'll start building the houses and barn while they're laying the track."

Drew said, "It's possible, Mom. After they build the bridge, they'll send the construction crews ahead of the ground preparation teams. The railroad's top priority is to build the miners' village and the mining operation, but they could send one of the teams to work on the houses and barn."

Boney said, "I reckon the railroad wants to start mining coal as quickly as possible, so it must take a lot of men to get it done."

Drew nodded as he replied, "When they build the spur to Butte City, they used more than a hundred and fifty men. And they didn't have to build a mining operation, either. I wouldn't be surprised if they have almost double that number of workers by the time the last work train arrives."

Gabrielle then asked, "Are the trains already on their way, Drew?"

"The first one that brought the engineers and the workers to build the bridge along with all of their equipment and material is probably already on its way back to Brainerd. Then there will be a steady stream of trains carrying more workers and a lot more material."

Boney asked, "Do they ship everything all the way from Minnesota?"

"Most of it. But some will come from Washington, and they'll buy a lot of the lumber locally."

Gabrielle looked southward and wondered if any of the trains had already arrived.

———

Fast Jack was holding his new Winchester with his travel bag at his feet, and his bedroll hung over his back as he watched the familiar landscape pass by. He knew the train would soon arrive in Glendive, and it wouldn't be long before he heard the whistle alerting the two brakemen that their services would soon be required. Then after they did their job and the train slowed to walking speed, he'd hop out of the boxcar.

But Jack had failed to notice that there weren't any brakemen to be warned because the train was equipped with the new Westinghouse air brake system. So, Jack was still waiting for the loud blast as he watched Glendive's easternmost buildings roll past and thought the engineer had made a mistake. Then he wondered if the man in the cab was trying to go for his brakeman kill record.

As he snickered at the idea, Jack watched the Glendive station pass by and suddenly realized that the train wasn't going to stop until it reached the construction camp. What made it worse was that he didn't even know how far west it was from Glendive. But he wasn't about jump from the boxcar at this speed and risk suffering the same fate as those eleven brakemen.

After the last building was out of sight, Jack began counting the clacks as the steel wheels crossed the seams between the rails. Each rail was eighty-eight feet, and if he reached sixty, it would be a mile and then he'd restart his count. He hoped to hear that long whistle sound before he reached fifty-nine.

Jack was getting seriously frustrated when he reached his ninth sixty-count and still hadn't heard that damned whistle. He was reconsidering his decision not to make the jump when he finally heard the long-awaited whistle. So, he stopped counting and waited for the three or four toots which let the brakemen know how many brake wheels they'd need to spin.

Jack still hadn't heard any short, sharp notes from the locomotive's steam whistle when he felt the train beginning to slow. It was only then that Jack realized there were no brakemen on the train.

But when he realized that he would be at least ten miles from Glendive, Jack modified his plan. He'd stay in the boxcar until sunset, and then he'd mix in with the workers when they lined up for chow. As he ate, he'd chat with some of them in the slim chance that he might learn something about Drew Campbell. Whether he got more information or not, he'd hop on the empty work train when it returned to Glendive for water and coal.

He didn't want to be spotted by anyone in the large work camp as he left the boxcar but didn't know which direction the spur was headed. So, he had to wait until he spotted the construction camp before making his stealthy exit.

It was another six minutes before the work train came to a stop, but when he looked south, Jack didn't see the work camp. So, he stepped across the boxcar floor, leaned out of the door facing the Yellowstone River and spotted the tents. It was larger than he'd anticipated, and he noticed that they'd already started building a bridge.

After spotting the camp, Jack picked up his travel bag and returned to his hiding spot. He set the bag and his Winchester on the floor, and then laid out his bedroll. After stretching out on his sleeping bag, Jack closed his eyes and listened to the chatting workers as they walked past the boxcar. It wasn't long before he unintentionally drifted asleep.

———

The workers had unloaded most of the freight before the workers were called to chow. Luckily for Jack, his boxcar bedroom was one of the two that would be emptied in the morning.

357

So, as Jack was snoozing, the workers were sitting around a large campfire filling their stomachs as they chit-chatted like a squad of gray-haired old biddies. Among the large group of laborers was the newly hired Jimmy Lynch.

Jimmy had been uneasy when he entered the passenger car with the other workers, but to his relief, he wasn't treated any differently. So, by the time he reached the bridge site, he was just another hard-working, underpaid laborer. They may have been a rough crowd, but they were mostly good men.

He still limped because of his injured calf, but Jimmy didn't let it slow him down as he helped build the camp and then started working on the bridge. For the first time in his life, Jimmy felt as if he was doing something worthwhile.

As Jimmy was the only worker who had lived in Glendive, he became a point of reference for the gossip about Ira Butler and the brakeman who had miraculously survived his accidental fall. Jimmy managed to avoid saying anything about the Remys and had limited Drew's involvement. But it wasn't until tonight that Fast Jack Hickman's name entered the conversation.

As he was talking to Walt Guzman and Sven Johannsen, Sven said, "Hap Tomlinson told me that he heard Campbell didn't fall by accident. Did Campbell talk to you about it, Jimmy?"

Jimmy nodded and replied, "He was gonna tell Sheriff Hobson that the engineer tried to kill him. Drew said he was called Fast Jack 'cause he had a reputation for killin' brakemen. Butler gave him six extra months' pay to keep quiet about it."

Walt asked, "Do you know if Fast Jack is still workin' for Northern Pacific?"

"John Knudsen told me that when he got back to Minnesota, they fired him."

Sven said, "I reckon Fast Jack would be mighty pissed off if heard that Drew Campbell was still alive. He might be so mad that he'd wanna get on the next train to Glendive and finish Campbell off."

Walt said, "Maybe he'll be on the next work train," and then asked, "Do you know what he looks like, Jimmy?"

"Nope. I never laid eyes on him. But if he's stupid enough to show up lookin' for Drew, he's only gonna find a .45 from Drew's Colt."

Sven and Walt snickered in stereo before the conversation veered to the number of painted ladies working in Glendive.

———

Fast Jack was still dozing when a wolf's howl leaked into the boxcar and then entered Jack's dreamworld. Soon, his

359

giant dream wolf was growling as it prepared to sink its six-inch-long, knifelike fangs into Jack's neck. But just as the canine monster leapt, the short nightmare abruptly ended. Jack's heart was pounding as he bolted upright, cracked his head on the small lift crane and collapsed back onto his bedroll.

———

Gabrielle rested her head on Drew's chest and said, "Our new home will be a ninety-minute ride to Glendive."

Drew asked, "Does it make you nervous being so close to town?"

"No, not at all. I know you're still anxious to find your calling, so I was wondering if you were thinking of finding work in town. You once said that you were going to see if a blacksmith would hire you."

Drew kissed her forehead before replying, "I was trained as a blacksmith and actually enjoyed the work, but it didn't stimulate my mind. Oddly enough, when I was working in the maintenance yard, I satisfied that need when I worked on the locomotives. I even spent hours studying the mechanics of the steam engine and how it transferred its power to the wheels."

Gabrielle smiled as she said, "Maybe you should use your money to build your own blacksmith shop next to the barn. But instead of forging horseshoes, you could make a small locomotive."

Drew grinned as he said, "And I could build a tiny railroad to give our children train rides, too."

Gabrielle laughed before she quietly said, "Maybe I'm already carrying your train's first passenger."

Drew gently stroked her flat tummy as he said, "Then I'd better start working on the locomotive as soon as we move into our new home."

As Gabrielle snuggled even closer, Drew couldn't imagine being any happier.

———

When Fast Jack recovered from his self-inflicted noggin-knocker, he took a few seconds to run his fingers over the large bump on the top of his forehead. He avoided creating another skull hill by sliding out from under the crane before slowly standing and then hurrying to the south facing door. After sliding it open a few feet, he unbuttoned his britches and emptied his overfull bladder onto the ground.

As he secured his fly, Jack looked at the moon and guessed it was almost midnight. He muttered a profanity before he closed the door and returned to his hiding place to have a cold supper.

Jack was chewing on his last slice of salted pork as he altered his already modified plan. He had to be out of the boxcar before it was unloaded, so after he finished eating, he'd exit using the southern door and wait for the loud bell used to wake up the workers. Then he'd join them for breakfast before sneaking back onto the work train for the short trip to Glendive.

It was just ten minutes later that Jack spread his bedroll on the dry ground near the coal car and sat down. His Winchester was laying on the bedroll and his hat was perched on his travel bag because it was too painful to wear.

Because he wasn't tired, Jack passed the time thinking about shooting Drew Campbell. He still had to find out where Campbell lived before setting up his ambush plans, so they were generic mental images. And while it may not be the same method that he'd used for disposing of the other eleven brakemen, Jack was sure that number twelve would be much more satisfying.

––––––

When the morning bell sounded across the camp, Jack popped to his feet and after gently pulling on his hat, he tied his bedroll, slung it over his back and then picked up his Winchester and travel bag.

He briefly thought about storing everything in one of the empty boxcars but didn't want to risk having them stolen. But instead of walking around the front of the locomotive, Jack headed to the back of the train. When he reached the last car, he set his travel bag on one of the siding's crossties, and then sat on the northern rail with his repeater on his lap.

As he focused on the camp, Jack spotted the cooking fire and then watched as the workers begin to slowly emerge from their tents. He'd wait until they lined up for chow before he joined them for breakfast.

But before the queue formed, Jack saw workers being gathered together and assumed they were being ordered to empty the train before having breakfast. He stood and was about to hide behind the train when he spotted two men walking away from the camp. Jack stared at the pair, and when they headed toward the locomotive, he realized who they were. The engineer and fireman were going to prepare the locomotive for the return trip.

Jack knew the train wouldn't move for another thirty minutes or so, but he wasn't about to risk having to make that long walk to Glendive. So, he walked behind the train and made his way to one of the empty boxcars.

———

After he climbed into the locomotive's cab behind Joe Chambers, fireman Spoon Fuller picked up his large bucket spade and said, "Maybe I'm seein' things, Joe. But I swear I just saw Fast Jack Hickman standin' near the caboose."

Joe snickered as he opened the firebox door and then replied, "If you saw somebody back there, he was most likely a hobo lookin' for a ride. Fast Jack is back in Brainerd and is probably sleepin' off a bender after gettin' laid off."

Spoon waited until Joe started the fire before throwing his heavy load of coal into the firebox. As he rammed his shovel into the diminished black pile, Spoon asked, "Do you believe those stories about Fast Jack?"

Joe was closing a valve as he answered, "Nah. The N.P. wouldn't have hired him if they were true. They only fired him 'cause Bill Jensen was makin' such a stink about Campbell."

"But Campbell didn't die, so they could have hired him back."

Joe grinned as he said, "That only made it worse 'cause Campbell coulda raised hell, too."

As Spoon shoveled and the fire grew hotter, Fast Jack Hickman snuck into an empty boxcar. He then settled into a dark corner and waited for the train to return to Glendive.

———

Jimmy was one of the men who was unloading the last of the equipment. As he and Walt Guzman lugged a crate to the bridge site, Jimmy passed within twenty feet of the man who was planning to kill his first real friend. But even if Fast Jack hadn't been hidden by the boxcar's wooden wall, neither Jimmy nor Walt would have recognized the engineer.

After setting the crate with the other building materials, Jimmy and Walt hurried to take their place in the growing chow line.

———

Joe Chambers tapped the large glass gauge and said, "We'll have enough pressure pretty soon, Spoon. Let's get some chow before we start rollin'."

Spoon tossed another load of coal into the firebox, closed the heavy door and then waited for Joe to leave the locomotive before he stepped to the ground. As they walked to the camp, Spoon glanced at the end of the train but didn't see anyone. Yet despite Joe's assertion, Spoon still believed he'd spotted Fast Jack Hickman. And even if he was wrong, he was still bothered because the man was holding a rifle.

As they soon would be taking the train back to Glendive, Joe and Spoon walked past the line of laborers and picked up their plates, cups and utensils. After they joined the early diners at one of the long tables. Joe and Spoon dug into their mystery stew.

Spoon swallowed his first bite of bread before saying, "I mighta been wrong that the feller I saw at the back of the train was Fast Jack, Joe. But I know for sure that he was carryin' a Winchester. And I ain't never seen a bum with a rifle."

Joe grinned as he replied, "Maybe the N.P. sent a special agent along to make sure we don't steal their train."

Spoon snapped, "It ain't funny, Joe! What if that feller is plannin' to shoot us? Maybe we oughta look in all the boxcars before we start rollin'.'"

Joe took a gulp of coffee before saying, "I don't wanna waste the time, Spoon. If you're so worried, you can check 'em out when we're takin' on water and coal in Glendive. And if you find your gun-totin' hobo, you can tell the sheriff."

Spoon mumbled, "I still think it was Fast Jack," then dumped a spoonful of stew into his mouth.

———

Jimmy and Sven were carrying a twelve-foot-long support beam to the bridge as the empty train left the turnaround and headed back to Glendive.

They set it in place, and as they were walking back to retrieve another piece of the growing structure, Sven said, "We weren't the only ones thinkin' about Fast Jack, Jimmy. When we were eatin', I heard the fireman talkin' about him to the engineer."

Jimmy quickly asked, "Did you hear what he said?"

"Sure. He was tellin' the engineer that he saw somebody with a Winchester at the back of the train he figgered was Fast Jack. But the engineer made fun of him and said the man with the rifle was a special agent."

THE BRAKEMAN

As Jimmy looked at the train rolling eastward on its way to Glendive, he recalled what Sven had said last night. He'd suggested that Fast Jack Hickman would be so angry that he'd take the next train to Glendive and shoot Drew.

The remote possibility that the fireman had actually seen the murderous engineer carrying a Winchester was still foremost on Jimmy's mind as he and Sven lugged a shorter beam to the base of the bridge.

By the time they dropped it where the construction foreman pointed, Jimmy decided to return to Glendive as soon as possible to warn Drew. He knew it was unlikely that the fireman had seen Fast Jack Hickman, but Jimmy wasn't about to risk his friend's life by hoping the man wasn't Hickman.

So, as they headed back to waiting pile of materials, Jimmy said, "I gotta get back to Glendive, Sven."

"Why? Is your leg botherin' ya?"

"Yeah, but that's not the reason. I need to talk to Mister Cloverfield."

Before Sven could ask another question, Jimmy spun around and headed to back to the bridge to see the foreman. He didn't want to quit, but he would if Mister Cloverfield refused to let him leave.

When he reached the chaotic but organized construction area, Jimmy approached Abe Cloverfield and waited.

As soon as the foreman finished giving instructions to two of the builders, Jimmy loudly said, "Mister Cloverfield, I gotta talk to you."

Abe asked, "What do you want?"

"I think Fast Jack Hickman is on the train that just headed back to Glendive, and he's gonna try to shoot Drew Campbell."

Abe stared at Jimmy as if he'd lost his marbles before he asked, "What made you come up with that crazy notion?"

Jimmy felt a bit silly after hearing the foreman's question, but still firmly answered, "The fireman thought he saw Fast Jack standing at the back of the train carrying a Winchester. I know he mighta been wrong, but I'd never be able to live with myself if Drew gets shot."

Abe was ready to point out the near impossibility of that happening but seeing the determination in Jimmy's eyes gave him pause. Then he recalled the deep respect John Knudsen held for Drew Campbell which added to his delayed decision.

So, after twenty-seven seconds had passed, Abe said, "You ain't gonna get paid, but we can afford to do without ya for a couple of days. And tell Charlie Baker I said it was okay for you to borrow one of his horses."

Jimmy quickly said, "Thanks, Mister Cloverfield," spun on his heels and then awkwardly trotted to the camp.

———

The empty work train slowly pulled into Glendive and Joe Chambers waited until the water tower's pipe was close to the water tank before using the air brakes to stop the train.

As he and Spoon oversaw the watering and loading of coal, Fast Jack slipped out of his boxcar hideout and was soon walking along Main Street in search of a diner.

———

Charlie Baker had lost a few horses to deserting workers, so he walked with Jimmy back to the bridge to confirm Abe Cloverfield's authorization. So, more than fifteen minutes had passed before Jimmy rode away from the camp. As he headed to Glendive, Jimmy hoped that the fireman had seen a special agent, a ghost, Bigfoot or anything else instead of Fast Jack Hickman.

But he didn't even know what Hickman looked like. So, when he reached Glendive, he'd tell John Knudsen what he heard and hope that he'd met the man. His next stop would be the Tidwell Livery where he'd ask if anyone bought a horse in the last hour. If they hadn't, he'd visit the smaller liveries. If none of them had sold a horse, he'd return to the camp as the Don Quixote of Montana Territory.

———

As Fast Jack ate at the counter in Finney's, he was talking to his neighboring diner. He'd claimed that he was a brakeman and had just learned that his pal Drew Campbell was still alive and living in Glendive.

He took a sip of coffee and then asked, "I gotta be leavin' soon, so do you know where I can find him?"

Henry Benedict, like most townsfolk, knew where Drew lived, but he was suspicious of the stranger. He said he was a brakeman, but he had a travel bag, a bedroll and a Winchester.

So, he nodded and replied, "He bought himself a small ranch about a mile east of town."

Jack grinned as he said, "Thanks, mister."

He dropped a quarter on the counter and then stood and slung his bedroll over his back. After picking up his travel bag and Winchester, Jack quickly left the diner.

Henry watched him leave and wondered if he should tell Sheriff Hobson about the stranger. But then he figured his misdirection was good enough and returned to his breakfast.

After leaving Finney's, Fast Jack saw the empty work train rolling away from the station. He wasn't concerned because he knew one would be arriving each day for the next few days. So, he set his bedroll and travel bag on the boardwalk and then sat on the bench in front of the barbershop.

Jack was very pleased when he'd learned that Campbell was living on a ranch about a mile out of town. He should be able to find it easily and then shoot him without the risk of being seen. Then he'd just walk back to Glendive, board the next work train and return to Minnesota. He'd decide on his final destination before it pulled into Brainerd.

If the ranch had been three or four miles away, Jack would have rented a horse. But he didn't want to waste any money, so he stood and after strapping his bedroll onto his back, he snatched his travel bag and crossed Main Street. Jack was in a good mood as he walked east along Second Street.

———

Just as Fast Jack was leaving Glendive to search for Drew's non-existent ranch, Jimmy Lynch turned his borrowed horse onto Main Street. As he rode to the Northern Pacific office, Jimmy searched for a lone stranger carrying a Winchester but didn't spot any potential Fast Jack Hickmans before he pulled up. After dismounting and tying off the horse, Jimmy hopped onto the boardwalk and then stepped into the N.P. office.

John was sitting behind the desk in his private office with the door open, so when Jimmy entered, John was surprised to see him.

He immediately stood, hurried into the outer office and asked, "What happened, Jimmy? Did you get fired?"

Jimmy shook his head and as he removed his hat, he replied, "No, sir. I'm okay. But I heard that the engineer who tried to kill Drew might be here to shoot him. So, Mister Cloverfield let me borrow a horse to find him."

John's face registered his shock as he exclaimed, "*Fast Jack Hickman is in town, and he wants to shoot Drew?*"

"I'm not really sure, Mister Knudsen. It's just that I didn't wanna take a chance that it's true. The fireman on the work train that just left saw a man he thought was Hickman, and he was carryin' a Winchester. If he was right, then he musta just got off the train. Do you know what Hickman looks like?"

"No. Does he have a horse?"

"No, sir. I was gonna go to the liveries and ask if a stranger bought a horse."

"That's a good idea. Let me know what you find out."

Jimmy nodded and then yanked his hat back on and hurried out of the office.

———

While Jimmy was beginning his livery inquiries, and Fast Jack was walking out of town, Drew and Gabrielle were riding south to visit the site of their new home. Boney and Francine had remained behind ostensibly to inventory what they'd be taking with them. But it was really because Francine thought the couple should have more private time together.

As they neared Section L162-10, Drew asked, "Do you want to ride into town and buy some new clothes, Brie?"

Gabrielle desperately needed more clothes but still replied, "I'll wait until after our house is finished, and we have to go Glendive and buy furnishings."

"That may not be for another month, sweetheart."

"I think my old dresses will survive that much longer, Mister Campbell."

Drew grinned as he said, "I wouldn't mind if the cloth disintegrated, as long as I could watch, Mrs. Campbell."

Gabrielle smiled as she shook her head and then replied, "I'm sure you wouldn't object. And besides dresses and furniture, there is something else that I'd like to buy for our new home."

"I'll gladly buy you anything except a new husband, ma'am. So, what is your wish?"

"Chickens."

Drew chuckled before saying, "I wasn't expecting such a fowl reply, Mrs. Campbell. But it's a good idea. Having a steady supply of eggs is a lot better than searching the forests for turkey nests."

"And we wouldn't need to go hunting when you crave poultry for supper."

Drew smiled and said, "With all of our turkey leftovers, 1890 may arrive before I have that craving again."

As Gabrielle laughed, she hoped nothing would ever interfere with their happiness.

———

Fast Jack had been walking east of town for more than thirty minutes yet still hadn't seen any signs of Campbell's ranch. When he looked behind him, he guessed he was around a mile and a half out of Glendive.

After Jack made one last scan of the eastern horizon, he turned around and as he started back, he grumbled, "I'll bet that lousy bastard is still laughin' for trickin' me."

Jack may have been furious for being misled, but Henry Benedict's decision to send the stranger on a wild goose chase had also saved Fast Jack from being spotted.

———

After Jake Tidwell and then Fred Brown had told him that no one had bought or rented a horse, Jimmy was thoroughly disappointed after Gus Twitchell told him that no one had rented one of his three horses that morning, either. So, as he walked away from The Happy Horse Livery, Jimmy thought the fireman had been mistaken after all. And even though he'd lost a day's pay because of the unnecessary search, Jimmy believed that the peace of mind was worth the three dollars.

As soon as he reentered the Northern Pacific office, John quickly asked, "What did you find out, Jimmy?"

Jimmy removed his hat and answered, "Nobody bought or rented a horse from any of the liveries. So, he ain't here, Mister Knudsen."

John leaned back and then said, "Maybe you should ask Sheriff Hobson if anyone reported having his horse stolen."

Jimmy hesitated before saying, "I suppose I could. But I ain't sure if the sheriff would wanna talk to me."

"I suppose you're right. But you could ride to the ferry and ask the ferryman if he carried anyone across the Yellowstone."

Jimmy nodded and quickly said, "That's a good idea. I'll go ask him," before he turned, tugged on his hat and walked out of the office.

After Jimmy closed the door, John sat behind the front desk and wondered if someone in the construction camp was just having a little fun at Jimmy's expense.

———

Fast Jack was around a half a mile east of Glendive when Jimmy rode out of town on his way to the ferry.

Shortly after he started back, Jack had figured out the real reason why Henry Benedict had lied to him. So, as he approached the town, Fast Jack decided to get a room at The Yellowstone Hotel. Then he'd leave everything behind and head to the nearest livery to ask where he might find Drew Campbell. And he'd come up with a better story for asking about him, too.

———

Jimmy pulled up next to the ferryman's shack, and as he dismounted, Josh Brockman stepped out of his crude office.

He quickly identified Jimmy but just said, "It'll cost ya twenty cents, mister."

Jimmy replied, "I only need to know if you took anybody across in the last couple of hours."

Josh's eyes narrowed before he asked, "What's it to ya? Are you up to no good?"

"No, sir. But I heard that some feller is lookin' to shoot Drew Campbell, and I wanted to make sure he didn't leave town."

Josh's eyelids opened wider, and his eyebrows rose as he asked, "Somebody else is plannin' on shootin' him? What for?"

"It's the engineer who made him fall off the train. So, did you take any strangers across?"

Josh shook his head as he answered, "Nope. I ain't had a single customer this mornin'. And I reckon after the railroad builds that bridge, I might never get another one."

Jimmy dug in his pocket and handed the ferryman a quarter before he said, "Thanks," and then mounted and headed back to Glendive.

Joshua watched him ride away for a few seconds before he slid the four-bit piece into his pocket and returned to his shack.

———

Fast Jack was taking his room key from the desk clerk as Jimmy rode past The Yellowstone Hotel and soon pulled up in front of the N.P. office.

After he stepped through the doorway and before he even closed the door, Jimmy said, "Nobody took the ferry all mornin'."

John wasn't surprised and replied, "It's too late for you to head back, so why don't you leave the horse at Tidwell's and then come back here. Okay?"

"I'll take him over to Fred Brown's barn 'cause that's where I board Homer. I'll be back in ten minutes or so."

Jimmy tipped his hat before he turned, opened the door and left the office less than a minute after he'd entered.

As he led the Northern Pacific's horse to Brown's Livery, Jack Hickman exited the hotel and headed to Tidwell Brothers Livery. As he approached the large barn, Jack was confident that his newly created reason for asking about Campbell wouldn't arouse any suspicions.

He soon passed through the wide doorway and spotted Amos Tidwell who was lugging a full pail of horse muck to deposit on the free manure pile outside.

Amos set the malodorous bucket down and then asked, "What can I do for ya, mister?"

Jack smiled as he replied, "I worked with Drew Campbell and felt really bad when I heard that he died. What made me feel downright guilty was that I hadn't paid him back the ten dollars I borrowed from him. So, you can imagine how happy I was when I heard he was still alive. I figgered as soon as he got back, I'd give him the ten dollars I owed him.

"Then I heard he quit and was livin' in Glendive. So, I hopped on the first train headin' this way to see him and pay my debt. But I don't know where he's livin' and figgered a liveryman is the best person to ask."

Jake hadn't been in the livery when Jimmy paid his visit and Amos had headed to Frank Green's smithy to pick up their horseshoe order.

So, with no reason to be suspicious of the stranger, Jake replied, "If you wanna talk to Drew, you got quite a ride ahead of ya, mister. You'd have to take the ferry across the Yellowstone and after about twenty miles, you'll reach the end of the mountains. Then you gotta ride west for another ten miles or so before you spot the cabin where he's stayin'."

Fast Jack was surprised but didn't want to ask another question as it might cause the liveryman to become suspicious.

So, he nodded and said, "I thought he lived in town, so I don't have a horse. Can I rent one for a couple of days?"

"Sure. Let's go out back and I'll fix ya up."

As he followed Jake outside, Jack believed Campbell's actual location was even better than the phony ranch. Now he wouldn't be rushed after bushwhacking the brakeman. And if he was lucky, he'd find some valuables when he searched Campbell's body and his cabin. Jack wasn't curious about why Drew lived so far from Glendive, and never considered that he might not be living alone.

————

As Jake was saddling a horse for Fast Jack, Jimmy returned to the Northern Pacific offices and took a seat on one of the two straight-backed chairs before the outer office desk.

John smiled and said, "I know you feel disappointed and maybe a bit foolish, but it's still good news that the fireman was wrong."

Jimmy replied, "I reckon so. And I ain't even gonna mind when all the other fellers make fun of me when I get back."

"Good. And now that you're staying in town for the night, you can use Mister Butler's apartment if you'd like."

"That's okay. I already paid the month's rent for my room at Bascom's, so I'll stay there."

John nodded and then asked, "How's your leg holding up?"

Jimmy raised his foot up and down a few times before answering, "It's doin' better than I coulda hoped for. I reckon it's because of the poultice Mrs. Remy put on under the bandage."

"I can see that. So, are you getting along with the other men in camp?"

"Yes, sir. Except for a few troublemakers, they're good guys. I feel like I belong there, so I really appreciate you askin' Mister Cloverfield to give me a job."

John grinned as he said, "You should thank Drew more than me, Jimmy."

"I know. But I don't reckon I'll ever be able to thank him enough. He shoulda shot me, but instead he had Mrs. Remy fix my leg and then treated me like a friend. He said he wasn't forgivin' enough to be a preacher, but I don't think there's a preacher in the whole country who's as forgivin' as Drew."

"I agree with you, Jimmy."

Then John looked at the wall clock and asked, "Do you want to come with me when I go home for lunch?"

Jimmy was startled by John's invitation but worried that his wife wouldn't feel comfortable having him in their house, so he replied, "That's okay, Mister Knudsen. I'm gonna head over to Bascom's and let Mrs. Bascom know I'll be stayin' there for the night."

John understood why Jimmy had declined his offer and replied, "Okay. But stop by after lunch and tell me how the bridge is going."

Jimmy smiled as he stood and said, "I'll see you later, Mister Knudsen," and then headed for the door once again.

———

Fast Jack had ridden the rented horse back to the hotel to retrieve his travel bag, bedroll and especially his Winchester. He had just entered his room when Jimmy stepped onto the boardwalk. And the ballet of coincidences which prevented Jimmy from spotting Fast Jack continued when the ex-engineer mounted his rented gelding after Jimmy turned onto Fifth Street on his way to Bascom's.

But as Fast Jack headed to the ferry, Amos returned to the livery carrying the burlap bag of horseshoes. He set the heavy load on the dirt floor and then said, "I reckon this oughta keep us goin' for a couple of weeks."

Jake said, "I reckon you're expectin' me to put 'em on the rack."

"I lugged 'em, so it's only fair you store 'em."

Jake grabbed the sack, grunted and as he carried them to the horseshoe rack, he said, "Some friend of Drew's showed up and rented the sorrel. He's gonna ride out there and give Drew the ten dollars he owes him."

Amos sharply said, "I don't think he's Drew's friend, Jake. Jimmy Lynch stopped by a little while ago and asked me if anybody bought or rented a horse. He told me that the engineer who tried to kill Drew might go lookin' for him to finish the job."

Jake dropped the bag of horseshoes and exclaimed, "I feel like a damned fool! *What should we do, Amos?*"

"If we tell the sheriff, he's probably gonna think we're loco. I don't know where Lynch is, but I think it's best if we headed over to the Northern Pacific office and told Mister Knudsen."

Jake nodded before the brothers hurried out of the barn.

———

Josh wasn't about to argue with a man carrying a Winchester, so he accepted Fast Jack's a quarter and then led him and the sorrel onto his ferry.

As he pulled the barge across the Yellowstone, Josh looked south towards Glendive hoping to see the sheriff or Jimmy Lynch leaving town. But the road was still clear when his boat bumped against the northern dock.

After his passenger mounted and rode away, Josh expedited his return crossing hoping someone would catch the bastard before he reached his biggest tipper.

———

Just forty-six seconds after Jake and Amos walked into the outer office, John Knudsen raced out the door, leaving the task of closing it to one of the Tidwell brothers.

He had just turned down Fifth Street when he spotted Jimmy leaving Bascom's and waved frantically to give him advance notice of what he was about to tell him.

Before he saw John's excited wave, Jimmy had already realized what had inspired Mister Knudsen's rushing approach.

So, as soon as John was close, Jimmy asked, "Did you see Hickman, Mister Knudsen?"

John huffed, "No, but someone just rented a horse from the Tidwell's."

Jimmy quickly replied, "I'll get my horse and ride to the ferry. If it's Hickman, I oughta catch up to him before he's halfway to the Remys' cabin."

John said, "Good luck," and then watched as Jimmy ran to Fred Brown's livery.

———

Drew and Gabrielle were holding hands as they stood beside the stake which marked the site of the future home when Drew said, "I can't believe it's been less than three weeks since I was tossed off the roof of that boxcar. But it was a very fortunate fall, and if I knew where he was, maybe I should send a thank you letter to Fast Jack Hickman."

Gabrielle replied, "I'm even happier that you survived that fall, but if I ever saw that murdering engineer, I'd still shoot him."

Drew laughed before saying, "So, would I, sweetheart. But he's somewhere in Minnesota, and I don't think any of our rifles have a seven-hundred-mile range."

"Then he'd better stay in Minnesota if he knows what's good for him."

Drew was still smiling as he said, "Let's head home for our turkey lunch."

Gabrielle nodded and then they walked to Mallard and Henna and mounted without realizing that Fast Jack Hickman was just five miles away rather than seven hundred.

———

Jack was unfamiliar with the horse, so he didn't push the sorrel as he had a long ride ahead of him. But if he'd known that Drew was just over the horizon, he would have dramatically increased the animal's pace.

So, as he leisurely rode across the Northern Pacific's land grants, Jack seemed more like a tourist than an assassin. He figured he'd have enough daylight left to reconnoiter the ground surrounding Campbell's cabin and then find the best place to set up his ambush.

———

By the time Jimmy mounted Homer and left the northern dock, he was four miles behind Fast Jack. But unlike Jack, Jimmy trusted his horse. And even though he believed that Drew was thirty-four miles away, Jimmy still had Homer at a fast trot as he chased after Fast Jack.

He hoped that Hickman was riding more slowly than he was, and if he was, Jimmy expected to spot him within a half an hour.

———

Drew and Gabrielle were pulling away from Fast Jack until Drew spotted a large trout leap out of the creek in a vain attempt to snatch a sparrow out of the air.

He pointed and shouted, "Did you see that?"

Gabrielle looked toward the creek and then replied, "No. What was it?"

Drew said, "It was the biggest trout I've ever seen, and he just tried to have a sparrow for lunch. Let's head over there, and maybe we can have him for our supper."

Gabrielle laughed, and as they headed to the creek, she said, "I'm sure the fish is waiting patiently for you to lift him out of his watery home."

Drew grinned and replied, "He probably would consider it an honor to be eaten by such a beautiful woman."

Just before they pulled up, Gabrielle said, "So, I guess that means you and my father will be eating turkey for supper."

Drew was on Gabrielle's left when they dismounted and led their horses to the edge of the creek. When they looked down, they didn't find the leaping trout waiting to be scooped out of the water. But if they'd glanced to the south, they would have seen a rider appear over the horizon.

It was then that the geometrics which controlled the line of sight came into play.

———

Jimmy Lynch was relieved when he spotted Fast Jack but didn't want to gain ground so quickly. So, he slowed Homer to a pace that was just a little faster than Jack's. Jimmy knew he'd still catch up to Hickman long before he reached the Remys' cabin.

Just as Jimmy slowed, Fast Jack was startled when he spotted someone standing near the creek in the distance, yet he was too far away to realize there were two people. But Jack immediately assumed he was looking at Drew Campbell and pushed the horse into a canter.

Jimmy didn't notice Jack's added speed for almost a minute. And when he did, he assumed Fast Jack had spotted him and was trying to run away. So, he popped Homer's flanks to equal Hickman's new pace, so he wouldn't lose sight of him.

———

Drew smiled and said, "I guess it's turkey for supper after all."

Gabrielle looked at him and replied, "You should have worn your waders, Duck Man."

Drew chuckled and after he stepped out of Gabrielle's field of vision to mount Mallard, she suddenly pointed and exclaimed, "Drew, there's a rider coming from the south, and he's moving fast!"

Drew quickly turned, spotted the rider and said, "He could be bringing us a telegram from Alistair. Or maybe it's John Knudsen coming to tell us about a change in the agreement."

"But why would he be riding so fast?"

"I guess he was surprised to see us here and didn't want us to leave before he caught up with us."

Gabrielle focused on the approaching rider as she said, "He could be Jimmy Lynch, Drew. But maybe he didn't change his ways as you believed. I think we should get our Winchesters just in case."

Drew replied, "I'm sure Jimmy isn't going to revert to his bad way of life, Brie. But it won't hurt to have our Winchesters ready."

Gabrielle nodded before she stepped to Henna and slid her '73 from her scabbard and Drew pulled his '76.

———

Jack was about a mile out when he realized there were two people ahead of him, and one of them was a woman. He immediately believed he'd been mistaken in his assumption that he'd found Drew Campbell and slowed his tiring horse.

Jimmy was concentrating on Fast Jack, so when he noticed Hickman suddenly reduce his horse's speed, he suspected the evil ex-engineer had decided to fight it out. But after a half a minute had passed and Hickman hadn't even looked back, Jimmy couldn't understand why he'd slowed down. It was then that he spotted a couple and their horses about a half a mile in front of Fast Jack. Even though they were too far away for him to identify, Jimmy was sure they were Drew and Gabrielle. He knew he had no chance to stop Hickman, so all he could do was to warn Drew by firing some warning shots.

Fast Jack was about four hundred yards from the couple and had just noticed that the man and woman were each holding a Winchester. But before he could identify Drew, he heard three rapid gunshots echo from behind him. He looked back and spotted a rider about a mile away racing towards him. Jack assumed the shooter was Drew Campbell and immediately forgot about the couple. He quickly reversed course and then pulled his Winchester from the scabbard.

———

As soon as Drew saw the distant rider firing into the air, he exclaimed, "I think that's Jimmy Lynch and he's warning us."

C. J. PETIT

Before Gabrielle could say anything, Drew quickly mounted Mallard and raced after the unknown rider who was charging at Jimmy.

Gabrielle hurriedly climbed into her saddle and chased after her husband.

Jimmy knew he'd warned Drew when he saw Fast Jack suddenly turn around. Then he did the smartest thing he'd ever done when, instead of reaching for his Winchester, he holstered his Colt and then pulled Homer into a sharp U-turn.

Jimmy's wise decision also convinced Fast Jack that he was chasing Drew Campbell. But he was well out of Winchester range, so he pushed his laboring sorrel into a full gallop.

Drew was about three hundred yards behind the unknown rider when he set Mallard to matching speed. He wasn't gaining on the stranger yet, but knew his black gelding was much fresher and could maintain the torrid pace longer. Drew looked back to check on Gabrielle and wasn't surprised to find her and Henna just a few yards behind him.

Fast Jack realized he wasn't gaining on the man he believed to be Drew Campbell and could hear the rented horse's labored breathing. So, he had no choice but to pull up. And his exhausted horse slowed, Jack watched in frustration as Campbell escaped. But just as he was about to slide his unfired Winchester back into its scabbard, he heard thundering hoofbeats behind him. He quickly twisted in his saddle and spotted the man and woman with their Winchesters just two hundred yards away. He still didn't know who they were, but before his horse came to a full stop, Jack jumped to the ground and levered a cartridge into his Winchester's firing chamber.

As soon as Drew saw the stranger begin to slow, he reduced Mallard's speed, and after Gabrielle caught up to him, she brought Henna into a matching pace.

Then just a few seconds later, when Drew saw the rider leap from his saddle and work his Winchester's lever, he shouted, "Pull up, Brie!"

When Fast Jack heard Gabrielle yell back, "Okay, Drew!" he realized that he'd been chasing the wrong man. So, he aimed his Winchester at the brakeman and waited for him to come within range.

Drew and Gabrielle quickly dismounted before she asked, "Do you recognize him, Drew?"

Drew stared at the waiting stranger for a few seconds before replying, "It could be my brain just playing tricks on me, but I think he's Fast Jack Hickman."

Gabrielle immediately asked, "If you're right, why would he even be here, Drew?"

"If he was a sane man, he wouldn't be. But any man who makes a hobby out of killing brakemen is far from sane. I reckon that after he found out I was still alive, he was determined to keep his record intact."

"How can you be sure it's him?"

Drew handed Mallard's reins to her, and then replied, "I'll go ask him," and then stepped away from Mallard.

Gabrielle exclaimed, "Don't go out there, Drew!" but knew it was pointless.

Drew began slowly walking toward Hickman and hoped he wasn't an expert marksman with a Winchester '76 aimed at him.

Fast Jack was surprised and enormously pleased when he saw Campbell walk away from the woman and their horses. He didn't understand what had inspired him to become an easy target, but it didn't matter. He just hoped the brakeman continued his approach until he was within range.

Drew didn't stop walking as he shouted, "Who are you and why are you pointing your rifle at me, mister?"

Fast Jack was surprised that Campbell hadn't recognized, so he yelled, "I'm the same feller who thought he killed ya a few weeks ago, Campbell!"

Drew continued his slow, steady approach as he shouted, "You failed then and you won't kill me this time either, Hickman! If you had half a brain, you'd mount your horse and ride back to Glendive and then take the next train back to Minnesota."

Jack didn't bother answering but centered his sights on Campbell's chest. He was about a hundred and sixty yards away, but the proprietor at Sorensen & Sons Firearms had told him the Winchester '73 could hit targets beyond its published effective range of a hundred yards. But Mister Sorensen hadn't explained the purpose of the ladder sight. So, when Drew neared the hundred-and-fifty-yard mark, Jack's carbine was around fifteen degrees lower than it should have been when he squeezed his trigger.

When Drew saw the Winchester's muzzle flare, he knew it was too late to move out of the bullet's path, so he was relieved when the ground six feet in front of him erupted like a miniature dirt volcano. Then he dropped to the ground and after setting his sights on Hickman, he cocked his Winchester's hammer.

Fast Jack cursed when he knew his shot had fallen short. But as soon as he saw Campbell drop into a prone firing position, Jack quickly fell onto his belly. But when he tried to set his sights back onto the brakeman, Jack couldn't even see him. The only way he had a chance of shooting him now was to expose himself, and Jack believed it would be suicidal to make himself a target.

Drew faced the same dilemma after Fast Jack dropped out of sight. But after hearing the sound of Hickman's Winchester and seeing his bullet land short, Drew was reasonably sure that his protagonist was using a '73. So, as the standoff continued, Drew was thinking of the best way to make use of that advantage.

Fifty yards behind Drew, Gabrielle understood why the shooting had stopped. After a brief deliberation, she turned, mounted Henna and then began a curving route to flank Fast Jack.

After Jimmy heard a gunshot, he'd wheeled Homer back around and soon spotted Fast Jack laying on the ground with his rifle pointed toward Gabrielle and their two horses. He set Homer to a slow trot and pulled his Winchester from his scabbard before he saw Drew on the ground with his rifle aimed at Hickman. When he saw Gabrielle mount her horse, Jimmy levered a .44-40 cartridge into his Winchester's breech and then nudged Homer into a fast trot.

Drew's dilemma ended when he saw Jimmy turn around, so he shouted, "The rider who fired those shots to warn us is coming up behind you, Hickman! Stand up without your Winchester and we won't shoot!"

Drew didn't expect Fast Jack to comply, and Jack might not have if he hadn't seen Gabrielle riding to his right with her rifle. And even if Campbell was trying to trick him about the other shooter, he knew he was trapped.

THE BRAKEMAN

So, he immediately yelled, "Okay! I'm standin' up! Don't shoot!"

Drew, Gabrielle and Jimmy all heard his loud surrender, but were still surprised when they watched Fast Jack lay his Winchester on the ground and then slowly rise to his feet with his hands in the air.

Drew quickly stood and began striding towards him with his '76 still pointed at Hickman's chest.

Gabrielle turned Henna towards Fast Jack and slowed her to a walk as she kept her '73 aimed at the man who'd tried to murder her husband.

Jimmy knew Drew and Gabrielle had the situation under control, so he released his Winchester's hammer and then returned it to its scabbard and slowed Homer to a walk.

The man in the middle was extremely nervous as he watched Campbell drawing closer. He'd tried to kill him twice and failed, and Jack couldn't believe the brakeman wouldn't want his revenge. So, Fast Jack's eyes were locked on Drew expecting him to fire at any moment.

Drew wasn't about to fire, but as soon as he started walking toward Fast Jack, Drew had already what he would do with him. Drew knew that Hickman wouldn't change his ways as Jimmy had, so he wasn't about to let him go. The man had not only tried to kill him twice, but he'd gotten away with murdering other brakemen. He just didn't know how many.

After he bound Hickman's wrists, he and Jimmy would take him to Sheriff Hobson and have Hickman charged with attempted murder. And he had two eyewitnesses to confirm his accusation which should guarantee his conviction.

The female eyewitness had pulled her Morgan mare to a stop when she was around fifty feet away so she could hear what Drew was going to do with Hickman. She only hoped her husband behaved like a lawman and not a preacher this time.

When Jimmy brought Homer to a stop fifty yards behind Fast Jack, he tipped his hat to Gabrielle even though she wasn't looking at him.

Adding to Jack's fear of being shot was his growing concern that he would lose control of his bladder. So, as he watched Drew Campbell and his threatening Winchester step ever closer, Fast Jack quickly squeezed his knees together.

Drew saw the sudden movement and exclaimed, "Don't move, Hickman!"

Fast Jack's terrified anticipation exploded and neither his mind nor his knees were able to prevent the warm flood that filled his britches. But he was so petrified that he hadn't noticed his unintended misfire.

Jack began to shake as he yelled, "Don't shoot me!"

When Drew saw the spreading dark stain on Hickman's pants, he loudly replied, "I won't shoot you, Hickman. Besides you already shot yourself."

Jack was relieved to know he wasn't about to be shot but was confused by what he'd heard until he felt the spreading dampness below his waist.

Drew then said, "Take three steps back and then you can put your hands down."

Fast Jack wasn't so fast when he took the three steps and then slowly lowered his hands. He just watched as the hated brakeman grabbed his Winchester from the ground.

Drew still kept his eyes on Hickman as he loudly asked, "Can you bring Mallard close, Brie?"

Gabrielle replied, "I'll be right back," and then slid her Winchester into its scabbard before riding away.

Jimmy then walked Homer a little closer to see if Drew needed help with Fast Jack.

Drew glanced at the sorrel and asked, "Where'd you get the horse, Hickman?"

"I rented him from a liveryman named Jake."

"Do you have any spare britches in your travel bag?"

"Yeah. But I ain't gonna change 'em and my underpants in front of a woman."

"You don't have to worry because I wasn't expecting you to take them off. I only asked because I wanted to use the dry britches to protect the Tidwell brothers' saddle."

Jack glared as he asked, "Are you gonna put me in the saddle and then take me into the forest and hang me?"

Just as Jimmy pulled up, Drew replied, "Don't tempt me. I'll take you to Glendive and have you charged with attempted murder. I don't think they'll send you to the gallows, but I reckon you'll spend the next decade in the territorial prison."

Jack may have been somewhat relieved that he wasn't going to hang, but he wasn't happy with the idea of being locked in a cold cell for ten years, either. So, he lapsed into silence as he tried to think of a way to avoid any form of punishment.

Jimmy then asked, "Do you need me to do anything, Drew?"

Drew smiled as he replied, "You can take the spare britches out of Hickman's travel bag and cover the sorrel's saddle seat. But before you do that, I'd like to thank you for warning us."

"I wish he never reached the ferry. I was lookin' all over but didn't find him anywhere. It wasn't 'til Mister Knudsen told me

Jake Tidwell rented a horse to a stranger that I tried to catch up to him."

"I'm still grateful, Jimmy."

Jimmy grinned and then dismounted and led Homer to the sorrel.

When Gabrielle arrived, Drew handed her his Winchester and asked, "Could you put this where it belongs, Mrs. Campbell? If Hickman tries anything, I'll shoot him with his '73."

Gabrielle nodded and after sliding Drew's '76 into Mallard's scabbard, she asked, "Can I assume you'll want me to return the cabin while you and Mister Lynch take that bastard to jail?"

"If you don't mind, ma'am. I should return before sunset."

Gabrielle said, "I'll be the obedient wife…this time," before she turned Henna to the north and rode away.

As she rode by, Jimmy waved and was happily surprised when Gabrielle not only returned his wave, but even added a big smile.

———

An hour later, as he rode between the brakeman and his friend, Jack still hadn't figured out how to avoid being jailed and was growing desperate. But as they approached the ferry, Jack had an epiphany. That brakeman had survived a long fall

399

and then being swept downriver for miles. And he wouldn't fall sixty feet or stay afloat that long, so he should have no problem using the Yellowstone as he path to freedom. The river would wash his britches, too.

Josh Brockman had been anticipating a return passenger, so he hadn't left the northern dock. But he was surprised to see three riders, and one of them was his favorite customer. So, he was already expecting a good tip before they arrived.

After dismounting and leading their horses onto the dock, Drew handed Josh a silver dollar, which was even a larger tip than he'd hoped to receive.

Drew then turned and said, "You can board first, Jimmy."

Jimmy nodded and then carefully led Homer onto the bouncing barge.

Jack then said, "I reckon you want me to go next."

"Yup."

As Jack stepped onto the barge with the sorrel, he looked at the Yellowstone and had second thoughts about using it as an escape route. But he immediately decided it was better to take his chances with the angry river than spending years in prison. But when he'd assessed the risk, Jack hadn't taken into account that Drew owed his survival to his ugly, waterproof garb. If he had, he might have welcomed joining the prison population.

When Drew walked Mallard onto the ferry, he paid no attention to where Jack was standing. And as soon as Josh Brockman began pulling on the rope, Drew added his own strength to bring the heavy ferry across the river.

Jack waited until the flatboat was close to the middle of the Yellowstone before he quietly stepped over the side and let the current sweep him away.

Six seconds passed before Jimmy glanced downriver, saw Fast Jack and shouted, "He jumped in the river, Drew!"

Drew and Josh immediately stopped pulling and turned their eyes eastward. When Drew spotted his prisoner, Fast Jack was already struggling to stay afloat as his jacket soaked up the icy water.

Josh loudly said, "He ain't gonna make it."

Drew was sure that the ferryman's assessment was correct but didn't say anything.

Fast Jack could swim, but only using the crawling dog paddle. So, after sliding into the frigid water, he began using his only stroke to reach the northern shore. But he soon realized that he wasn't making much progress. So as the Yellowstone dragged him away from the ferry, Jack started treading water hoping to find some floating debris.

That desperate hope soon disappeared when he felt his waterlogged coat pulling him beneath the surface. He frantically tried to avoid being taken to a watery grave, but his panicked splashing only shortened his time he could remain afloat.

The three men on the ferry watched as Fast Jack Hickman struggled to avoid the inevitable for a few more seconds before he was swallowed by the Yellowstone just a couple of hundred yards away. But only Drew recognized the irony of Jack's drowning death. And if he'd known that Ira Butler had suffered a similar fate, Drew would have been seriously spooked.

They observed the river for another thirty seconds before Drew said, "Let's finish crossing and then we'll tell John Knudsen what happened."

———

John said, "I didn't tell you because I wasn't sure that the stranger who rented the horse was Hickman, much less that he was planning to kill Drew Campbell."

Sheriff Hobson replied, "I still wish you told me, Mister Knudsen. I only found out 'cause Jake Tidwell mentioned it to Deputy Pope."

"If that man was Hickman, he'd have a long ride ahead of him before he reached the Remys' cabin. So, it probably won't be until tomorrow morning before we find out if Jimmy Lynch was right."

"I just hope Lynch wasn't just headin' that way to shoot Campbell himself. You forget he rode out there with Early to kill Campbell and the Remys."

John shook his head as he said, "Jimmy's not the same man, Sheriff. He…" but stopped when the door began to open and then exclaimed, "Drew! Jimmy!"

Sheriff Hobson whipped his head around as John quickly asked, "What happened?"

Drew took off his hat and then replied, "Gabrielle and I were visiting the site of our new house and didn't notice Hickman until Jimmy fired some warning shots. By the time Fast Jack reached us, Brie and I both had our Winchesters.

"After Hickman took one long-range shot at me, we both dropped to the ground and had a short standoff. But when Gabrielle flanked Hickman and Jimmy pulled up behind him, Fast Jack knew he was trapped, so he gave up."

Sheriff Hobson asked, "Did you leave him at the jail?"

Drew shook his head as he replied, "I told him that I was going to take him to the jail and have him charged with attempted murder. But when we were taking the ferry across the Yellowstone, he tried to escape by jumping into the river. He didn't get very far before he disappeared beneath the surface."

Sheriff Hobson stood, said, "That was a stupid thing to do," and then pulled on his hat and left the office.

John quietly said, "You almost drowned in the Yellowstone because Fast Jack tried kill you, Drew."

"I know. But when he pulled back on that throttle to throw me off the boxcar, he didn't care where I died. And if it wasn't for Jimmy's warning, he might have succeeded this time."

John smiled and said, "I'll make sure everyone in town knows what you did today, Jimmy. And when the spur is finished, come and see me about the secretary job. Okay?"

Jimmy grinned as he said, "Okay, Mister Knudsen."

"And stop calling me Mister Knudsen. My friends call me John."

Jimmy blushed as if he was a shy adolescent boy trying to talk to a pretty girl before John asked, "Do you want me to notify my boss about Fast Jack, Drew?"

"It's up to you, John. I'm going to take the sorrel back to Amos and Jake and then head home to tell Gabrielle what happened."

John grinned and said, "When you're on the ferry, be careful not to trip and fall into the Yellowstone."

Drew pulled on his hat as he said, "I only go swimming in the Yellowstone when I'm wearing my duck suit," and then shook Jimmy's hand and said, "You're a good man, Jimmy Lynch."

Jimmy smiled, and as he watched Drew leave the office, he decided that he might take John's offer after all.

John then stood and said, "I'm going to send a telegram, but not to my boss. I'll wire Alistair MacLeish to let him know what happened."

Jimmy followed John out the door and as the new manager headed to the Western Union office, Jimmy mounted Homer and rode to Fred Brown's livery.

———

After dropping off the sorrel and pooh-poohing Jake Tidwell's heartfelt apology for renting the horse to Fast Jack, Drew rode out of Glendive.

Drew stayed dry and upright on his return crossing of the Yellowstone. As he helped pull the barge along, he hadn't even bothered looking downriver for any signs that Fast Jack Hickman had somehow miraculously survived. Drew believed that he'd earned his place in hell.

It was mid-afternoon when Drew waved to the ferryman and rode Mallard away at a medium trot. He was anxious to talk to Gabrielle and hoped she wasn't angry at him for not bringing her along.

———

Gabrielle wasn't even disappointed when she started back to tell her parents about the bizarre confrontation with Fast Jack. But even though Drew said he was going to charge Hickman with attempted murder, she still was concerned that her husband might change his mind.

So, after giving her stunned parents the news and answering their many questions, Gabrielle said, "I hope Drew doesn't decide to forgive Hickman and let him leave town on the next train."

Francine replied, "I know he's a compassionate man and gave Lynch a change to become a good man. But I can't imagine that he'd forgive a man who came all this way to kill him after he learned his first attempt had failed."

Gabrielle sighed and then said, "You're probably right, Maman. But a man who would be so vindictive that he'd do something like that might come back after he gets out of prison. What if he shows up again when Drew and I have a houseful of children?"

Boney patted his daughter's shoulder and said, "You're just worrying too much about something that will never happen."

Francine quickly added, "You should be thinking about your houseful of our grandchildren."

Gabrielle smiled as she said, "I still wish that Drew pushed Hickman into the Yellowstone rather than taking him to jail."

As her parents laughed, Gabrielle knew that her husband would never even think of pushing that evil man off the ferry.

———

The sun was setting behind the mountains when Drew pulled up in front of the cabin, dismounted and tossed Mallard's reins over the hitchrail.

He removed his hat, opened the door and when he found his family sitting at the table, he said, "Things didn't go quite as I had planned," before closing the door.

As he hung his hat, Gabrielle asked, "You didn't let him go, did you?"

Drew stepped close to his wife, kissed her and after taking a seat, he replied, "No, ma'am. But I didn't leave him with Sheriff Hobson, either."

Gabrielle glanced at her mother before asking, "Did he escape?"

"He attempted to escape by diving off the ferry but never came close to the river's shore. I told John Knudsen and Sheriff Hobson what had happened before I left Glendive."

Gabrielle was relieved that the crazy man would never return but didn't comment on the irony of his death nor on the eeriness of her wish which she'd expressed to her parents.

Instead, she said, "I'm just glad you're home, Drew. Now you can take care of Mallard while Mom and I start preparing supper."

Drew smiled, stood and said, "Yes, ma'am," before standing, grabbing his hat, and then leaving the cabin.

———

Hours later, Gabrielle's heart was still racing as she laid her head on her husband's heaving chest and quietly said, "Before you returned, I told my parents that I wished you'd pushed Hickman into the river instead of taking him to jail. I know it's irrational, but I still feel guilty for having said it."

"It may be unreasonable, but I can understand why it would bother you. When I watched him drown, it was so ironic that I felt a bit spooked myself. But at least we won't have to worry about Fast Jack making another attempt to kill me after he's released from prison."

"I was worried about that possibility, too."

Drew kissed her forehead before saying, "I can't promise you that the rest of our lives will be free of worry, sweetheart. But what I can promise you is that I will always love you."

Gabrielle sighed and then whispered, "And I'll always love you, Drew."

As Drew slid his fingers through Gabrielle's long black hair, he had no idea of what those future worries might be. His only concern was how he would be able to provide for his perfect wife and their children.

But even as he drifted off to sleep, fate was already working to solve his future seven hundred miles away in Brainerd, Minnesota.

———

June 10, 1884

Gabrielle watched as the dozens of construction crews erected the assorted buildings of the mining village and asked, "I don't understand why we aren't allowed to see our new house before it's finished, Drew."

"Neither do I. But I'm sure they're almost done by now. And after seeing all of those freight wagons heading over there for the past few weeks, I'm sure that you'll be happy with our home."

Boney said, "Mister Cloverfield said he'd let us know when the houses were ready. But I was surprised when he said that he'd have his men load our things."

Francine then said, "I was surprised, too. They've been treating us as if we were royalty."

Boney grinned and said, "You are royalty, sweetheart. You're a princess while I'm just a lowly commoner who was granted the honor of becoming your husband."

As her mother laughed, Gabrielle said, "I guess the Northern Pacific is trying to make up for the way Butler treated us."

Drew nodded but suspected that there was another reason for the work crews' deferential treatment. He had a feeling that Alistair and his adoptive father were the more important reason than just the N.P. trying to make amends. What drove his suspicion was a letter he'd received from Alistair a couple of weeks ago.

Fergie had written about his family and passed along additional details about the spur and coal mine. He'd also wrote that his father had been very impressed by what Drew had done since being tossed off the boxcar. But the last paragraph in the letter was a bit puzzling.

Alistair explained how critical the maintenance shop was to the Northern Pacific. It was almost as if he was trying to convince Drew to return as a foreman. But it was so vague that Drew wasn't sure of Fergie's reason for praising the large workshop.

In his reply, Drew hadn't asked Alistair about it, but suspected that his friend would offer an explanation in his next letter. And hopefully, he and Gabrielle would be living in their new home when it arrived.

———

Two days later, just as the family sat down for lunch, there was a knock on the door.

Boney quickly stood, walked to the door and when he pulled it open, he saw Abe Cloverfield's smiling face.

Boney hopefully asked, "What can I do for you, Mister Cloverfield?"

"I just wanted to let you know that I'll be sendin' over some men to load up your wagon in the mornin'."

Gabrielle quickly asked, "So, can we finally go and look at our houses now?"

Abe smiled as he replied, "I was just gonna say that you need to look at the houses before you decide what you want to load into the wagon, ma'am," and then tipped his hat before heading back to the large construction site.

Boney closed the door and as he walked back to the table, Gabrielle excitedly said, "I can't wait to see our new homes!"

Drew smiled and said, "I hope you can wait until after the horses are saddled, Mrs. Campbell."

Gabrielle kissed Drew before she began to wolf down her lunch.

———

Gabrielle's excitement hadn't shown any signs of diminishing as they rode eastward. And when they made the turn toward Glendive, it even rose a notch or two.

And even though they were still ten miles from the northern border of Section L162-10, Gabrielle exclaimed, "I can almost see our house, Drew!"

Drew smiled as he said, "I reckon that means those folks who still believe the earth is flat are right after all."

Gabrielle's brow furrowed as she replied, "I did say 'almost', Mister Campbell."

Drew winked at his pseudo-angry wife, and after she smiled, he turned his eyes southward. Even though he'd agreed to two small houses and a barn, Drew suspected that Alistair's interpretation of 'small' was a lot different than his. If the Northern Pacific was simply honoring the agreement, the houses and barn should have been completed two weeks ago.

———

Fifty minutes later, the rooftops of the Remys' house and the barn rose above the southern horizon.

On cue, Gabrielle pointed and exclaimed, "There's your new house, Maman and Papa!"

Francine replied, "I can see it and the barn, too, Gabby."

Boney added, "Both of them look a lot bigger than I expected."

Before Francine could reply, Gabrielle exclaimed, "There's our house, Drew!"

Drew chuckled at his wife's enthusiasm before asking, "Do you wish to be carried over the threshold, Mrs. Campbell?"

"No. It would only delay my inspection. But you may carry me across the barn's threshold if you'd like."

Drew smiled, but as more of the houses came into view, he whispered to himself, "You really went overboard, Fergie. But at least the privies aren't oversized."

As he scanned the property, Drew noticed two unexpected structures. There was a room-sized brick building behind the barn and a bridge had been built across the stream. He was almost surprised they hadn't built a windmill and pump while they were at it. At least it gave him and Boney something to work on.

The surprises continued when Francine said, "There are even rocking chairs on the porch, Boney."

Boney replied, "And there's a stovepipe, too. Do you think there's a new cookstove inside?"

Gabrielle noticed their house's stovepipe and then spotted a second, smaller pipe jutting out from the roof near the back of the house. But she didn't say anything because she was so absorbed in her visual exploration.

Drew was also silent as he studied the two houses. They were similar in design; but weren't the same size. The house they'd built for him and for Gabrielle was noticeably larger. He suspected Alistair had them add a couple of bedrooms for their children.

They were crossing Section L 162-9 when Boney loudly asked, "Do we explore each of our new homes separately or together?"

Drew was almost shocked when Gabrielle replied, "We can all discover what's inside your house first, Papa."

Boney grinned and said, "We'll do a quick tour and then you and Drew can visit your new home privately. When you're finished, we'll see what surprises are in the barn. You'll find us sitting on our porch using our new rocking chairs."

Gabrielle could only nod as she was too excited to speak.

Drew may not have been as excited as his wife, but he was sure that he was more curious. They'd seen many heavily loaded freight wagons pass by their cabin carrying materials for the houses and barn. But judging by the size of the buildings, they probably missed even more wagons. And maybe they made use of Josh Brockman's ferry as well.

He was still estimating the number of large wagons it would have taken when they pulled up before the first house, dismounted and tied their horses' reins to the hitchrail.

Boney then took Francine's hand and smiled before they climbed the three steps onto the covered porch. As soon as he opened the door, the second round of surprises began.

Before they even stepped over the threshold, Francine exclaimed, "It's already furnished!"

The Remys' amazement continued as they entered the main room with Drew and an equally astonished Gabrielle walking behind them.

Gabrielle's big brown eyes were even larger as she scanned the room. And even Drew was surprised by the furnishings which included a large rug in the center of the room.

Francine rushed through an open doorway and exclaimed, "Boney, I can't believe it! There's a new cookstove, cupboards, a pantry, a cold room and even a pump near the sink!"

When Boney caught up to his wife, he said, "This is beyond anything that I could have possibly expected, Fran."

415

After discovering a new set of pots and pans in one of the cupboards, Francine delayed her kitchen exploration to inspect the other rooms.

Gabrielle took Drew's hand before they followed her parents down a short hall. They watched as Francine opened the first door and then pull Boney inside.

As her parents gushed over the furnished bedroom, Gabrielle looked at Drew and said, "Now I wish I'd decided to visit our house right away."

Drew smiled as he replied, "We'll discover what's inside our home in a few more minutes, sweetheart."

Gabrielle said, "I hope so," just before her parents left their bedroom.

The adjacent room was empty, but when Francine opened the door across the hall, she squealed like a teenager and exclaimed, "A real bathtub!"

Gabrielle may have been anxious to explore her own home but hearing her mother's joyous reaction was well worth the delay.

As Francine entered the bathing room, Boney smiled and said, "I think we might be here for a while. So, we'll see you after you visit your house."

Gabrielle said, "I'll try not to keep you waiting too long, Papa," and then turned and hurried away.

Drew's longer strides allowed him to catch up to his anxious young wife before they reached the front door.

As they walked across the hundred-yard gap between the houses, Drew looked toward the barn and tried to imagine the brick building's purpose. He hoped to discover its function after he and Gabrielle discovered whatever surprises might be waiting for them inside their new home.

When they stepped through the doorway, Gabrielle gushed, "Our house is furnished, too!" before she hurried to see the kitchen.

As Drew followed Gabrielle, he was ashamed for feeling somewhat disappointed. While it was much more than he'd expected from the Northern Pacific, there was little difference between their main room and the Remys'.

But as he watched Gabrielle excitedly flutter about in her new kitchen, which was also much like her parents', his disappointment vanished. Her happiness was all that really mattered.

Unlike her mother, Gabrielle opened every one of the cabinet doors. After finding a matching set of pots and pans, and one with glassware, she discovered a cabinetful of tableware. It wasn't fancy by any means, but it was a welcome surprise.

Gabrielle took a peek into the cold room before saying, "Now let's see our bedroom, husband."

Drew smiled as he replied, "As you wish, my lady."

When Gabrielle mentioned their bedroom, Drew suddenly remembered asking John Knudsen about Butler's four-poster. But that had been a month ago, so John may have forgotten his request.

Just a few seconds later when Gabrielle opened the first room's door and exclaimed, "I forgot about the bed!" Drew knew John hadn't forgotten.

Gabrielle slowly approached the massive quilt-covered mattress and as she ran her fingertips across the covering, she said, "I can't wait until we share this bed again, Drew."

Drew smiled as he replied, "I'd ravage you on our bed right now if your parents weren't waiting for us."

Gabrielle kissed him before saying, "We'd better leave before we make them wait a lot longer."

Drew said, "Quickly," before they hurried away from soft temptation to explore the rest of their home.

As Drew had suspected, the next room was already furnished as a nursery. After finding a large cast iron bathtub and sink in the small room across the hall, there still were two more rooms to explore.

And as soon as they opened the door to the middle room, Drew discovered the first of Alistair's surprises. After noticing Ira Butler's rolltop desk and matching chair, he spotted what seemed to be a draft table and a tall cabinet with at least a dozen two-foot-wide, two-inch-high drawers.

As they entered the room, Drew found a bookcase with an entire shelf full of technical manuals which was even more confusing than the draft table.

Gabrielle said, "This looks like an office or a workroom, Drew."

"I know. But I don't understand why Alistair sent the draft table or all those technical books."

"Why do you think Alistair sent them?"

"Before we even left the cabin, I suspected that Alistair and his father had planned to build larger houses than what was on the agreement. But when I saw the bridge across the stream, I knew he had done much more than just increase the size of the houses."

"I didn't even notice the bridge. But what's a draft table?"

"It's what engineers and architects use when they draw the blueprints for their designs. I'm not an engineer and never even met an architect, so I can't figure out why it's here."

419

"Maybe there's a letter somewhere to explain why he sent it."

"I hope so. Let's explore the other room and if we don't find one, I guess my curiosity will have to wait until we move in and have more time to search for a letter."

When they entered the last mystery room, Drew laughed and said, "At least I understand this room's setup."

Gabrielle smiled as she replied, "The worktable and gun rack can stay until we need the room for our second baby, Mister Campbell."

Drew grinned as he said, "Yes, ma'am. But I think we've kept Mom and Dad waiting long enough," and then took her hand before they left the gun room.

As soon as they saw Drew and Gabrielle step onto the porch, Boney and Francine left their rocking chairs.

When they met, Francine asked, "Was it as nice as our house, Gabby?"

"It was almost the same except for the two additional rooms. One was furnished as an office and the other as a gun room."

As the two couples headed to the barn, Drew focused on the brick building with renewed interest. After finding the draft table and technical books, Drew was even more curious about what he might inside.

When they entered the large barn, Boney said, "Jacques and Jean will be happy to have a roof over their heads and walls to keep out the wind. And there are enough stalls for all of the horses, too."

Despite Drew's anxiety to see what was inside the brick building, he was able to remain calm as they toured the barn's interior. After Boney climbed the ladder and discovered a large number of bundled hay stacks in the loft, Drew finally gave in to his insistent curiosity.

So, before Boney descended the ladder, Drew said, "I'm going to see what's inside that brick building," and trotted out of the barn.

Gabrielle quickly followed, so she would be able to watch Drew's reaction when he opened the heavy door.

As he swung it open, Drew only partially satisfied his curiosity when he looked into the dark room. There was a large anvil, a forge with bellows, a drum for making charcoal beside a large barrelful of charcoal, and a wall lined with tools. So, it had everything a well-equipped blacksmith shop needed. But there were other pieces of equipment and tools that he recognized from his years working in the Northern Pacific maintenance shop, too.

He was still trying to understand the setup when Gabrielle asked, "Did Alistair have them build you a smithy, Drew?"

"It's more than just a smithy, Brie. It looks like a combination blacksmith shop and the train maintenance shop back in Brainerd."

Drew stepped deeper into the workshop and was still puzzled as to why Alistair had it built and stocked. And seeing two large, open crates full of damaged locomotive parts didn't help. He hoped Alistair left a letter of explanation somewhere, but if he hadn't, Drew would post a letter to his friend and ask why the workshop existed.

He was still staring at the crates of broken parts when Boney and Francine entered, and Boney said, "It looks like your friend wants you to be a blacksmith, Drew."

Drew turned, smiled and replied, "I think Fergie has something else in mind. I just have no idea what it is. Let's go see that bridge before we ride back to the cabin."

Drew was still trying to unravel the mystery of the workshop as the two couples passed the large corral and headed toward the creek.

As they approached the bridge, Gabrielle said, "It looks strong enough to support one of those loaded freight wagons."

Drew stopped thinking about the workshop and studied the structure of the bridge. It didn't take long for him to understand the reason for its robust appearance.

He smiled at Gabrielle and said, "The bridge was built using some of the spur's rails and crossties."

Boney asked, "Why wouldn't they just use some of the hardwood from the forest?"

"The crossties and rails were readily available, and it probably only took them a couple of hours to build it because they're railroad men."

When they were closer to the bridge, Drew pointed and said, "I think they set a crosstie on each side of the stream for support. Then they laid about a hundred crossties on the ground leaving a one-inch gap between them. After laying the bottom of the rails on top of the crossties, they drove spikes into each of the crossties and then just rolled it over and set the bridge onto the supporting crossties."

Gabrielle said, "It must have weighed more than a ton, so how could they lift it across the stream?"

"They probably had a mule team drag it across the creek and then used a large A-frame, pulleys and the mules to lift it into position. But I'm not an engineer, so that's just a guess."

Gabrielle smiled and said, "It's probably a good guess, Drew. So, let's walk across the bridge once before we head back."

———

On their way to retrieve their horses, Drew glanced at the baffling brick building and knew he'd go crazy if he had to wait for a letter from Alistair. So, he decided to do a quick search of their new house but would limit it to the room with the draft table.

So, as they walked toward the Remys house, Drew said, "Brie, before we ride back, I'd like to look around in the office in our house. Hopefully, I'll find a letter from Fergie that will explain why he had that workshop built."

Gabrielle smiled as she replied, "I'm not surprised. It was obvious that not knowing its purpose really bothered you."

Then Boney said, "We'll wait for you on the porch."

Gabrielle said, "We won't keep you rocking too long, Papa," before she and Drew split off and headed to their house.

As they approached their front porch, Gabrielle asked, "What if you don't find a letter, Drew?"

"I'll write a letter to Fergie and have to wait for his reply. But I'd rather post a long letter of gratitude than a desperate plea for an explanation."

"If there is a letter, where do you think it is?"

"My guess would be the cabinet with all those drawers or the rolltop desk from Butler's apartment. You can check the desk while I search the cabinet. Okay?"

Gabrielle said, "Yes, sir," just as they reached the porch steps.

Less than a minute later, Drew opened the cabinet's top drawer and found it full of blueprints but no letter.

Before he checked the second drawer, Gabrielle lifted the rolltop desk's cover and exclaimed, "I found the letter, Drew!"

Drew spun around and Gabrielle handed him the envelope simply addressed 'TO DREW'.

Drew was grinning as he removed the letter and gave the empty envelope back to Gabrielle.

After unfolding the pages, he read:

My Dearest Friend,

I'm sure that when you spotted the houses and barn, you realized why they weren't the small houses you'd expected to find. Yet I believe you still were surprised to discover they were filled with furnishings. And when you entered this room, you probably were a bit confused as well. I imagine you were even more baffled by what you found inside the brick building, assuming you've already gone there. So, I'll explain why I decided to have it built and stocked as it is.

425

Before we were reunited, I was already planning to ask you to return to Brainerd to work beside me. And it wasn't simply because you were the best friend I ever had. It was because you were also the smartest person I ever met, and the one with the greatest potential.

But it wasn't long before I realized you weren't about to leave your new home. So, after discussing it with my father, we decided there could be another way to let you reach your potential and hopefully benefit the Northern Pacific in the process.

I knew you already have skill working with iron, but the crates of broken parts in the brick building aren't meant to be converted into horseshoes. And they aren't waiting for you to repair them, either. Their purpose is to serve as examples which would allow you to improve their designs or to create something new to replace them. But because you aren't employed by the Northern Pacific, you will own all of your creations. All I ask is that you give the N.P. the first chance to purchase the design.

When you open the cabinet's drawers, you'll find blueprints of locomotives, rolling stock, and other railroad assemblies. There are also copies of the patents for many of the parts which you can use as guides for your own patent applications. And inside the large case in the corner of the room you'll find a complete set of engineer's drawing instruments.

Now that you have the tools and materials you need, let your mind go to work. And I won't be surprised if you patent inventions that have nothing to do with trains.

And if you decide to bring your family to Brainerd to meet my family, in the bottom right-hand drawer of the rolltop desk you'll find an envelope with four Northern Pacific passes.

Forever you friend,

Fergie

Drew handed the letter to Gabrielle and said, "Now I understand the purpose of the brick building."

As Gabrielle began reading the short missive, Drew said, "Fergie is more confident in my abilities than I am."

Gabrielle didn't reply until she finished reading, and then set the letter on the desktop, smiled and said, "Don't underestimate yourself, Drew. I have even more confidence in you than Fergie does. And I'm sure that when you start doing something which makes use of your abilities, and especially your imagination, you'll realize that I'm right."

Drew took her hands, kissed her softly, and then said, "At least I won't be wearing a rubberized duck suit while I work."

Gabrielle smiled as she said, "That duck suit saved you for me. So, even if you never wear it again, we'll always keep it."

"Yes, ma'am."

Gabrielle then glanced at the draft table and asked, "Before you start inventing things for locomotives, could you draw a blueprint for an improved chicken coop?"

Drew chuckled and then replied, "It'll be a challenge, but I believe that I'll be able to create a comfortable chateau for our chicken community. And you might find it interesting to know that chickens were involved in the Miles City scandal a couple of years ago."

Faith smiled, said, "You can tell me about the conniving chickens while we're walking, Mister Campbell."

Drew grinned and began telling her the story as they left the office and then the house.

_____

As they rode back to the cabin, Drew told Boney and Francine about the letter. But it was just a small part of their ongoing conversation which mostly was focused on their new houses and barn.

Francine asked, "Does your house have a heat stove in the bedroom, too, Gabby?"

Gabrielle replied, "Yes, Maman. And each room had a kerosene lamp just like yours, too."

Boney grinned and said, "I was impressed with our large bed. But when we return, I have to take a gander at your giant four-poster."

Francine laughed and then asked, "Gabby, did you…" but didn't finish the question when Gabrielle quickly shook her head.

Boney snickered, but Drew just grinned as they both assumed Mrs. Remy was about to ask if he and Gabrielle had enjoyed a brief frolic on the four-poster. Drew was impressed that his wife hadn't blushed after she'd interrupted her mother's query.

Gabrielle quickly asked, "When we get back, are you going to tell Mister Cloverfield we're ready to move, Papa?"

"Drew and I can ride to the construction site and let him know, and we'll take care of the horses when we return."

Francine said, "We'll still fill our wagon, Boney. But least we won't be bringing the cookstove."

Boney nodded as he replied, "We can do some of the loading before sunset so we can leave early in the morning."

———

After Boney and Drew unsaddled the four horses, they didn't bother harnessing Jacques and Jean to move the wagon. They just wrapped the leather straps around their waists and rolled it to the front of the cabin.

They managed to load more than half of what Boney and Francine had decided to bring with them before they were summoned to supper.

Before they began eating, Boney said grace, thanking God for their food and then added, "And we are even more grateful for all the abundant blessings we have received after You guided Drew to our family."

Drew wasn't embarrassed by Boney's personal prayer because he believed it wasn't just a twist of fate that had sent him plummeting into Cabin Creek and then stolen the canoe.

After a quiet amen, the family shared their dinner and engaged in a lively conversation about tomorrow's move. What surprised Drew was that no one expressed any sadness for abandoning the only home they'd ever known.

———

Drew blew out the lamp and then joined Gabrielle who was waiting beneath the blankets.

After she laid her head onto his chest, he said, "I was impressed that you didn't seem embarrassed when your mother was about to ask you if we had enjoyed ourselves on the four-poster."

Gabrielle smiled as she replied, "I wasn't embarrassed because that wasn't what she was about to ask me."

Drew was still clueless, so he asked, "Then what was she going to ask you before you cut her off?"

Gabrielle quietly laughed before answering, "You are a smart, well-read man, but you still have a lot to learn about women, Drew. Do you want some time to figure out what my mother was about to ask me?"

Drew saw it as a challenge, so he said, "Alright. But it shouldn't take me very long."

Drew began his rapid hunt with Mrs. Remy's aborted question of 'Did you' and began attaching different verbs in alphabetical order starting with 'ask'. His brain rushed past 'bring', 'call', 'do', and 'eat' before he dropped the alphabetized method and settled on the most likely short verb of 'tell'. *Tell him what?*

Then the brilliant light of revelation parted his dark mental clouds and Drew looked into Gabrielle's dark eyes and excitedly whispered, "Are you carrying our baby?"

Gabrielle nodded and then placed his hand on her abdomen before replying, "I was planning to tell you after we moved into our own home."

Drew kissed her and then said, "I love you, Brie. And you've made me happier than I ever could have imagined. So, now I'd better get started creating and inventing to provide for you and our first child. But only after I design and build your impressive chicken coop, of course."

Gabrielle smiled as she said, "I love you, too, Drew. And you've made me just as happy."

Gabrielle then closed her eyes and as she listened to her husband's heartbeat, she couldn't imagine a life without him. And before she drifted into sleep, Gabrielle said a silent prayer to thank God for her husband and the new life growing inside her. Then she asked that when He welcomed them to His heavenly home, it wouldn't be for a very long time because she'd already found her own heaven with Drew.

EPIOLOGUE

After Drew's impressively designed poultry palace was populated with a dozen demure hens and two strutting roosters, he began what would become his life's work.

By the time Gabrielle gave birth to Alistair James Campbell on the 27th of January, Drew had already had his first two patents approved. The first was for an improved pressure relief valve that could replace two of the older designs. The second was for a safer link-and-pin coupler that was also less susceptible to theft. Drew sold both patents to the Northern Pacific. And there had been no need to haggle after receiving their initial, generous offer for each of the patents, either.

———

On the 8th of May, exactly ten years after Drew shook his hand before leaving St. Thomas, James Stewart was sitting at his desk opening the day's mail. The first two pieces were bills, and one of them was overdue.

Mister Stewart sighed, but his mood instantly improved when he glanced at the third envelope's return address and read, 'Drew Campbell' on the first line.

He was smiling but a bit disappointed when he slid just a single sheet from the envelope. But when he unfolded the letter, his chin dropped and his eyes bulged when he found a check for twelve hundred and sixty dollars.

James was so stunned that it took him almost a minute before he slid the check off the page to read Drew's short missive.

Dear Mister Stewart,

This is only a small token to express my gratitude to you and all of the kind souls at St. Thomas. Each of you did much more than teach me how to think and behave. You were also models of how we should treat others. While I may not have reached those lofty standards, I'll keep trying.

But God has blessed me more than I could possibly deserve by giving me a wonderful wife whom I will love forever. He then blessed us with a perfect son, who has become the joy of his grandparents, whom I consider my own mother and father. And as if that wasn't proof of His generosity, He guided me onto a path that led to a fulfilling career.

With all of my heart, I thank each of you,

Drew Campbell

———

On the 18th of August, Josh Brockman lost his beloved ferry when a violent thunderstorm pummeled the barge with enormous hailstones which punched dozens of plum-sized holes in its hull. He didn't bother trying to repair the ferry as it would be too expensive.

So, after Josh began working at the Tidwell brothers' livery, the only way to reach Glendive was to make the long ride to use the railroad's bridge. But it wasn't long before a Northern Pacific construction team arrived. And when they left six days later, there was a well-built trackless bridge across the Yellowstone that could support a heavy wagon. Drew never asked, but he assumed the bridge was yet another Fergie surprise.

———

John Edward Campbell arrived exactly 364 days after Alistair James was born. Their first daughter, Francine Marie joined the family on the 11th of June in 1887. But instead of correcting male-female imbalance, on the 9th of April the following year, Gabrielle gave birth to James Andrew. Another attempt to even the playing field on the 30th of January of 1889 when Mary Anne loudly announced her arrival. But all hopes for a 50-50 mix were dashed when Drew and Gabrielle welcomed Nathan Bonaparte into the world on the 1st of June in 1890.

God then took pity on Gabrielle and decided that Nathan would be her last delivery. It wasn't until she'd gone almost a year without conceiving that Gabrielle was able to thank Him for His decision. While she believed that if God was a woman, there would be only three little Campbells in the house, Gabrielle still loved each of their children as much as she loved her helpful, loving husband.

While Gabrielle was bringing new life into their family, Drew had continued inventing. When he'd started, his time was equally split between the workshop and the office. But it wasn't long before he began spending more time at the draft table than he did at the furnace. By the time Gabrielle finished having babies, Drew worked almost exclusively in the office, which also gave him more time to spend with Gabrielle and their children.

Drew also began to expand his area of creativity, so over those first six years, Drew had sixteen patents to his name.

THE BRAKEMAN

The Northern Pacific had bought six of them, and the others were still in Drew's name. But he'd licensed those ten to different companies on a royalty basis, which gave his family a steady, healthy income.

———

While they never used the Northern Pacific passes to visit Alistair's family in Brainerd, Drew and Alistair would arrange to meet in Bismarck whenever their wives weren't about to have a baby. It made windows of opportunity difficult, but they still managed to get together four times before Nathan arrived.

On each of those reunions, the Campbells and Remys would be accompanied by either John Knudsen's family or Jimmy Lynch's wife and two children.

———

When seven-year-old Alistair and six-year-old John complained that it wasn't fair that they had to share their room with their two brothers while their two sisters had a room to themselves, Drew hired a construction firm to add two more rooms to their house. Then, to keep the peace and avoid complaints from Francine and Mary, after Drew moved the four boys into the two new rooms, he converted their vacated bedroom back into a gun room.

While he would never point any of the assorted rifles, carbines, or his long-barreled Colt at another man, he and Boney still enjoyed hunting in the nearby forests. But he'd only donned his waders to try his hand at trout fishing once before he realized he lacked the patience. And even though his fishing days ended before they really began, he still kept his waders and the other pieces of his duck suit. After Gabrielle had him to put on a waddling, quacking duck show for the children, it was rare for a week to pass without being asked for an encore.

Yet even his duck suit wasn't as popular as one of his unpatented creations. Drew built a small railroad for their children. It had a locomotive that used a gasoline-powered engine to pull three box cars and a caboose along its route. And instead of rails, the Campbell Express followed deep ruts making it easier to add spurs.

And despite the train's five-mile-per-hour speed, neither parent was concerned that that one of their children might fall. In fact, tumbling off a moving train was considered to be a sign of a happy future.

BOOK LIST

1	Rock Creek	12/26/2016
2	North of Denton	01/02/2017
3	Fort Selden	01/07/2017
4	Scotts Bluff	01/14/2017
5	South of Denver	01/22/2017
6	Miles City	01/28/2017
7	Hopewell	02/04/2017
8	Nueva Luz	02/12/2017
9	The Witch of Dakota	02/19/2017
10	Baker City	03/13/2017
11	The Gun Smith	03/21/2017
12	Gus	03/24/2017
13	Wilmore	04/06/2017
14	Mister Thor	04/20/2017
15	Nora	04/26/2017
16	Max	05/09/2017
17	Hunting Pearl	05/14/2017
18	Bessie	05/25/2017
19	The Last Four	05/29/2017
20	Zack	06/12/2017
21	Finding Bucky	06/21/2017
22	The Debt	06/30/2017
23	The Scalawags	07/11/2017
24	The Stampede	08/23/2017
25	The Wake of the Bertrand	07/31/2017
26	Cole	08/09/2017
27	Luke	09/05/2017
28	The Eclipse	09/21/2017
29	A.J. Smith	10/03/2017
30	Slow John	11/05/2017
31	The Second Star	11/15/2017
32	Tate	12/03/2017
33	Virgil's Herd	12/14/2017
34	Marsh's Valley	01/01/2018
35	Alex Paine	01/18/2018

Printed in Great Britain
by Amazon